KT-497-989

An
Untamed
State

Roxane Gay

corsair

CORSAIR

First published in the United States of America by Black Cat, an imprint of Grove/
Atlantic, Inc.

First published in Great Britain in 2014 by Corsair
This edition published in 2015 by Corsair
1 3 5 7 9 10 8 6 4 2

Copyright © Roxane Gay, 2014

The moral right of the author has been asserted.

*All characters and events in this publication, other than
those clearly in the public domain, are fictitious
and any resemblance to real persons,
living or dead, is purely coincidental.*

All rights reserved.
No part of this publication may be reproduced, stored in a retrieval system, or
transmitted, in any form or by any means, without the prior permission in writing of
the publisher, nor be otherwise circulated in any form of binding or cover other than
that in which it is published and without a similar condition including this condition
being imposed on the subsequent purchaser.

A CIP catalogue record for this book
is available from the British Library.

ISBN: 978-1-4721-1982-7 (paperback)
ISBN: 978-1-4721-1983-4 (ebook)

Printed and bound in Great Britain by Clays Ltd, St Ives plc

Corsair
An imprint of
Little, Brown Book Group
Carmelite House
50 Victoria Embankment
London EC4Y 0DZ

An Hachette UK Company
www.hachette.co.uk

www.littlebrown.co.uk

For women, the world over

Kingston upon Thames Libraries	
KT 2170291 8	
Askews & Holts	03-Jul-2015
AF THR	£7.99
ST	KT00000818

Part 1
Happily Ever After

1

Once upon a time, in a far-off land, I was kidnapped by a gang of fearless yet terrified young men with so much impossible hope beating inside their bodies it burned their very skin and strengthened their will right through their bones.

They held me captive for thirteen days.

They wanted to break me.

It was not personal.

I was not broken.

This is what I tell myself.

It was hot, nearly a hundred degrees, the air so thick it felt like warm rain. I dressed my son, Christophe, in a pair of miniature red board shorts and a light blue T-shirt with a sailboat across the front. I covered his smooth brown arms and his beaming face with sunscreen. I kissed his nose and brushed his thick, dirty-blond curls away from his face as he pressed his palms against my cheeks and shouted, "Mama! Mama! Mama!" My husband, Michael, the baby, and I said goodbye to my parents, told them we would be back in time for dinner.

Michael and I were taking Christophe to the ocean for the first time. We were going to hold him in the warm salt water as he wiggled his toes and kicked his chubby legs. We were going to throw him toward the sun and catch him safely in our arms.

My mother smiled from the balcony where she watered her plants, wearing a crisp linen outfit and high heels. She blew a kiss to her grandson. She reminded us to be safe.

We put our son into his car seat. We handed him his favorite stuffed animal, a little bulldog named Baba. He clenched his beloved toy tightly in his little fist, still smiling. He has his father's temperament. He is usually happy. That is important to me. Before getting into the car, Michael double-checked that Christophe was strapped securely in his car seat. He put our beach bags into the trunk.

Michael held my door open. When he closed it, he pressed his face against the window, and blew air until his cheeks filled. I laughed and pressed my hand against his face through the glass. "I love you," I mouthed. I don't say those words often, but he knows. Michael ran around to his side of the car. After he slid behind the steering wheel and adjusted the rearview mirror so he could see the baby, he leaned into me and we kissed. He rested an arm on the armrest between us and I idly brushed the golden wisps of hair on his arms. I smiled and rested my head on his shoulder. We drove down the long steep hill of my parents' driveway and waited quietly for the heavy steel gates, the gates keeping us safe, to open.

In the backseat, Christophe cooed softly, still smiling. As the gates closed behind us, three black Land Cruisers surrounded our car. The air filled with a high-pitched squealing and the smell of burning rubber. Michael's tanned knuckles turned white as he gripped the steering wheel and looked frantically for a way out. His body shook. The doors of all three trucks opened at the same time and men we did not know spilled out, all limbs and gunmetal. There was silence, the air thin, still hot. My breath caught painfully in my rib cage. There was shouting.

Two men stood behind our car, machine guns raised. Michael pressed his foot against the gas pedal to move forward but a tall man with a red bandana across the lower half of his face, a man holding a machine gun, pounded his fist on the hood of the car. He left a small dent in the shape of his closed hand. He glared at us, then raised his gun, pointed it directly at Michael's chest. I threw my arm across Michael's body. It was a silly, impotent gesture. Michael's eyes were bright, and arcs of tears trembled along his lower eyelids. He grabbed my hand between both of his, held me so fiercely it felt like all those slender bones would be crushed.

Two men slammed the butts of their rifles against the car windows. Their bodies glowed with anger. The glass cracked, fractures spreading. Michael and I pulled apart, waited tensely, and then the windshield broke, the sound loud and echoing. We covered our faces as shards of glass shattered around us, refracting sharp prisms of light. Michael and I reached for Christophe at the same time. The baby was still smiling but his lips quivered, his eyes wide. My hands could not quite reach him. My child was so close my fingers thrummed. If I touched my child, we would all be fine; this terrible thing would not happen. A man reached into the window and unlocked my door. He started to pull me out of the car roughly, growling as the seat belt held me inside. After he slapped my face, he ordered me to unlock my seat belt. My hands shook as I depressed the button. I was lifted up and out of our car and thrown onto the street. The skin covering my face stung.

My body deflated. My body was just skin stretched too tightly over bone, nothing more, no air. The man sneered at me, called me *dyaspora* with the resentment those Haitians who cannot leave hold for those of us who can. His skin was slick. I couldn't hold on to him. I tried to scratch, but my fingers only collected a thick layer of sweat. I tried to grab on to the car door. He slammed his gun against my fingers. I yelled, "My baby. Don't hurt my baby." One of the men grabbed me by my hair, threw me to the ground, kicked me in my stomach. I gasped as I wrapped my arms around myself. A small crowd gathered. I begged them to help. They did not. They stood and watched me screaming and fighting with all the muscle in my heart. I saw their faces and the indifference in their eyes, the relief that it was not yet their time; the wolves had not yet come for them.

I was pulled to my feet and again I tried to break free, I tried to run, to reach for my son, to feel his skin against mine just one last time. I shouted at him through the broken window. I shouted, "Christophe!" banging my fist against his window so he would look at me. I said the things any mother would say to her child in that moment even though he was too young to understand any of it. My voice was stripped raw. He stared, reaching for me. He kicked his legs. I studied the dimples over each of his knuckles. I broke free and pulled the rear door open, wrapped the seat belt around my hand as a strange pair of hands tried to pull me loose. The man on Michael's side hit him in the face with a closed fist again and again. Michael slumped forward, his forehead pressed against the horn. The horn wailed, the whine of it filling the air. A thick, dark stream of blood slowly slid from my husband's forehead, down between his eyes, along his nose and over his lips. In the backseat, Christophe started crying, his face burning a bright red.

The cold steel of a gun barrel dug into my skin. I froze. A voice said, "Go easy or we kill your family. We kill everything you've ever loved." I did not move. The gun dug deeper and deeper. I unclenched my fingers and stood. I stared at my family. I do not love easy. I raised my hands over my head. My thighs trembled uncontrollably. I could not move. A hand grabbed my neck, pushing me toward a waiting vehicle. I turned to look back, a sudden calm filling me. Michael slowly raised his head. I looked at him hard, wanted him to know this was not how our story would end. He shouted my name. The desperation in his voice made me nauseous. I mouthed *I love you* and he nodded. He shouted, "I love you." I heard him. I felt him. I watched as he tried to open his door but passed out again, his body slumping.

My captors put a burlap sack over my head and shoved me into the backseat. The delicate construction of bone in my cheeks throbbed angrily. My skin hurt. My captors told me, in broken English, to do as they said and I would be back with my family soon. I needed to hold the fragile hope that I could find my way back to my happily ever after. I didn't know any better. That was the before.

I sat very still as two men flanked me. Their muscular legs pressed against mine. Each man held one of my wrists, so tightly they would leave dark red circles. The air was filled with the stench of sweaty young bodies and my blood and the sunscreen I had rubbed into my child's skin. Before I passed out I heard cold laughter, my son crying and the desperate wail of the car horn.

//

I opened my eyes and couldn't see anything but bright spots of light and gray shadow. My head hurt. I gasped and began thrashing wildly as I remembered where I was, my baby crying, my husband. The burlap sack made it difficult to breathe. I needed a breath of clean air. A strong hand grabbed my shoulder, shoved me back into the seat. I was warned to sit still. I began to hum. I hummed so loudly my teeth vibrated. I rocked back and forth. A hand grabbed the back of my neck. I rocked harder. Someone muttered, "She's crazy."

I was on the edge of crazy. I hadn't fallen in yet.

I was scared, dizzy and nauseous, my mouth dry. As the car lurched I leaned forward and vomited, bile seeping through the burlap, the rest dripping down my shirt. I was repulsive, already. The man to my left started yelling, grabbed me by my hair, slammed my head into the seat in front of me. My mouth soured as I tried to protect my face.

And then, inexplicably, I thought about my friends in Miami, where Michael and I live, and how they would talk when news of a kidnapping reached them. I am a curiosity to my American friends—a Haitian who is not from the slums or the country-side, a Haitian who has enjoyed a life of privilege. When I talk about my life in Haiti, they listen to my stories as if they are fairy tales, stories that could not possibly be true by nature of their goodness.

My husband and I love to entertain, dinner parties. We cook fancy meals from *Gourmet* and *Bon Appétit* and drink expensive wine and try to solve the world's problems. At least we did this, in the before, when we were less aware of the spectacle we were and when we thought we had anything even remotely relevant to say about the things that tear the world apart.

At one such party, where we entertained his friends and my friends, some of whom we liked and many of whom we hated, everyone drank lots of wine and danced to a fine selection of music. We ate excellent food and engaged in pretentious but interesting conversation. Talk turned to Haiti, as it often does. We sat on our lanai, illuminated by paper lanterns and candles, all of us drunk on the happiness of too much money and too much food and too much freedom. I was on Michael's lap, draw-ing small circles on the back of his neck with my fingernails, his arm around my waist. Everyone leaned forward, earnest in their desire to understand a place they would likely never visit. One of my friends mentioned a magazine article he read about how Haiti had surpassed Colombia as the kidnapping capital of the world. Another told us about a recent feature in a national magazine on the kidnapping epidemic—that was the word he used, as if kidnapping were a disease, a contagion that could not be controlled. There were comments about Vodou and that one movie with Lisa Bonet that made Bill Cosby mad at her. Soon everyone was offering their own desperate piece of information about my country, my people, about the violence and the poverty and the hopelessness, conjuring a place that does not exist anywhere but the American imagination.

That night, I buried my face against Michael's neck, felt his pulse against my cheek. He held me closer. He understood. There are three Haitis—the country Americans know and the country Haitians know and the country I thought I knew.

In the back of the Land Cruiser the day I was kidnapped, I was in a new country altogether. I was not home or I was and did not know it yet. Someone turned up the radio. A song I recognized was playing. I began to sing along, wanted to be part of this one familiar thing. Someone told me to shut up. I sang louder. I sang so loud I couldn't hear anything around me. A fist connected with my jaw. I slumped to the side, my head ringing. I didn't stop singing though my words slowed, slurred.

I was supposed to be at the beach with my husband. I was supposed to wrap my legs around Michael's waist as he carried me into the ocean and away from the shore while our son napped. I would trace his jaw with my fingertips and my lips. I would taste the salt and sun and sea on his skin and he would hold me so tight it hurt to breathe. We would ignore everything around us and he would kiss me like he always kisses me—hard, with purpose, the soft of our lip flesh bruising, pulpy, his tongue in my mouth, a hand twisting through my hair possessively. He always tries so hard to hold on to me because he does not realize I am with him always. We are a lock and key. We are nothing without each other. When the sun became too much, when our desire became too much for that moment, I would pull away and we would climb out of the water, our bodies heavy. We would lie on the hot white sand with our sleeping son between us. The salt from the sea would dry on our skin. We would drink something cold and bask in the perfection of our happily ever after.

But we weren't there. I wasn't there. I was alone in a country I did not know, one that did not belong to me or my father, one that belonged to men who obeyed no kind of law.

We drove for hours along winding, narrow roads. The men discussed financial matters, speculating as to the kind of ransom I would fetch. A hand grabbed at my breast, slowly swelling with milk, and I sat straight up, my spine locked. I whispered, "Do not touch me." There was a laugh. A voice said, "Not yet," but the hand squeezed harder. I tried to pull away from the violation but there was nowhere to go. I was in a cage, the first of many.

"You're never going to get away with this," I said, my voice already hoarsening.

There was laughter. "We already have."

III

We stopped on a noisy street. My kidnappers pulled the burlap sack off my head and I swallowed as much air as I could. I squinted as my eyes adjusted to my surroundings. The sun was still out but fading into pink along the horizon. It was beautiful how the color stretched across the sky in sweeping arcs. I stared into that pink, wanted to remember everything about it, until a hand grabbed my elbow. I winced, stumbled forward.

A few people in the street stared but no one moved to help me. I shouted, "This is not right," knowing my words were useless. There's no room for such distinctions in a country where too many people have to claw for what they need and still have nothing to hold.

My captors walked me through a dark room with three couches and a large, flat-screen television. A woman sat on one of the couches in a red tank top, denim skirt, and flip-flops, the kind with a high chunky heel. My eyes widened as I watched her watching me. She didn't look surprised. She shook her head and resumed watching her program, some kind of talk show.

In another room, four men played cards. There were bottles of Prestige beer on the table and an overflowing ashtray. One of them licked his lips as we walked by. We passed through a child's bedroom. My breasts ached uncomfortably. I thought about Christophe, my sweet baby boy, whom I hadn't yet weaned, who hungered for his mother's breast and could not be satisfied.

Finally, we reached a room with a small bed along one wall and a large bucket against the other. There was a small window covered with bars looking out onto an alley, and below the window a faded poster for the Fanmi Lavalas political party, bearing the likeness of a man I didn't recognize. They threw me in this room and closed the door. They left me in a new cage. I immediately grabbed the doorknob, twisting it frantically. The door was locked. It was impossible not to panic. I started beating the door. I was going to beat that door down but the door was strong and my arms were less so.

When I was completely worn-out, I sank to the floor. The heat overwhelmed me. Already, my clothes clung to my body. I could smell myself. The edges of my face were damp with sweat.

Heat takes on a peculiar quality during the summer in Port-au-Prince. The air is thick and inescapable. It wraps itself around you and applies pressure relentlessly. The summer I was kidnapped, the heat was relentless. That heat pressed up, so close against my skin. That heat invaded my senses until I forgot nearly everything, until I forgot the meaning of hope.

★ ★ ★

I waited and tried not to imagine what could happen to me. I could not allow myself to think of such things or there would be no reason to believe I would be saved. Instead, I tried to remember why my parents would ever return to the country they once left, the country they once loved, the country I thought I loved.

There is this truth. I know very little of my parents' lives as children. They are not prone to confession. My mother and father are both from Port-au-Prince. They grew up poor. There were too many children and not enough of anything. They were often hungry. They walked to school barefoot and were teased for having dirty feet. My fathers' parents both died when he was young, in ways that disgusted him, in ways, he once told us, that showed him that the only way to survive this world is by being strong. His mother, he said, was a weak woman and his father was a weak man and it was their weakness that led to their deaths, the father from liver failure due to a fondness for rum and the mother from heart failure from loving the wrong man too much. My father has lived his whole life determined to be nothing like them, no matter what it cost the rest of us.

My mother's father died when she was six. Her first step-father died when she was eleven. Her second stepfather died when she was fourteen and her third stepfather died when she was eighteen. Her mother has been living with the same man for more than twenty years, but refuses to marry him. Her concern is understandable. My grandmother and the man I know as my grandfather live in a small, two-bedroom apartment in the Bronx where she has lived since she first came to the United States. She worked as a housekeeper for a Jewish family in Manhattan and sent for her twelve children one by one. When the youngest finally set foot on American soil she started taking classes at a local community college, determined to do more with the remainder of her life than clean the messes of the lives of others.

My parents came to the States separately, my father, Sebastien, when he was nineteen by way of Montreal then Queens and my mother, Fabienne, by way of the Bronx. They flew here on Pan Am. They saved the airsick bags embossed with the Pan Am logo and marveled, when they shared these parts of their history, at how similar their stories were.

Once upon a time, my parents were strangers in a strange land but they found each other. They found love, meeting at a wedding where my father, taken by her strange smile and the careless way she moved on the dance floor, asked my mother if he could drive her home. She was accompanied by her sister, Veronique, who would later become my godmother. The sisters sat in the backseat of my father's Chevelle, giggling the entire way because, as my mother would later tell me, Sebastien Duval was so very serious.

A week after that first meeting, my father told my maternal grandmother he was going to marry her daughter. He courted my mother, always visiting her at her mother's apartment, where she lived with several of her twelve siblings. My father wore a neatly pressed suit and tie. He was often nervous and it charmed my mother that she created such uncertainty in a man otherwise brimming with confidence.

They mostly sat on a plastic-covered couch and talked, quietly, while the younger of my mother's siblings ran around with too much energy in a too small apartment. Three of her brothers, older, glowered at my father anytime they walked through the room and sometimes made idle threats about the bones they would break if my father stepped out of line. My parents had little privacy. Their romance blossomed between shared breaths and touching thighs and unwavering glances while life in that cramped apartment raged around them.

It is a wonder they were able to fall in love. Falling in love, my mother says, requires its own private space. She and my father had no choice but to carve that private space for themselves where there was none.

Though my father made his intentions plain early on, he waited six months to propose. On the day he asked my mother to be his wife, my father took her to see *The Towering Inferno*. She loved Steve McQueen, thought he was a very handsome American. My parents held hands throughout the movie, my father brushing his fingers across my mother's knuckles. This gesture made her heart race, my mother said, because it was the most intimate moment they had ever shared. As he walked my mother back to her apartment, my father began to talk of how someday, he was going to build towers, only his weren't going to burn. No. His towers were going to soar into the sky and nothing, he said, nothing would make him happier than having my mother by his side. Though most people don't realize it, my father is the wild and romantic partner in their relationship. My mother said nothing and they continued walking along empty New York streets.

Later they stood, quietly in the foyer of my mother's building as my mother considered my father's words. He waited, his forehead sweaty, his suit hanging loosely from his narrow frame, his body becoming smaller and smaller as his hope faltered. My mother enjoyed the quiet tension of the moment. She was not being cruel. She had spent so much of her life always surrounded by too many people clamoring for someone's attention, clamoring for everything a person could need, never getting enough. All she truly longed for was quiet and space and she knew my father would provide those things for her. My father's hand shook as he slid a modest diamond on her finger. He held her wrist gently, his thumb resting against the slightly curved bone. He said, "I am an ambitious man," and my mother replied, "I believe you are."

A year later, they married, and a year after that, my father graduated from City College of New York with his degree in civil engineering, took a job at a large construction firm in Nebraska. He took my mother away from everything she knew but even though she didn't believe in fairy tales, he was her Prince Charming.

Where he went, she followed.

||||

The first thing Michael heard was a terrible, high-pitched whine—a car horn, maybe, though something was off about the sound. His head ached dully and there was something wet on his forehead, streaming along the left side of his nose and down his face. He sat up, tried to focus but all he could see was bright light, splintered. There was crying, the sound of a child crying, his child crying, he realized. Broken glass on his legs, one piece, buried in his knee. It didn't hurt but it looked strange, almost beautiful as it refracted a narrow beam of light.

He closed his eyes then slowly opened them again. He looked at his hands and noticed his wedding ring and tried to remember who he was wearing the ring for and then it all came back—his son, smiling in the backseat, his wife, Mireille, her small hand on his forearm, her wide smile, how she bit her lower lip when she was nervous, the glint in her eye when they argued and then the armed men, a rifle butt aimed at his head, his screaming child in the backseat, but most of all, the look of terror in Mireille's eyes as she was taken away by two armed men.

Michael opened his car door, hands shaking, and stumbled out, couldn't balance, fell to his knees. There was a gnawing in his chest, a sharp pain just beneath the breastbone. "Christophe," he whispered. Michael fumbled with the back door, quickly unstrapping Christophe, touching him everywhere, trying to make sure the boy wasn't hurt. When he was sure Christophe was fine, Michael held the screaming child to his chest. He tried to form words that would make sense to a baby. Christophe could not be consoled. The car horn began to fade away as Christophe's shrieks pitched higher, his little body shuddering as he tried to breathe and cry at the same time. Michael started walking into the mass of people who had gathered. "Help me," he said hoarsely, and then he took a deep breath, covered Christophe's head with his hand and shouted in a voice he could not recognize as his own, "Help me. Help us. My wife has been taken."

The gathered crowd just stared, some shaking their heads. His hands shook the entire time he was typing the code, blood and sweat in his eyes, but the gates slowly opened once more and Michael ran up the steep incline toward his in-laws' house. He pounded his fists against the door—as large and imposing as ever, ornate mahogany, this detail clearer than others for some reason. He was wild with panic, didn't know what to do, didn't understand any of it, didn't understand why he and Mireille weren't still on their way to the beach for a perfect afternoon.

One of the housekeepers, Nadine, answered the door with a smile that quickly drifted into a hard line as Michael ran past her and found Mireille's father, Sebastien, in his study. Michael tightened his grip around his son. He fell to his knees, blood, sweat, even tears dripping from his face onto the immaculate marble. "They took her," he wailed, rocking back and forth. "They took her," he said again, this time the last of his words falling silent.

Sebastien paled for a moment but quickly composed himself. He was Sebastien Duval. Composure was his only choice. He had learned that long ago. Sebastien cleared his throat and immediately picked up the phone, began dialing. He was calm, had always believed in the benefit of behaving rationally regardless of the circumstance. He looked at the crying man in front of him, the man with a thick body and blond hair and easy smile. Sebastien Duval stood, holding the phone, and pointed down at Michael. "Pull yourself together," he said. "This matter will be handled." He said these words as if they could possibly be true.

Michael wiped his face with his T-shirt and stood, carefully. The ache in his head was sharper now. His whole face hurt. "Handled? My wife, your daughter, was just kidnapped. We have to call the police, the American embassy, the president, every goddamned body. We have to do something more than *handle* this."

Sebastien held up his hand, spoke a few, clipped words in French to whoever was on the phone, then hung up. "The negotiators are on their way," he said. "The police have been notified. We must remain calm or the kidnappers will take advantage of our weakness."

Until that moment, Michael had not understood the vastness of the world and how small a place he held in it, in a country where he barely spoke the language, where women could be stolen from their families in broad daylight. Michael shook his head. "This isn't happening," he said, clenching his jaw. Michael tried not to think of Mireille's petite frame, of what could be happening to her. His wife was strong. Her will was iron. He knew that. He held on to that.

Christophe had stopped crying but he breathed in stuttered gasps, his eyes pink around the edges. "Mama mama mama," he said.

"I know," Michael said, kissing Christophe's cheek. "I want Mama too."

When the negotiator arrived, American, dressed in a dark, perfectly tailored suit, a doctor had already been to the house to see to Michael's injuries. Mireille's mother, Fabienne, sat with Michael and Christophe while Sebastien stalked back and forth across the room. The negotiator, who introduced himself as Mr. Evans, sat and opened a large black briefcase and pulled out a sheaf of paper, and what they later explained was a recording device to use on the telephone.

"We have to get ahead of the threat," Evans said. "If we have a better sense of who is behind this, we'll have a better chance of retrieving the victim quickly."

"The victim has a name," Michael said, tersely. "Her name is Mireille, and she needs to be *retrieved* today."

The negotiator nodded. "Of course that's what you want, sir, but that's not quite how things work down here. Negotiation is a process and you should be prepared for this to take time."

"How much time?" Michael asked, loudly. "Quantify time."

"Sir, please, stay calm," the negotiator said. "I know what I am doing."

Sebastien stopped pacing and stood quietly, rubbing his chin. "I am loath to negotiate with these animals. I pay one set of kidnappers and soon they'll be coming for my entire family— my wife, my other daughter, my nieces and nephews. There is a great deal at stake here."

Michael stood, his entire body vibrating with frustration. "I'll pay. Whatever it takes. I will pay now. I don't care about any of that bullshit. I want my wife back."

"We have to wait for the ransom demand," the negotiator said, "before we can do anything. At that time I will ask for proof of life and we will begin to negotiate. You have to be patient, Mr. Jameson. I am very good at my job. I will get your wife back."

Michael looked at his father-in-law, refused to look away. "I want to make the decisions on this matter."

"You know nothing of this country," Sebastien said. "There is little you can do to help."

Michael fixed Sebastien with a hard stare. "I know my wife," he said. "I will not be ignored."

Sebastien waved his hand in the air and resumed his pacing. "Let us not argue," he said. "We must wait and we must be prepared."

He sounded confident, and looked at Michael without blinking. Michael swore he wouldn't blink first.

‖‖‖‖

It was not personal. That is what I told myself as I waited for something to happen, for someone to come find me, save me, set me free.

Kidnapping was a business transaction, one requiring intense negotiation and, eventually, compromise, but I would be safe. I would be returned to those I love, relatively unharmed. There was ample precedent for hope.

One of the accountants who worked for my father, Gilbèrt, was kidnapped the previous year. His kidnappers originally asked for $125,000, but everyone knew it was simply a starting number, an initial conversation. Eventually, with professional assistance and proof of life, his family paid $53,850 for Gilbèrt.

My parents' friend, Corinne LeBlanche, was kidnapped not long before I was taken. She and her husband and five children lived in Haiti year-round. She always swore, to anyone who would listen, that were she ever kidnapped, her husband, Simon, best meet her at the airport with her passport and children once she was returned because she would never spend another night in the country. Simon was a fat, happy, prominent business-man who owned a chain of restaurants and gas stations that did quite well. He laughed when Corinne made such declarations. He didn't yet understand how these things went differently for women. She and the children now live in Miami. She called me when Michael and I returned to the States. Even though we said very little, we spoke for a long time.

Two years ago, the matriarch of the Gilles family was kid-napped. She was eighty-one. The kidnappers knew the family had more money than God. They failed to realize that she was frail and diabetic. She died soon after she was abducted. Every-one who knew her was thankful her suffering was brief, until the kidnappers, having learned the lesson that the elderly are bad for business, kidnapped her grandson, who at thirty-seven promised to be a far more lucrative investment.

When my cousin Gabby was kidnapped, her family paid and she was released in less than two days. We marveled for weeks at what a mercy that was. She had always been a frail girl, prone to fits of crying and long depressive spells where she took to her bed and kept her room shrouded in darkness. After the kid-napping, though, Gabby never cried and she seemed happier, somehow. It was a miracle, her mother said. The rest of us did not know what to think.

My negotiations would be somewhat more complex and far more costly. A good family name and a prominent father, they come at a high price even if, in those early days of my kidnap-ping, we had no idea just how high the ransom would be.

My father works in construction so his office in Port-au-Prince isn't well appointed—it's mostly just a space with a door. The floor is covered in cement dust and bits of gravel. Shelves crammed with three-ring binders, blueprints, and his engineering textbooks from college line the walls. On the coatrack, there are three hard hats—the one from his first job in the United States, the one his company gave him when he retired, and the one he bought when he started his own company. When we were kids, my brother and sister and I loved to wear our father's hard hats. They were always too big but it was fun to pretend we were just like our father, that we too could build great things.

In my father's office there is also a desk—wide, made of cherry, polished until it gleams, an imposing contrast to the rest of the office. Each time he hires a new employee, my father invites them to a brief meeting in his office, where he sits behind his shiny desk. He laces his fingers behind his head and stretches his legs and calmly tells the employee he will never pay a ransom, not for himself, not for any member of his family. He smiles and says, "Welcome to Duval Engineering." He wants the people who work for him to know the only money they will ever receive from him is money they earn through sweat and hard work.

My sister, Mona, works with my father. She's an engineer too. We were all surprised when she agreed to work with him. She was always the rebel, wearing makeup and short skirts and piercing her ears too many times, the one who openly defied our parents with her *wild ways*. She is also smart and loyal. Mona and my father don't necessarily get along but my father is getting old and he trusts blood, says family is the only thing you can trust in a country like Haiti. He is a liar of the highest order. Family is one of many things you cannot trust in a country like Haiti. Mona spends half of every month in Port-au-Prince and the other half in Miami with her husband, a Cuban artist named Carlos, whom we call Carlito because it drives him crazy. Mona is my best friend. Wherever she has gone, the whole of our lives, I have tried to follow. Michael and I moved to Miami because she was there. Wherever she is feels more like home.

When Mona started working for Duval Engineering, all I could think of was something terrible happening to her. Mona always laughed off my concern, said the day she stopped feeling safe in the country where her parents were born, she'd leave for good. As I sat in that crazy-hot room, waiting for something to happen, I wondered if Mona felt safe. I wondered if she knew how unsafe I was, if Michael had called her yet, if she had flown to Port-au-Prince to wait with our family for my release. I knew one thing for certain—she would want me to fight because I would want her to fight if she were in my place.

My mother is terrified of being kidnapped—the threat of it haunts her. She finds the indignity of captivity unbearable. She is a woman who covets her privacy, and to be surrounded by strange men, to be exposed to them in any way, is not an experience she believes she can survive.

When my mother and I had conversations about kidnapping in the before, I got angry. I told her there were people who needed her. I told her if she were kidnapped, she would have no choice but to survive. I told her nothing truly bad happens when someone is kidnapped, that a kidnapping is only a matter of time and money and that she would always have both. This was when it was easy to speak wrongly on such things. In the after, I understood my mother's fear more clearly. She knew my father too well.

When my mental accounting began to frighten me, I sat on the narrow bed and tried to pretend I was in Miami, hiding in a host's bedroom at an awkward dinner party. I was waiting for Michael to find me, something I forced him to do often, but then a tall man strode into the room like he owned everything in it and I was right back in my cage. He wore a tight pair of jeans and a T-shirt with the likeness of Tupac on the front. His eyes were wide and soft brown, like you could see right through them. Just below his left eye was a thickly braided scar that trembled when he spoke. An automatic pistol was tucked into his waistband. He looked at me and smiled.

"I am the Commander," he said.

I nodded slowly and before I could stop myself, I said, "Commander of what? Where is your army?"

He crossed the room and grabbed me by my throat, pulling me to my feet. I slapped at his forearms but he tightened his grip. My face grew taut as I struggled to breathe. When he was satisfied with his display of authority, he shoved me back onto the bed. He wiped his hands, spat on the floor. He laughed. "Let's try this again. I am the Commander. Today, I am the Commander of you."

"Like hell," I snapped. I bit my lower lip. I wanted nothing more than to repeat my question but I could still feel his fingers holding my throat closed. The edges of the room were dark and fuzzy.

The Commander sniffed loudly, leaned in real close. "How come you don't cry? I was certain there would be tears already."

"I do not waste my tears."

He began pacing. He pulled his gun from his waistband and waved it toward me. "Your family," he said. "They will pay a lot of money for you. U.S. dollars."

I watched his frenetic pattern back and forth across the room. I looked him right in the eye. "My father doesn't believe in paying kidnappers. You should know that."

The Commander approached me again. He pressed the gun flat against my chest, slowly dragging it between my breasts. I wondered if he could smell my milk, on the verge of leaking. He licked his lips. "Your father will pay for his youngest daughter. I am to understand you are his favorite."

The word *daughter* lay heavy on his tongue, took on a repulsive shape.

I dug my fingernails into my thighs and hoped my father would be a better man than I knew him to be, would ignore his convictions, would pay, and quickly. I hoped I did not know my father as well as I feared.

The Commander sat next to me, our thighs touching. I tried to move away but he grabbed my thigh, his fingers digging into the meat of my body. "I've been to Miami," he said. "A fine city."

I stared at the terrible scar beneath his eye. I tried to memorize his features, his clothing, his shoes—Skechers. I recognized the logo. These details felt important. I had to go the bathroom very badly but I didn't want to ask. I did not want to ask my kidnappers for anything.

The Commander tapped my knee with his gun. He repeated himself, said, "I've been to Miami."

I inched away again.

He grabbed my elbow. "Sit still."

I shrugged. "I've been to Miami too."

I did not want to tell him anything about my life. I did not want to tell him about my home with the silver palm trees in the front yard and small pool in the back where we swam with Christophe, or how on Fridays and Saturdays my husband and I got a babysitter and went to South Beach, where we ate expensive dinners and danced salsa all night, or how some days we were surprised to hear someone speak English, so varied were the tongues of the city. I did not want him to know anything about me.

The Commander grabbed the bone of my chin. He forced me to look at him. His eyes were strangely warm; not even the scar could make his eyes ugly. He said, "Don't play games. We know everything about you, where you live, where you work, where your husband works."

I pulled away. "Somehow I doubt that."

He reached into his pocket and proffered a cell phone. "Call your family."

My hands shook as I dialed the numbers. The phone rang once, twice, and then I heard my father's voice. "It's me," I said.

The Commander plucked the phone from my hands. He said, "We will not negotiate. We want one million dollars for the beloved daughter of one of Haiti's favorite sons."

Whatever my father said amused the Commander greatly because his smile grew wider and wider. He handed me the phone.

I said nothing. I had nothing to say.

"You will have to be strong," my father said.

I marveled at his ability to state the obvious, to say the most useless things.

"I'd like to speak with my husband," I said.

There was a pause and then Michael said, "Babe," and I closed my eyes, imagined sinking into his voice, imagined being safe again.

"Christophe . . ."

"He's fine. I'm holding him right here."

I listened as carefully as I could, trying to make out my son's breathing.

"Are you okay?" Michael asked. "Have they hurt you?"

"I'm fine," I said. I wanted to be careful and calm. I wanted to say something important, something that would help Michael find me, something he would remember and hold on to. I said, "I'm not that far from you. I am not far at all." The Commander grabbed me by my hair, yanking hard. I did not make a sound even though my scalp burned. Christophe was listening. I did not want my child to be frightened. Michael shouted my name over and over.

The Commander said, "One million dollars. We will call in two days to make arrangements for payment." He hung up and released his grip, shoving me to the floor. He waved his men out of the room and just before he locked me in my cage, he wiggled his finger back and forth, said, "You are not as smart as you think you are."

I was alone again. I had two days and then I would be returned to Michael and Christophe and we could find our way home. I could survive two days with these men. I could.

My parents spent most of their lives trying to find their way home too. They wanted to return to their island, their people, their food; they yearned for the salt of the sea on their skin or at least my father did and my mother learned to want for what he wanted.

It is not easy to be the child of immigrants who, for most of my life, wore a longing for home nakedly. After they were married, my parents headed to the middle of the country because sometimes, to find home, you must first go farther afield. In Nebraska, a landlocked, flat place filled with thick, pale, cheery people, they were alone, far from everything they knew or loved but they were going to be happy. My father does not understand obstacles, doesn't believe they exist. He cannot even see obstacles. Failure was never going to be an option. He often says, "There is nothing a man cannot get through if he tries hard enough."

He built skyscrapers. We'd move for a year or two while he oversaw a new project, and come back to Omaha for a year or two, all our lives, all so he could reach higher and higher. My father said, "There's no telling how high a man can reach if he's willing to look up into the sky and straight into the sun." On the day of the ribbon cutting for his first skyscraper, my father stood with my mother, side by side, their bodies practically melded together. He held his arm around her waist, his hand resting possessively against her stomach. My brother and sister and I ran in frantic circles around them, buoyed by the excitement of a tall building and an oversized pair of scissors and our father, wearing his hard hat and a well-tailored suit. My parents stood staring up at the tower of steel and glass gleaming brightly beneath the high sun. My father said, "I told you I would build you a monument to the sky," and my mother murmured, "Yes, Sebastien, you certainly did." She once told me there was something very attractive about an ambitious man. I think she confuses ambition and ruthlessness. That night, we went out to dinner after the ceremony and my parents spent most of their time sitting with their foreheads touching in their own world. My parents are not warm people. They love hard and deep but you have to work to understand the exact nature of that love, to see it, to feel it. That day was the first time I realized my parents loved each other more than they loved us though I couldn't know then the price I would pay for that love.

ЖНI

Even hours after he stalked out, the Commander's threat lingered, trapped in the thick heat of my cage. I whispered my father's words. *There is nothing I cannot get through if I try hard enough*. My chest throbbed, my breasts still swelling, rock hard. Leaking milk spread over the cotton stretched across my chest. I had never planned on breastfeeding Christophe but when I first held him, so soft and mewing, his tiny lips quivering as they sought my breast, I couldn't help but hold him to my chest; I couldn't help but give him what he needed. Now, my son was alone with his father, needing me and there was nothing I could do. I gritted my teeth.

Growing up, my father told my siblings and me two things—I demand excellence and never forget you are Haitian first; your ancestors were free because they took control of their fate. When he came home from work each night, he'd find us in our corners of the house and ask, "How were you excellent today?" We needed to have a good answer. If he approved, a rare thing, he smiled, squeezed our shoulders. If he disapproved, he'd remove his glasses and rub his forehead, so wearied by our small failures. He would say, "You can be better. You control your fate."

His disapproval was constant and quiet and exhausting. Mona and Michel largely ignored my father's demands but as the youngest, I took him very seriously, made myself sick with the pursuit of perfection, the better he might love me for it. I had near-perfect recall of most everything I ever saw or heard or read—I was just lucky in that way. It wasn't so difficult to become excellent. My memory drives the people in my life crazy because I remember everything, always, in exacting detail. My memory was a gift until it became a curse, until no matter how hard I tried, I couldn't forget things I desperately needed to forget so I might survive.

One day, when we were fooling around, my brother and sister and I found a secret world about a mile from where we lived— an undeveloped tract of land with a small creek and lots of trees, all beyond a steep hill. People would go there to throw away their junk so there were always new, interesting things to play with and explore. We called it Pitfall, like the Atari game, and whenever we were done with our homework, we would jump on our bikes and head to a place where we weren't Haitians in America or Americans in Haiti, where we could make our own rules and draw our own maps. We only wanted to understand some small part of the world.

As I waited for something to happen, I began to draw a mental map of where my kidnappers were holding me, to make sense of this world I wanted no part of. That's what my father would want—for me to take whatever control I could. Starting at the door, I pressed my hand against the wall and began counting out the number of paces it took to walk the length of each wall— seven steps, ten steps, seven steps, ten steps. I tried to memorize these measurements; I tried to understand the terrifying shape of the walls holding me.

I wasn't tall enough to look out the window so I overturned the large bucket and stood on it. The window looked onto an alley littered with trash. Occasionally I saw the legs of a passerby. When I banged on the window, no one paid me any mind. "Help me," I shouted, until my throat hurt. "Please help me." Sometimes, a pair of legs stopped then quickly walked away.

This was not the Haiti my parents wanted to return to, this land of mad indifference. They remembered the country differently, almost fondly, and the beauty of their island only blossomed the further through time they moved away from it. Like most people, they, or at least my father, created a Haiti that only exists in his imagination—a country that would willingly embrace him.

When I graduated from high school, my parents returned to Port-au-Prince. He had his fill of working seventy hours a week, answering to white men who would never promote him even though he gave them more than twenty years of his life. My father started his own construction company and it soon became the largest, most successful firm in the country. He was the triumphant son, returned. He would reshape the country into the home he remembered, the unvarnished one. It was easy for my father to overlook the country's painful truths because they did not apply to him, to us. He left the island with nothing and returned with everything—a wife, children, wealth.

There is this truth too. My mother was reluctant to return to Port-au-Prince. The oppressive heat and the promiscuity of the capital, so many people living in such close quarters—it troubled her. She hated how everyone was always preoccupied with everyone else's lives. It would be different this time, my father assured her. They were together. They had money. My mother resigned herself to my father's dreams as she has always done.

After she returned to Haiti, I often wanted to ask her why my father's dreams were more important than her own, but the question would have hurt her more than her answer would have helped me. It wasn't until I was taken away from my husband and child that I realized we were all going to pay the price for my father's dreams.

I grew bored staring out the window, being ignored. I sat on the bucket and wondered what time it was. It felt like days had passed since we decided to go to the beach. The air was thick enough to fall into. The walls were slick with moisture. I heard a television and in the distance, a radio, cars speeding past. The music was familiar though I couldn't quite make it out. My bladder burned. My scalp throbbed. My face felt broken, the various pieces of me loose and coming apart. I crossed my legs tightly, wondered how my captors expected me to relieve myself. I could not handle pissing in a bucket, being forced to stay in that hot room with my own stink. That was what I thought because nothing much had yet been asked of me.

I did not want to ask my kidnappers for anything but I did not want to soil myself. I wouldn't be able to last much longer so I walked slowly to the door and pulled on it. It was locked. I exhaled slowly, knocked three times, waited. I started dancing from foot to foot. I knocked again, more loudly.

When the door finally opened, a young man, maybe twenty-five, not much younger than I, stood in the doorway. He too had a gun tucked into the waistband of his pants. He smiled, not unkindly.

"I need to use the restroom."

The man cocked his head to the right and turned. He motioned for me to follow. I walked with small steps, tried to memorize everything I saw. We passed the kitchen, where men still sat with dark glass bottles in front of them. They sneered as I walked by. The same man who leered at me earlier licked his lips slowly. I tried to ignore the line of fear weaving itself into my spine. Already my senses were sharpening. I smelled the danger.

The bathroom was small and unclean. The air was sour. There was a window, small, but I could still fit. I could try. And then I could run and get free, find my way home. A surge of hope flared through my breastbone. As I tried to close the door behind me, my escort stopped the door with the toe of his boot.

"Door stays open."

My face burned, heat rising up through my neck. "You cannot be serious."

He ran his fingers along the handle of his gun. I knew I couldn't hold out much longer. I was desperate. I bit my lower lip. My hands shook as I pushed my jeans and bikini bottoms down my thighs.

We were supposed to go to the beach, Michael, Christophe, and I. We were supposed to be at the beach, bathing beneath the sun while Michael ogled me in my new bikini. The bikini was a gift—black and chic with narrow, pleated folds along the front. He gave it to me the night before we left. I was in bed wearing a pair of his boxers and nothing else, one leg crossed over the other, bouncing my foot, watching him pack. He always packs for us, says I have no sense of how to arrange things in small spaces. Rather than get annoyed with how I pack, mostly by throwing piles of clothing into the suitcase and sorting it out upon arrival, he handles the packing.

When Michael finished with our son's suitcase, he threw himself on the bed next to me and slowly pulled the bikini out of his pants pocket, first the top then the bottom, dangling them over my face as I grabbed at them, giggling happily. "A beautiful body deserves a beautiful bikini," he said. We had already been married for five years, but I still blushed. He has always made me feel like the only beautiful woman in the world. I held the top against my chest, admiring the sleek design. I draped the bikini bra around his neck and pulled him toward me, hooking my leg over his, pulling him closer, pulling him into me, my heart pounding, his heart pounding, him on top of me and inside me, both of us quiet but breathing hard and something about the heavy silence of the moment made me feel everything that much more.

The man watching over me stared, the left side of his lip rising unattractively. I bit my lip harder, tasted blood, and tried to cover myself with my arms as I hovered over the toilet seat. The pressure between my thighs was unbearable. I tried to relax. I tried to breathe, to give in to the humiliation. I tried to let go but I couldn't. All I could feel was that man's eyes on my body, seeing parts of me I only showed my husband. "My husband is going to kill you," I said. "He is going to tear you apart with his bare hands." A wave of dizziness rocked me and I grabbed the sink to steady myself. My escort laughed, stepped inside the bathroom, closed the door behind him.

A fresh wave of panic rose inside me and finally I was able to relieve myself. I wiped quickly and flushed and moved to the sink to wash my hands. I stared at my reflection as I ran my hands under the lukewarm water. A bruise was spreading beneath my right eye and there was a thin cut along my forehead. I patted my damp hands over my face and wiped them on my jeans. I held on to the sink. My escort moved behind me. I looked up and studied him in the mirror. I gripped the sink more tightly. Our eyes met in the mirror. I refused to look away. He planted his hands on my shoulders, squeezing hard. He rolled my muscles beneath his fingers. It was not pleasant.

"You should thank me."

I nodded. I tried to ignore my instincts, tried to think of every possible outcome for anything I might say. I could be smart or I could be stupid; neither alternative would end well. I chose stupid. "I'm not going to thank you for a damn thing let alone taking a piss." I hoped the coarseness of my words might add some steel to my spine.

My escort laughed, sliding his hands down my bare arms. His hands were surprisingly soft. I looked at his fingernails, long but well manicured. He did not give the impression of a man who works hard. I had never felt anything so off-putting but then, I was only beginning to catalogue my discomfort. I had an inadequate frame of reference.

I stood straighter, forced my chin forward, continued to hold his gaze in the mirror, foolishly hoping bravado might save me from the inevitable. "Take your hands off me."

When he grabbed my hair and pulled my head back, my body understood what would happen next. The body holds a certain wisdom the mind does not. I threw my arms in front of my face as he pushed me forward, tried to slam my head into the mirror. The glass shattered. Tiny shards burrowed into my arms, creating tiny but very sharp dots of pain. It was hard to focus. I could only think of one word, *fight*. He pulled me toward him and I saw myself in the fractures of glass that remained. I already did not recognize myself. Seeing what fear looked like in my eyes was an honesty I wasn't prepared for. I whispered, "You will survive this." My escort began fumbling with the waistband of my jeans, his fingers pressing against the bones of my hips as he tried to tug my pants down. I kicked back and connected with his knee. He growled, muttered angry words. The barrel of his gun dug sharply into the back of my neck. "Enough," he said. "Fight me and you will regret it."

I kicked again. He wouldn't pull the trigger. He couldn't pull the trigger. My life mattered. I had one damn thing worth something to the men holding me. "You can't shoot me," I said, "or you won't get paid." I twisted from side to side trying to get away, reaching for the door. If I could make it into a different room, I would be safe. All I had to do was open that door.

He grabbed my hair again, practically lifting me off my feet. All my life I've been the small girl with the big mouth and both of those things were working against me. My escort was much bigger. All the men I had seen, I counted seven, were much bigger. They had lean and long bodies and strong hands and angry mouths. Once, they had been good boys. I needed to believe that. Thin streams of blood trickled along my forearms. My skin began to swell around the shards of glass.

"You do not understand your position," my escort said. "I will teach you."

He pulled me against him. His chest was tightly muscled, more like stone than the meat of a man. He shoved his hand down the front of my jeans, grabbing at me, forcing a finger inside of me. The intrusion was painful and unexpected. A wet sound curled in my throat as I tried to free myself from his grip. Finally, I found air. I screamed loud enough to make the walls shake.

He shoved his gun back in his pants and used his free hand to cover my mouth. "Make one more sound and you will regret it."

I ignored his threat, screamed into the palm of his hand as he forced his fingers deeper, feeling around for something he could not find. He burned my neck with the heat of his breath.

Suddenly, the bathroom door flew open and the Commander stood, glaring. My escort stopped, seemed to shrink into himself. I no longer felt his breath on my neck.

The Commander looked at my escort and shook his head. "This is not how we do business."

My escort pulled his hand out of my pants and pushed me away. Another man appeared in the hallway. I straightened my clothes, smoothed my hair. I refused to bow my head. I walked steady. I would not falter. The Commander ordered the newcomer to take me back to my cage. As I was led away, I looked back. My escort rubbed his fingers beneath his nose, smiled, nasty man.

Alone again, I sat on the bed. I was calm. I was calm. I was calm. I began carefully picking glass from my arm and setting the thin shards in a small pile on the floor next to my feet. When I finished, I looked at the small pyramid of bloody glass I had built. It was almost beautiful. There was a sharp ache between my thighs. Another wet scream curled in my throat but it felt important to stay calm, calm, calm. I covered my mouth with my hand and began rocking back and forth.

I waited. I had nothing but the memory of a strange man's fingers inside me, twisting, reaching, taking. I prayed this would be the only terrible thing I had to carry.

It had grown dark. No one came for me. I was thirsty, so very thirsty. I was hungry. I was tired. My body ached. All I could think about was the hot breath of a man I did not know on the back of my neck as he forced his fingers inside me and how he was going to come for me and no matter how hard I fought I would not be able to stop him.

I guessed Michael would be giving Christophe a bath, a bottle in the absence of my breast, putting the baby to bed. I wondered if Christophe would fall asleep easily without me. I talked to my son every night as he fell asleep, told him important and silly things so he could hear the sound of my voice, so he could always know I loved him and chose to spend time with him. Michael would talk to Christophe as he fell asleep. My husband would do that for me but it would not be the same. Christophe would know I wasn't there.

I had to go to the bathroom again but the ransom for that small dignity would be high. A car raced through the alley blaring music. I was so tired. My body felt heavy. I lay on my side, my back to the wall so I could keep my eye on the door. I waited and waited and tried to ignore everything my body needed and would soon have to endure. In the before I took the sanctity of my body for granted. In the after my body was nothing. It was a matter of time. I had known that from the moment I was taken. The waiting was worse than anything I could imagine. My imagination was still quite limited then. That is no longer the case.

||||||

Waiting. It was terrible. The house was quiet, too quiet, a cavernous and echoing shell without Mireille. Michael had never gotten used to his wife's family's wealth. When they were in Miami it was easy to pretend his wife was more like him, middle-class, born and raised. Sure, they lived a nice life but they worked hard. In Haiti, there was no way to pretend. The opulent homes, the cars and the drivers and people always waiting on you hand and foot and beach houses bigger than most people's houses back in the States and everyone wearing designer everything and so many unspoken rules about how to behave. Half the time, Michael was afraid to open his mouth for fear of saying or doing the wrong thing around people he knew nothing about. Miri always assured him he was fine but he felt out of place around his wife's family and secretly suspected they didn't think he was good enough for her though Lord knows they were too mannered to admit it.

Michael sat up in the large bed he normally shared with Miri when they visited her parents. He could almost see the outline of her body in the sheets, feel her feet stretched over his legs. Next to him, Christophe slept fitfully, twisting around. Michael frowned. Normally their son slept peacefully.

The laptop on his thighs was warm, the fan whirring softly. Michael's eyes were dry and heavy. Too much time had passed. He continued scouring the Internet for as much information as possible about international kidnappings and ransom and proof of life—developing a bewildering vocabulary for a nightmare he had never imagined, not even in his darkest moments of trying to understand his wife's country.

The sharp pain just beneath Michael's breastbone would not go away. Every sound startled him from his stupor, but only briefly. Mostly, he thought, "This can't be real. This is not happening. This cannot be real."

Earlier, after a cursory visit from a pair of police officers who took a few notes and promised to "investigate," Michael and his in-laws waited for a phone call that did not come. The kidnappers were sticking to their schedule. It would be another day still before they would know where to bring the ransom, how much that ransom might be, a ransom Sebastien seemed unwilling to pay. Michael couldn't allow himself to even consider such a possibility. It made no sense. Sebastien had to be posturing. Michael pressed his hand against the baby's chest. No father would refuse a ransom for his child, especially no father with so much money at his disposal. He shook his head. "No," he said into the quiet room. "No." They were going to get Mireille back, soon, and this would be over, forgotten. They would go home to their real lives. They would forget all about this place; finally, they would be free of it, forever.

If he could just hear Mireille's voice for a few seconds, the tightness in his chest might loosen. He might breathe again. He might let go of the nagging realization that all this was too far beyond his control.

Kidnapping. The word didn't even feel real. When Michael called his parents just before putting Christophe to bed, they listened in disbelief, promised to pray for Mireille even though they weren't usually much for praying, not anymore. The more he thought about it, Michael could not think of a single person he knew who had much faith at all. He was starting to understand why. "You get her back, no matter what," his mother, Lorraine, said, her voice steely. "You get her back right now and then you get on a plane with my grandson and bring your family home."

Michael promised he would and his parents pretended they did not know how hollow those words were.

His head still hurt, and the wound on his forehead itched beneath the gauze. Michael closed the laptop and set it on the floor. There was too much online, too much to know and see—stories of people held hostage for years, tortured for no reason at all, ears cut off, human trafficking. Michael rolled onto his side, pulling his son into the warm cave of his body. He closed his eyes and reached for the empty space just beyond the child. He could almost feel Mireille's skin against his, how she smiled in bed when she turned toward him, her chin jutting gently forward, her lips slightly parted, eyes half-lidded. She was the most beautiful girl and she was his. Her smile. That's what he would focus on. Before long, Michael had drifted into a sleep as fitful as his son's.

The call to make arrangements for the ransom came the next morning at 10 a.m., as promised. Sebastien answered the phone and the negotiator picked up a second receiver, started the recording equipment.

"We have your daughter. The price is one million dollars U.S. We are ready to make arrangements for the delivery of the money and the return of your daughter."

Sebastien tried to stay calm. He looked down at his hand, saw it was shaking. He frowned, shoved his hand in his pocket. "We don't have that kind of money," Sebastien said.

"Let us not play these games. They are beneath us."

The negotiator gave Sebastien a look and Sebastien nodded, clearing his throat. "We are willing to pay one hundred and twenty-five thousand dollars, not one penny more. Hear me clearly."

Michael hovered near Sebastien; his eyes were glassy with panic, more of the naked, wild emotion that made Sebastien Duval so uncomfortable.

"One hundred and twenty-five thousand," Sebastien repeated. "And I want my daughter back within the next twenty-four hours." He swallowed hard and hung up.

Michael's eyes widened. "Are you insane? You're trying to bargain them down?" He rushed at his father-in-law, swinging his arms, but the negotiator stood between the two men, gripped Michael's arms until he stilled.

"This is how these matters are handled. You have to trust my expertise," the negotiator said.

The three men stood in uncomfortable silence staring at the phone. It did not ring.

"This is sheer lunacy," Michael muttered. "This is not how we're going to get Miri back. You didn't see them and their guns. They aren't messing around."

Sebastien raised his hand in the imperious manner that drove Michael crazy. He wanted to break all the fingers in the man's hand. He clenched his jaw, forced himself to stay calm. Circles of sweat spread from beneath his arms across his back.

A few minutes later, the phone rang again. Sebastien counted to ten, then picked up the phone. "Yes," he said.

"The ransom for your daughter is one million dollars U.S. We will not negotiate."

Sebastien had always been able to make difficult decisions. When he left everything he had known, he had been nothing more than a boy, really, always hungry, his feet caked with dirt at the end of each day. He abandoned his nothing of a life to start anew in a strange country where he still had so little but knew it was possible to hope. He found his way, had made everything of himself.

"If that's the case, I'm afraid there is nothing more for us to discuss," Sebastien said, avoiding Michael's stare. "That was my only offer. I expect my daughter returned to me within twenty-four hours, unharmed."

Sebastien hung up the phone. As always, he would do what was necessary to protect his family, his entire family. Michael kicked a chair across the room and stormed out. Sebastien tried to ignore the doubt, so unfamiliar an emotion, tearing at the edges of his resolve. "This is the right choice," he said softly. He wasn't going to lose everything he had worked for to thieving losers, only to be left with nothing of a life again.

卌|||

I sweated everywhere—beneath my arms and between my thighs, along my spine. My breasts still leaked. My body was weeping but whenever I felt like crying I bit down on my knuckles until the pain distracted me. What little air there was grew so thick I thought I might die. My chest tightened ever more.

As a child, I felt that strange sense of suffocating, often. There was the heat of a Nebraska summer and there was the heat of Port-au-Prince and they were two very different things.

Every summer, my parents took us to Haiti during the worst possible time—June and July. We always began packing in early May. It was easy to sift through our clothes—nice outfits for church and visiting distant relatives, swimsuits for the beach, T-shirts and shorts to play with our cousins. The more difficult packing was the various goods we were expected to bring—American movies on videotape and later, DVD, Gap clothing, large bottles of olive oil and industrial-sized bags of rice from discount warehouses, small electronics, Nike sneakers, cornflakes, Tampax, all the things that were outrageously expensive and eagerly coveted in the motherland, what my siblings and I called Haiti, always with a smirk. My mother coordinated the packing efforts, putting these goods in suitcases large enough to accommodate the body of a large adult male, perhaps two. At the airport, we would stand in line with all the other *dyaspora* and their unfathomably large suitcases. I found the whole affair mortifying and tried to stand as far away from my parents and their embarrassing luggage as possible. It was easy to spot the Haitian families not only from the suitcases, but from the hovering masses of American-born children hiding in plain sight at a comfortable distance.

Before every trip, my parents reminded us of the proper etiquette for children in Haiti. They did not want us to draw undue attention to ourselves. They wanted us to be seen and not heard, speaking when spoken to, never speaking out of turn, never raising our voices or being disrespectful. Despite their best efforts we always drew attention to ourselves. My brother tried to sag his jeans until a stranger in the airport grabbed him by the ears and hitched his pants up to their proper place, sucking her teeth and shaking her head. Mona and I wore low-cut T-shirts and large hoop earrings and short skirts. All three of us wore headphones, listening to music our parents disapproved of. We answered our parents in English when they spoke to us in French.

The airport in Port-au-Prince was the worst place on earth for spoiled children. It was the only place we ever visited where you had to go outside after getting off the plane and before entering the terminal. The moment we started walking down the hot metal staircase, the unbearably thick air wrapped itself around our bodies, seeping into our pores. The walk across the tarmac was interminable as the throng of Haitians, elated or miserable about returning home, pushed us forward. We waited in an endless customs line overwhelmed by the heat and the smell of so many sweaty people in cramped quarters and then, outside the airport as we waited for a cab or a relative to pick us up, it was like being thrown into the middle of a riot, everyone shouting, waving their hands wildly in the air, ignoring the rules of polite conduct and personal space.

We always stayed with my mother's favorite sister. Tante Lola married well and owned lots of property. There was a guesthouse with its own pool behind her house and we installed ourselves there for weeks at a time.

This is the Haiti of my childhood—summer afternoons at the beach, swimming in the warm and salty blue of the ocean. We ate grilled meat and drank Coke from green glass bottles, biting the rim, enjoying the sound our teeth made against the glass. We played in the sand and my sister and I chased my brother up and down the beach while our parents cheerfully ignored us. There is a picture of me sitting on the beach. I am fourteen, skinny, just starting puberty, late bloomer. I am wearing the first bathing suit I have ever been allowed to choose for myself. It is blue, one piece, cut high at the hips but modestly. There is a strap around my neck that reaches down to a threaded knot between my collarbones. I am wearing sunglasses because I want to look sophisticated. I want to stare at cute boys as they come out of the water, without admonishment from my parents. My

knees are pulled to my chest. I am also wearing a straw hat with
a matching blue band, a gift from my father. I saw the hat while
we were driving through the city on the way from visiting one
relative to another. A vendor had what seemed like hundreds
of hats displayed on a large tarp. I started tapping the window
with my hand excitedly. I begged my father to pull over and suddenly he did and I grinned like a crazy person. We all piled out
of the car and hovered around the display, each trying to decide
on the perfect *chapeau*. I would wear the hat every day for the
rest of our trip and back in the States I would wear my perfect
hat for the rest of the summer until school started and a classmate teased me about my sombrero and then the hat found its
way to the back of my closet, crushed by sneakers, a black sock,
a softball helmet.

In another picture, my sister and I are standing on the beach,
arm in arm. Behind us, my parents' beach house in Jacmel is
being built and the concrete frame of the house stands, win-
dowless. My mother is on the long veranda, already finished.
She is waving, her arm midair, her fingers curled toward us. I
am fifteen. Mona is eighteen. It is Mona's last summer before
college. She is radiant. She can taste freedom, which is all we
ever wanted, freedom from our parents, from the endless trips
to Haiti, from our parents' rules. Our ingratitude, in the face of
our happiness, was fairly staggering. In the picture, we are both
wearing two-piece bathing suits, matching. Mona convinced my
parents it would be fine to allow us to wear bikinis because we
were good girls. Mona was not really a good girl. I knew that, always waited up for her when she snuck out at home in the States
to drive around in the backseats of cars with American boys.
When she came home, she smelled like beer and cigarette smoke

and my mother's perfume, which she sprayed behind her ears and knees and under her elbows. Mona taught me about kissing and going to third base and wrote silly words on my back with her fingers as she taught me everything important. She told me about kids who didn't have to be home by eight, who didn't have to spend their Saturdays in a stupid basement surrounded by other miserable Haitian kids. In the picture, Mona's lips are nuzzling my ear. She's whispering, "You'll be free soon too." My childhood was very different from that of my brother and sister. By the time I was old enough to want to feel free, my parents had relaxed many of the strict rules they enforced for Michel and Mona. Michel is not in the picture because he was already in graduate school. When he went away to college, he never really came home. Sons are different, my mother says. They always look for home somewhere else. Daughters, though, a mother can count on. Daughters always come home.

This is the Haiti of my childhood—my father building toy boats and pointed hats for us from palm fronds. He taught us how to eat sugarcane, how we had to peel the thin bark and suck on the fibrous core. He took us to an old woman's house and bought *dous*, a sugary fudge, wrapped in wax paper. We ate so much of it our mouths wrinkled. Back in the States, he was always serious, always wearing suits and shiny shoes, rarely laughing, rarely home because he had to build and outwork and outthink the white men he worked with. In Haiti, my father was a man who eagerly removed his shoes and rolled up his slacks to climb a palm tree to gather coconuts. One by one he would throw the coconuts down. My mother held the fruit high over her head and slammed them down on a sharp rock and when the hard shell cracked open, she would pull the coconut apart and peel the coconut meat from the shell, handing each of us large pieces. We hated coconut but we ate it anyway.

This is the Haiti of my childhood—my mother sitting with her sisters, gossiping about everyone they ever knew, their childhood friends and where those friends were now, their current friends and neighbors, former lovers, the people they worked with, their husbands, their fathers. My mother always glowed, her fair skin tanned, eyes bright, hair hanging down past her shoulders. Only in Haiti do I remember her laughing nakedly, talking openly, easily, in a way that was so foreign to us. Mona and I always hid nearby trying to hear every word of the adult conversation. Listening to my mother and aunts talking made us feel like we knew her.

Driving through Port-au-Prince is a precarious affair. There are more people than room on the road. There is no order, no patience, no civility. Anytime we climbed into the backseat to go somewhere, I felt wound up with nervous energy. I sat between my brother and sister gripping their thighs as they held on to their door handles, their knuckles white. It wasn't the wild driving that scared me, though. It was the angry mobs swarming our car whenever we slowed at an intersection or to make a turn from one narrow street to another. No matter where we went, our car was always mobbed at street corners by men and women and children, hungry and angry and yearning to know what it might feel like to sit in the leather seats of an air-conditioned luxury sedan. My father saw himself in those people. As we grew older, we saw ourselves in those people. The bones of our faces were the same. My father would open his window just a crack to throw out *gourdes* and sometimes, American dollars. He would try to pull away in the wake of the desperate clamor to reach for that money. I remember seeing a man with one leg and an enormous tumor beneath his right eye disfiguring his face and the way he slammed his hands against my window and stared at me with such disgust. I waved to him and he spit on the window, a thick globule of white saliva slowly sliding down the window. He shouted something I didn't understand. My sister turned my head, held me in the crook of her arm. "Look straight ahead," she said, and so I did. I looked straight ahead at the backs of my parents' heads and the crowded street before us and I tried to forget how brightly the rage and frustration pulsed off the man with the broken body on the corner.

We loved Haiti. We hated Haiti. We did not understand or know Haiti. Years later, I still did not understand Haiti but I longed for the Haiti of my childhood. When I was kidnapped, I knew I would never find that Haiti ever again.

ℍℍℍℍ 卌||||

In the cage there was no time. I don't know when I fell asleep. There were only the walls threatening to close in on me and the heavy stillness of the air. I lay alone on the narrow mattress, my body lonely for my husband. We had not slept apart in years.

Michael and I met in graduate school—he was getting his master's degree in civil engineering and I was attending law school. There was no reason for our paths to cross, but there he was, standing outside my office, looking for Kendra, the woman I shared a tiny office space with. Mutual friends set them up on a blind date and she was running late on her way from the law library to meet him. Michael leaned in the doorway, his large frame filling the space.

He smiled, asked why he had never seen me before. I said something about the improbability of billions of people in the world. He asked me out right then.

I couldn't help but laugh. I said, "Are you really that guy?"

"If it means getting to take you out, yes, ma'am. I am that guy."

I was lonely. I was not good with men or dating or interactions of any kind with other people. Until Michael, my hardly romantic history consisted of four men who were not memorable in any way. I leaned back in my chair and took my glasses off, set them on my desk. I pointed to the stack of books on my desk. I said, "I'm in law school. I don't date." My hands grew sweaty so I slid them beneath my thighs.

Michael stepped into my office and leaned against the edge of my desk, close. Too close. I smelled his cologne and the soap he used. A strange warmth rose up through my neck. I looked up. "Have you heard of personal space?"

He crossed his arms across his chest. "You are feisty."

I rolled my eyes. "That's what men always say when women don't fall at their feet swooning."

"Do women still swoon?"

"If you have to ask . . ."

He laughed, a full, throaty laugh that filled the small office. Before we could continue our banter, Kendra appeared, looked from me back to Michael and raised an eyebrow. Michael stood, awkwardly, hovering near my desk, but he never stopped looking at me or through me. He and Kendra introduced themselves, made small talk while she packed her bag so they could leave for their date. I was irritated. He still kept staring at me.

"What are you looking at?" I asked.

He gave me a *look*. I turned away. I thought about his hands, what they might feel like on my arms, against the small of my back, elsewhere. My irritation grew. Michael and Kendra left and I stared at the door for a few moments thinking about how his laugh and his smell lingered. I decided he had an unnaturally large head. Suddenly, he appeared in the doorway again. "I have to make this fast. Go out with me. There will be swooning."

Although most everything about him irritated me, from his arrogant smile to his Republican style of dress—a button-down shirt and sensible khakis—still, I accepted his invitation, said, "I will give you one evening to make me swoon."

He tugged on my elbow and took my hand and kissed my knuckles. His breath warmed me.

I pointed to the door. "Go away. Your date is waiting."

He disappeared again, quickly reappeared once more. "I like that you are already jealous."

Hours later, I called Mona and told her about the arrogant American who asked me out while picking up another woman for a date. She laughed, said, "You've finally met someone you actually like. I hear it in your voice."

"I have not," I said, stuttering.

Mona laughed harder. I wished she would stop. "I'll remind you of this conversation, someday," she said.

I ignored the fluttering in my chest and hung up on her. Ending phone conversations abruptly is a bad habit of mine.

At the end of our first date, dinner, movie, ridiculous conversation, I stood just inside my front door. Michael stuck his foot between the door and the jamb, leaned in and kissed me. His breathing was loud and heavy, his breath warm on my face. He clasped my neck. His pulse throbbed against my throat. I sighed and he whispered, "I do believe you swooned."

Mona told me not to play hard to get when I told her about the date. "Girls have to put out, these days," she said. "You know what to do, don't you?"

My tongue grew dry. "Of course," I said. "I know lots of things about men and women."

"Miri, shut up. You are not seriously a virgin."

I hung up on my sister, my face burning hot.

Michael and I had our second date at a popular bar downtown that used to be a theatre after I ignored him for a few days and he suggested I was playing hard to get and I tersely informed him I was not familiar with that game.

As we sat waiting for the waitress to bring our drinks, Michael said, "You never confirmed whether or not there was swooning."

I patted his chest. "Again, I say, if you have to ask . . ."

I drank my first drink quickly—a stiff gin and tonic with a splash of grenadine for which Michael teased me mercilessly. "You're basically drinking a Shirley Temple," he said. When I tried to kick him beneath the table, he grabbed my ankle. His hand was warm. My eyes widened. He nodded smugly, said, "I have lightning-fast reflexes." I tried to kick him with my other leg. He grabbed that ankle too.

We sat there, my ankles in his hands. I continued to sip my drink, making enthusiastic noises. Finally, I said, "This is awkward." Michael released my ankles. I immediately felt colder. We continued drinking and I looked Michael up and down, stabbing a plastic sword in his direction. "I bet you're one of those guys whose bedroom at home is still decorated with all the trophies you won in high school, playing some macho sport like football. And you were the big man on campus, and you dated hot girls, and you've never been unpopular a day in your life."

He grinned. "Do they give trophies for football?"

I shrugged. "I don't know."

"Wrestling."

"Come again?"

"I wrestled in high school and college. And yes, my mom has kept my trophies and awards and such in my room at the farm. And yes, people tend to like me. Is that so bad? You like me."

I dropped an ice cube in my mouth, chewing it loudly. "I don't even know you. So far, you are mildly tolerable."

"We can remedy that." Michael leaned back in his seat and told me his life story, the good and bad of it.

His openness was frightening. Americans are so fond of confession without considering the consequences. I didn't tell him much about myself; there wasn't much to tell. I had always been a good girl, focused on being excellent.

Before long, the alcohol went straight to my head and I stopped making sense. I have never been good at holding my liquor. When the bartender threw us out at closing, Michael said, "I should get you home."

"Now would be a good time for you to take me to your place so we can wrestle." I giggled and flexed my arms. "Maybe I will win a trophy."

I expected him to say something chivalrous. Instead, Michael opened my door and spilled me into my seat. As we drove, I sang along with the radio. I always sing along when I hear music no matter where I am—grocery stores, malls, dental offices. It is either a charming affectation or a terrible one, depending on whom you ask.

"You have a nice voice."

I turned to look at Michael. I rested my hand on his thigh, my fingertips reaching inward. "You, sir, are a liar."

"No really."

I began singing more enthusiastically and lowered the zipper of his slacks, sliding my hand between the folds of fabric. I had seen it in movies. Michael stiffened at my touch. My hand tingled. He gripped the steering wheel more tightly. He sighed softly, and I squeezed my fingers around him but then I wasn't sure what to do next so we stayed like that until we didn't.

Michael's apartment was spare but clean—an old love seat, a large television, and an array of stereo components. In the spare bedroom, there was a drafting table, a futon, and lots of athletic gear—a basketball, dumbbells, a weight belt, some sort of cryptic-looking exercise machine that seemed neglected. We stripped as we stumbled to his bedroom and by the time we fell onto the bed we were naked. I could feel every inch of my skin. It was so strange but I didn't want that feeling to go away. We were not shy. I kissed him wetly, running my hands over the muscles in his shoulders. I said, "You have such nice shoulders. You have very pretty shoulders. Did you know that?"

Michael held himself above my body, his muscles flexing attractively. "How drunk are you?" he asked.

I traced his breastbone with my fingernails. "Do you care?" Before he could answer, I rolled over onto my stomach and looked back at him. My head felt heavy and I buried my face in the pillow. I giggled and said, "Your shoulders really are so pretty. You are a pretty, pretty princess."

He pressed his thumbs along my sides and worked his hands up my back like he was trying to push me out of my own skin. I reared, tried to pull him into my body with my leg.

"You have beautiful skin, beautiful brown skin," he said, his voice barely above a whisper.

When I woke, the room was painfully bright. I covered my eyes with my arm, rolling away from the window. The bed was unfamiliar. I rolled to the other side, slowly moving my arm, taking in my surroundings. I tried to remember where I was. I tried to make sense of the thick, sour taste coating my mouth, my lips, my teeth.

"Good morning," a voice said.

My own voice didn't seem to work. I mumbled incoherently.

I was naked and quickly pulled the sheet tightly around me, sat up and pulled my knees into my chest. One layer of fog evaporated. I slowly began to recognize Michael, those pretty shoulders, his ridiculously appealing hair, his face, open and eager to please. He brushed stray strands of hair out of my face and tucked them behind my ear. He kissed the tip of my nose. He said, "You are lovely to look at first thing in the morning."

My stomach rolled uncomfortably. I leaned back against the headboard and closed my eyes. "You didn't take me home last night?"

"You asked me to bring you to my place."

I buried my face in my hands, began rubbing my temples. "I drank too much. This is unusual for me but I don't remember anything after you holding my ankles in the bar. And something about trophies."

Michael tugged on the sheet that had fallen around my waist. The throbbing in my head trumped modesty. "You were a wildcat. And you called me a pretty, pretty princess."

I shook my head violently, then instantly regretted that decision. I rolled out of the bed and began grabbing for my clothes. I dressed quickly and made an awkward goodbye with a half-assed apology. As I walked home I tried to reassemble my dignity. By the time I reached my house I had sweated most of the gin. My hangover stink was terrible. I needed to wallow so I fell onto the couch and passed out after cursing myself for my inability to interact normally with men.

Hours later, a loud knocking at my front door brought me out of my still-drunken stupor. "I'm coming," I said hoarsely, carefully finding my way to the front door while trying to maintain my balance. The sour stink lingered. I opened the door a crack and peeked out. Michael stood on my porch holding coffee, which he passed me through the narrow opening.

He smiled. "I came to make you something to eat."

I accepted the coffee and inhaled the rising steam and waved my hand. "No food."

He pushed the door open and slipped inside. As I closed the door, I muttered, "What is it with you and personal space? Come on in, why don't you."

Michael stood in the foyer, his hands shoved into his pockets. "You look terrible."

"Thanks. Tell me—when you come to the home of a one-night stand uninvited, is that stalking?"

Michael laughed. "You're the lawyer in training but I'm not a one-night stand."

I arched an eyebrow. He cupped his hand around the bottom of my coffee cup and raised it to my lips. "Drink." I took a small sip. The coffee made my mouth taste even worse.

"We didn't have sex last night," he said.

I slapped Michael's chest hard. My hand stung. I shook it loosely. "You could have told me that hours ago."

He shrugged. "This was more fun."

I turned to walk away, muttering, "Asshole," but he grabbed me by my waist, pulling me into his arms. I dropped my cup and a thin trickle of coffee began to spill onto the beautiful wooden floors, something exotic the original owner said when my father bought the place for me. Michael pulled his fingers through my hair, stretching my face taut. He kissed me so hard I felt his lips in my spine. It was the kiss of a stranger and I wanted it and I wanted him. I have always played hard to get because other people terrify me but right then, I didn't have the energy for my usual nonsense. I reached for his waistband, drawing myself into his body.

Between kisses, I said, "I look and smell hideous right now."

My eyes were dry and sore. My head continued to throb dully. Everything was fuzzy and distant and then it wasn't. Michael started pushing me back toward the staircase. He bit into my neck and fumbled with his jeans, trying to shove them down with one hand while he pulled my pants down with his other hand. The edge of a step dug into my back painfully. I ignored it. Then he was inside me and I gasped as he opened my body, a sharp ache spreading up through my stomach and down through my heels and he was shoving his tongue into my sour mouth, groaning loudly while he fucked me steady and hard. His hair brushed my forehead and my neck and I arched into him like I was hoping to conjoin our rib cages. He showed me how little I knew about him.

When he came, he pressed his sweaty forehead against mine, slowly turning his head from side to side. He said, "God, I'm going to marry you," and I gasped softly and sank into the mild panic he inspired. He continued moving inside me, breathing hotly on my face, inhaling my ugly hangover sweat, and the earnestness and inappropriateness of his words and his mouth on my neck and his fingers between our bodies and my thighs nearly made me come too.

I wanted to cry. I wanted to sleep. Michael's body grew heavier on top of mine. I had to push him off me, finally, because the pressure of the step digging into my back became too much. I started crawling up the stairs. I said, "Are you coming?" He looked down at his cock, hanging half stiff, coated with a thin layer of blood. I blushed, said, "I must have started my period."

I wouldn't tell him he was my first until our wedding night, when finally, in our room, I shouted, "Jesus, just rip it off," after endless minutes of his awkward fumbling with my dress. Michael calmed himself; he was patient, found a way through the silk to my skin. We did not make it to the bed. Even though we were tired and drunk, we fell to the floor and just before he entered me, I grabbed his chin, was reminded again of the weight of the rings on my finger. I said, "You are the only one."

He smiled softly, kissed my chin, said, "You're the only one too, babe."

I grabbed his chin again. "No. I need you to hear me. You are the only one."

Michael paused. His body trembled against mine. He drew his fingers down my face and paused at my lips, sliding his thumb into my mouth. "Seriously?"

My face warmed. I looked away.

He shook his head. "Mireille, you are utterly impossible. You should have said something."

"I just did."

"Miri, if I had known, I would have waited, I would have been more of a gentleman. I didn't know."

"You know now and you were perfect." I spread my legs, wrapping them around his waist, pulling him inside me.

After the first time we made love, Michael bounded up the stairs after me, saying, "Blood doesn't scare me." I pointed him to my bed, said I was going to jump in the shower. He said, "You look beautiful." I ignored him. In the shower, I stood under the hot stream of water, my arm against the wall, my head against my arm, trying to make sense of how fairy tales begin.

卌卌

A new day, a rough hand pulled me to my feet by my hair. My scalp screamed, had already withstood so much. I tried to stand, disoriented. Again, I didn't remember falling asleep. I still couldn't breathe. I ached. I wanted a moment of clean, fresh air. I wanted water. I smelled sharp and sour. My stomach rolled.

The Commander shoved a phone into my hand. "It has been two days," he shouted. Thick strands of saliva flew out of his mouth, wrapped around each word. "Why doesn't your father pay?"

I shrank, trying to find an answer that might satisfy us both. That answer did not exist. "I told you. My father will not negotiate. You are wasting your time. You stole the wrong woman."

The Commander grabbed my arm and twisted it behind my back. The pain was so sudden I gasped. The muscles in my shoulder twisted uncomfortably and I tried to do anything to make my body stop feeling like it was being pulled apart.

"Call your father," he said.

I tried to dial the number using my thumb. It was hard to focus on the numbers and the pain at the same time, hard to figure out how to manage either. I was not going to cry. That's what I kept telling myself. I was sick of those words. When my father answered, I said, "It's me." I looked at the Commander. "What do you want me to say?"

He twisted my arm harder. I bit my lip but tried to make no sound, no sound at all. "I want your father to hear what is happening to you while he wastes time negotiating or not negotiating, as the case may be. I am the one who does not negotiate, not him."

I was shoved against a wall and dropped the phone. The impact threw me off balance but still I was silent. The Commander handed me the phone again. "Tell your father. Tell him how you're being treated."

When I looked at the Commander closely, I realized how young he was. Not even the hideous scar beneath his eye could hide how little he knew despite how much he knew, that he was, in his skin, more boy than man. I told myself he could not force me to do anything. He could not make me dance for him. Or it was that the Commander did not understand how I knew my father, a man who has put great faith in himself. That faith has always been richly rewarded. Performing my distress for my father to demonstrate how badly I was being treated would serve no purpose. I am, or I was, very much like my father. I shook my head. I did not waver. I did not look away. I held the phone to my ear again and said, "I am fine and being treated as well as can be expected, but I am ready to come home."

"We hope to have this situation resolved soon," my father said, calmly. "Stay strong." His ability to remain calm under any circumstance has always surprised me. During my thirteen days of captivity I spoke to my father several times. His voice never wavered.

I wanted to ask for Michael but I did not want to give the Commander the satisfaction of knowing what or who mattered most. I tried to think of something funny I could say, something clever. I couldn't. I was violently hungry so I said, "Tell my husband to get in the kitchen and make me some damn dinner."

The Commander gave me a look. In that stifling hot room, I was instantly cold.

My arm was wrenched so tightly the bone seemed to stretch away from my shoulder socket. The pain made all the air in my chest disappear. The room went white and then black and then white again. I ended the phone call and only then did I give voice to my agony.

The Commander released his grip and I fell to the floor clutching my arm. I tried to curl in on myself. The Commander rubbed his chin and stared down at me. He planted his boot on my head. "You will not enjoy the consequences of your petty defiance."

He sounded like a movie villain. I laughed and the Commander left me there, cackling hysterically.

I often laugh when it is inappropriate. The first time Michael brought me to his parents' farm, three hundred acres between Lincoln and Grand Island, he took me on a long walk around the property. We saw the corrals and outbuildings and acres and acres of pasture, an abandoned tractor, a couple of small oil derricks. As we walked, we held hands and he told me stories of hot summer days working with his father, early to bed and early to rise. He told me how once, when he was a boy, it was so cold, the cattle froze to the ground right where they stood. I laughed and laughed imagining a herd of cows trapped in shrouds of ice across the pastures. Michael's face fell. We were silent for the rest of the walk and he began to walk faster. I had to run-walk-step to keep up with him until finally I was tugging at his shirt.

Michael and his parents are proud of their land. His family's roots, my husband told me on our first date, are so deep, they reach straight through the earth to the other side. My father feels the same about his land in Haiti though the roots on an island are, perhaps, not as strong because they have less to hold on to.

The Jameson family farm is beautiful—everywhere you look, shades of green and gold and brown as far as the eye can see. Day and night, you hear the rustle of corn and soybean stalks as sweet as the ear can hear. And then there's the stink of the pigs and their filth. Just after they're fed, the pigs start to squeal. The sound is so high-pitched and heartbreaking, it makes my skin crawl. You can't hide from the truth of life on the farm. We are animals and we eat animals and in order to eat animals you need to keep and kill animals. It took several visits before I was able to eat a meal at my in-laws' table without feeling nauseous. I once joked, "This is the circle of life," as we sat down to dinner and Glen, my father-in-law, informed me we were eating beef from a freshly slaughtered cow. Michael and his parents nodded and said, "Amen."

My sarcasm doesn't really work in the country.

The day Michael told me about the frozen cows I grabbed hold of his elbow and pulled until he stopped. "Did I say something wrong?"

Michael shrugged out of my grip and stalked off. Over his shoulder, he shouted, "I need to be away from you right now. You can be so mean."

I made my way back to the house slowly, trying not to think about the way *mean* sounded coming from Michael, like I had committed a sin for which there could be no forgiveness. I found his mother in the kitchen baking a pie. I stood in the doorway and asked if there was anything I could do to help. She gazed at me curiously as she kneaded a thick mound of dough, said, "We don't get much of your kind around here." She paused, slapped the dough hard, sending white puffs of flour everywhere.

My face burned hotly and my chest tightened. "Do you mean law students?"

"Your clever talk won't do you any favors here." Lorraine paused, wiping her hands on her apron. "I don't think you're going to last. My son is having a little fun. He's always wanted to go to the islands."

I didn't know what to say so I excused myself, went and sat on the porch. The longer I sat there, the angrier I became. When Michael found me, I was crying.

That night we lay next to each other, angrily, in his childhood bed, the detritus of his youthful accomplishments watching over us, me staring into his broad back. Every time one of us shifted, the other shifted in the opposite direction.

Finally, I sighed loudly. "Maybe we are trying too hard to make this work. You let your mother believe we are casual and that's fine if we are casual but you say one thing to me and let her believe another and so you can see, I hope, why that makes me doubt you."

He turned on his side, propping himself on one elbow. He put his hand on my stomach. "Is that what you think?"

I turned away. "Yes, Michael. That is exactly what I think."

"Sometimes," Michael said, "you say the stupidest fucking things."

I sat up so quickly I felt dizzy. "Excuse me? Did you just call me stupid?"

Michael got up on his knees, pushed me onto my back, and straddled my waist. "No, I did not." The whites of his eyes glowed. Frustration pulsed from his skin. He looked very different, dangerous. It excited me. He grabbed my arms and pushed them over my head.

I tried to extract myself from his grasp, my heart beating faster than I thought a heart could beat. "Have you lost your mind?"

He shoved my wrists deeper into the old mattress. The bed creaked. I wondered what his mother might say if she could see her son the way I have seen him. We fucked hard and angry, his hand sweaty, covering my mouth to keep me quiet. I didn't know him until that night. I did not truly love him until that night.

Later, after he fell asleep, I found one of his old T-shirts and a pair of shorts. My sneakers were waiting neatly by the front door. In the driveway, I looked up into his bedroom window for a long while. There's a gravel road that circles his parents' farm. In the deep of night, I started running, enjoying the sound of the gravel spreading away from me with each footfall. When I finally stopped running, it was still dark but the air felt cooler, thinner. I was covered in sweat and the threadbare T-shirt clung to my body. Michael was waiting on the front porch. He looked exhausted and his hair stood on end. He jumped down the porch steps and pulled me into a long embrace, burying his face in my damp neck. When I tried to push him away, he only held on to me more tightly. I have always appreciated how he never lets me go. I need that. My natural instinct is for flight and the safety of solitude.

"I thought you left," he whispered.

I shook my head. I could feel sweat and him on my inner thighs. "Where would I go?"

We sat on the porch stairs. I said, "I'm tired." In the distance, we heard the echoing call of a rooster and then another. I shivered. "Your mother hates me."

"No she doesn't. She's slow to warm. There's a difference."

His answer bothered me. I slid out of his embrace and stood. "It's not that simple and if you don't understand why this bothers me, we have a problem."

Back in his bed, we lay side by side, pretending to sleep.

When it became clear I was, indeed, more than a fling, Michael's mother sat me down on her sunporch for *a serious conversation*. She brought out a pot of tea, pound cake. She sat uncomfortably close, our knees touching. She said, "I'm sure you're a nice young woman," and I said, "Yes, ma'am, I am," and she said, "I'm sure your parents are very proud of you," and I said, "Yes, ma'am," and she said, "You'd be opening yourself up to a whole lot of trouble if you took things any further with my son."

I shifted in my seat. "I don't mind trouble."

Lorraine took a bite of pound cake. She set her fork down and it made a soft, unexpected sound. A small constellation of crumbs dotted her lower lip. "Marriage is hard. Life is long."

"Michael and I are not talking marriage."

She ignored me. "His father wants him to take over the farm someday. Could you be happy out here? Could you be a farmer's wife? There aren't a lot of people who look like you. We don't have a problem with it the way you think we do but you and my boy would be making things a lot harder for yourselves if you took things any further."

I did not know what to say. I pretended to not understand the exact nature of her objections to our relationship. We finished our tea and cake. When I offered to wash the dishes, she groused, "I can handle washing a couple plates and mugs. I don't need any damn help."

On the drive home, Michael turned to look at me. "I'd love for us to live out there, someday. We could help my folks out, have a real nice life."

The seriousness in his voice frightened me. The bucolic scenery frightened me. I stared out my window at the passing cornfields. Every few moments some terrible insect made a new, wet mess of itself on the windshield. After a while, I said, "You do know we could never live out here, don't you?"

He laughed. "You're kidding, right? The farm is my home. It's the one place where I'm the most me."

We didn't talk for a few miles, just listened to the rumble of the highway. "How would you feel if I asked you to move to Haiti? That's my home, at least in some ways."

Michael cleared his throat. I closed my eyes and hoped we wouldn't say things that couldn't be unsaid.

"That's different," Michael said.

My fingers numbed. "Different how?"

"The farm has running water and reliable electricity. The farm is not a hellhole. The place isn't run by criminals. Come on, babe. It's not the same thing."

I had not known Michael capable of saying unnecessarily cruel things. Normally I was the one who said unforgivable things and he was the one who forgave. This shift intrigued me.

I shoved my hands beneath my thighs. "I see."

We were quiet for the rest of the drive. When he dropped me off, he tried to kiss me. I turned my cheek, didn't let him touch me. He didn't ask if he could come in, knew he had crossed some kind of line. He sat in the driveway for hours. I watched from behind the curtain, waited for him to muster the manhood to apologize. He didn't. I turned off the lights and still I watched him. He went home eventually. Before I went to sleep, I sent him an e-mail—"You, sir, are an asshole."

Days would pass before we spoke again, days during which I stared at my phone and willed him to call, willed him to apologize, willed him to plead for my forgiveness and make whatever was wrong between us right. I willed myself to make a similar gesture but I couldn't. I hold grudges. When he didn't call, I focused on my studies, on being excellent. I should have never let him distract me with his pretty shoulders and talk of swooning. The law made sense. Michael did not. Days turned into weeks. I vowed to never speak to him again. I wrote irate e-mail drafts I did not dare send where I called him terrible names and detailed his failings in increasingly petty ways. I sent him an e-mail asking, "What the hell are you doing?" He wrote back, "I'm thinking, trying to decide if we can make this work. We come from different worlds." I replied, "Don't bother coming back to my world."

We had not spoken in twenty-seven days. I was very un-
pleasant to everyone I encountered. I didn't answer my parents'
phone calls. When I spoke with Mona I answered her questions
in terse one-word answers. She said, "Should I come visit you,
kid, and beat this guy up?" I told her not to bother. I told her I
was done with him. I wrote even angrier e-mails that went un-
sent. I was done with American men as a dating species.

And then Michael found me in the law library. I didn't need
to look up to know he was standing over me. The warmth of his
body was too familiar. "I am so sorry," he said. "It's been way
too long since I've seen you." His voice cracked. I was not interested in his acts of contrition.

I stood knowing I was going to speak without thinking. I
couldn't stop myself. I refused to look him in the eyes. He tried
to reach for me but I slapped his hand away. "Don't," I said.
"Don't you dare."

"I have behaved very badly. Let me try to explain; I needed
some time to think. I'm not good with disagreement or complications and I . . . I needed time."

I stabbed my finger into his chest, hard. "You could have
fooled me. Let's be perfectly clear here. You pursued me." I
punctuated each word with my finger. He winced. I didn't care.
"You're the one who told me to take the chance and then I did
and you say something cruel and, even worse, ignorant about
the place my family is from. You think you know anything about
Haiti because you've watched some shitty news reports? You
don't call me for nearly a month, don't even bother to explain
that you need time. Where do you get off?"

People were staring. My voice was loud and tight. I did not
care that I was in a library or that my peers were staring or

that Michael seemed genuinely apologetic or that I was probably overreacting. I have a temper. I do not handle being scorned with any kind of grace. I stuffed my heavy laptop into my bag and grabbed a handful of books. He grabbed my arm and I narrowed my eyes, looked down at his hand. "Don't touch me." He refused to let go. I arched an eyebrow and looked him right in the eye. "If you do not unhand me, I will scream. You know me well enough to know I am not afraid to make a scene."

I walked out of the library as fast as my legs would carry me, my rage building, filling my mouth with such heat.

To his credit, Michael ran after me. He stood in front of my car door with his arms across his chest.

I started crying and when I cry I am ugly and when I feel ugly I get meaner. "Get out of my way." I refrained from calling him names.

Michael refused to move. I threw my keys at his chest and they bounced off his body and clattered on the pavement. He said, "Go ahead, make a scene," and so I did. I made a spectacular scene.

Alone, in a stifling hot cage, my arm so sore the pain was the only thing I could focus on, I would have given anything to be a farmer's wife, anything at all.

︱

This is how a fairy tale ends.

Hours passed after the phone call to my father. I walked around my cage. I tried not to move my arm, the bones of which felt loose and very out of place. I ran in a small circle, pretended I was outside breathing fresh and clean air. I listened to the sounds of the street. There was a family with an infant nearby, one who cried a great deal, and maybe a nightclub. Sometimes I heard the faint, tinny sound of fast dance music for hours on end. I closed my eyes and thought about every single hair on Christophe's head, how when my ransom was paid, I would count every last one of my child's hairs. I thought about how he fell asleep when I fed him, sighing softly. I thought about Michael drawing me a warm bath, washing my back as I sat with my cheek against my knees. It had been two days since I last cleaned myself, stood under warm water, two days since I had eaten. Earlier that morning one of my captors brought me a bottle of warm water. I drank it greedily, until my stomach ached and expanded uncomfortably. It was not long before I was thirsty again but I knew I could not ask for more, could not give those men a sense of what I needed.

When the first man came, I knew who it would be. I was jumping up and down in place, singing the song I heard playing in a nearby home earlier, "Mon Colonel," by Sweet Micky. I stopped jumping as the door opened, and stepped away from the intruder, kept moving until my back was against the wall. He closed the door behind him. I thought *fight*.

"The Commander has a message: you should have played the game. Those who play the game don't get hurt. You got me into a lot of trouble, so I am going to enjoy this."

He bared his teeth. My fingers found their way into fists, curled around my fear, held my fear close. I tried to find a way out of the moment, tried to do something with time that would change the circumstance or slow things down long enough for me to find a way out. He rushed at me and I ran for the door but the man was quick too, shifted in front of me, laughed. Once again, my runner's thighs failed me.

"I don't mind a little chase." He rubbed his hands together. I would never forget that sound, the empty whisper of soft hands preparing to do hard things.

He stalked me around our tiny cage in a cage in a cage. He was silent, his focus singular as was mine. I was covered in sweat and rotting milk. I stank. I tried to anticipate his every move but eventually he grew bored of playing cat to my mouse. He grabbed me and threw me on the bed. I fought him and he laughed louder, said he would never forget me. I scratched and kicked and screamed and spit in his face. He only laughed more. He stripped me of my clothing, stripped me bare, and then he stripped me of something I cannot name, flipping me onto my stomach, pulling me up by my hips, forcing my thighs apart with his, forcing himself inside me. He ripped me wide open. Everything tore. All I could think about was my body, how the first time in my life I understood the very weakness, the utter fragility of human flesh.

With his arm pressed against the back of my neck, forcing my face into the mattress, I tried to breathe, tried to free myself but there was nothing I could do. He took a very long time. He grunted with each thrust and there were many. When he finished, he patted my ass, squeezed hard, left quietly. Before I could move, before I could hope for an end to what had begun, there was another man who simply climbed on top of me without ceremony. I tried to crawl away but he was too heavy. My screaming, he said, bothered him, so he shoved his fist in my mouth, making my jaw feel like it was coming apart. I thought *fight*. I fought.

The third man made me get on my knees on that filthy floor like an animal. He wanted my mouth. I looked down at my thighs and saw blood in the dim light. I hardly understood it was mine. We are not supposed to recognize our own blood when spilled in such a way. He held a knife to my throat, told me to forget I had teeth. I ignored his threat and tried to bite down. He pressed the blade into the skin at the base of my throat, and drew his knife to the left. I gasped and he shoved his cock down my throat before I could stop him. My eyes watered and I gagged but I did not cry. It was impossible to breathe. I wanted to surrender but I could not. I clawed at his thighs. When he was finished all I could taste was the betrayal of my mouth.

I began to realize what survival demanded of me. I said, "I will survive this," and someone else in the room laughed. There was the lighting of a cigarette. I turned my head and realized there was an audience. Sitting on the floor, legs crossed in his lap, was the Commander, smoking, watching. He did not move or look away. It was almost like he wasn't there.

The next two men threw me back on the bed, spread my legs wide, laughed at what little fight I had left, my pathetic efforts to protect myself. I tried to count how long each man took so I would be better prepared the next time they came. I needed to know. It was hard to hold on to so many numbers—thirty-four, nineteen, fifty-seven, seventy-nine, sixty-three. I could no longer scream. My voice was already hoarse so the sound I made caused me to cringe. It was the sound of something lost.

This went on for hours and hours.

There was a man named TiPierre. He told me his name. Other than the Commander, he is the only one who told me his name. He said he was sorry I was being treated so poorly. He spoke quietly, with kindness. Kindness is deceptive. We were alone. He lay next to me on the narrow bed. I was perfectly still. I thought *mercy* though I did not ask for it. I was a wild thing, without self-pity. TiPierre touched me like a lover. I fought him the hardest, found something inside myself to resist even though I had no energy left. He was quiet, calm, kissed just above the bleeding cut on my shoulder, kissed around the bruises on my neck. He said, "I only do this because I must." He said, "Put your arms around me." I did because I needed someone to hold on to even if it was a transgressor. I held on to him and I trembled. I had no choice. I was lost. He said, "Relax, it will be easier," but I couldn't relax.

Nothing would have made that night easier, nothing.

Later, he sat on the edge of the bed pulling his T-shirt over his head. "The Commander wants me to take you to him but first you must clean yourself. Get dressed," he said.

I pulled on my clothes. My body was not my body; it was less than nothing. I followed TiPierre back to the bathroom. Everything sounded muffled. The taste of blood and men filled my mouth, ran between my teeth. My feet were bare. Something gritty collected between my toes. When TiPierre looked away, I started running toward where I thought the front door was. Hobbled as I was, I did not get far. TiPierre grabbed me by my shoulders. He said, "Be smart," and steered me to the bathroom holding me by my hair. The mirror in the bathroom was still shattered and what remained was still stained with my blood. I did not bother to look at myself.

He nodded toward the bathtub, handed me a small towel and thin bar of soap. I looked up at the small window. If he left me alone, I could try to fit through the small space. I could hoist myself up and out of this hell. I could be free. TiPierre closed the toilet lid and sat, looked to the floor as if this fraction of kindness would forgive his trespass. My eyes smarted as I disrobed and handed him my clothes.

"I'd like to be alone," I whispered. "I need to be alone."

TiPierre shook his head and swallowing my anger, I climbed into the shower. I willed myself not to look at him or the window or to imagine anything beyond.

The water was lukewarm, the pressure weak. I lathered the soap and tried to clean myself. Everything hurt. I hissed as I washed between my thighs. My skin was raw, gone completely. I knew even then that there would be nothing left of me by the time they were done. It was not long before there was a knock on the door. I wanted to beg for mercy but again I did not. I simply turned off the water, dried myself, put my soiled clothes back on.

My hair hung in my face as I followed TiPierre to the Commander's room. He said, "Don't fight the Commander or it will be too much for you." He squeezed my shoulder gently, kissed my forehead. His lips were moist.

The Commander's room was clean and well lit. He lay on a large bed covered with a red satin bedspread, laughing at something on the television, a big flat screen surrounded by expensive electronics equipment. I had never met one until I was kidnapped, but self-proclaimed leaders of men don't seem to have original ideas for spending their money. The Commander was bare-chested, wore only a pair of cargo shorts. He leaned against a stack of pillows, his hands clasped behind his head. He barely looked up at me as TiPierre shut the door, locking me in a new cage.

"I love American television," he said. "So silly, all of it."

I turned to look at the screen, recognized an older episode of *Friends*.

"I will never understand women like you," he said. "You make your lives so much more difficult than need be."

"I doubt you understand women at all," I said, softly.

He wagged his finger at me. "I have a problem finding women who will satisfy my particular, shall we say, appetites. The women in this country, they don't like certain things, won't do certain things. Haitian women are proud and stubborn and hard. You American women, though, you will do anything. This is what I hear."

"Please don't hurt me," I stuttered.

The Commander laughed. "Now you want to play nice?" He patted the empty space next to him.

I shook my head. "I'm not coming anywhere near you. You can go straight to hell."

The Commander sighed, stood. "You certainly haven't learned your lesson."

I stepped backward, fumbled for the doorknob. He was wrong. I had learned. I had learned so much. "I've learned my lesson, I swear." I started babbling nonsensically.

He laughed. He grabbed me, threw me over his shoulder, and dumped me on the bed. I tried to breathe. He brought the back of his hand to my face, bone against fresh bruises. I winced.

"You don't need to do this," I said. "I know the rules now. I will play your game, say whatever you need."

He removed my clothes, almost politely, and knelt between my bare thighs, lit a cigarette. This cannot happen, I thought. This is not possible. Smoke curled around the Commander's face. He was a *chimère*, a ghost. "If only you had learned your lesson sooner." He ashed his cigarette on my stomach.

Only then did I understand the kind of man he was, what he enjoyed taking from women. I finally understood fear. What is truly terrifying is the exact knowledge of what will come and being unable to save yourself from it.

Grabbing hold of one of my thighs, he forced me open, stretching my hipbones. He held my skin taut. I tried to push his hands away, to scratch his wrists, to crawl off the bed, to get away. He held the cigarette so close to my skin, the heat seared. My flesh rose. I began to sweat again, the air filling with the smell of soap and sweat and smoke. The smell of my own flesh burning was almost a comfort. I was alive. There was something of me left to burn. I screamed and screamed.

When there was no more of his cigarette, he pressed the flaming tip to my stomach, twisted it until my body extinguished that fire.

"No more," I said with what I could find of my voice. I was delirious and undone. The smell in the room made me sick. I could hardly hold on to myself. "I have a child. I have a child who is not yet a year old," I said. "I'm still breastfeeding." It was important to remind this man I was not merely meat for him to butcher. I was a woman. I was a mother and a wife and a daughter. I needed him to leave something of my body for those who loved me.

"You have no idea what will happen to you if your father doesn't pay," the Commander said. He almost sounded sad.

He climbed on top of me. He bit my chin. I moaned, turned away from him. He told me to open my eyes, to see him. I refused. He bristled, said, "As you wish." He said, "You shall not know kindness from me." I planted my hands against his chest to hold him off, to save some piece of myself. He was a sharp blade. I was a tender wound. I couldn't keep count. I finally surrendered to the pain, spreading sharply between my thighs and straight into my heart. I opened my eyes and inhaled sharply. As I passed out, the Commander hovered over me, smiling. Finally, I thought, as I drifted into a place where I felt nothing but still, somehow, ached. There was nothing left to count.

~~HHH HHH~~ ||

Michael and I took our first trip to Port-au-Prince after dating for a year. Michael insisted on meeting my parents. I tried to prepare him. I explained how he would see things he might never see in the States, difficult and painful things. I explained that there is nowhere in the world both as beautiful and as ugly, as hopeful and as hopeless. He did not quite understand what I meant but he tried and I tried. I hoped he would understand he could not love me without loving where I am from.

In the weeks before our trip, Michael read travel books and surfed the Internet and took notes. He'd point to a hat and say *le chapeau* and in the driveway, he'd pat the hood of the car and say *la voiture*, and when we woke up in the morning he'd say *je t'aime*, the words always sounding square and strange wrapped in his thick midwestern accent. It was very charming. We had a lot of sex.

He filled an entire suitcase with bottled water.

As I watched him packing, I said, "What the hell are you doing?"

"I don't want to get sick."

"We're not going off the grid, Michael. My parents have plenty of distilled water. That's all we drink."

He shook his head, and zipped his suitcase shut. "Just in case," he said, patting his bag proudly like he was making an intelligent decision.

Miami International Airport often feels like Port-au-Prince. It is crowded and hot and forever under construction though nothing seems to change. Everyone is irritable and sweaty and talking too loudly, often trying to carry too much to some impoverished country where the people have too little. As we stood in line, Michael kept tugging my sleeve, whispering into my ear loudly, "Look at that suitcase. Look at *that* suitcase. How are these people going to get on the plane?"

I laughed. "The rules are different for these flights. Haitians ignore the rules anyway."

He rubbed his chin thoughtfully and started taking pictures with his cell phone. We sat in first class and Michael grinned like a little boy; it was his first time. I squeezed his hand. His smile always brings out the best in me. Michael had a happy childhood and that helped him become a happy man. My parents love that about him; they love his joy, his red cheeks and his easy smile, the way he isn't intimidated by anything. They call him Mr. America.

I tried to ignore my nervousness. I talked fast, so fast, trying to remind Michael of all the things he should and shouldn't do.

He said, "Relax, babe. I've met the parents before."

I leaned back. "You haven't met Haitian parents."

As we descended into Port-au-Prince, we switched seats and Michael stared down at the beautiful blue water and then the capital, sprawling in from the edge of the island.

"Are you ready for this?"

He nodded eagerly. I hoped for the best.

We walked across the tarmac, white heat billowing around us in waves. By the time we reached the terminal, where the air-conditioning wasn't working, Michael was dripping in sweat, his hair clinging to his red face. We waited in customs for what seemed like hours, the line shuffling forward with people cutting at random or clustering when they saw someone they recognized or when they simply wanted to improve their chances of ever getting out of the airport.

Michael wiped his forehead and shook his head. "This is insanity."

I held his arm. "Baby, this is the easy part."

At baggage claim, my parents' chauffeur, Nelson, waved to us eagerly. When he tried to take Michael's suitcase, Michael said, "I've got this," and Nelson frowned.

"Let him take your bag," I said.

Michael let go of the handle and shifted uncomfortably. A fresh bead of sweat trickled down his neck. We followed Nelson through a throng of people gathered near the airport entrance, cabdrivers trying to grab tourists' bags to hijack fares, vendors selling Haitian flags and straw hats, armed police trying to keep the chaos to a dull roar. Dozens of young men stood behind a fence shouting to people they recognized and strangers alike.

The drive to my parents' house was long and bumpy, the sun-scorched concrete of Port-au-Prince stretching around us.

Nelson spent most of his time with one hand on the horn and one arm hanging out the window so he could gesture angrily when someone cut him off or otherwise got in his way. I stared at Michael as we drove, saw his wide-open eyes, how he seemed to be holding his breath. Everything was as dirty and broken as I remembered until we entered my parents' neighborhood and the city quieted. The streets were cleaner, more orderly, the cars nicer, the concrete walls towering even higher than the homes themselves. Michael relaxed visibly, loosened his grip on my hand. At the gate at the foot of their driveway, Nelson honked the horn and slowly, the steel gates opened. We drove up the long, narrow drive. As the house came into view, Michael said, "Holy shit, this is a castle," and I said, "Welcome to Port-au-Prince."

My mother has ideas about men and women. When a woman lives with a man before they are married, my mother believes she's engaged in a *concubinage*. This sort of arrangement upsets her greatly. Michael and I pretended we were not living together until we married. During our first visit to the motherland, we had to sleep in separate rooms.

When he realized this, Michael pulled me aside. "Seriously?"

I squeezed his arm, kissed his chin. "You'll be fine."

He pouted. "I can't sleep without you. You've ruined me."

"I suppose you won't be getting much sleep then."

My mother found us in the hallway, Michael's arms around me, me on the very tips of my toes, my lips pressed against the hollow of his neck. She cleared her throat and we pulled apart, an uncomfortable heat spreading through my face and scalp. My parents do not know me as someone who is open with her affection. They do not know who I am with Michael.

Forever the perfect host, my mother gave the grand tour as someone saw to our luggage. We walked across the marble floors, and once again, I took in the impeccable décor, the teak ceiling fans spinning lazily and filling each room with a strange hush, the bright and evocative Haitian artwork on almost every wall. Behind the house there was a sitting area with teak benches, a fire pit, an open, grassy area, a brightly tiled, rarely used swimming pool. The two housekeepers, Nadine and Wilma, shuffled quietly through the house, neither seen nor heard unless they were needed. I pretended such servitude didn't make me uncomfortable, offered them kind smiles whenever they passed by.

We sat on one of the teak benches across from my mother. Nadine brought us cold drinks. When my father came home from work, he joined us, performed as he always does for guests, creating from his imagination a Haiti that does not exist, or perhaps once existed and is fading away, a jewel in the middle of an ocean with white beaches and clear blue warm water and a strong, resilient people—a Caribbean Camelot.

"I had no idea people lived in such luxury," Michael said, gripping my hand tightly.

It would not be the last time he made that statement. Americans have such strange ideas about the world beyond their borders.

After dinner, I stood with my mother on a balcony listening to the mystery of the city around us.

"You love this man."

An unexpected smile spread across my face. I looked down at my hands. "He's the only man I've ever loved."

Before bed, I kissed Michael good night in the hallway just outside of his room.

"Come visit me later," he whispered.

I shook my head and backed away. He refused to let go of my hands until he absolutely had to. I laughed. "You'll have to be a big boy and sleep all by yourself tonight."

"You'll miss me," he said.

"Not as much as you'll miss me."

He peeked out of his door once more, his hair, which needed to be cut, falling into his face. "Damn right," he said. And then he whispered loudly, "Please stay."

I wanted very much to sleep next to him but knew my parents would disapprove. They would think less of him and in the before, I cared about such things. I blew Michael a kiss and quickly raised my shirt, flashing my breasts. He flashed a lazy smile and began waggling his tongue. I skirted to my room before we got into trouble.

My chest ached as I lay, alone, in the middle of my bed staring at the ceiling fan. An hour passed and I still could not sleep. I cursed Michael for making me *that woman*. The house was still and quiet. I paced until my calves grew sore, then slowly opened my door. The hall was dark and empty. I was thankful for the marble floors. I carefully made my way back to Michael's room, every sound making me paranoid.

He was lying on his side, asleep, facing away from the door. I stepped out of my pajamas and slid beneath the sheets next to him. His body, his warmth, and the smell of his skin were reassuring. I kissed his forehead, pressed my lips to the bone of his cheek. He stirred lightly, wrapped his arm around me, pulling me closer. I traced his lips with my fingers, so soft.

Michael slowly opened his eyes and was about to say something but I said, "Shhh." He slid one of his hands through my hair and kissed me with an uncommon urgency. He kissed me like he was trying to swallow me whole and I gave in to it, to him, his breath in my throat. I was feverish. He pushed me onto my back and dragged his fingers across my collarbones, touched me so softly. I brushed his hair away from his face and wrapped my legs around his waist and we lay like that for a long while, skin to skin, looking at each other. Normally we tear at each other when we make love but that night, we were different, we were soft, we were silent. I held him so tightly I thought our bodies might knot together. When I came, I cried. I was not used to crying. The tears felt strange as they streamed down my cheeks and down my neck, into my ears. It terrified me how much he made me love him, how much he made me step beyond myself and into him, into us.

After, we lay together, hot, still fevered, sweaty. The air was thick with the smell of us. I faced away from Michael, my spine against his chest. I couldn't stop crying. He kissed my bare shoulder.

"Baby, what's wrong."

I pulled his arm around me, holding him tightly, covering his hand with mine, sliding my fingers between his. I couldn't explain what I was feeling. Finally, I pulled myself together, kissed his fingertips. Quietly, very quietly, I said, "You are the only man I have ever truly loved."

"Look at me."

I shook my head.

"Look at me."

Slowly, I turned to him.

He ran his finger along my hairline, down my neck to my arm. I shivered. I wanted him again. "Why do you say that like it's a bad thing?"

I buried my face in his armpit. He smelled like soap and sweat. I mumbled, "You better not hurt me," then I said, "If this isn't serious, don't you lead me on."

Michael raised himself onto one elbow and smiled. "I made my intentions known to you the first time we made love."

"I am terrified of loving you this much."

He kissed my neck and he sank his teeth into my skin and sucked so hard he would leave a bruise. I didn't stop him, wanted him to mark me. We made love again. We were still silent but we were not gentle. As I drifted asleep, he said, "We can be terrified of this much love together."

Sometime later, Michael shook me awake. "I hate for you to leave," he said, "but morning is coming."

I grumbled and grabbed his wrist, tried to make out the time on his watch.

He leaned against the headboard and watched as I got dressed—my tank top, a pair of his boxers, so I could take something of him to my room with me. Michael cleared his throat. "When we get married, you won't have to sneak out of my room when we visit your parents."

I shrugged, smoothing my hair. "If we get married."

I walked around the bed and he jumped up, stood between the doorway and me. "Don't."

"Don't what?"

"Shut down. I know how you feel about me and you know how I feel about you. We don't have to play games." He pointed to the bed.

I planted my hand against his chest and stood on my toes to kiss him once more. "I'm not an easy woman to love," I said.

I'm not sure if I was apologizing or warning him. I rubbed my thumb across his cheekbone and left.

As I crept back to my room, my mother cleared her throat. "You are a bit old," she said, "to be sneaking around."

I made some silly excuse about walking around because I couldn't sleep and quickened my step until I was safe in my room. Outside, the sky had turned a pale blue gray.

At breakfast, Michael and I sat across from each other, flanked by my parents. They were both reading the newspaper, occasionally sharing an interesting news item.

Michael poured two liberal scoops of sugar into his coffee, stirring lightly before taking a sip. "How did you sleep last night, Mireille?"

That uncomfortable heat returned to my face, the whole of my upper body. I narrowed my eyes. I wanted to kick him under the table but my leg wouldn't reach. "I slept fine, Michael, and you?"

He grinned widely. "Best sleep of my life."

I arched an eyebrow, stopped pretending to be irritated, leaned forward. "The best?"

Michael leaned forward too. "The very best."

I took a sip of my own coffee, too hot, bitter, excellent. "It must have been the island air."

"I hope I sleep that well every night while I am here."

Even though my cheeks burned, I couldn't stop myself. "I hope so too. I really do." My fever returned.

My mother set her newspaper down. "Honestly, Mireille."

Michael and my father bonded instantly over their mutual love of concrete and all things construction. That afternoon, we drove out to the provinces where my father was building an orphanage and a school in Jérémie for an American NGO. Jérémie is remote and isolated, about 125 miles from Port-au-Prince. It took hours and hours to get there—abominable roads. Michael and I sat in the backseat of my father's Land Cruiser, sweating, our thighs sticking to the leather seats. It was too hot to even hold hands or sit close to each other. His hair clung to his face, which was even redder than it had been at the airport. My father had the air-conditioning on but it did little to cool us.

My mother turned around, looked at Michael, and said, "*Il est rouge comme une tomate.*"

I glared at her.

Michael wiped his forehead. "Is it always this hot?"

From the front seat, my father nodded. "We are blessed with a lot of sun."

The roads became narrower and narrower, less paved, jolting us back and forth. About thirty miles from Jérémie, we had to drive across a dry riverbed where children ran and played and chased our vehicle. A stray goat ambled by. Michael waved eagerly at the kids, his forehead against the glass.

"When it rains, this riverbed floods," my father said, "and then no one can get to Jérémie."

Michael and I looked out our windows and up into the cloudless sky.

We walked through the construction site and my father puffed his chest out, shook Michael's shoulder excitedly. "You see," he said, "there is much work to be done but great things are happening here."

Michael smiled politely but as we drove through Jérémie to get to the construction site, he saw the run-down buildings, paint peeling, the streets filthy, and crowded with so many people mobbing our car whenever they could. He could only shake his head, over and over, muttering, "This is unbelievable." He did not know how to make sense of any of it. Neither did I.

My mother and I stood in a nearly finished classroom trying to stay cool while the men continued surveying the site, talking about the long-term viability of structural integrity and completion schedules and other matters that were beyond our understanding.

"Your young man is nothing like your father," she said.

I smiled. "No. No, he isn't."

On the drive back to Port-au-Prince, we passed the schoolchildren again, seven or eight little boys in T-shirts and shorts, playing soccer near the edge of the dry riverbed, shrieking happily as one scored.

"Stop the car," Michael said.

We slowed. My father turned around. "What is it?"

"I just want to get out for a minute."

My father frowned but stopped. Michael jumped out of the car and walked toward the children rolling his sleeves up. I got out and stood near the edge of the makeshift pitch, watching my boyfriend as I shielded my eyes from the sun with my hand. One of the young boys kicked the soccer ball toward Michael and soon he was playing with those boys like he was a child himself. When he scored a goal, he threw his hands in the air and started running around in a circle. The little boys followed, their hands in the air too. I took dozens of pictures, couldn't help laughing. Michael came and grabbed me, and soon we were both playing soccer with the kids, stirring up small clouds of dust as we passed the ball back and forth. A group of older kids and adults began to gather around us. A tall, thick-bodied, blond-haired man was not a common sight in the provinces. The crowd cheered both teams equally, laughing loudly whenever one of the boys stole the ball from the *blan*. After a while, my father approached us, pointing at his watch. I sighed. We said goodbye to the small crowd, waving until our arms ached.

In the backseat, Michael turned to me. His shirt was soaked all the way through. "I like it here," he said.

I did not care that we weren't alone. I leaned into him and kissed his lips, my hand against his chest. "So do I."

For most of the trip, Michael was wide-eyed, trying to cope with the country and the startling contrasts—so much beauty, so much brutality. Everywhere we went, he stared, at the garbage in the streets, the complex webs of electrical wiring overhead, huge estates with unbelievably high walls around which *bidonvilles*, shantytowns, sprawled as far as the eye could see, and everywhere, so many people, desperate, angry, hungry, scratching. There was a promiscuity that was, when you spent too much time thinking about it, impossible to bear.

I told myself he wasn't afraid to see beyond the gritty surface of the city, because of how he would get out of the car and talk to the roadside vendors all over the city, selling everything that could be sold on brightly colored tarps, or standing near their merchandise hanging from concrete walls. He tried to be a good sport—loved the children, their youthful eagerness, how they all spoke like little adults. He loved the beautiful women and the music and the art and especially the food, which he made me promise to cook for him. I needed to believe that meant he loved me enough to love my country.

Michael spent a little time each day at my father's company, learning about my father's business. He tried to hold conversations with Nadine and Wilma and they were instantly charmed. They mostly forgot about the rest of us. By the end of our visit my mother said, "If Nadine and Wilma even thought Mr. America was going to sneeze, they would be waiting with a handkerchief."

I said, "Michael is very easy to love."

We spent our afternoons at the beach, lounging on wide couches, drinking rum and eating fruit and swimming together in the warm salt water. Michael openly ogled the women in their bathing suits walking tall, looking good. Once, he whistled, and said, "Haitian women are the most beautiful women in the world," and I said, "Obviously." I buried him in the sand up to his neck and straddled his entombed body, teasing him as he struggled to free himself. When he finally did climb his way out of the tightly packed sand, he carried me over his shoulder and threw me into a crashing wave and then fell on top of me, and we lay there, in the surf, beneath the beating sun and he said, "I'm going to love you forever," and I believed him. I believed in our happily ever after.

My father took us on an overnight trip to Cap-Haïtien and we toured the nearby Citadelle, a mountaintop fortress built in the early nineteenth century by Henri Christophe, a man who once declared himself king of Haiti, a man for whom we would eventually name our child. As Michael and I stood on the roof, we could see straight to the ocean. There, on what felt like the top of the world, we were surrounded by green and blue and the sweeping peaks and valleys of the mountains around us. It was warm and sunny, but the air was thinner, easier to breathe.

I held Michael's arms, squeezed. "You see," I said softly.

He nodded, covered my hand with his but later that night he also said, "I am so ready to go back to the States."

We were standing in the driveway, while I smoked.

I frowned. "You seem to be having a good time. You said you like it here."

Michael shoved his hands in his pockets. I watched as he tried to backpedal. "I am, I do, but you have to admit, this is a lot to take. Did you see the beggars at the market?"

I stepped toward him, flicked my cigarette, and put my hands on my hips. "What, exactly, is a lot to take?"

He looked up at the sky like he hoped something in the stars might offer him counsel on the right thing to say. "Never mind," he said.

"Right," I said, stalking away. I did not sneak into his room that night. At breakfast the next morning, I refused to look him in the eye, ignored his attempts to make nice.

On our last evening we walked along the street just outside my parents' estate. Michael shook his head and rubbed his forehead. "How do people like your parents survive the guilt of living like this?"

I looked around us, at the high, gated walls on one side and everything else on the other. I squeezed his hand. "I have no idea."

"I couldn't bear it," Michael said.

I wanted to tell him I don't think anyone can, not really. I wanted to tell him I saw the exact same things he did, that this country was a lot for anyone to take, but it was easier to pretend I didn't.

Back in Miami, Michael dropped to his knees and made a big show of kissing the filthy airport floor. He whispered, "Thank God we're home."

I walked away in disgust. We didn't speak on the flight from Miami to Omaha or on the drive from Omaha to Lincoln. We stopped in front of my house and sat in the car, silently. He tried to say something and I held my hand up. I got out of the car, struggling to pull my suitcase from the trunk. When he tried to help me, I said, "Don't you dare. I do not need your help."

Michael didn't leave, though. He sat in the car waiting for me to cool off. I watched him from my living room window, parting the curtains just an inch or two to see how long he would sit out there. This is how we argued in the early going, at a remove. It was well after midnight when I walked out to the car in my pajamas. I tapped on his window. He was asleep, his arms folded across his chest. I knocked on the window again. When he didn't wake, I knocked louder. He opened one eye and I twirled my hand in a circle. He yawned and rolled the window down.

"Come inside already."

"You forgive me?"

I smacked his shoulder. "No, but there's no point in your spending the night in the car, either."

We lay next to each other in a familiar bed for the first time in two weeks. I put as much distance between us as possible. When he tried to reach for me, I shoved his hands away.

"Why are you so angry?"

I sat up and turned on the light. Michael winced, covering his eyes with his hand. I pointed at him as I got out of bed and started pacing. "Is that seriously a question?"

"Maybe I was a bit dramatic. Okay, fine, I was rude at the airport but I don't think my reaction was entirely unreasonable. The trash, the heat, the power going out all the fucking time, the people *everywhere*, always wanting something."

I went to the bedroom window and stared down at the quiet street below, determined to pick a fight for no reason. "After everything I showed you, that's what you remember?"

Michael sat up. "How could I forget? We had a blast but we were surrounded by misery. That is hard to take. I'm just being honest."

"Michael, if misery is all you saw, you weren't looking closely."

"I looked plenty close, Mireille, and saw many beautiful things but I also saw terrible things. I can't pretend otherwise. You shouldn't expect me to."

"Right," I said, still pacing.

"As if you haven't said bitchy things about where I am from. You laughed about frozen cows, cows who died where they stood."

I grabbed a shoe from the floor and threw it at his chest. Michael caught the shoe and dropped it by the side of the bed, the corners of his mouth lifting.

"Don't you laugh and don't you bring up those poor frozen cows," I said, my voice rising sharply. "I swear to God. I get it now, how they died was very sad, but it is not remotely the same thing. We're talking about a country, filled with people I am a part of."

"I'm not sure what to say here. You're going to jump down my throat no matter what I say. Surely we can talk about this like adults."

I grabbed my pillow from the bed as well as the duvet, hoping Michael would freeze without it. "Don't bother saying anything, Michael. You should just kiss the carpet or something to show our bedroom how grateful you are to be at home, alone in

your bed, like an adult." As I ran downstairs, I shouted, "And
don't bother coming after me."

I sat on the couch and stared at the ceiling wondering if Michael would follow, if he would apologize, if he would show me
he understood how he hurt me, if he could see we weren't so
different in how we felt. I fell asleep waiting.

||||| ||||| |||

was returned to my cage, locked inside. I was a bloody beast. My cage was madly hot. I held the air in my hands, tried to shape into something that might save me. I was naked, my clothes in a neat pile on the floor next to the small pile of glass shards I had built. My body throbbed as I dressed, as I tried to cover what could not be covered. Everything hurt. My breasts were so full of milk, I thought my skin might stretch so thinly, they would burst open. It hurt too much to sit so I dropped to the floor and slid beneath the bed. It was cooler there, dark. I hoped I might disappear or die.

I waited for my father to pay the ransom or for my husband to find me. I stared at the door and thought, "It has been long enough. Someone will come. I will survive this." I waited for salvation. No one came. It grew dark outside again. When I closed my eyes, all I could see was everything that had been done to me so I tried to keep my eyes open. I was so weary. I slept fitfully.

This morning after rose slowly. I was still beneath the bed. My cage was still madly hot. I whispered my name, my child's name, my husband's name, my child's name, my husband's name, my name. I whispered these names over and over. The door opened and I froze. I tried not to cry out. My muscles tensed. I saw a pair of boots, the Commander's. He lifted the bed with one arm. I already knew his strength. "Come out from under there." I slid out slowly then rose to my knees, paused, held on to the mattress and stood, shakily. When he looked at me I did not look away. I did not cower. He would not break me. I could not be broken. These men had kidnapped the daughter of Sebastien Duval. Even as I became less and less that man's daughter, my ambition to survive was my only emotion. I swallowed everything else, put it far beyond anyone's reach, even mine.

The Commander handed me a copy of *Le Nouvelliste*. I stared at the date—10 Juillet, 2008. Three days. Only three days had passed.

"Hold the paper in front of you," the Commander said.

I was too tired to refuse. My arms shook as I held the newsprint to my chest. The Commander took my picture, the flash blinding me, then grabbed the paper and shoved a cell phone into my hand.

"Now," he said. "You call your father and say what must be said."

I nodded. When my father answered, I said, "Hello," but could barely hear myself. The Commander grabbed my shoulder and squeezed, hard. I swallowed. My throat was too raw. I tried to think of the necessary words, the correct combination of words the Commander wanted my father to hear. I looked up at my captor. I am very stubborn. I said, "May I speak with Michael, please?" There was shuffling and then I heard my husband's voice. My knees buckled and I fell on the bed, a stinging pain rushing between my thighs. "It's me," I said.

"How are you? We're working on getting you freed. I swear to God, I'm doing everything in my power."

"Michael, stop talking. I need you to hear me. Please come get me. Hurry."

"I'm trying, baby. There have been . . ." He paused. "We're working on getting the money together as fast as we can. You're going to be okay. Everything is going to be okay."

It was the absurdity of his words; it was how little he understood my circumstances. I hung up.

The Commander folded his arms across his chest, shook his head. He crouched down until we were eye to eye. "You have not yet learned." He smiled, traced the line of my face from my ear, down along my jawbone.

I turned away, my skin a hot, pulsing streak where he touched me.

The phone rang and I answered. It was an unfamiliar voice. "This is the negotiator. Please hand the telephone to the person in charge. We are working to resolve this situation as quickly as possible."

"It's for you."

My captor scowled, took the phone. "What is taking so long to get me my money?" he asked.

I listened to one side of the conversation, to the back and forth about the value of my life. The Commander handed me the phone again. He lifted my shirt. I looked down and noticed a large bruise purpling just to the right and down from my navel spreading around toward my back. I did not try to cover myself. I had no need for modesty.

The Commander moved behind me, his lips against my ear. "Say what must be said."

My father was talking to me, going on and on about the futility of negotiating with men without morals. The Commander began to press the bruise. The pain was breathtaking. I was covered in sweat, filthy, exhausted, starving. I was a mass of desperate need. I needed to step out of my skin, abandon my body the way my father was abandoning my body. The Commander pressed harder and harder until I couldn't control myself. "Daddy," I said, gasping. "Please pay for me. Please. I cannot stay here."

I begged my father to save what was left of me. Once again, I had an audience while I endured the humiliation, the threat of his indifference.

I tried to force the Commander's hand away from my body but he only applied more pressure. I screamed. I couldn't speak but I screamed. Something wet seeped down the inseam of my jeans, a sharp smell. I wet myself. My father shouted my name, telling me to be strong, telling me he loved me. His lies enraged me into silence. Michael came on the phone. The Commander released his grip and I limped away, my hand over my bruise like that might protect me. I went to a corner, pretended I could hide. Pain continued to throb across my stomach. I leaned against the wall. "Oh my God, Michael, you need to hurry. You need to hurry." The Commander's fist connected with my chin and the phone fell out of my hands, fell to the floor and I fell to the floor, all falls down.

The Commander and his men left me alone and I stayed in a loose heap on the floor; I couldn't move. I stared at my engagement ring. It was nice to look at something beautiful. I still had something from my life to hold on to even if it was a silly bauble.

We were engaged on a Thursday. Michael had been gone for two weeks, consulting on a project in Germany as part of his apprenticeship. With the time difference and my workload as editor for the law review and the work he was doing, we hardly spoke. It staggered me, how much I missed him, his voice, his body, his face. Missing him made me uncomfortably aware that this man I had so little in common with had become a necessary part of my happiness.

Michael came home near midnight. I heard him at the front door and turned onto my side, pretended to be asleep. He climbed the stairs, leaving his suitcase in the hallway. He undressed and crawled into bed and kissed my forehead. He shook me awake but I refused to open my eyes.

"I know you're awake," he said, turning on the light.

I turned into my pillow, mumbled, "I don't like you anymore."

He tried to tickle me and I squirmed but soon I was laughing and kicking the covers off and we were wrestling and I tried to ignore how terrifying it was that in one ridiculous moment, I was happy again. I was the worst kind of cliché. He let me win the wrestling match and I straddled his waist, pinning his arms over his head. I grinned, shaking my head when he tried to kiss me.

"No, no, no," I said. "My mouth is for men who stay home, where they belong."

"What about the rest of you?"

"The same."

"You should let me go."

"Why?"

"I have something to give you."

I kissed his lips softly, let go of his wrists, and pressed the palms of my hands to his cheeks, tried to memorize his bone structure. I smiled. "What do you have to give me, baby?"

I assumed he was going to say something wildly dirty but instead he said, "Hold that thought," and carefully slid me off of his body. He went to his pants, fumbled with them, and returned with his hands behind his back. "Close your eyes."

I shook my head, tried to see what he was holding.

"Close your eyes."

I folded my arms across my chest. "If you went to Germany and brought me back a beer stein, I am going to break it over your head. When I open my eyes I expect to see a German chocolate cake and nothing else."

He laughed, too hard, shifted nervously. Finally, I closed my eyes and waited for what I hoped was an excellent souvenir from his time in the Fatherland. Somewhere along his ancestry, Michael's people were German though he never expressed much affinity *auf Deutschland*. I closed my eyes and held my hands in front of me. He knelt on the bed next to me and cleared his throat. I opened one eye and he kissed just beneath it, whispered, "Close your eyes." I shut my eye again. He held my left hand, kissed each knuckle. He slid something cold and solid onto my finger. I was so surprised I immediately felt nauseous.

I pulled my hand away and opened my eyes. "Michael, what are you doing?" My voice rose. "What the hell are you doing?"

"Hush," he said. "For once, don't say the first thing that comes into your mind. Listen."

He told me all the reasons he wanted to marry me. He said he would have given me a ring the first time we made love because he had always known he was going to marry me and he said he didn't mind that I think I am a difficult woman to love and then I stopped hearing him. The ring felt comfortably heavy on my finger. I didn't look at it because I didn't care what it looked like. I only cared that it was there.

I stared at him and thought about the long speech I had prepared that morning about slowing down, taking some time to evaluate our feelings and priorities, a speech I prepared to better manage the terror of realizing, with a certain finality, that we weren't playing at this love thing, that I was inconsolable without him.

"You can say something now, preferably something like yes."

I nodded slowly and then the moment overwhelmed me. I wanted nothing more than to run. I've always loved running, loved how much it hurts, how good it feels when I stop, how much running makes me feel I have everything I could ever need in my very own body. I slid out of bed and ran down the stairs and out the front door. I ran down the street in my bare feet in the cold night wearing a tank top and pink flannel pajama pants. The moon was full and high and I ran so fast I worried I might outrun my happiness. I didn't run long, just enough to make my heart pound. When I returned, Michael was sitting on the front porch in a T-shirt and boxers holding my jacket, which he threw to me as I walked up to him shivering. "So is that a yes?" he asked, drily.

"Yes," I said. "Of course it's a yes."

He stood and wrapped my jacket around me and shook his head. "I will forever tell anyone who asks about how we got engaged that you ran into the night like a wild woman."

I grabbed his T-shirt and started walking backward and fell back into the grass, pulling him on top of me. I said, "With you, yes, I am a very wild woman."

Our engagement party was held at my parents' beach property in Haiti, a beautiful blue and white cottage only a few yards from the ocean. A long veranda stretched from the house to just near the water's edge and on either side, white, gauzy tents were erected to accommodate more than three hundred of my parents' closest friends and family. His parents, Michael decided, probably wouldn't have enjoyed having to make the trip but really, he was protecting me from what they would think of the country. Americans either love Haiti or they hate Haiti. There is no room for ambivalence. Given his mother's disposition we were fairly confident about where she would stand.

Wide glass bowls filled with light hung along the length of each tent. Lit torches extended along the shoreline as far as the eye could see. Beneath the tents, the tables were covered with linen tablecloths and elaborate flower arrangements of calla lilies and white roses. There was a buffet with Haitian delicacies and someone's interpretation of American food—tiny hamburgers Michael stuffed into his face all night even though he loves Haitian food. The champagne was cold and flowed freely. By the end of the night, everyone was floating. It was easier to pretend this was the way life was for everyone. It was a beautiful affair. My mother, who loves to entertain, outdid herself and enjoyed a crowning moment; her friends would talk about the party for years.

As we pulled up, Michael dressed in a tan linen suit with a French blue shirt, me in a white linen dress, strapless and long, he took in the spectacle of wonder and light, said, "This is just incredible."

As Michael and I entered our engagement party, all the banter and social calisthenics stopped for a moment as the crowd stared at us. We walked down the stairs slowly, and I gripped Michael's hand. The crowd parted and we made our way to my parents. Everyone stared, whispering. Word spread quickly when I got engaged. It was such a coup, my mother told me, finding an American, a white man. When she said this, I told her, "You've been in Port-au-Prince too long." She only laughed and said, "The world is the same everywhere, Mireille. This will be good for your children." I hung up on her.

We spent the evening being congratulated. The whole situation infuriated me but I was a good Haitian daughter so I smiled politely. We were given lots of advice about where to have the wedding and where to live (Port-au-Prince) and what to name the children (after my mother and father) and we continued smiling politely and kissed many cheeks. By the end of the evening, we were exhausted and ready to elope. When the dancing started and people began gathering on the dance floor, Michael and I sat at our table, finally alone.

"My face hurts," I said. "I hate these people."

Michael nodded wearily. "I need to learn how to speak French faster. I think they're talking about me."

"They are," I agreed.

One of my great-aunts started heading toward us with a look in her eye that let me know we were about to receive more advice about starting our lives in Port-au-Prince even though we had a fine, nicely settled life in the States. I had no more small talk in me. I was out of patience for the comfortable lunacy of such a beautiful party on a perfectly groomed beach in the middle of a land of starving people. The futility of my comfortable guilt was always with me. I stood and pulled Michael after me. The night had finally turned cool, some of the humidity lifting. Michael removed his jacket and threw it over his shoulder. We walked along the beach, following the endless line of burning torches. The air was thick with smoke and salt. The farther we got from the party, the more we could hear the ocean, how it quietly crept to the shore over and over. We found a small outcropping of rock.

Michael shook open his jacket and set it on the rock for me. I stepped out of my shoes and sat down. I pulled my knees to my chest and looked out onto the water.

A boat quietly floated by, filled with laughing teenagers.

"This is the Haiti I love, Michael—the water, the warm nights. I want you to know it has nothing to do with all that back there."

He sat down next to me, kissed my bare shoulder. "I know you."

We could still hear the music in the distance.

"You are the Haiti I love," Michael said.

"Would you live here with me?"

He was quiet for a moment. The waves lapped the shore softly and in the distance we could hear the party still going, the rhythmic strains of *konpa* reaching us. "Yes, Miri, I would."

I held Michael's hand and kissed his knuckles, remembering the enthusiasm with which he kissed the ground in the Miami airport. It took weeks to forgive him even though I too was generally relieved the moment I stepped back on American soil.

"You are such a liar but I love you for saying that," I said.

We married six months later, in Miami. As we walked out of the church, they played "This Must Be the Place" by the Talking Heads and Michael serenaded me, singing about home as the place he wants to be, always with me.

‖‖‖‖‖‖‖‖‖‖‖‖‖‖

Their early courtship kept Michael on his toes. He liked the chase, the push and pull. He liked her eyes and her neck and her sharp tongue, how she was always ready for . . . something, he wasn't quite sure. Mireille did her best to keep Michael away but he persisted, showing up at the law library, her office on campus, even her house one night.

It had been a long day on campus and Mireille was exhausted, lonely. She had hours more work ahead of her, no one to talk to, nothing to occupy her attention but legal briefs and precedents. Her only job, her father said when he bought her the house, was to be an excellent student, so that's what she did. There was no time for romance even though she found herself thinking of Michael, hoping he might suddenly appear, wherever she was. Romance would come later, she hoped.

Michael was sitting on the concrete stairs leading up to her porch. She was so lost in thought she startled, jumped back as Michael cleared his throat.

Mireille held her briefcase closer to her body and bit her lower lip.

"Are you stalking me again?" she asked.

Michael grinned. "I'm stubborn. I like you."

She stepped around him and slid her key in the lock, turning it slowly. "I thought we went over this a few times. I don't have time for a relationship right now. I'm almost done with school and then I need a job, who knows where, and first-year associates don't get to have lives."

Michael stood and took Mireille's bag from her. "You spoke, I listened, now it's my turn." He followed her into the house and carefully set her bag down, then rubbed his hands together. "I'm going to make you something to eat." Before Mireille could protest he raised his hand. "I know you haven't eaten."

He pushed her into the kitchen and forced her into an empty chair. There were several wine bottles on the counter, resting in a stainless steel rack. He hummed as he inspected each bottle, finally deciding on a Pinot Noir. Michael held the bottle against his chest as he uncorked it, then he poured Mireille a glass. She was tired and all argued out after a long day of working on a legal brief for moot court. She sat quietly as Michael busied himself in her kitchen cooking something from the sad assemblage of available ingredients—some pasta, green onions, a few soft tomatoes, a block of Romano cheese of questionable origin.

As he cooked, Michael talked. "The way I see it, I need to prove my case that we should date, get married, have babies, and live happily ever after."

Mireille raised her glass in Michael's direction and nodded, leaned back and crossed her legs. "This should be good."

He argued a very good case for himself and cooked a very good meal. They drank two bottles of wine. Mireille had never been much of a talker before she met Michael, never trusted anyone would be interested in what she had to say, but something about his manner made her open up the lonelier parts of herself. Her face grew numb. Michael's face flushed from the warmth in the kitchen. Finally when their words grew slower, eyes heavy, Michael stood, said, "I better get out of your hair. I've imposed long enough. I rest my case, as you might say."

She stood too but stumbled. Michael caught Mireille in his arms. She wanted to hold his hand. "I am not the lush I appear to be," she mumbled. "You keep catching me on days when I haven't eaten much."

They walked to the front door and stood facing each other. Mireille held on to the belt loops of his slacks, her forehead against his chest. "You made a very strong case but I can't do this." She sighed, and looked up and pretended not to notice how he wore his disappointment, nakedly. There was a quiet pause.

"Well," Michael said, his voice cracking, "I guess you really mean it." Mireille bit her tongue and nodded. Michael kissed the top of her head, tracing the edges of her face with his thumbs. "I really like you."

"Don't make this hard. You're a nice guy and you deserve a nice girl. I am not a nice girl."

Michael nodded. "I see." He leaned in, pressing his lips against Mireille's. She couldn't help but open her mouth to him, clasping the back of his neck.

Suddenly she pulled away and opened the door. "I really cannot do this." Michael stepped outside. Mireille grabbed his shirt just before he stepped off the porch. "I am lying."

Michael closed his eyes for a moment, and stepped back inside, his breath wrapping around them. Mireille reached past him and locked the front door. She turned off the foyer light. She started for the staircase and reached back. His fingers found hers. Upstairs, they undressed without talking and crawled beneath the sheets. She lay with her head on Michael's chest, her legs twisted through his.

"You have no idea how good this feels," Mireille whispered.

He kissed her forehead and held her tighter. "Look how we fit," he said, before they fell asleep.

That was the thing about them, Michael thought, whiling away the hours until Miri was freed from her captors. He and his wife fit even though there were any number of reasons they should not. Michael stood in his father-in-law's office, holding the phone, the dial tone echoing into his sweaty palm. He heard something in Mireille's voice, something he had never heard before. She was afraid and her fear chilled him. She was normally so fearless. Something terrible was happening. Michael thought again about how well he and his wife fit, about how she overcame herself to be with him, how this couldn't possibly be how their story ended.

He set the receiver down, grabbed Sebastien by the shoulders, and shoved him against a wall, causing a brightly colored abstract painting to fall to the floor. "She is your child!" Michael shouted. "She is my wife, the mother of your grandchild. Did you hear her? Pay them what they want. I am begging you." Michael shoved Sebastien again.

Sebastien could not look his son-in-law in the eyes. He could not explain to the American that he was doing what he believed to be right. He could not explain to the American that he was not dealing with men of honor, men who would respect an agreement. Sebastien allowed himself to be shoved. When Michael brought his fist back and tried to punch his father-in-law, Sebastien grabbed the younger man's wrist. Michael was surprised by his father-in-law's strength. Sebastien held fast and looked Michael in the eye. His voice was cold, steel, resolute. "I am doing what is best. There is more at stake here than just Mireille. If you would allow yourself to think clearly, you might see that."

"I don't know how you live with yourself," Michael said, shaking himself free from Sebastien's grip. "I'll find a way to pay the ransom myself."

Michael stepped away and as his breathing slowed, he picked up the phone again, quickly dialing their financial planner, Steve, in Miami—a midwestern transplant like himself. "I need to liquidate everything we have," Michael stuttered into the phone. He gripped the desk and ignored the people around him. He could do this one thing. He could get the money together and find a way to make contact with the kidnappers. He would work around Sebastien. Enough was enough.

Sebastien sat behind his desk, his hands trembling. He tried to forget the sound of his daughter's scream and what might have brought about that scream. He watched quietly as Michael made phone call after phone call. "You are wasting your time," he said at last, with a finality that made Michael shiver.

||||| ||||| |||||

After allowing me to bathe and wash my clothes in the bathroom sink, TiPierre brought me water, a bowl of rice. I was so hungry I grabbed sticky clumps of rice with my fingers, shoving them into my mouth. I didn't care if the food was drugged or poisoned. I needed something to fill the gnawing hollow inside me. He watched as I ate, smiled kindly. It was repulsive. When I finished, I felt sick, my stomach bloated. I wanted more.

He looked at me shyly, said, "I gave part of my share of the ransom to the others so they would leave you alone."

I tried to understand, tried not to hope but I was desperate. I allowed myself to believe he had rescued me. "Why would you do that?" I asked.

"I like you."

"You don't know me."

"I know you are brave."

I brought my fingers to my lips, shook my head. "This is how you would treat your mother? My child's mother?"

"The Commander needed to teach you a lesson. He is a very angry man. He does not like to be defied."

"He's an animal. He is capable of anything. Don't think he will ever respect you."

TiPierre stood and the tightness in my chest began to unravel. I needed to believe I was safe despite holding so much evidence to the contrary in my skin.

Instead of leaving, TiPierre closed the door. I started shaking, moved to the corner, to the false safety of two walls, tried to become part of that house, part of something bigger and stronger than myself. I held my hands out in front of me. "No," I said. "Don't." I said, "You said you paid for me to be left alone."

He wore Nike sneakers, green with a gold swoosh. He bent over and unlaced the shoes, stepped out of them, set the shoes neatly to the side. I wondered how he kept his home, if he was a clean and organized man. "You will be left alone. I can't keep the Commander away, but the others, yes." He pulled off his shirt. His torso was lean and long, his skin the color of caramel. He had a birthmark, dark red, in the shape of a ragged diamond, just under his navel. Under different circumstances, he would have been an attractive man.

"I don't want this," I said. Another man inside me would render me further undone.

"I bought you for myself." He smiled as if I were supposed to smile back, as if what would happen and who we were made sense. He walked toward me holding his hands open. "I will not hurt you."

I ran my hands through my matted hair and took a deep breath, again tried to find the right combination of words to save myself.

When he reached me, he traced the bruises on my face. "I've always wondered what it would be like to be with someone like you. I see you women, how you wear your designer clothes and your beautiful shoes and your dark sunglasses, your French perfumes. It's like the shit of this place doesn't touch you. You never see me but I am there, watching. You are all so beautiful." He pressed his lips against mine. I shrank from him, from the insistent heat of his tongue, the way he wet my mouth with his. "You are beautiful," he whispered, hotly.

He kept caressing my face. The gentleness of his touch over my broken skin made me shiver, broke me further. He kissed my forehead. His lips were cool. His fingers were soft and warm. If I closed my eyes, it would be easy to pretend the man before me was a lover, that our bodies belonged together.

I fought him. I swallowed the pain. I did not close my eyes.

Even before I was kidnapped I knew there were lots of ways the body can be broken—our flesh and bone are so weak.

Michael always said his mother had never been sick a day in her life. As a boy, he would come down with a cold or flu and she would tend to him and nothing would compromise her legendary immune system, her strong German constitution. When the call came that there was something wrong with Lorraine, Michael refused to believe. He said it wasn't possible. His mother was an impenetrable fortress, made of steel. That is who she was for him. He was inconsolable. There is no graceful way to deal with the fear of losing a mother.

Michael was in the middle of too many projects at work, he said, but mostly, he couldn't face his mother as her body fell apart. He told me this when we were in bed, trying to figure out how we could best help his parents. It is one of the only times I saw my husband cry in the before, one of the only times he had reason to cry. I held him, his voice cracking as he admitted he couldn't bear watching his mother die. "Oh my love," is all I could say, to see him like that, so exposed and so honest. I surprised both of us when the next morning, I said, "I'll go to the farm to take care of Lorraine."

It was easy enough to take a leave of absence from my law firm. I started the firm with four of my smartest lawyer friends—two immigration attorneys, two criminal defense attorneys, and one personal injury attorney. We were an odd mix but wanted to practice law and be damn good at it without sacrificing our entire lives. We each had offers to go to big firms in Chicago and New York but the thought of having to work a hundred hours a week, eating meals from damp Styrofoam containers in dimly lit offices, all in the name of getting ahead, earning money we would never have time to spend—it was too much. That wasn't why we had gone into the law. It's not that we were idealists but we aspired to be. We took the risk, pooled what money we had, and promised we could always take the time we needed for ourselves and our families so long as we gave our all when we were at work. We were lucky. The first few years, we did work crazy hours and didn't know how we were going to make ends meet but we were working for ourselves. Then we won some big cases. We developed a reputation—the sharks of Biscayne Boulevard. We were able to hire a handful of associates and two paralegals. We were able to breathe a little and live a little. Even my father, who had never approved of our starting our own firm, grudgingly acknowledged we had made a wise gamble.

My partners would manage my cases until I returned. I had a laptop and a cell phone. Any work I needed to do I could handle from anywhere. Michael and I flew back to Nebraska a couple of days before Lorraine's surgery. We said goodbye in the hall just outside my mother-in-law's hospital room. The air around us was stale and antiseptic.

Michael ran his fingers through my hair. "I don't know how to thank you."

I pressed a finger against his lips. "You don't thank me for being your wife."

He wrapped his arms around me and lifted me off the ground. "Yes, I do. I thank you. I'm going to miss you like crazy. I thank you." My arms circled his neck and we kissed softly and then we stood, my feet in the air, our lips barely touching. I wanted to say *do not leave me here*. I wanted to say *I cannot sleep without you*. I was silent. I patted his shoulder and straightened his tie. He set me down and smiled, almost sadly. "I know you're going to miss me too even if you won't say it." Before I could respond, Lorraine coughed loudly. We returned to her bedside and Michael held his mother's hands in his. He kissed her forehead and we stood, for a long while on either side of his bed, staring at each other. Finally, he patted the plastic bedrail. He said, "This is my mother." His voice sounded strangled. He looked like a little boy. The devotion of an only child runs so deep.

I nodded. "I will treat her like my own." Lorraine's lips wrinkled into a frown. "Mostly," I said.

He left the room, paused in the doorway, watching me standing over his mother. The room felt smaller and darker. Lorraine sat up, huffing as she tried to make herself comfortable. "I don't really expect you to stay."

I rolled my eyes and studied the pillow behind her head. I've seen movies. "Lorraine, I will be right back." I ran out of the room. I saw Michael standing at the end of the long corridor, waiting for the elevator. Hospitals are so quiet. I didn't want to shout his name but I didn't want him to leave. "Michael," I said, whispering loudly. He continued staring ahead. I called his name again, louder this time. Finally he turned and I ran toward him, my heels echoing loudly.

"What's wrong?" he asked.

"Nothing." I stood on the tips of my toes and wrapped my arms around him, held tight. He held me against him, sliding his hands slowly up and down my back. "I'm going to miss you too, like crazy," I said into his shirt. My husband is much taller, so I pulled him down until my lips met his ear, tried to memorize the steadiness of the pulse in his neck. Quietly, very quietly, I told him everything that needed to be said about how I feel about him and us and what it would be like to be apart from him and how I knew he was scared and it was okay for him to be scared but he would never have to be scared alone. I talked for a long time. It surprised me, how much I had, until then, left unsaid between us. I held my husband's face and looked into his eyes. I said, "Okay?" He nodded. I did not want to let him go. He had a flight to catch so he pulled away reluctantly, jabbed his finger against the elevator button. As the elevator doors hissed shut, he held his hand out to me, palm open and I held my hand over my heart.

My mother-in-law was in the hospital for just over a week. She was not a good patient nor was she popular with the doctors and nurses. She was scared and she is stubborn—a hellish combination. During the day, we watched soap operas and courtroom dramas and Maury Povich. Lorraine picked fights. I tried to be patient as she criticized my shoes, scowling at me as I walked to the window. "Those shoes are impractically high. Accept your natural height." When I leaned over to adjust her pillow, she wrinkled her nose and said, "That perfume of yours is too young for you, makes you smell like a teenage tart." I whiled the hours away, staring at my phone. When she was trying to get my attention, Lorraine said, "You have the attention span of a gnat; you can't even hold a damn conversation without staring at that thing." There were blissful moments when I stepped out to talk to Michael. When I returned to her room, she said I was keeping her son from his important work. She stared at my engagement ring and muttered, "That is an ice-skating rink you've got on your finger. You are probably going to put my son in debt."

By the third day, I had taken to wearing earbuds, pretending to listen to music, occasionally nodding my head. Lorraine smiled and said, "Your people do have a fondness for music and dancing."

I perfected saying, "Whatever you say, Lorraine."

When my mother-in-law was thirsty and too weak to hold the plastic cup, I gently held her head and brought the cup to her lips as she took tiny, careful sips. Her face was gray, drawn, her skin practically blue, paper-thin. I thought of my own mother and how unbearable it was to imagine her in a hospital bed, small and afraid, something dark and unknown eating away at her from the inside. When the pain was too much Lorraine pursed her lips and held her hand against the incision, shaking her head slowly. When she was hurting like that, we talked about Michael, wondering what he was doing, marveling at how well he was doing in his job. She told me about Michael as a little boy, so curious, always building things. He was a good boy, she said, and I said, "He is a good man." We were both happy, smiling. "At least you seem to really love him. You treat him right," Lorraine said grudgingly. I said, "Thank you, Lorraine."

The doctors treated the cancer aggressively so as soon as she recovered, she had six weeks of radiation and chemotherapy. Three or four days a week, we drove the hour or so from the farm to the hospital in Lincoln. I'd sit with her as the IV in her arm pumped poisonous chemicals into her body; I'd do a crossword puzzle or read, or stare at the wall wondering how much time would pass before I lost my temper. We got to know some of the other regulars who had their chemo appointments at the same time. Lorraine and I confused them as they tried to make sense of our connection. One day Lorraine told the woman next to her, "My boy married this one. I have no idea why," and the woman said, "Maybe because she's here with you." I wanted to high-five that lady.

After chemo, Lorraine spent hours in the bathroom, hugging the toilet. I brought her ice chips, wiped her face with cool cloths, played Willie Nelson tapes from a small boom box. Lorraine loves Willie Nelson, says he's the only man who would make her leave Glen. "Something about a man with long hair," she said, one afternoon, me sitting on the bathroom counter while she sat on the floor, with her back against the bathtub. I nodded, said, "I can see that." Michael has beautiful hair, shoulder length, thick and blond. He often wears the top half of his hair in a ponytail and lets the rest of it hang loose. When we're making love, Michael's hair brushes against my shoulder in such a way that makes my back arch at an unnatural but entirely pleasant angle.

There were times Lorraine was so weak she could barely stand. I helped her bathe, running a soft washcloth over her body as she sat in the tub, her knees pulled to her chest. The first time, she stood naked in front of me, shifting nervously, trying to hide behind her arms. I wore a tank top and a pair of shorts. "I never had a body like yours," Lorraine said, looking me up and down. Her ribs were beginning to protrude and her skin hung loosely but there was no shame in her body, none at all and that's what I told her. "I ought to be able to do this for myself," she said. I pulled my hair into a ponytail and pointed to the empty tub, said, "You ought to know when you need help." She scowled but got in the tub without much argument, said, "Don't make the water too hot. I don't want you to boil me." I started buying fruity soaps from a store in the city and each morning I'd say, "What fruit do you feel like today?" and she'd humor me, grumble, "Raspberries," or "Green apples," and we'd go from there. There is something terribly intimate about bathing another person. I learned almost everything a person could know about my mother-in-law's body—her scars and birthmarks and wrinkles, the single strand of hair behind her left ear. Sometimes I hummed as I washed her and if she recognized the song, Lorraine hummed along too.

Toward the end of her treatment, Lorraine lost all patience with everything. It was understandable. She was exhausted and completely worn down. We were in her bedroom, Lorraine in bed, me sitting in a chair next to her bed, flipping through a glossy magazine. This is how we started every day. Mornings were hard, her body always stiff and unwilling to move. There was the nausea, the aches of aging, and a variety of other complications that made having to get out of bed an ordeal.

"I'm tired of looking at you. I'm ready to go," Lorraine croaked.

I turned the page but didn't look up. "I'm ready for you to go too, Lorraine."

Lorraine sat up slowly, grunting as she moved her body. "Well. Look who's got teeth."

I set my magazine down and handed Lorraine her morning regimen of pills and a glass of water. "I've always had teeth, Lorraine. Unlike you, I don't feel the need to use them all the time."

She made a small sound but sat a little straighter, took her medication without complaint.

I stayed with Lorraine for four months, through the worst of it. It meant that Glen was able to keep the farm running. Michael came to visit every few weeks. He never stayed for long enough and we had no privacy. During his visits, I was usually so tired I wasn't good company. Even so, we made the most of our time together. We didn't bicker or talk about inconsequential things. We made frantic, quiet love trying to get enough from each other's bodies to get us through the time apart. It was never enough.

On the day I left, Lorraine and I sat at the kitchen table, eating cereal. We talked about the episode of *Survivor* we watched the previous day. I washed our dishes and she walked me to the front door. Glen was waiting to drive me to the airport in Lincoln. I wore a ridiculously high pair of heels and a tastefully slutty dress for Michael, and Lorraine didn't bat an eye. I was impressed by her restraint. I wasn't sure what to say as we stood in the doorway. Lorraine isn't one for demonstration. I told her I would call when I got in, that I'd call often. I meant it. She grabbed me and pulled me into a warm embrace. Just as quickly she pushed me away. She said, "Thank you for getting on my nerves for so long," and I said, "You're welcome, Lorraine." We have talked three or four times a week ever since. She is family.

The Commander called for me again. It was the seventh day. Every day more was taken from me. He forced me onto my stomach and handcuffed my wrists to the headboard. He left me there, bared to him as he talked, mostly incoherent, half-formed political ideas, angry barbs about wealth and women, the ramblings of a man without a real ideology.

"I don't understand women like you," he said, winding down. "You could have made things easier for yourself. Would it be so hard to play nice with me?"

"I don't understand men like you. You could have made things easier for me."

"You always have something clever to say, Mireille Duval. I like that about you."

"My last name is Jameson."

The Commander laughed. "My, how quickly things change. You people are all the same. You live in your grand homes looking down on us in the gutter. You think you control everything and can have anything."

"There is nothing original about you, not even your ideals," I muttered.

He waved his arm across his chest. "One day all of you will live like the rest of us. You will know what it's like to live the way the real people of this country do."

"As if you do, with your flat-screen televisions and Xbox systems?"

He grabbed me by my hair, yanking my head back. I hoped for my neck to break. "I can see it is difficult for you to learn your lesson. I will try again to teach you."

There was nothing he could do, I told myself, that he had not already done. I had not yet developed a respect for his cruelty. The Commander reached beneath his pillow and pulled out a long knife, the kind so sharp the blade hummed. He would open my body in a different, more terrible way.

I closed my eyes, breathed shallow, thought of my husband and son at home in bed, cool and clean and happy—the way both Michael and Christophe smiled at me with their whole faces. I made no sound. Later, the Commander left me cuffed to his bed and walked around the room naked ranting about how a change was coming, that the people would revolt. He drank rum from a dark brown bottle, grabbed my cheeks, and dug his fingers into my face, prying my mouth open. He poured rum into my mouth and I swallowed, willingly. It was not long before everything dulled. I did not mind when he doused the cuts on my back with alcohol. My skin burned. Before I passed out, I said, "My heart is safe. My heart is safe."

In Haiti, it is the father, not the husband, who gets the first dance at his daughter's wedding. Even though we were marrying in the States, I thought it would be nice to uphold the tradition. Mona danced with my father at her wedding and the way he moved her across the floor, both their faces shining, I wanted that moment for myself. When I told Michael a few days before our wedding, he rubbed his chin, said, "That's kind of twisted," and I slapped his arm. I said, "It's sweet."

My father and I danced to Etta James, "At Last," his favorite song. My mother beamed at us from her table, she and Mona sitting so close their faces were practically touching. I was nervous, so many people staring at us, so much aloneness with my father. This was something new for us, sharing a quiet moment. He smiled shyly as I held his shoulders and he held my waist and we swayed. He said, "I trust that with this man, your heart is safe," and I nodded, because it was, because I knew Michael would take good care of the softest parts of me I dared to give him. That night, with my father so relaxed, so happy, I thought my heart was safe with him too.

Later, I was dying or losing myself or both or maybe the two states were the same thing. I awoke slowly. I was as far away from being my father's daughter as I had ever been. My arms were stiff, stretched tautly. When I tried to move, it was difficult. My shoulder popped. I tried to sit up, realized I was on my stomach, my wrists still cuffed to the Commander's bed. I looked around and standing next to the bed was a young woman, couldn't have been more than twenty-two. She looked down at me with her hands on her hips, muttered something too softly for me to make out.

"Please, help me." The words felt dangerous in my mouth. I cleared my throat. "Help me."

She reached into a drawer in the nightstand and produced a small, silver key. She quietly unlocked each cuff and I winced as my arms fell and the blood rushed back to my shoulders, my raw, abraded wrists.

"Help me get out of here," I whispered.

She pressed one finger to her lips, nodded. She handed me my clothes. My hands shook as I dressed, tried to fasten the button on my jeans. When I couldn't, she moved toward me, reached. I stepped away, a rush of adrenaline shooting through me, but she shook her head, smiled softly, fastened my jeans for me. I grabbed her hand, didn't want to let go. Her skin was soft. I needed someone soft to hold on to, someone who wouldn't hurt me. I needed to believe a woman wouldn't hurt me. She didn't let go of my hand, pulled me after her.

We moved quickly but quietly. The house was still; the city was still, early morning. My heart beat so fast. I felt Michael's arms around me. I saw his smile. I walked toward his smile, the memory of it.

There were two sleeping men curled up on different ends of a long couch. They didn't stir. At the front door of the house, the young woman pushed me into the street. She said, "Run," so I ran. When I looked back, she shook her head, moving her arms like she was pushing me along. I had no idea where I was going. Even though it was early and still and silent, there were people in the street. As I ran past them, they stared. I cannot imagine what I looked like, bruised and bloody and barefoot, running, wild, so very wild, trying to get free, being chased even though I was not being chased.

The slums are an endless maze of narrow streets and alleys lined with small concrete block homes. The blocks rise up into a mountain and dark, narrow, winding staircases hold everything together. The sky is often blocked by a thick and tangled web of electrical wiring. Cars are parked everywhere, sometimes half on the sidewalk, half in the street. Women rarely move through the streets alone. It is not safe, not ever. When they do walk down the street, they often carry large buckets of water or baskets carrying goods to sell at La Saline market. Old women sit on concrete stairs, their heavy skirts bunched between their thighs as they stare at the goings-on or peel vegetables or feel the beating sun on their skin. The streets are covered in trash—plastic bottles, torn paper, shallow pools of dirty water, rusted coffee cans, discarded cigarette butts. Sometimes a stray chicken or goat carefully steps its way through the streets. When a car barrels down the street, anyone in the street jumps out of the way. The music is loud. Car horns wail regularly. The air is thick with the smell of too many people in too little space. Many of the walls are painted brightly; some of the walls have advertisements for Comme Il Faut cigarettes or a local church or barbershop. I ran through these streets and thought, "This is a Haiti I have never seen or known." It was a Haiti no one should have to know.

I came upon a small café and stepped inside. I refused hope but it was so close, so close my fingers felt electric. Michael's smile grew brighter. I had a husband and child and if there was kindness in the world, someone in the café would get me to them. Inside, two women sat at a small, square table smoking cigarettes as they stared at a television on a high shelf in one corner of the room. A tall orange drink sat in front of each woman. I tried to stand straight, tried to hold my head high, tried to sound strong. "May I please use your telephone?" I wanted to be polite. I wanted to sound like a woman who deserved to use a telephone to call her husband to come and save her. Another woman shuffled out from behind a bar along one side of the room. She was older, her hair gone completely to gray. She wore a pink T-shirt and white Capri pants, lots of gold bracelets dangled from her wrist. She looked at me carefully, then sucked her teeth, waved her arms like she was trying to sweep me out her front door.

"I want no trouble here," she said.

I tried to hold it together. "Please, my family can pay you money, lots of money."

She paused, nodded toward a small table in the corner. "Sit," she said. I did as I was told and sat carefully, tried to ignore the pain. I gripped the edges of the table. She brought me a glass of water, a napkin. I drank the water quickly, drank so fast my head began to hurt. She disappeared for a few minutes and when she returned she set a cell phone on the table in front of me. I closed my eyes and tried to concentrate, tried to remember the exact sequence of numbers between that moment and salvation. I pressed each number carefully, tried to steady my hands, tried to quiet my heart. As I pressed the last number I heard a familiar laugh. I looked up and saw the Commander standing over me, his hands on the butt of the gun tucked in the waistband of his pants. He tossed a wad of tightly rolled bills held together with a rubber band to the woman. I nodded slowly, took another sip of my water. I swallowed the rising bile. I tried to breathe.

The Commander sat across from me. He appeared calm, bemused.

"Don't look so disappointed. You were never going to get away. Your father may think he owns the city but I own *these* streets."

He snapped his fingers, ordered two drinks. When the proprietress set mine in front of me I did not bother to ask what it was. I simply drank it, fast. My limbs tingled as the alcohol took effect. The Commander leaned back, spread his legs wide, as if providing his arrogance room to stretch. He set a pack of cigarettes on the table. I reached for one without asking, and when I put the cigarette in my mouth, he proffered a lighter. I leaned into the flame, took a long drag, exhaled slowly. The cigarette made me dizzy. I inhaled again.

"Well, I enjoyed the run."

He set his gun on the table. "That is good. There is certainly a lot to see around here. I hope you took it all in, what you people hath wrought."

"Fancy words. You let me go on purpose."

He smiled, and I marveled, once again, at the exceptional whiteness of his teeth, how they gleamed, wetly sharp. "You are smart. I like that too."

I took another drag of the cigarette, ashed on the floor, crossed my legs even though it felt like something new tore inside me every time I moved. The cuts on my back wept angrily. "You are not going to let me go."

"Is that a question?"

I smiled. "No, it is not."

He motioned to the proprietress who brought us more drinks. It was all very civilized. We sat, talking, though not like friends.

"You wouldn't be here if it were not for your father's reluctance to pay what I am owed."

"I wouldn't be here if you hadn't stolen me from my husband and child." I pounded my fist against the small table. "You took me in front of my child," I said. "My child." It was more than I could take, sitting across from that man and his smugness, his righteousness and mine.

He waved his arm widely. "What about all the children who will never know anything but life here?"

I took a long sip of my drink, wanted to numb myself. "I did not create the problems in this country nor did my family."

The Commander laughed, reached across the table, took my wrist in his hand, and squeezed, hard. "People like you always choose to absolve yourselves. You are complicit even if you do not actively contribute to the problem because you do nothing to solve it."

I held his gaze. My rage engulfed my fear. The Commander was just a man, I realized, a small and petty man. "You are complicit too. Don't think for one second you aren't."

A strange expression crossed his face. He released his grip, shrugged, then looked up at the television. An episode of *Judge Judy* was airing. We watched, silently, drank, smoked many cigarettes. I wonder what we must have looked like, me and my battered body, the Commander and his arrogance, the anger hovering between us muted by the sharp counsel of a television judge. The laughter began just beneath my breastbone and soon my shoulders were shaking and finally I gave in, threw my head back and laughed so loudly I am certain they heard me for blocks and blocks.

As we exited the café, the Commander carried me, his arms hooked under mine. I kicked and tried to grab on anything with my feet. I knocked over chairs, a table covered with empty glasses, kicked the doorjamb of the entrance. I would have done anything, absolutely anything, to save myself from returning to the cage, to the men who used my body. There was one moment when I was facing the interior of the café as the Commander struggled to hold on to me. I could feel how frenzied I looked, my hair, flying from my head in every direction, the anger in my eyes, the white heat of it rolling off my body, threatening to burn everything around me. I stared at the woman who betrayed me. I shouted, "How could you? We are both daughters of Dessalines." She stood perfectly still. She did not blink. She did not look away with her dry eyes.

By the time we made it back to the Commander's house, I calmed. He would take me to his room filled with the trappings of his lack of imagination. His anger at my attempt to escape would be cold, cruelly measured. I accepted this.

A Jamaican friend, Elsa, once told me of a popular lullaby from her country about a mother with thirteen children. The mother kills one child to feed twelve, and one child to feed eleven, and one child to feed ten until she is left with but one child, whom she also slaughters because she too hungers. Finally, she returns to the middle of a cornfield where she slaughtered her other children, where the bones of their thirteen bodies lay. She slits her own throat because she cannot bear the burden of having done what needed to be done. After telling me this story, Elsa said, "A West Indian woman always faces such choices."

The Commander closed the door to his bedroom and stood against it, smiling. He is a man who smiles without any change in his eyes. His eyes are dull, uninteresting. There is not one original thing about the man except for the scar on his face.

There was a different way to fight. I knew I needed to find it, to live, to make it back to those from whom I had been taken. He pulled his gun from his waistband and began running his fingers along the length of the barrel, over the trigger, the slight curve of the handle, a beautiful affair with pearl inlays. I walked over to him and got on my knees.

I would fight by giving him that which he did not yet want. I feigned surrender. I held his wrist gently, pressed my lips against the underside. I became someone different, a woman who could satisfy a man with his desires. I held his wrist and opened my mouth and swallowed the barrel of his gun, occasionally massaging his arm. The gun was hard. My teeth scraping the metal made me cringe. I did not show my disgust. I was becoming a woman who could be disgusted by nothing. The gun oil was almost sweet in my mouth. It coated my tongue and filled my nose. Even though my throat was swollen, raw, I relaxed as best I could and I took the barrel of that gun into my throat. I looked up at the Commander, who gazed back at me curiously. He leaned against the door, relaxed. I tried to breathe and treated the gun like I would a lover. I choked myself on that weapon, making soft, wet, strangled sounds. I could see how much the Commander appreciated the display, how his breathing changed, the stiff rise of his pants.

I stood and held on to him by the waist of his jeans. At the foot of the bed, I undressed. I did not shrink from the way he looked at me. Though I had little experience with men, I knew I had a nice body or I did before. I took the gun from him, and our eyes met. He was guarded as he loosened his grip. I set the gun on the bed, yearning to be able to pull the trigger. I undressed the Commander the way a woman who could want a man like him might. I began to forget everything I had ever known and anyone I had ever loved. I became no one. I became a woman who wanted to live. That was my fight.

I kissed his chest and the palms of his hands and pressed my cheeks against the palms of his hands. I think he trembled. I lay on his bed and set his gun over my mound. I spread my legs. I offered myself to him. The Commander wrapped himself around my thigh. He traced the bruises and blisters along my inner thighs with the end of his gun. He penetrated me with his gun and I raised my hips. I grabbed his shoulder, squeezing the thick stretch of muscle. I endured the pain. I was no one, so the pain did not matter. He kissed my thigh over and over, drew his fingers around the bone of my knee.

When it was the right time, when I knew he wanted me desperately, I told him he should put his gun away. I told him he had no need for it. I told him he should become his gun. He liked this. He was rough because he is not a man who knows how to be gentle, who knows how to handle precious things. He was not a difficult man to understand. He held my hair in his fist and put his mouth on my neck and put his mouth on my lips. I opened my mouth to him the way I opened my body to him, the body he had already tried to break but could not break. I was silent. I pretended I did not feel pain even though the only thing I felt was pain. My hands were not my hands. My body was not my body. He was loud, made a sound from deep in his chest like a roar and then he was completely spent; his body was heavy and immovable on top of mine. I raged beneath him, staring at the ceiling. In what was left of my mind, I screamed. I was alive.

I made my choice. There is nothing you cannot do when you are no one.

||||| ||||| ||||
||

Sebastien Duval and Fabienne Duval née Georges each had twelve siblings. Their mothers' wombs were fertile countries unto themselves. Each sibling had at least two children. Several had more. Mireille's family was oppressive in size.

As news of the kidnapping spread throughout their circle, Mireille's bloodline began showing up at the Duval house early each morning, impeccably dressed. They were there to hold vigil and support the family. They were there to be seen holding vigil and supporting the family. They were a benevolent pestilence.

The family held court in the large sitting room, barking orders at the maids who held tongues silent and heads high as they brought tea and coffee, sweets and fruit. The family talked loudly, offering wild opinions, making idle threats, demanding change, trying to solve all of Haiti's problems in one sitting as is the way of Haitians when they gather. Michael hovered on the periphery, struggling to hold on to the conversations. After eight years with Mireille he could follow along when people spoke slowly, but with so many people, all talking so fast and furious, it was hard to make sense of anything. When he tried to interject, his mouth dried and he became overly conscious of his awkward French. When he spoke English, they mostly looked right through him.

Veronique, Mireille's maternal aunt and godmother, fell to her knees every so often, throwing her hands in the air as she offered up ecstatic prayers. Her sister Vivienne shook her head and rolled her eyes, and surreptitiously sent her own daughter, safe in Miami, text messages keeping her up to date on the spectacle. Lily and Mathieu, twins, sat side by side, whispering to each other about how this was what happened when you left the country of your birth and assumed you could return without consequence. They were Sebastien's siblings and they resented how few of his blessings he bestowed unto others. He called them the Handouts because their hands were always out.

Three of Sebastien's brothers, Etienne, Bernard, and Benjamin, were doctors—an internist, a gynecologist, a pediatrician. They liked to make jokes about what would happen if they walked into a bar. They stood in a corner, pretending to look busy so they would not have to hear about all that ailed their siblings and in-laws and on and on.

Emmanuel, Fabienne's youngest brother, was close to Michael in age. He was the only one who really tried to talk to the American who was largely distracted, his eyes constantly flitting across the room as if waiting for someone else to appear. Emmanuel had a flask of rum he offered to Michael, who drank from it eagerly. He gently jabbed Michael in the ribs with his elbow, said, "We'll get her back, man. They can't keep her forever." Michael took another sip of rum but said nothing.

Fabienne sat on a couch against the wall near the middle of the room, flanked by two of her sisters. She held her hands in her lap, one leg crossed over the other. The conversation around her was a persistent hum that refused to organize itself into distinguishable sounds. Her youngest daughter, her stubborn sweet girl, was out there in a city Fabienne loathed, a city she had sworn she would never return to but for the will of her husband. She knew what the curve of Sebastien's spine said and what he meant when his eyes wrinkled at the corners. He made her blood rise in ways that still made her warm, everywhere. He was a man who did as he was told when he came to their bed each night and she said, "In this room, you are just a man. You leave the rest of it beyond these walls."

But now, everything out there was spilling into every last part of their lives. This wasn't supposed to happen. Sebastien had assured her they were safe. Mireille was an American, mostly. Fabienne smiled, remembering how when Mireille was young, eight or nine, she would always answer her mother in English when they were in public, a spiteful thing all the children did to show their parents they were not like them at all. And then, fifteen years later, Mireille began answering her mother in French, no matter where they were. The petty insurrections were over. She loved all her children. Mona, her wild child, always saying, "But Mom," and asking, "Why?"—Mona who was still a good girl, as settled as she likely would be with the photographer, and Michel, the adventurer, always in some faraway place, trying to put distance, Fabienne understood, between himself and his father. Still, it was her youngest who took up most of her heart.

Fabienne longed for a simple pleasure, all her children in one place, safe, with her.

They didn't take Americans. That was how Fabienne had slept at night, knowing her daughters would always be safe when they were in Port-au-Prince. And now, she knew her husband had lied to her. So many years, following him to so many places, and he had repaid her with such staggering deceit. If she allowed herself, she would tear his eyes out and spit on his bleeding face. She breathed deeply. She loved him. She tried not to consider the satisfaction of his flesh beneath her fingernails.

Sebastien stood next to the couch, taking slow, careful sips from a small cup of espresso. He had to look calm. He had to be in control. Too many people in the room would be more than happy to see him fall, to plunder all he had built. One thing he had learned in this life—there were always barbarians at both sides of the gate.

He looked up from his reverie, but didn't dare meet the eyes of the woman who had stood by his side the whole of his life. There Fabienne sat, as beautiful as always, so elegant, her back straight, eyes flashing, dark hair streaked with silver. Her face older, but still, this was the woman he married without ever looking back, always faithful. When he looked at Fabienne, everything was good and quiet. He could step away from the rush of the fire he always felt at his back.

Always, in America, he had to prove himself to the men he worked with, then men he worked for, the men who worked under him, all men he could outthink on his worst day. He hated how they mocked his accent before clapping him on the shoulders, saying, "You don't mind, do you?" He hated how surprised they were when he did something excellent, and how they never stopped being surprised, even twenty years on. It was not easy to be a man like him in a country where everyone looked upon him with suspicion. Everything he had made of himself and still, these indignities choked him and filled his mouth with bitterness. The easiest decision of his life had been to return to Haiti, where at least, he would always be a man among men.

And now, his youngest child was in the hands of animals—the little girl who always looked up at him, followed him everywhere, did as he asked. Sebastien never imagined this could happen. Things were getting so much better throughout the country—even CNN said so. He paid various thugs to allow his trucks into certain neighborhoods so his workers could build what needed building. Every hour of every day he paid armed guards to watch the concrete plant and keep people from stealing too much. He paid bonuses and holidays and when a project finished early or under budget. He paid the customs agents to finesse the import of supplies he needed. He paid the women who fed his family and cleaned his home and he paid for their children to go to school, made sure they had strong roofs over their heads.

Always, Sebastien was paying money, small ransoms here and there, the price of doing business in Haiti. But this was too much—a million dollars, such a breathtaking amount of money. It galled him that men who had not worked an honest day in their lives would be so bold as to ask for a lifetime's fortune. But it wasn't about the money. It was about so much more and there was nothing he could say to explain what he meant. Sebastien rubbed his forehead. He was doing the right thing. He finally met his wife's stare and his stomach fell. They had spoken little since their daughter was taken. There was little to be said.

Fabienne stood and everyone hushed, watching as she crossed toward her husband. They wanted the spectacle to swell ever more garishly. When husband and wife were only inches apart, Sebastien smiled softly. He studied Fabienne's hands, still smooth, the hands of a much younger woman. And oh how her hands felt in his, so much smaller than his calloused hands, what a network of delicate strength. Sebastien set his espresso on the small end table and reached for Fabienne's hands but she swatted him away.

"No. You do not get to hold my hands, not until my daughter is safe, back in this house."

Sebastien shifted from one foot to the other, terribly aware of the barbarians staring at him, judging him no matter what he said, no matter what he did. He tried to reach for his wife again but she was resolute, holding her body in a rigid line. "I am doing everything I can to bring our child back to us. You have to trust me."

"No," Fabienne said. "The time for trust is over. Too much trust I have given you. End this, now." She could feel panic rising through her spine. "Now," she repeated, her voice high and sharp. "Goddamn you, Sebastien Duval. Bring home my child."

Sebastien was suddenly weary. All the stares had shifted from curious to accusing. He loosened his necktie. "Excuse me," he said, stumbling forward, and out of the sitting room. He kept walking until he no longer heard voices and finally, when he was alone, he collapsed.

HHHH HHHH HHHH
III

With the Commander I surrendered defiantly but with TiPierre I fought viciously, like the caged animal I was. I clawed at him and beat his body with my hands. I refused to lie still, twisting my body every which way. He was always calm, patient, as if he knew he would win but also knew I needed to fight.

TiPierre had a son close in age to Christophe. He told me about his child as he lay next to me on the tenth night, his arm heavy across my chest, one of his legs draped over mine. Even though I kept trying to free myself, he would not be moved.

"I love my boy," TiPierre said. "He lives with his mother. I live with her when she isn't angry with me. She is often angry with me. You know how women can be."

I was silent, my skin burning with the weight of his arm across my chest. I said nothing.

"You have a son. What do you want for your boy?"

"I do not have a child," I whispered. "I do not have a child." The constant ache in my breasts sharpened even though my milk was drying, I could feel myself losing this one last part of myself. I tried to figure out what I could say to make TiPierre stop talking, to make him finish what he had come to my cage to do so he could leave me alone to be no one and feel nothing.

He propped himself up on one elbow. "Why would you deny your own child?"

I turned away from the man, the boy really, next to me, the one who hoped that through the intimacy of confession he might bring about my desire. "I am not the mother of that child," I said, pulling my knees to my chest, trying to find my way to some silent place inside myself.

TiPierre abandoned his line of questioning and began tracing my shoulder with his fingers. I bit down on my knuckles, as hard as I could. It was an interesting pain, dull but steady.

"I would like to raise my boy in America. I don't want him to become like me, running the streets, living in all this," TiPierre said.

Ti Pierre was from Gonaives, came to Port-au-Prince as a *restavek*, sold into indentured servitude when he was a small boy, sold by his mother who loved him for one thousand *gourdes*, twenty-five U.S. dollars. He was no stranger to the buying and selling of the human body. As a boy, he worked, indentured, to a wealthy family who lived up on Montagne Noire. All day and night he worked, cleaning for them, and when he got older, cooking. At night, the bones of his fingers were curled in pain from scrubbing marble floors and climbing ladders to polish a crystal chandelier and washing the beautiful German cars he would never sit in. The father of the family who owned him used to beat him each evening with a whittled tree branch to remind TiPierre of his place, fifteen strokes, more if he had somehow displeased his employer. TiPierre did not go to school, never learned to read or write, had no friends. He forgot his mother who loved him, his father, brothers and sister, his real name. He ran away when he was sixteen, ran to the slums because in the slums he would be safe. Someday, TiPierre said, he would make his way to Miami, where he would be a deejay in a fancy nightclub. He would meet famous football players and rap stars and beautiful women who wear bikinis at night. He would play Benny Benassi and David Guetta and Chemical Brothers and wear sunglasses in the dark and jump up and down to the beat. Maybe, he said, I would come see him spin. Maybe I would be his girl and look pretty for him. Of course he thought he could buy me.

I was desperate to keep his body from touching mine more than necessary. He kissed my shoulder and fondled my breasts affectionately. I pitied him, how carelessly he had been loved, how easily he had been discarded, how little he knew of love or true desire. I loathed myself for my compassion. I loathed him for making me feel anything toward him at all.

I shook, silently, my hand over my mouth until my bitterness welled. "With you as his father, your son has a very good chance of turning out exactly like you."

TiPierre grabbed me by my neck, the V of his thumb and forefinger locked just below my chin. I tried to swat his arm away but he squeezed until my eyes bulged and I gasped hungrily for air. I was on the edge of something, a quiet blackness. I found comfort there.

"You are an animal just like the man you work for," I said hoarsely, relaxing into his hand, hoping TiPierre would kill me. I longed for him to squeeze just a little harder, to show no mercy. I was no one. My death would not matter.

He finally released his grip. I touched my neck, could still feel the pressure of his hand against my fingertips. He kissed my collarbone, and the new bruises blooming around my throat. "I am sorry," he said, "but what you said was not nice."

"We are not friends. We are not lovers. I do not choose this. I do not want you. My God, surely you can see that."

He was seemingly oblivious. TiPierre brought his mouth to my breast and began to suckle softly. I panicked, shoved him away, but he refused to stop, refused to hold any part of me as sacred. The ache began to lessen as he stole the milk from my body. The relief was so startling I could not bear it. I dug my fingernails into his shoulders and scratched so hard, I hoped I might find bone. He cursed and pulled away. I covered my chest with my arms, shaking again.

"You cannot do that. You cannot."

For once, TiPierre heard me. He shrugged, resumed talking about his son, and I let myself breathe. The son's name was Innocent Sylvain; he was nine months old. "I'll bring you a picture of my boy," he said.

I grunted. I did not want to see any evidence of the man in this animal.

"In a different world, our sons could be playmates but in this world, my son will someday end up working for yours."

"I have no son. Please stop saying I do."

TiPierre slid on top of my body again, pinning my wrists above my head.

My body could not take any more. I knew that. I knew his intentions. "No," I said. "No more tonight, I cannot."

He ignored me.

After hours of labor, when it finally came time to push, the doctor had to reach inside me to turn the boy around. The pain was so intense it rendered me silent. All I could focus on was the pain and then the doctor told me to push and I had so little energy left but I held on to my thighs and Michael held me, his sweaty forehead pressed against mine. As the baby began to emerge, my body felt like it was coming apart, like my pelvic bones were separating then fracturing. It was only after the baby was all the way out that I groaned, a loose and ugly sound. That is the pain I remembered on the tenth night, when so much had been done to my body. It was my only frame of reference for a pain more profound than the body should survive.

There was a time when I did not want a child.

My husband and I were young and successful in Miami. The life we were living was all I wanted for us. We were not careful but I thought my disinterest in motherhood would reinforce our irresponsible approach to birth control, which mostly involved hope and, once in a while, Michael pulling out.

I did not want a child.

A year and a half before I had Christophe, I had a miscarriage. Michael never knew.

I didn't even realize I was pregnant until everything had gone wrong. I was at the beach, running, when a tight fist twisted everything inside me and forced it out. I drove home, bleeding, thinking, "At least my car seats are leather," and when Michael wasn't home I was relieved. I sat on the toilet staring at my blood, drying in streaks almost to my knee.

I waited until I had a better idea of what to do. I waited for Michael to come home but he didn't so I undressed, stuffed my clothes in the trash and took a hot shower. I did not cry. It was for the best, that's what I told myself.

When I was pregnant with Christophe, I was feeling tired and irritable all the time. I thought it was work stress. There's always a steady stream of clients for an immigration attorney in Miami—so many people desperate to stay, desperate to bring the ones they love to the Promised Land even if they haven't found any promise yet. My caseload was insane after my leave of absence. If Michael didn't call me most nights to remind me to come home at a decent hour, I worked well into the night. I was nauseous anytime I smelled something citrusy or flowery or salty. I spent an entire day in my private bathroom, my forehead pressed to the toilet seat, my chest and back muscles sore from the heaving. I ignored the incessant ringing of my office phone and my cell phone and the chime of new e-mails pouring in every few minutes. After work, I stopped at Walgreens and bought a double-pack pregnancy test. I went to a gas station and peed on a stick and peed on another stick. The tests had those digital readouts that blink Yes or No so any idiot can determine if they are in the family way. I did not want a child. I got so angry I started crying because I don't love easy and loving a child or the idea of a child felt like it was too, too much.

I stayed in that gas station bathroom for a long time, until the smell of antiseptic cleaning products and stale piss and the cheap air freshener being sprayed into the bathroom at five-minute intervals with a soft puff made me sick. I wrapped the pregnancy tests in toilet paper and carefully placed them in my purse like they needed to be handled with care. When I got home, Michael was in the kitchen cooking dinner because he's the one who cooks most of the time. He smiled, his face pink and sweaty from slaving over a hot stove. He asked about my day and I sat at the kitchen table and told him how I was sick all day. He came over and held the back of his hand to my forehead, clucking, brushing my hair out of my face, and then he went back to cooking, smiling at me every few minutes, pretending not to worry.

When I miscarried, Michael was in Key West with friends for the weekend. I waited for him to come home because I forgot he would not be coming home. I did not cry. I ached and cramped all night but I scrubbed the bathroom clean, I scrubbed the bathroom and watched the red run pink and then disappear and I scrubbed the seat in my car and I took the trash to a Dumpster behind the 7-Eleven just outside our neighborhood. I bought a pack of cigarettes and drove home slowly. I smoked. When I pulled into my driveway, I got out and lay on our lawn, Bermuda grass, not at all comfortable. I stared up at the palm trees, which always look beautiful at night, and I smoked the whole pack. I held my hands over my stomach, tender and rotten, strange fruit.

By the time I was done smoking, my lungs ached and my teeth were gritty with tar and my fingers smelled terrible and still I lay on the grass. I said, "I do not care," and "I do not want a child." I lay there all night, until the sun rose and the sprinkler system turned on and soaked me to the bone and still I did not move. It was a Sunday morning so I listened as my neighbors started pulling out of their driveways to go to church. There are so many Catholics in Miami. I didn't move until my bladder felt so full I thought I might piss all over the lawn. I stood because Michael was trying some new lawn maintenance routine and I didn't want to ruin the yard.

When he finally came home late that night, Michael was bright red with sunburn, his hair blonder than usual. He was still hungover. He said, "I had the best time, babe. You should have come."

I lay on the couch in the dark. He dropped himself on me and I gasped and put my hand on his shoulder and he misunderstood the gesture and buried his head between my breasts, shaking his head back and forth, so I bit my lower lip and I did not cry. He asked me to rub his body with calamine lotion. He forgot to wear sunscreen and giggled like a teenager, when he told me this, like taking risks was still funny. The bedroom reeked of bleach but Michael didn't notice. He flopped on the bed face-first and I carefully straddled his waist and pushed his shirt up around his shoulders and slowly rubbed calamine lotion into his skin. He started snoring before I finished.

As I sat at the kitchen table watching my husband cook, pregnant a second time, I thought about my tendency to keep so much of our story to myself. I reached into my purse, felt the padded handles of the tests, set them on the kitchen table. I cleared my throat, then moaned softly as a wave of nausea hit. I took a deep breath. I said, "Michael," and he looked at me and I waved one of the pregnancy tests over my head. "We should probably talk about this." He dropped the sauce-covered wooden spoon he was holding onto the kitchen floor and I looked down at the red pattern it created, something that looked like a sunburst. He jumped up, throwing a fist in the air, and said, "Hot damn."

I felt a strange pang and I held my hand up again. "We should talk about what to do."

He stilled. "I don't understand."

"I don't want a child, you know that."

The sauce on the stove started bubbling. Michael ignored it. "But now we have one."

I shook my head and remembered coming home from running at the beach with my bloody thighs and how that blood changed me. I said, "I can't do this." I grabbed my purse and ran out of the house and got in my car and drove out of the neighborhood so fast I was certain I would crash into something and maybe I was hoping for that too so I wouldn't have to think or feel.

When I was young my father taught me never to cry. He first told me this while I was upset about something trivial but of great importance to a young girl—a classmate who I thought was my friend but who I caught making fun of me, my wild hair, calling me Don King with a group of popular girls. I lay on my bed, hearing their taunts for hours. My father came into my room, said we needed to be strong because as Haitians in America we would always be fighting; Americans wouldn't understand we came from a free people. He said they would always see us as slaves so we had to work harder, we had to be better, we had to be strong. He gave me a history lesson when I only needed him to commit some small act of kindness. He sat on the edge of my bed, as I hiccupped, my face streaked with tears. He said, "There is no room for emotion if you want to succeed in this country." He patted my thigh and said, "What happened to you was unfair and unkind but ambition is the only emotion that matters. You must learn this now." He walked away. I understood from an early age to keep my feelings to myself.

I threw the bottle of lotion against the wall and then I lay next to Michael, staring at the ceiling fan and its lazy revolution, creaking every third turn. In the dark, I looked down at my stomach and the swelling that would not come. I could not allow myself to feel anything. I said, "It's over," and I did not cry. Michael kept snoring. I went outside and slept in the backseat of my car that night. I don't know why but I wanted to be in a small space. Michael found me in the morning. When I rolled my window down, he narrowed his eyes and said, "What the fuck, Mireille?" I was still so tired. I said, "Call my office and tell them I'm not coming in today." I rolled the window back up and curled back into a ball and covered my eyes with my arm. I ignored Michael as he pounded his fists against the glass. I had my spare key with me so he could only harass me, looking like a crazy man in front of our good Catholic neighbors. He went back in the house and not too long later, there was another knock on the glass. I opened my eyes and saw Mona staring at me, hands on her hips.

"Open the door," she mouthed.

I knew she wouldn't back down so I opened the door and slid across the seat. We were quiet for a while. Michael sat on the front porch, looking bewildered.

"So, kid, what are we doing sitting in the backseat of your car?"

I shrugged, stared out my window.

"Do I need to get Carlito to beat Michael up? Did he hurt you?"

I shook my head, closed my fingers into tight fists.

Mona closed the distance between us and grabbed my chin between her fingers, forced me to look at her. "You are freaking me out. I need you to start talking."

"Michael would never hurt me."

"Then who did?"

Tears welled in the corners of my eyes. I wiped them away. I refused to cry. I looked out the window again and whispered, "The thing is, Mona, I did not want a child so I don't know why I feel like this."

"Oh honey," Mona said. My sister brushed a long strand of hair from my face, tucked it behind my ear. She has always taken care of me. The day my father told me never to cry, Mona came to my room and washed my face with a cool washcloth and tickled my back and made me smile. She told me everything was going to be okay and that she'd help me with my hair, which she did. She said, "Fuck those white girls and fuck what Dad said." She told me I could cry whenever the hell I wanted. I almost believed her.

In the backseat of my car, I sighed. "So that's that."

"What does Michael say?"

I looked through the windshield at my husband, sitting on the porch staring at my car with such intensity I thought he might be able to hear us. "He doesn't know."

"Jesus Christ, Miri. You have to tell him."

"You know, my friend Elsa once said babies don't come easy. I know what she means now."

"Tell your husband, kid."

I turned and fixed Mona with a hard look. "You can never tell him. Never. I don't want him to know. I don't want to talk about it. I just want to sit here."

Mona sighed, pulled my head into her lap, and began lightly stroking my hair. "One day you're going to go crazy with everything you don't want to talk about. You really are."

I closed my eyes.

Sometime later, Michael knocked on the window again. Mona rolled it down and he said, "What the hell is going on?"

"She's having a bad day, work bullshit. You need to be gentle with her for the next few weeks, Michael."

He reached through the window and pressed the button to unlock the doors, and walked around to the other side. "Move over."

I did, reluctantly, and immediately felt ridiculous being so cosseted by my husband and my sister.

"So," Michael said. "Since when do you have your sister lie to me?"

Mona snorted. I glared at her. They each took one of my hands and the longer we sat there, the more the ache in my belly dulled.

I am not easy to love but I am well loved. I try to love well in return.

The day I found out I was pregnant with Christophe, I drove to a nearby hotel and checked in and paid with my credit card. I wanted to be found. I knew Michael would go online to see if I was spending money. I rolled back the comforter because my mother says hotel comforters are extremely unsanitary. I sat on the bed and read the leather-bound folio with all the important information about the hotel. There was a business center and a concierge and in-room dining. If I needed incidentals like a toothbrush and toothpaste, sewing kit, they would bring these items to me at no cost. I needed incidentals so I called the front desk. The buttons on the phone felt strange to the touch, sticky with human oils.

When they arrived, I arranged my incidentals neatly on the bathroom counter—toothbrush, toothpaste, Q-tips, shower cap, shampoo, sewing kit. I returned to the bed, turned on the television and scanned the Pay-Per-View options. There was lots of porn involving complex configurations and various fetishes. Michael has a fondness for porn with white men fucking black women though he pretends he's indifferent to pornography. There's a folder on his laptop's hard drive labeled "Zebra." He thinks I don't know. I love that he thinks he has secrets I don't know about.

I still did not want a child but I held my hands over my stomach just below my navel and pretended I did not feel a little hope, pretended I did not wonder if the child were a boy or a girl, what that child might look like. I wondered if Michael would find me, if he would care, if he would understand why we could not keep this child, why even if we did keep the child there was a good chance the child wouldn't stay kept. I had grown superstitious about such things after the first miscarriage, secretly scouring the Internet for explanations, trying to understand the exact nature of my culpability. I would call Mona late at night, sharing my theories, and she would tiredly tell me it wasn't my fault, that lots of women miscarry. I wanted to believe her. I always want to believe my sister. I looked at my watch. Two hours had passed. I brushed my teeth. I flushed the pack of cigarettes I had in my purse. I made a cup of instant coffee and the smell instantly made me nauseous. I threw up and just as I was pressing a cool washcloth against my forehead I heard a soft knock at the door. I peered through the eyehole and saw Michael. I pressed the palm of my hand against the door, wondering if he could feel me. He knocked again, so hard I worried the door might splinter. He wasn't going to leave so I opened the door.

He looked me up and down and said, "You look terrible, too skinny."

I didn't have the energy to respond.

Michael rubbed his forehead. He said, "You make me crazy," and I said, "I know," and I thought about how small my life would have been if I had never met him, small but easily contained.

"There is something you should know."

He turned to face me. He looked serious. I went to the window, played with the long plastic rod for opening and closing the drapes, rolling it back and forth between my fingers.

"They lie when they say every view in Florida is a beautiful view."

"I like the view from where I'm sitting."

I half laughed and pulled the drapes closed. "Always the charmer."

Michael stood and came to me, wrapped his arms around me. "I don't care what it is, so long as you talk to me."

I patted his chest but did not move my hand away. He was warm, solid. "Our lives are good. We shouldn't mess with the equilibrium of what we have."

He covered my hand with his. "You don't sound at all like yourself. You're kind of worrying me. Are you going to tell me you're having an affair?"

I looked up, gave him what I hoped was a rather furious look, and stomped over to the dresser, grabbed the empty ice bucket and threw it at Michael's head.

He ducked, looking sheepish. "Okay, okay. That wasn't fair. I just don't understand what's going on."

My stomach churned. I said, "There was a baby once, Michael. I didn't know the baby was there and then I did but it was too late." I leaned against the door, with my hands behind my back. When he tried to move toward me again I shook my head, said, "No, don't."

"I don't understand," he said.

I shrugged and slowly sank to the floor, stretching my legs out in front of me. I was so tired. "The weekend you went to Key West."

Michael sat back down on the bed. I watched as he tried to recall the events of that weekend. "Goddamn, Mireille." His hands clenched into tight fists. "Goddamn you. I knew something was wrong. You should have told me."

"We can't do this, Michael. You don't know how hard it was."

"You didn't give me a chance to know, did you?" he said, peevishly.

I shrank. I was not going to cry. I rubbed my face, squeezed hard.

Michael sat down next to me on the floor.

"I didn't mean it like that," Michael finally said after an awkward silence, caressing my arm.

I pulled my arm away. "Yes, you did, or you should have."

"Would you really consider not going through with this pregnancy?"

I shrugged. Michael pressed one of his hands to my stomach and I traced his knuckles with my fingertips. I was so tired I curled up and rested my head in his lap. I fell asleep quickly. In the morning, I found myself in the hotel bed, Michael sitting up, staring at me.

"Why are you staring at me?"

"You have to stop."

"Stop what?"

"Making decisions for us as if you're the only one in this relationship."

I sat up. My head hurt. I was still tired. "I don't do that."

"Yes, actually, you do. I want us to have this child but this is a decision we need to make together, period. You should have told me about the miscarriage. You should have let me help you and you didn't and I have a real goddamned problem with that."

I was not used to Michael taking a stand. He's not a pushover, but he knew what he was getting into before we married and picks his battles. I was so surprised to see him unwilling to tolerate my bullshit, I blurted out, "You're right. I'm sorry."

Michael's eyes widened. "Say that again?"

"You are right. I am sorry," I said, exaggerating each word.

He nodded. "Well, good."

"Anything else?"

"I planned on having a long argument so I'm going to need a minute."

I squeezed his thigh. "Very funny, babe." I closed my eyes again and was racked by a fresh wave of nausea. I stumbled out of bed and into the bathroom, stubbing my foot against a corner, wincing, and then puking into the toilet. Michael was right behind me, knelt, held my hair away from my face. I stared into the toilet. "This is your fault."

He massaged my shoulders gently. "Yes, it is."

"To be clear, I am going to make your life miserable. I am

telling you this in advance so you can better appreciate my apology."

Michael handed me a cup of water. "Yes, I know," he said. "I am happy to be miserable if it's with you."

I vomited again.

The first trimester was interminable. I was always tense, afraid to do anything for fear I would kill my baby, sick all the time, unable to eat. At work I was distracted. I lost eleven pounds. I am naturally thin so I looked like someone was starving me. We couldn't find an obstetrician we liked so we spent many late afternoons leaving work early only to sit in the waiting rooms of various doctor's offices across Miami looking for a doctor who wasn't weird, rude, creepy, or indifferent. After one obstetrician basically hit on me in front of Michael, making a horrible comment about how a pregnant lady can't get pregnant, we worried there were no competent obstetricians in all of Miami.

Whenever I felt a twinge or cramp I panicked, made Michael take me to the emergency room. They got to know us by name at the University of Miami hospital. I was so sick even Michael started to wonder if going through with the pregnancy was a good idea. In my tenth week, I spent an entire day cramping. I saw blood and left work, drove myself to the hospital. The emergency room was crowded. It was the first really hot day of the year. There is some correlation between sweltering heat and medical catastrophes in Miami. I was surrounded by a bewildering range of people displaying visible, bloody injuries. I waited, mildly panicked. Michael was in a meeting, his assistant told me, and not to be disturbed. I politely told her to please go ahead and disturb him but for some reason he didn't get the message or she didn't deliver it. An hour passed, the pain intensifying. I became wildly panicked, tried not to hyperventilate. The pain was familiar. I was losing the baby, alone, in a hot, smelly waiting room surrounded by crazy people.

Michael finally called, sounding cheery, which did not help. "What's up?" he asked. "I'm on my way home."

"I'm sitting in the waiting room at the hospital. How about that for what's up?"

He instantly became serious, asked where I was, but I was not at my best. I hung up. He kept calling back but I didn't answer because I was tired and sweaty and unreasonable. If I spoke to him I'd say something regrettable. I turned my phone off when the vibrating became annoying.

I was still in the waiting room when Michael ran into the ER, tense, sweaty, his shirt wrinkled and damp, his tie hanging loosely around his neck. He found me hunched over, my face in my hands, and sat next to me, resting his hand on my back.

"I found you. You're still waiting? You had me so scared. You hung up on me. Seriously, Miri. You are unbelievable. There's a time and place for hanging up on me when you're mad. Being in the ER, not so much." He talked so fast I could barely make out each word.

I didn't answer, just leaned against him, held his leg tightly, irritated but glad to have someone to share my misery with, glad to be with him. Michael wrapped his arm around me and kissed the top of my head. "Okay," he said. "I'll be angry later but so we are clear, there will be a lot of anger." He tapped his foot impatiently, staring at his watch every few minutes.

After fifteen minutes or so he went to the receptionist, pointed back at me, said something I couldn't make out, poked the counter with his finger, pointed back at me again, and soon we were ushered somewhere closer to medical attention. The emergency room physician said the cramping was likely due to the baby's position in the womb, that there wasn't much they could do beyond prescribing bed rest. She decided to keep me overnight for observation. In my room, Michael held my hand, tracing around where the IV needle pierced my skin. I was exhausted and scared and in a foul mood. I couldn't even hold a conversation. I just lay on my side, shivering even though the nurse brought me several blankets.

I'm not sure what it was but something about his face and the calmness in his features made me irrationally angry. I could not stand the sight of him. My stomach cramped again and I pulled my knees closer to my chest, hissed softly.

"What can I do to help?"

"Get out, just go. You're driving me crazy with the hovering."

"I'm not leaving you, Miri, not going to happen."

I growled. "Michael, I swear to God, if you do not leave this room immediately, we will have a problem."

He shook his head, gave me his well-practiced look of exasperation, one I normally mimic, which irritates him no end. When he stood, his knees cracked and I thought *good*.

"Are you sure?"

"Yes, I am quite sure. Go home. I'll see you tomorrow or whenever. If I make it through the night. Did you know that in the eighteen hundreds, forty percent of women died during childbirth? I am probably going to die."

He stood, awkwardly, shifting his weight from foot to foot, his hands shoved in his pockets, unsure if I was testing him. "Aren't you being a little dramatic?"

I turned to look at him. "Why are you still here?'

Michael took his hands out of his pockets, leaned over the railing, and kissed my forehead. "I'm going, I'm going." He paused in the doorway. "Should I come back in an hour?"

"Good night, Michael."

As he shuffled out of the room, I pulled the pillow off my face and sat up, said, "I cannot believe he actually left," and, "Asshole." I stared at the television on mute, sulking, grinding myself into a complicated and bitter mood that had been slowly festering all day. I played with my phone, checked for text messages from Michael, and when there were none, threw the phone across the room. It made a racket as it hit the wall and then fell to the floor, the case cracking into several pieces. It wasn't long before I was lonely and feeling sorry for myself. I kept looking at the door, hoping Michael would come back. I chastised myself for sending him away. I felt sorrier for myself. I got angry again. During that first trimester, I spent almost every moment experiencing the entire spectrum of human emotion. It was the kind of thing that could put a woman off children forever.

A couple of hours later, a nurse breezed in, a redhead named Laura who smelled like mints and cigarette smoke. She refilled one of my IV bags and chattered pleasantly as she did whatever nurses do when they're looking at your chart and messing with the IV machine and keeping you from having a moment's peace. I missed smoking. I wanted to grab her arm, pull her to me, and suck the nicotine out of her body.

"Why is your gorgeous husband standing guard outside your room, looking pitiful, instead of in here with you?" she asked.

I frowned. "My stupid husband went home."

"Unless I'm thinking of the wrong guy, he is standing right outside your door." She smiled down at me, patting the railing.

Just like that Laura and her delicious cigarette scent were gone. My mouth watered. I wondered if I had imagined her—an oasis of forbidden vice. I swung my legs over the edge of the bed and stood carefully, gripping the IV pole for balance. The floor was cold. I took small steps as I made my way to the door. My legs were rubbery. The wheels of the IV pole squeaked lightly. I cringed. When I reached the doorway, I was sweating. I held on to the doorjamb and looked into the hallway. There to the left was Michael, standing, leaning against the wall. He was, indeed, looking pitiful.

I cleared my throat and he stood straight.

He pointed at me. "What the hell are you doing out of bed?"

"You said you were going home."

"No. You said I was going home. You're not the boss of me."

I looked up at my husband, eyes wide. "Oh, I'm not?"

"Not today."

I bit my lower lip. Michael is very sexy when he gets mouthy. He says the same thing about me. "Stop standing in the hallway. It's weird. Come back in the room. I'm bored."

He shook his head, crossed his arms across his chest. "Not until you do something for me. Raise your right hand."

"Excuse me?"

"You're a lawyer. This is not a stretch. Raise your right hand and repeat after me. 'I, Mireille Duval Jameson, apologize for being mean to my loving, devoted husband.'"

At the nurses' station to the right of us, three nurses leaned forward, eavesdropping. I'm pretty sure they were smirking.

"I'm not saying that."

"Do you want me to stop standing in the hallway being *weird?*"

I shrugged.

"Do it," Michael said.

"Fine, whatever. I, Mireille Duval, apologize for being mean to my loving, devoted husband."

"Very good. I'll let the abbreviation of your last name go for now. Say, 'I will stop being an asshole.'"

I wrinkled my nose. "You first."

He raised his hand higher. "I will stop being an asshole."

I laughed. I couldn't help myself. "Fine. I will stop being an asshole."

He stepped closer. "You missed me. Admit it."

There was a sudden twisting just below my navel, one that was all too familiar. My knees buckled. I gripped his arm, said his name as I gasped.

"Enough messing around," he said, steadying me. He was calm. "I'm a terrible husband. You're not supposed to be out of bed." He lifted me, nodded toward the IV pole. "You hold that." Michael carried me back to my hospital bed.

Before he set me down, I said, "Wait, baby. Yes, I missed you. Kiss me."

My husband looked at me. "I love you."

The way he said it reminded me of who we are together. I clasped the back of his neck and he lowered his lips to mine and wanted to hold his breath inside me forever.

When we pulled apart, I was flushed all over. "Now you can put me down."

Michael laid me down like a precious thing. I slid to one side of the bed, reached back, patted the empty space next to me.

"Come hold me and also tell your child to stop giving me such a hard time."

My husband wrapped himself around me. I held his arm across my stomach. He covered the gentle rise of my stomach with his hand. He said, "Stop giving your mother a hard time, little baby." I slid my fingers between his and finally said what I had been thinking since I learned I was pregnant again. "I'm terrified, Michael. I am absolutely terrified."

It felt good to push my fear into the air around us.

"Shhh," he said. "The three of us are going to be just fine."

It was the first time either of us had acknowledged there were three of us. We were a little family even if we had no idea what we were doing. Somehow, that made me feel better. In the before, it was so damn easy to believe in happily ever after.

𝍸𝍸𝍸 𝍸𝍸𝍸 𝍸𝍸𝍸
||||

I made myself forget everything I could no longer bear to remember—love, my husband's sleeping body, his smile, my child's fingers, how our baby laughed, how much it calmed me to poke his chubby cheeks while he nursed, feel his sweet, warm breath on my skin. I made myself forget the baby album Michael and I made just for the two of us—pictures of Michael and me in bed, my swollen belly a coaster for his beer cans, countless pictures where I am raising my middle finger to my husband, a few dirty pictures, the ultrasounds we labeled with the word *Blob* and the week of pregnancy, a staged photo where we dressed up like cave people, another one where Michael took a picture of me literally barefoot and chained to the kitchen stove. I made myself forget how when he took that picture he joked, "This is the only time we'll ever see you near a stove." I forgot my mother and hiding in her skirt as a little girl and the grip of her hand as we walked together and my father lying in bed next to me, reading while I was sick, and my friends, the parties we had, the dancing, the wine, falling asleep in our backyard and waking up beneath a canopy of palm fronds, cooking with Michael, him standing behind me, his hands covering mine, his nose buried in my neck, as we chopped onions and carrots and red peppers and leeks.

I made myself forget for as long as I could and then, alone in my cage, as the heat of the day rose and filled the room, it suddenly all came back to me, who I was and who I loved and who I needed. The memory of my life, the weight of it, threatened to break my body more than any man could. I needed to be no one so I might survive. I needed to hear the voice of someone who loved me but could not ask for such a thing. I waited.

The sky darkened when the Commander appeared. I became two women—the one who remembered everything and the one who remembered nothing. This required a delicate balance.

As a child, my mother would take us to the park in our neighborhood on Tuesdays and Thursdays and sometimes Saturdays. We walked together through the well-manicured subdivision, all holding hands, my mother, my brother, my sister, and me. Sometimes she made comments about the lawns, the ones that were a bit unkempt. Occasionally a neighbor driving by would honk their horn and wave and my mother would smile brightly, wave her hand energetically, and then she'd look down at us and say, "Americans are so rude with their horns." My mother loved America but did not care much at all for Americans.

At the park, she sat on a bench and read while the three of us played. There was a balance beam and for years it was nearly impossible for me to traverse. No matter how hard I tried, my body was unwilling to walk that straight line without falling to one side or the other. The ground beneath the balance beam was covered in soft wood chips, and on the walk home I often found myself brushing the clinging wood from my clothes. One day, when I was nine, we arrived at the park and I was determined to walk the line. I took off my shoes, having decided the shoes were the problem. I wiggled my toes and they brushed against the soil and wood chips. I did side stretches like Mrs. Polanski made us do in gym class and then I stepped up carefully, holding on to my sister's head until I could steady myself. From the corner of my eye, I could see my mother had set her book down. I turned to her and smiled. She nodded and stared at me intently. She stared at me so hard, I was certain her will alone would get me to the other side.

I closed my eyes and stretched my arms out to my sides. I imagined I was flying and slowly, I began to move forward. I did not lift my feet at first, just slid forward along the smooth painted wood. I had not yet fallen. I felt emboldened. I took a real step, faltered a bit, tensed my arms. Then I took another step and another step and another until I was at the end of that balance beam. When I reached the end, I jumped up and threw my fists in the air. I landed on the beam perfectly and the thrill of it filled my chest with a feeling I hardly knew how to understand. My mother was never one for affection but she stood and came to the end of the beam where I still stood, flush with the simple, careless joy of my small accomplishment. She wrapped her arms around me and lifted me in the air. She whispered into my hair.

★   ★   ★

The Commander stood in the doorway and motioned for me to follow. He did not grab me or touch me at all. I took small, careful steps.

"You may call your family," he said. He handed me a new cell phone and left me in his room, affording me a small amount of privacy. I dialed the eight numbers and waited as the phone rang. My father answered but I did not want to hear his voice, or a single word he had to say. I asked for my husband and waited and when Michael came on, I wanted to break down but I could not.

"I wanted to hear your voice."

"Baby, we're working on getting you back. I swear."

I wrapped an arm around my waist. The whole of my body was so tender. "Don't," I said. "Just stop. Tell me about our son."

"He's right here," Michael said. "He misses you. He's been very quiet, knows something is wrong but he is okay. Your mother and I think he said his first word, *toast*, only it sounded like *yost* but still, he pointed to bread when he said it. I'm pretty sure he is the smartest baby ever."

I smiled, then stopped myself. It was too easy to fall into his voice, to pretend I was anywhere but abandoned to animals. "We did good with him, Michael. He's the best thing we will ever have done. Don't let him forget who I was, no matter what happens."

Michael's voice pitched higher. "What are you talking about, Miri? What's going on? I am doing everything I can. You have no idea."

I swallowed hard. I wanted to tell him something, everything. I wanted him to know I was losing myself, that I was all torn apart but I did not want that to be the last he knew of me. "I just don't want him to forget me. I don't want you to forget me." I laughed hoarsely. "I'm not going to be all noble and tell you to move on quickly and forget me if I die."

He started to say something but I interrupted. "Don't talk. Listen." I walked to the farthest corner of the room. I lowered my voice, turned away from the door, the Commander, what had been done to me. "I have always been in love with you. I wanted you to know that. You and our son are the only things that matter and I hope you don't forget any of it."

"You're scaring me, Miri. What's going on? If they lay one hand on you, I swear."

I held my hand over my heart as if that might protect the pulsing muscle of it. I wanted to say, *what do you think is going on?* I didn't. I said, "I'm fine. I did not want how I feel about you to go unsaid, not this time." I heard movement behind me but I did not want to turn around. I wanted to stay with my husband, with his voice. "Tell me you're a pretty pretty princess."

He laughed, a sad empty laugh. He spoke slowly, said, "I am a pretty pretty princess."

My hands felt so empty and yet I could feel the shapes of my husband and my son against my palms. "Michael, I mean it. Don't let him forget me or this would all be in vain."

"We are coming for you. Hold on, Miri. That's all I ask. Hold on."

A heavy hand grabbed my shoulder and I winced. I nodded slowly, bit my lower lip. "I have to go, Michael."

As the Commander took the phone I heard my husband saying my name over and over. I turned to look at the man before me. "You married an American," the Commander said.

"Yes, I did."

"And he loves you; the two of you have a son."

My skin chilled. Something invisible began to wrap around my neck. "Yes."

"If your father does not pay soon, I may have to take his only grandson. Maybe then he'll be compelled to pay. Men are strangely moved to preserve their bloodlines, though in your father's case, it's hard to say."

When I was a little girl, my mother also told me the story of a little girl and a magic orange tree. This little girl's mother died when she was born and as fathers often do, her father remarried a woman, who, as stepmothers are wont to be, was cruel and quite evil. The stepmother rarely fed the little girl. One day, after she got in trouble with her stepmother, the little girl ran to her mother's grave and cried and cried, her tears soaking the ground covering her mother's body as she fell asleep. When she awoke in the morning, an orange seed fell from her dress into the tear-soaked soil and immediately a perfect green leaf appeared. The little girl started singing to this leaf and it blossomed into a tree. The more she sang, the higher the tree grew. She sang telling the tree how to grow. She ate oranges, delicious oranges from the tree. She knew the tree was her mother. When she brought some of her perfect oranges home, her stepmother demanded to know where the little girl had gotten the oranges. The little girl was a good girl so she took her stepmother to the tree and the greedy stepmother tried to take all the oranges for herself. Again the little girl sang and the tree swept the evil stepmother into its branches and killed her because the tree was that little girl's mother and a mother will do anything to protect and provide for her child.

★   ★   ★

I had to try to forget who I was forever. There was no delicacy or balance with a man like the Commander. I inhaled deeply. I became no one again. I traced the scar beneath his left eye and I held his chin and looked him in the eye. I did not raise my voice. There was no need. "If you touch my child, I will kill you. Whatever happens to me happens but you cannot harm my child." I dug my fingernails into his chin. "If my father doesn't pay, I will call my bank, I will pull together what money I can. I will find a way. I don't know how but I will find a way. It won't be what you want but it will be more than you have. You also have me. Let that be enough. Let me be enough."

My voice was steady. I was calm. I had begun to realize I would never see my family again. It was easy to offer myself in the place of my child.

The Commander arched an eyebrow and slowly pushed on my arm until I released my grip. He took off his shirt and flexed his pectoral muscles. "Now things are getting interesting. It is a very touching thing to see a mother sacrifice for her child." He planted his hands on my waist, pressed his fingers into the bruises there.

I did not flinch. I felt nothing. I held his gaze. "It is not a sacrifice."

When he pushed me onto my knees, I slowly sifted through every memory of the life I had once known. I wiped each instance away.

"I think I will keep you," the Commander said. I grabbed at my chest for a moment because my heart seized uncomfortably. I thought my heart might stop. I hoped for such mercy. Just as quickly the tightness eased, began to spread outward. I tried to remember why my heart hurt so much. I saw the faint outline of all I loved but it was far away, the edges blurry. It was not easy but I forced myself to erase those blurry edges too.

I was no one.

𝍸𝍸𝍸
𝍸

Michael's father first took him hunting when he was nine. They drove up to Michigan's Upper Peninsula for a week and spent their days in a freezing-cold deer blind, their fingers and faces numb. His father stood behind him, helping Michael hold the rifle in the hollow between his shoulder and collarbone. His father said, "The key, son, is to breathe. Inhale when you pull the trigger and exhale when you release." His father told him to respect what you're killing, that taking a life was no small thing. When Michael shot his first deer, he cried, inconsolably, salty tears and mucous freezing to his face as he and his father climbed down out of the deer blind and went to the slaughtered animal, a respectable eight-point buck.

The animal's glassy black eyes were wide open and staring at Michael. It was a terrible thing to see. He and his father knelt on the ground, frozen leaves crunching beneath their boots. His father took Michael's hand and held it just over the entrance wound, its edge blackened, a thin stream of blood streaking the buck's muscled torso. "You took a life," his father said, "but you did it well. There is no shame in this. You hear me?" Michael nodded, poked his finger in the wound where it was still warm, slick. They drove home with the buck in the truck bed. Every once in a while Michael would look back at it, those glassy black eyes still wide open, staring at him. He once told Mireille he did not feel shame though he did feel sorrow for the life he had taken.

Michael, restless, still waiting, remembered Mireille's stories about her cousin Victor, the son of an uncle in Jacmel. It was an open secret that Victor associated with *the wrong element*, spent most of his time in the slums running with a gang, was known to handle certain delicate situations requiring an indelicate approach for the Duval family.

When Michael finally understood Sebastien wasn't going to capitulate, he called Victor, who showed up an hour later with two imposing friends, JoJo and Patrick, who spoke little and chewed on toothpicks. Sebastien barely acknowledged his nephew but Fabienne, always the epitome of politesse, kissed Victor twice on each cheek, asked after his parents and siblings. Michael and Victor hugged in the awkward way of men who are marginally acquainted and Victor slapped him on the back, leading Michael out of Sebastien's earshot.

"This is a terrible thing, man. Anything I can do. I like my cousin. She's one tough lady, always talking so smart."

Michael laughed halfheartedly. "That's Miri. We need to find her. It has been way too long."

Victor studied his phone for a moment, hit a few keys, then shoved it in his pocket. "Fuck that guy. He's always looking down his nose even though he comes from the same shit as the rest of us." He squeezed Michael's shoulder. "We're going hunting tonight."

When night fell, Michael dressed in dark clothing and left Christophe with his grandmother. He kissed his son and whispered into the boy's head, "I am going to find your mother." Michael ignored the tightness in his chest, a tightness that never seemed to go away in this strange place where his wife was missing. He climbed into a car with Victor and his friends. As they drove down the driveway, Victor handed Michael a ski mask and a pair of dark leather gloves.

"What are these for?"

Victor grinned. "You can't be showing that pretty hair and those pretty hands where we're going."

Michael nodded as if he understood. Victor also handed him a Glock 9 mm pistol, the weight of which felt good in Michael's hand, heavy. He traced the barrel with his fingers, inhaled the scent of gun oil as they drove through the worst parts of Port-au-Prince hunting for a woman who could not be found in a place where everyone was an expert at hiding.

Every so often, they turned down a narrow street or alley and stopped. Victor, Patrick, and JoJo pulled red bandanas over their faces and the four men knocked on doors, threatening to kick them down. Michael always stood near the back, standing at full height glowering and sweating beneath his mask, his gun tucked into his waistband, the grip visible. Victor flashed Mireille's picture and shouted a barrage of questions and wouldn't stop until he got the answers he wanted. The answers were always the same. No one knew anything.

"We are in the Wild West," Michael thought after they stopped at a run-down, one-story house that looked more like a rambling shack. The door was flung open and a loud television blared into the street. A young man sat in a lawn chair near the front door, cradling a beer. He barely looked up as the four spilled out of their car. Victor didn't bother with a mask this time. He simply walked up to the young man, who stood and grinned.

"Victor, man, sa k pase?"

"M ap boule, TiPierre. M ap boule. Look, man. M ap chache kouzen mwen." He handed TiPierre a picture of Mireille.

TiPierre whistled low. "Li anfòm."

"Chill, that's my blood." Victor looked back over his shoulder. "And that's her husband. Don't be bringing that around him. Just tell me, does Laurent have her?"

TiPierre looked at the picture again and shook his head. "Nah. We got out of that. Too much legwork, too many crying bitches." He held two pinched fingers to his lips and pretended to inhale. "We're into something else now."

Victor kicked the broken glass at his feet then looked TiPierre in the eye. "If I find out you're lying and your crew took one of mine, pral gen yon gwo pwoblèm, okay?"

TiPierre nodded. "I hear you, Victor. I hear you. We wouldn't mess with your family. Like I said, too many crying bitches, always wanting to go home, thinking they're too good for you, asking for bottled water and shit. No thanks."

Victor stepped around TiPierre and peered into the house, where a woman sat on a couch watching television, holding a young child. "Your woman let you back home?"

"Today," TiPierre said, laughing. "I don't know about tomorrow."

Victor rubbed his chin. "Where is Laurent these days?"

"He's living with his sister, laid up with some lady. You know how he is."

"How he can get women with that face of his, I don't know." Victor shook his head and took one last look around before fixing TiPierre with a hard stare. "We've got to get going but if you hear anything, you get in touch with my guys. Don't fuck me on this."

TiPierre smiled, didn't blink. "I got it, man. I got it."

Back in the car, Victor rubbed his forehead and turned to Michael. "Someone's lying but I don't know who. All these motherfuckers do is lie until they start believing they're telling the truth."

Michael fingered the grip of the gun again. "I could kill a living thing to save my wife," Michael said. "I would feel neither shame nor sorrow."

Victor nodded and started the car. "We'll see if it comes to that. We have more hunting to do."

They drove off into the night, the only sound Victor tapping the steering wheel to an indeterminate beat. Michael held his wife's picture in the palm of one hand and the gun in the other. He would feel nothing at all until he found his wife.

|||| |||| |||| |||| |||| |

I stood beneath the weak stream of lukewarm water, scrubbing my clothes, trying to rinse away all they had seen. When I finished, I wrapped myself in a towel and returned to my cage under the careful watch of an armed escort. They could see the wildness in me, how it shrouded my body, how my body was nothing, how I was capable of anything. I randomly clawed and hissed to remind them that I knew I was an animal. Sometimes, I spit. I did not care.

Alone, I set my clothes on the end of the bed and waited for them to dry. I refused to look at my body. I hurt enough to understand. Outside, it was fire hot and raining, a heavy, pounding rain and the air was thick with the smell of it. Children ran down the alley, their feet splashing in puddles.

I was no one so I had little to think about. I sat carefully on the edge of the bed and tried to make sense of living in that cage for the rest of my life, of being meat and bones for a man with cruel appetites. I could do it for the child who belonged to the woman I had been. It was nothing at all to make that choice for her, for him, for his father.

What you can never know about being kidnapped is the sheer boredom, the violent loneliness, the unending hours alone with nothing to do, nothing to look at, no kindness to be found. To distract myself, I started reciting parts of the Immigration and Nationality Act I had memorized. I thought of my favorite legal statutes and then I reached the limits of such memory. I thought about the ongoing cases I was working. I thought about my clients, so many of them willing to do anything to stay in the United States.

After listening to their stories, I always told them I understood what they wanted, that I was a child of immigrants, that we were more alike than different. It was a gentle lie. I told them I would fight for them and I did even though I had no idea, at the time, of what I was truly fighting for.

One of my first well-paying clients was a woman named Chloe Kizende. She was Congolese, the daughter of a wealthy diplomat, and seeking asylum, running from aimless and blood-hungry rebels who were tearing her country apart and doing terrible things to people from families like hers. She sat across from me, in her finely pressed linen suit, her hair piled regally atop her head in thick braids. She was in Miami, she said, because at least the heat was somewhat familiar. I could smell her perfume as we spoke, expensive. She spoke with an English accent. I had so little empathy for her situation, as we sat in my air-conditioned office, me wearing my own finely pressed suit. I thought of how nice it must be for her to buy her way out of a hell too many people were trapped in. That irony was not lost on me as I whiled the hours and days away in my cage between one horror and the next. I finally understood humility and how little I once possessed.

I had to stop thinking about my old life. I was no one. I had no career. I had nothing. I was nothing. I said these things to myself over and over and over. My stomach growled. I had eaten so little over so many days. I made myself forget the taste of every perfect thing I had ever eaten—*pain au chocolat* in Paris, beans and rice in Little Havana, my mother's *griyo*, thick steaks grilled on the back patio of the farmhouse, Michael's elaborate pasta dishes. I made myself forget what it was to be full, to be satisfied. I chewed on a fingernail. There was a knock at the door and the Commander appeared. He crossed his arms across his chest. I crossed my arms across my chest.

I looked up and glared then looked away. I wanted to be alone.

"You don't look happy to see me."

I looked down at my bare legs, tried to pull the thin towel around me and down my legs a little more. "You shouldn't sound so disappointed, *Commander*. I might start to think you're getting ideas about me."

"Maybe I would like to keep you more than I want the money. You offered yourself to me, after all."

I raised my head. "I offered myself in exchange for a child's life. There is a difference."

He shrugged. "The reason matters little to me."

There was no choice for me. I could not return to a family I no longer knew. I could not survive the rest of my life in a cage. "I don't care what happens to me."

The Commander laughed, a grating sound, higher pitched than seemed fitting for a man of his stature. "You care, very much, even if you do not realize it."

"You know nothing about me."

He shrugged. "I imagine you are hungry."

My hunger was so intense it could have consumed me but I did not respond. He took me by my elbow and pulled me to my feet. In the kitchen he pointed to an empty seat. The woman who had untied me days earlier was standing at a small stove. When I saw her I lunged toward her hissing, frothing at the mouth. She shrank from me, looked down. "That's right." I shouted. "Don't you look at me after what you did."

The Commander grabbed me and forced me into a chair. "My sister was acting under my direction."

I sat, gritting my teeth as I crossed my legs. I tried to breathe through the pain, a constant, a second skin, overwhelming me completely. He had a sister. He had people to whom he belonged. It made no sense.

I twisted my rings back and forth trying to clear my head and understand what he wanted from me. He always wanted something. There was always a ransom to be paid.

The Commander sat across from me. "Negotiations with your father have stopped. He refuses to pay and I have compromised too much already. I understand why he is so successful in business. He is a man of conviction." The Commander scratched his chin. "I must say I admire his resolve—to sacrifice his own child, my goodness." He reached across the table and grabbed my left hand. "We are going to get to know each other very well as you become accustomed to your new life."

I closed my eyes for a moment. I sat still. I burned. My heart became smaller and smaller and it ached and blackened. My heart was no longer safe; it never had been. I opened my eyes and stared up at the ceiling, the dim lamp hanging loosely, wires exposed. "You are lying."

He held his hands open. "I have no need to lie. I have never lied to you."

The scar beneath his left eye pulsed, slithered across his face and swelled like something serpentine. I tried to pull my hand away from his but he tightened his grip and then he used his other hand to remove my rings. Before I could stop myself and remember I was no one, I stood and reached across the table for that part of myself I was still holding on to. "Don't take those," I said. He held the rings, cupped in his hand, and raised his arm. I stepped around the table and jumped up, tried to reach his arm. He laughed, began dancing around the small kitchen, taunting me.

His sister said a name I didn't recognize. She said, "Stop being childish." He ignored her.

Beads of sweat trickled down my face and neck, pooling in the new, deep hollow above my collarbones. I was so hungry. The air in the kitchen thickened with the smell of grease. The Commander grew bored and grabbed me, twisted me around and pulled me against him, my spine curved sharply against his chest as I tried to break free. His breath was hot on my neck. "You have no need of these rings now that you belong to me."

The towel wrapped around me began to loosen. I dug my bare heel into his foot. He wore pristine white sneakers. "My father is going to pay the ransom. I know he will. I will not belong to you. Let me go."

The Commander dragged his tongue from my neck, along the bone of my jaw, up to my ear. The smell of his saliva repulsed me. The texture of his tongue repulsed me. The sticky wet sound repulsed me. He held me tighter, like he was trying to pull my body into his. "I would be happy to reunite you with your husband and child in order to further compel your father to pay or you can honor our previous arrangement."

My fingers slowly uncurled. The thought of my husband and child in this hell was beyond imagining. "Leave her family alone. Don't mention them. Don't even think about them."

He pushed me into an empty chair and leaned against the edge of the table. "Don't you mean your family?"

I didn't answer. The woman at the stove, my tormentor's sister, set a plate of food in front of me—rice and chicken in sauce. My stomach growled loudly and my mouth watered. The food steamed, making me even hotter.

She set a fork to the left of my plate. "Eat," she said, gently.

When I was young, we had an uncle in Cap-Haïtien. He owned a store, sold phone cards and convenience store items at outrageous prices and did well for himself. I once overheard my mother say he also sold other things and the way she said it made me think he was a gangster of some kind, trafficking in something exotic like stolen electronics or maybe even drugs. Our parents would send us to our uncle for two or three days each time we visited Haiti so we could see more of the country. The drive, overland, was a long, miserable affair. By the time we arrived we were always cranky and bickering.

During one visit, Tante Lola's driver dropped us off and drove away smirking, his radio blaring as he weaved through the narrow streets and headed back to the capital.

My brother and sister and I stood in our sweaty, wrinkled

clothes in front of my uncle's store, staring up at the hand-painted sign, MARCHÉ ABRAHAM. I stood in the middle and reached for their hands. I was always in the middle, protected by them. In the store, a large ceiling fan twisted lazily, doing little to move air. There was no room to move. There was no way to make sense of the inventory, a bizarre collection of items bearing little connection to convenience. My uncle came out from a back room, his arms wide open. "My beautiful nieces and nephew, welcome." He pulled us into his arms and hugged us tight, said, "Come, come."

His house was attached to the back of the store and he led us through a small courtyard and into the house, where our cousins, all four of them, were engaged in a serious game of Monopoly. We asked if we could play and Victor, the oldest, sneered at us. "This game is in French." Michel sneered right back, made it clear we spoke French and could play just fine. We became a team, the three of us against the four of them, played well into the night, trading insults. We slept beneath mosquito netting, my siblings and I in the same bed, me in the middle again, sleeping curled against my sister, who held my hand. In the morning, we woke and found that there was no water left in the cistern. My uncle pointed down the block to a public water pump. The three of us carried a large ten-gallon paint bucket to the pump, filled it, and struggled to carry it back, our muscles straining from the weight of water, the heat of the island, the incredulity of having to carry your own water to do something as simple as wash your face. We spent our whole day that way, ferrying water to do every little thing. There was never enough water.

Back in the capital, we begged our parents to never send us there again. My father's disappointment was palpable. He sat the three of us on a couch, all bare legs and knobby knees. He frowned down at us. "You are all so very spoiled," he said. "It is only an accident of birth that makes it possible for you to enjoy your lives the way you do." We were young. We had no idea what he meant.

In the Commander's kitchen, I grabbed his sister's wrist. She looked down at me. "A different accident of birth could put you in my place," I said.

She did not try to pull away. She gently unpeeled my fingers and set my hand on the table. I wanted to tear the skin from her face so I could see the blood of a woman who would stand by and do nothing while another woman endured what was being done to me.

The Commander dragged a finger along my bare shoulder. I brushed his hand away, and he grabbed a fistful of my hair pulling me toward him. I curled my fingers around the fork, raised it high, and stabbed it into the backside of his hand. He yelped loudly and began hopping, waving his hand in the air as he flung the fork against the wall. I turned my attention to the food in front of me and began eating with my hands, my fingers quickly slicking with grease. I ate so fast, like something starving, feral. That is what I was, from the Latin *fera* for wild animal, something menacing, existing in an untamed state.

The Commander sat down again, shaking his head, smiling happily. "I will enjoy taming you."

The woman set a glass of water in front of me and I drank greedily, washing the sticky rice down. I set the glass on the table. "You cannot tame me. Know that."

He sneered and started eating. He chewed slowly, wiped his mouth every few bites. I dreaded what would come next. The stink of the food decaying in my mouth, that kitchen, our bodies and sweat, made me crazy.

As he ate, the Commander told me about his father, a man prone to drink and something of a womanizer, but intelligent and charming. The Commander's father worked as a chauffeur for a wealthy family and also did other odd jobs. Sometimes, when his employers were out of the country—Paris, New York, Montreal, Miami—the Commander's father would pick up his children in the black Mercedes of his employer and drive them around the city. They would roll slowly past the presidential palace and head high into the hills where the wealthy lived. His father often said, "Look how these people live. Never forget what they choose to deny you."

I rolled my eyes. "My father grew up in a shack with a dirt floor, never had a moment to himself, shared that tiny place with his parents and twelve siblings. You are not the only man to grow up wanting or hungry or angry. My father earned everything he has."

The Commander slammed his fist against the table and our plates jumped. My water spilled and spread across the table in a beautiful pattern. We stared at each other for a few moments, the only sound in the r   dripping over the edge of the table. "Even now, when he has a ndoned you, you defend your father?"

"I have not been abandoned."

He reached for a napkin and carefully wiped his mouth. "Let us test your theory. I will call your father. If he answers, we can assume he is still willing to negotiate. If he does not answer, you can accept I am not lying."

"I don't see how that makes any sense. There could be any number of reasons why they don't answer the phone."

"If your child were kidnapped, would you be anywhere but near the phone?"

I shifted in my seat, longed for my clothes, some way of covering my body, shielding myself from the waking nightmare. "Go ahead. Call." I was defiant and righteous. My father loved me. Even though I was no one, my father loved me.

He put the speaker on and set the phone between us. The phone rang and rang and rang. A strange sensation began to rise up from my rib cage. I pushed my food away from me and leaned forward. I was starving but had no appetite. The phone continued to ring. I idly rubbed the empty space where my rings were supposed to be. I missed the weight of them already. I missed the man who placed them on my finger. I forced myself to forget him again. I was no one. The Commander pursed his lips and shrugged. He moved to end the call but I grabbed his arm. "Wait."

He sat back, slid the phone across the table to me, a cocky smile creeping across his lips. The phone continued to ring. I don't know how long we sat there listening to the dull echo of the phone ringing but eventually the ringing became a busy signal, the steady pulse growing louder and louder in my ears until the sound threatened to pierce my eardrums. My hands shook as I ended the call. The Commander stood, came back around to me. He held my chin gently, tilted my face up. "As I told you, your father is unwilling to pay a reasonable ransom for the return of his youngest daughter. It is a shame he is not the father you deserve. It is a shame you will continue to pay for his sins."

The Commander tried to pull me to my feet but I pushed him away, stepped around him, and went to his bedroom. I did not need him to lead me. I was no one so I knew where I had to go. I knew what I would be made to do.

####### ⊪⊪⊪⊪⊪⊪
⊪⊪II

After the Commander fell asleep, I found my towel and wrapped it tightly around me. An armed guard stood outside the bedroom door and he took me back to my cage. The house was quiet save for a radio playing in one of the rooms upstairs. My clothes were stiff and dry and I carefully pulled them on, finally felt less anxious. I tried to remember the name of the woman I had been. I could see the shape of that name but nothing more. I sat on the bed, leaning against the wall. It was slowly becoming easier than I might have imagined contemplating the rest of my life in a cage, to hope that life would not be a long one.

My father was asleep next to my mother, safe, their bodies cool and connected. My husband was asleep with our child or he was awake and worrying. I had to stop thinking of them as my family. I had to continue forgetting everything about them—the wrinkle around Michael's right eye, the black and gray streaks of my mother's hair, my father's laugh, my child, the softness of his bare feet against my cheeks, the steel of my father's voice, the coldness in his eyes. One by one, I tried to erase each of these memories. I tried.

I drifted asleep, fitful, but was woken by TiPierre straddling my waist. His boundless, persistent desire angered me. My temples throbbed. "No fucking more. You've had enough of me."

He held my arms by my sides. "I paid for you. You are mine."

I was weary of men claiming ownership of me. "Talk to the Commander. I'm certain he will tell you to leave me alone."

TiPierre laughed. "It seems you have seduced him. We are all to leave you alone. He is out, though, handling important business. There's no reason why I shouldn't have one more night with you."

I went limp. "Let go of me. I won't fight, not if this is the last time."

I felt him smiling in the darkness. "See? I am not so bad, right?"

He loosened his grip on my wrists. I pulled my hands free and held his face in my hands. He was warm, his skin smooth. TiPierre leaned down, brushed his lips against mine. I tried not to scream, tried to relax. When his tongue traced my lips, I turned my head to the side just slightly and tightened my grip on his face. I grabbed at the meat of his cheek with my teeth. I bit down as hard as I could, determined not to let go until my teeth met. TiPierre roared and grabbed my shoulders, tried to shake me loose. I squirmed beneath him but I did not let go. I tasted blood, his skin came loose, a sanguine taste coated my teeth. His hand circled my throat and squeezed and I had to let go but my whole body flushed triumphantly. I tried to bring my knee up between his thighs, hard, but then he punched my face once and twice and a third time. I couldn't focus. My ears rang. When I opened my eyes, everything was dark and blurry. TiPierre lay on top of me with his forearm against my throat.

"You lied to me, American whore. You are not worth the price I paid. I'm glad I lied to your cousin. You can rot here."

I scratched at his arm, scratched hard, felt narrow lengths of his skin coming away from his body. "My cousin?" My nostrils flared as I imagined someone looking for me. I could be free soon. Then I smelled TiPierre's anger.

"Don't worry about that. Worry about me!"

I didn't dare to hope people were looking for me. I did not dare. "You are insane to think I could ever want you."

He pressed down harder. "I was good to you."

The absurdity finally made me hysterical. I started laughing again. There was so much laughter while I was in that cage, crazy desperate laughter that became keening each time.

TiPierre rolled off me, cursing, and stood, moved near the doorway and turned on the light. I squinted. I looked up. My face swelled and my cheekbone felt like it had shattered beneath his fist. A thick flap of skin hung loosely from his face. I wanted to rip it all the way off. If he came near me again, I would. I would tear his body apart before enduring him inside me again. His anger filled the room but my anger engulfed his. I sat up and stared at him, bared my teeth. I hoped they were bloody.

"You will not touch me again," I said.

He cried out, hoarsely, and ran toward me. I quickly jumped off the bed and tried to stay just beyond his reach. He stumbled around the room and even though it hurt to move, I was fast.

This is what I know—the body is built to survive. An unknown energy pulsed just beneath my skin. I whispered, "I will survive this."

When he finally caught me, he slammed my body against a wall and my vertebrae rearranged themselves. There would be bruises on my back. The bruises would be deep. He lifted me off the ground and slammed me into the wall again. My laughter returned. His eyes were glassy with rage. So were mine.

"You think this is a game?"

I spit in his face, smiled as the saliva slid along the curve of his nose and over his lips. He flipped me around so I was facing the wall. His hands were everywhere.

I tried to twist my body free. I kicked my legs back trying to make contact with his knee. "You have no right," I said, angrily.

His hands fumbled with my pants and he pushed them down my thighs.

"I have every right," TiPierre said. "You think you're too good for me? Is that what you think?"

I couldn't stop laughing. I don't know why. Too much was beyond my control. There we were, alone with the stink and sweat of ourselves. "I am too good for you," I said, defiantly. It was hard to catch my breath I laughed so hard. Then I stopped. I said, "She is married. She has a husband she loves. She will never want you. Never."

He unzipped his pants and leaned into me. I understood what he was about to do, what he could still take from me. I reached deep down inside myself. I do not know the exact location of my soul but it was near there. I screamed, "No," so loudly the walls of the room shook. The ground felt unsteady.

"What is going on here?" a loud voice behind us asked. It was the Commander. The relief I felt was so sweet and so immediate it sickened me.

TiPierre released me and I fell to my knees. I had no strength left. I could not even hold up my head.

"I thought I made myself clear."

TiPierre tried to stutter an excuse but the Commander cut him off. "You disobeyed me." He cuffed TiPierre across the face, right where I bit him. TiPierre straightened himself, glared at me, tried to protest. The Commander hit him again, then grabbed TiPierre by the neck, walked him to the door, shoved him out of the room. "I will deal with you later. Don't think I won't."

The younger man left the room in a bitter wake. I was alone in my cage again with the Commander. He pulled me to my feet and pulled my pants up. He held my chin, turning my head from side to side. He sucked his teeth. "That boy has no finesse. I cannot blame him. The streets are all he knows."

My legs faltered again and I had to hold on to the Commander. I mumbled something but couldn't form the right words. He swept me into his arms and carried me to his room, placed me in his bed like he was a good man. He covered me with a blanket like he was a good man.

I said, "I am very tired. Please get it over with, whatever you're going to do." There was not much life or fight left in me. I stopped caring.

The Commander brushed my hair from my face. He lay next to me and told me a story about his mother, who scrubbed the floors and washed the clothes and cooked the food for a man like my father. He told me how a man like my father treated his mother like a whore because that's the kind of thing men like my father can get away with. The Commander said his mother is old now even though she is not old, more ghost than woman.

When he finished talking, I said, "Your mother did not deserve the unwanted attentions of a man like my father." I said, "I did not deserve the unwanted attentions of a man like you. It is often women who pay the price for what men want."

The Commander grunted, turned on the television, started watching a poorly dubbed movie. I stared into the darkness for a very long time, terrified of how he would touch me next. I fell asleep thinking about the man who was another woman's husband, the man I could not forget no matter how I tried to remove every trace of him from my memory. His name lingered in my mouth and in my eyes and in my hands.

I awoke to the smell of coffee, sharp and bitter. I tried to remember the taste of coffee, the taste of anything. My face throbbed and I touched my cheek gently. I tried to remember where I was. Nothing looked familiar. I reached behind me. There was a man and he had a name, a name I loved. I remembered his smell but I was alone. I had a name but I could not recall it, either. I was no one. I sat up and was so dizzy I had to lie back down. I curled on my side, pulled my knees to my chest, covered my body with the blanket next to me even though it was so hot, I was sweating everywhere, between my thighs, beneath my breasts, under my chin. I thought of Alaska, of sitting in a lawn chair on an iceberg and how it would be cold and dry even on a warm sunny day. I had never been to Alaska but I imagined the country to be cold and green and white and blue. "I will never see Alaska," I said to the empty room.

It was the twelfth day though I could not be certain. I had lost count. Time no longer mattered. I was no one and had no reason to measure time or the days between who I had been and who I had become.

"Would you like to try to call your family today? I am quite certain, if they bother to answer, they will tell you they are still coming up with the money. You will see, once and for all, that I am not lying to you."

I threw the covers off and slowly sat up, leaning against the headboard.

I shrugged and held my hand out. When he handed me the phone, it was yet another cell phone. I wondered if the Commander had an infinite supply of mobile devices. When I called, a man answered. I tried to remember what I should say to him. He knew it was me. He knew my name. I tried to remember how to say his name.

"We are so close, Miri. I swear we are."

He was my husband but I couldn't be sure, not of anything. I tried to hold on to what I hoped I knew. "You didn't answer the phone yesterday."

"What are you talking about? We are always by the phone."

A rush of anger overwhelmed me. Things were clearer now. "You're lying," I said. "You're going to leave me here."

Michael made a hoarse choking sound. "That is not true. You have no idea, baby."

The woman I was would have believed him but the woman who was no one could not. "I want you to leave the country, Michael. Take your son and leave and don't you ever come back to this place, not ever."

"I thought you weren't going to be noble. You're scaring me. I'm not going anywhere without you," Michael said. He said something else but none of it mattered.

I hung up and pulled the sheet around me and went to the window. It was covered with black iron bars. Children, bare-chested and wearing long shorts, played soccer in the street. Every time they smiled, I saw a flash of perfect white teeth. I pressed my hand against the window. I wanted to forget all I knew of children, of how they laughed with abandon, even when playing in the filthy streets of Bel Air.

The Commander stood behind me. His smell was becoming familiar. It was the smell of a cruel man, surprisingly clean. He wrapped his arms around my waist and pressed his lips to my bare shoulder.

"As you can see, I have not lied to you. I never will."

I did not turn around. "I would like to go home. You will never be able to rest if you keep me here. You will never know what I might do."

He tightened his grip, held me closer. He sank his teeth into my shoulder like he was trying to gnaw the meat from my bone. When he lifted his head, a perfect ring of pain throbbed in the small indentations of his teeth.

"I am a businessman. If your family had transacted their end of our business, you would have gone home unharmed, untouched. They chose not to. I appreciate your threat but I can say the same to you. There are people you love and as long as they are in this country, they are within *my* reach."

A small boy, adorable, no more than five, grabbed the soccer ball and held it high over his head, started running in a tight circle, giggling while the older boys chased him. For a too-brief moment I remembered playing soccer with Michael and a group of little boys on a dusty riverbed. I forced myself to forget that too.

I turned to face the Commander. "You cannot keep me here forever." It sounded like a question and I hated myself for it.

He led me back to his bed and dumped me in the center of the mattress unceremoniously. He handcuffed my hands to the headboard, each click echoing loudly. "We shall see how long I can keep you here," he said, smiling, almost sweetly.

‖‖‖ ‖‖‖ ‖‖‖
‖‖‖ ‖‖‖

When the Commander finally freed me again I sat up and nearly fell over as blood rushed to my head and arms. A sharp ache spread across my skull. I exhaled loudly and I stretched my arms out in front of me. A dark red and brown band of raw skin circled the skin and bone of my wrists, naked without their shackles. I felt dangerously free. I looked at my hands, my fingernails torn and ragged, caked with blood and someone else's skin. My hands shook. My whole body shook. The word *mercy* clung to my lower lip again, hung loosely, daring to fall. I had less than nothing left.

I only needed to ask and the Commander would grant me some small measure of mercy, not enough but enough. If this was the rest of my life, there was no need for further fight. There would be no easy life but there could be an easier life. From the bed I could see the sun was at its highest. I looked at the clock on the DVD player. It was four in the afternoon. Time meant very little.

The children were not playing in the street. The sky suddenly darkened and rain started to fall at a diagonal in heavy sheets. I wanted to stand in that rain. "I'd like to stand in the rain," I said without realizing I had spoken aloud. The Commander grabbed me by my shoulder and told me to get dressed. I did. He pushed me out of his room and down the dark hallways to the front door. Once again, I tried to memorize everything, just in case I could find a new way out for myself. The thought of escape was a foolish hope and I held on to it dearly. Desperation and foolishness are nearly the same.

We stepped out onto the street and the Commander released his grip. "Remember your son and husband and what I could do to them," he said, evenly. He raised his T-shirt, revealing his gun, and leaned against the door, under the narrow eaves of the house. I stood with my arms wrapped around myself. I raised my face to the sky and let the rain fall over me. There was a space between the clouds. Pale shafts of sunlight appeared. The rain continued to fall. It was the heaviest rain I had ever seen. I pulled my hair out of its loose ponytail. My clothes soaked and clung to my skin. I did not mind. An old woman with skin so loose it wrapped her bones in folds stood in the doorway of her small block of a home. When she looked at me, I saw real sadness in the lines of her face. I stared at her until she looked away. The rain was warm. I stuck out my tongue. The rain washed my mouth clean. There was not enough rain to wash the rest of me clean. I was filthy. I was hopeless.

I stood in the rain until the clouds cleared. As far as the eye could see, waves of steam rose from the pavement. "You'll have to thank me for this," the Commander shouted from where he stood watch. I did not turn around but I nodded. There would always be ransoms for any dignity or peace. I was not my father. I was willing to pay.

Eventually, the Commander grew bored with his generosity and came to get me from the middle of the street. As he pulled me toward the house, I said, "No," and began grunting like an animal. I forgot how to speak. I only knew I did not want my body forced back in that cage with the other animals. I dragged my heels. I scratched at his bare arms and he flexed his muscles. The scar beneath his eye moved again like it was trying to reach the other side of his face. In the doorway, I grabbed for the doorjamb with my hands and feet. I grunted louder. The Commander bloodied my knuckles with the butt of his gun and then he hit me over the head.

Michael loves concrete, loves making concrete and testing the compressive strength. The compressive strength is the most important performance measure. The testing is important because engineers need to trust that the bridges and buildings they design and build will stand the test of time. When we first started dating, Michael endeavored to teach me everything he knew about concrete. I did not have the heart to explain to him I had already received a similar education from my father. "Concrete," he likes to say, "is the purest expression of man's strength." I ask, "What is the purest expression of a woman's strength," and he says, "You." Once, he brought me twelve slender concrete cylinders. He called it an unbreakable bouquet. I loved him so fiercely in that moment.

I did not pass out when the Commander slammed the butt of his gun against my skull. I was breakable but unbroken. I fought even harder, kicking at the walls as he dragged me to his room. I kicked one wall so hard I left a large indentation. I was a breaker of concrete. I found the compressive strength of the concrete in those walls—that of a woman who is no one divided by the memory of the woman she used to be, the woman torn from her husband and only child.

In his room, the Commander punished me for my tiny rebellion. I did not make a sound. I was no one. Then it was dark and I was alone. I could not close my eyes. When I closed my eyes, all I could see, smell, feel, was the Commander forcing himself on me again and again, his seed staining my thighs, his teeth in my skin, his saliva on my face, his blades and his fire. All I could hear was the unnatural calm of his voice, how he always spoke carefully, how he treated me as both lover and enemy—the only way he could, I think, understand a woman. I tried to forget the Commander for just one moment and instead I tried to remember my name or the names of everyone or anyone I had ever known, loved, needed. I remembered nothing.

"Mercy," I whispered even though I was alone. I needed to say the word. I needed to know I could say the word. The utterance was not a prayer. It was more audacious because I yearned to be answered.

Beyond the closed door I heard the sound of paper shuffling; I heard this sound for more than two hours. I covered my ears but I still heard that sound. Every possible thing conspired against me.

Something soft was dropped on my face—my worn and filthy clothes. "Get dressed," a voice said. It was not the Commander. I did not know his men's voices well enough to make sense of this man though my body knew him. My body knew all of them. My bikini bottoms had long been forgotten. I stepped into my jeans quietly and pulled my shirt on, whimpering softly as the fabric fell over my skin. The man grabbed me by my elbow, dug his fingers into me even though that small cruelty was not necessary. He led me to the kitchen. On the table there were two cash counters shuffling money at a blurry pace, and an unfathomable number of stacks of hundreds and twenties, U.S. dollars.

I stared down at the ground, my bare feet. I was ready to say *mercy* to the Commander if he was going to throw me to his wolves once again. Right then, I would have done anything to save myself from the unkind attentions of all those men. The Commander sat at the head of the table wearing a dark pair of sunglasses. My escort shoved me toward the Commander and I stumbled into the kitchen, fell against him as he pulled me into his lap, held me against him, his arm across my stomach. I tried to pry his arm off me, strained to free myself from his embrace. He sank his teeth into the back of my neck and squeezed my breasts, less swollen now, hollowed. I inhaled sharply. The men around the table murmured their approval.

In the far corner, TiPierre stood sullen, glaring in my direction but avoiding eye contact like a spurned lover. A large bandage covered his cheek.

I nodded toward TiPierre. "How's your face?" I rasped.

He jumped at me but the Commander shook his head, snapped his fingers once, and TiPierre stilled, remained in his corner.

I no longer gave a damn. I said, "Good dog. Heel." I stuck my hand in the fire. I was willing to burn.

The Commander cleared his throat. "You will soon be free."

There was a new, louder ringing in my ears. It drowned out the sound of everything in that room, the angry men, their voices, the cash machines still doing their work of calculating my worth. I said nothing, felt nothing.

"Did you hear me? It seems your father has finally found a reason to pay for his youngest daughter."

I shook my head, still numb. "You said the negotiations ended."

He squeezed my breasts again. "Perhaps I lied to you, after all."

I tried to remember my name. I needed to remember my name but I couldn't. It was locked somewhere I could not reach.

The Commander stood and pulled me after him. I resisted, trying to dig my heels into the slick floor. He threw me over his shoulder, ignoring my flailing limbs. His men cheered. "I think I will enjoy you one last time," he said.

When he was done, I sat on the edge of his bed, staring into the distance. I said, "You should have killed me."

Once upon a time, my life was a fairy tale and then I was stolen from everything I've ever loved. There was no happily ever after. After days of dying, I was dead.

Part II
Once Upon a Time

||||| ||||| |||||
||||| ||||

I ran down an unfamiliar street, my bare feet slapping against the pavement. I was free even if I did not know it yet or my body was free and my mind was in the cage. It was hot, early evening, the hush of a day ending. I ran over shards of broken glass, felt my skin come neatly apart. I bled. My feet were slick. I did not stop running. The Commander told me to run until I could not run anymore so that is what I did. My thighs burned. It was strange to be able to move so freely, to breathe fresher air. I wanted someone to find me. I wanted to stop. I kept running. When I passed people standing in their doorways or ambling down the street, I stiffened, knew they could not be trusted. I ran. I saw a cross rising into the sky, reaching up. A church would be a safe place. I hoped.

I was so tired. I was loathsome. I was not a person. I was no one. I was nothing. Sweat dripped down my face, burning my eyes, rolling uncomfortably into my ears. I took the stairs into the church two at a time, leaving bloody footprints. It was dark and quiet in the chapel, where it smelled faintly of incense. In the far corner, there was a thin line of light and the silhouette of a door. I paused, leaning forward, panting heavily. I swallowed hard. I followed the edges of the room toward that sliver of light. I wanted to find something perfect behind that door. I wondered if I might find someone masquerading as God. My stomach was hollow. I was so hungry. I thought about the sensation of a dry disc of communion wafer on my tongue. When I reached the door, it was warm to the touch. Music was playing, Barry Manilow, singing about the Copacabana. My mother loves Barry Manilow. When I was a little girl, she had his records, and sometimes I caught her staring at them, tracing Barry's face with her finger. I knocked on the door three times. I knocked so hard it made my knuckles ache. I drew blood. I marveled I could still bleed.

An older man finally answered. I tried to concentrate on who I had been before I became no one. There was a name and the memory of it lingered on my tongue. "Help me," I said. The man looked at me carefully, reached for me but I stepped away and bumped into a wall. I hissed. There was a name of a woman I had once been. I rubbed my forehead, wanted so desperately to remember the name so someone who knew who I had been might come for me.

"Please say something," the stranger said, staring at me curiously.

"I need help," I said, hot air rushing from my chest.

The stranger shook his head. He said, "I don't understand you."

I repeated myself. My chest tightened. I looked back toward the church doors, hoping the Commander hadn't chased me down again. I wanted to barricade myself in the sanctuary.

"What is your name?"

I pulled what remained of my shirt tightly around my body, what remained of my body. "Mireille. Kidnapped."

He approached me again and wide threads of fear knotted around my throat.

"Don't hurt me."

The stranger smiled kindly. He was a small man, his white hair trimmed neatly. He wore a pair of dark slacks, a dress shirt, and a tan cardigan with thick wooden buttons. "You have nothing to fear from me. What is your last name?"

There was a man who knew the name that had once been mine, a man with an easy smile and blond hair he wore too long, blond hair that curled in his face in the morning. When this man said the name that had once been mine, the sound came from deep in his chest. The sound of my name in his mouth spread easily, was full of joy. I remembered a little boy who also had curly hair, both brown and blond. His cheeks and thighs were chubby. I leaned against the wall behind me and sank into a tight crouch. I could see their faces, hear that blond man with the easy smile calling out to the woman I had been, calling out to me before I became no one. "M m m m . . . ," I said. I took a deep breath. "Michael." The name came out awkwardly, sounded like three different names rather than one.

The stranger removed his glasses and looked at me closely. "My goodness. I think I know you."

I tried to give him some way of making sense of who I was. I was so lost.

He nodded eagerly. "Yes, yes. I met your father at the Haiti-Cel gala. He is a good man. I heard about the kidnapping, terrible business."

"Please call Michael," I said. "Please."

The stranger was a preacher at the church, was up late writing his sermon, he said. He excused himself and quickly returned. "I have called your father and he is on his way. God brought you to safety."

I did not look up. "There is no God," I said. I stood, my legs stiff and sore, moved away from the preacher. I did not want to be alone with this man I did not know in a small room. I did not want him to hurt me. I did not want to have to do something terrible to keep him from hurting me. The preacher called for his wife and she sat with me as we waited. It hurt to sit against the curved hardwood of the pew, in such a false place. The preacher's wife clasped her hands in her lap, asked if I needed anything. She tried to see to my wounds but I refused. I wanted no part of a stranger's skin against mine. I said, "I am fine, thank you." I wanted to be polite. It was important to be a good reflection of my family. Somehow, I remembered that too, that once, I was a good Haitian daughter.

Time passed. I wanted to close my eyes, relax, but I was not safe. I was not safe. It was best to stay awake. I gripped the pew in front of me. I tried to breathe. Suddenly, I heard a desperate voice shouting a name and pounding footsteps. I stood and turned slowly. A man who seemed familiar ran through the church's doors, followed by my father and a man I did not recognize. These men knew who I had been.

I stood and stared and said, "Michael?"

"Yes, baby, it's me."

"I need help. I am not safe," I said, as loudly as I dared.

Michael looked stricken. "I don't understand," he said. "Take a deep breath."

I whispered my name several times, tried to find a way to fit myself into that name, tried to hide the truth. I was no one, a woman with no name, no family.

Michael tried to pull me in his arms but I backed away. I wanted to run again. I was terrified. I could not trust these men. My husband's face wrinkled. He held his hands up. "It's me, baby. We're here to take you home. You're safe now," he said as if he understood the meaning of the word. He saw the fear in my eyes. He could see. He smelled the rot of me. He closed his hands into tight fists and said, "My God, what happened to you?" his voice echoing through the chapel.

I pointed to the two men behind him. "Who is the man with my father?" I needed a precise accounting of everyone who could hurt me.

Michael shook his head, rubbed his jaw, covered in stubble. "I'm not understanding what you're saying but that man, where you're pointing, is the hostage negotiator."

I looked at Michael again. He seemed more familiar. The man who used to be my father was increasingly familiar as well.

"Days," I said, softly. "How many days?"

Michael looked down. "We can talk about that later. Let's get you out of here."

"How many days has it been?"

"Thirteen."

I held my stomach and faltered, to truly know how much time had passed. Michael caught me, steadied me. "Let go of me," I said, shrieking. "Don't any of you touch me."

The three of them started speaking at once. My husband told me how good it was to have me back. My father told me how strong I was, as if I needed his appreciation of my strength. I had a calculation for my strength he would never understand. The stranger was silent. They were all liars. My father shook hands with the preacher, holding both of the man's hands between his, promising a donation to the church, an additional ransom. He could barely look at me. Later he would tell me the bruises made him sick to his stomach. I would say, "Your hands are on them."

The men surrounding me didn't know what to do with me. I could see that. I wanted to be away from my father and his money and his convictions that had brought us all to this empty church.

My legs trembled and I sat again in a pew across the aisle. Michael sat next to me; he was too close. I needed something from him. I needed him to know what to do for me. I tried to think of another name. I knew it well. It was a good name but I couldn't find a way to say it.

"Picture," I said.

Michael shook his head. He looked so helpless. "Picture? Mireille, you're still not making much sense but I want to understand you, I do."

I took a deep breath, tried to start again, tried to find a way to speak the same language as the man beside me. "You have a child."

He nodded. "We have a son, yes, baby, we do."

I shifted uncomfortably, wanting so much to say the right thing. "What is the boy's name?"

Michael slid closer. "Look at me," he said.

I turned to face him but couldn't hold his gaze, looked down at my hands.

"We have a son and his name is Christophe. He misses you very much."

"Christophe," I said, softly. In my head I said the name over and over. "Like Henri Christophe, the man who declared himself king."

"That's who we named him for."

My father cleared his throat. Michael waved his arm, ignored him.

"Is he okay? Was he hurt? Do you have a picture?"

"He's fine, with your mother." Michael reached for his wallet and pulled out two pictures of a small boy, a smiling boy. My hands trembled as I took one of the pictures and stared at it and said the name *Christophe* once more.

"May I have this?"

"What? Of course."

I was so tired. My eyelids were heavy. I clutched the picture tightly, rubbing my thumb over the child's face. I knew him, of course I knew him even though I erased as many memories of him as I could, tried to strip my heart of his face and smile and the warmth of his breath. I wanted to tear the picture into tiny pieces and eat each one so the child would always be with me.

Finally, Michael said, "We should get you out of here." He slipped out of his shoes, knelt, and held my cut feet in his hands, wrapped a handkerchief around each foot. He helped me slide my feet into his shoes. It felt good to be afforded this small protection.

The three men ushered me into the car, hulking around me. I shook. As we pulled away from the church, I pulled myself together as much as I could and said, "Please take me home so I can shower."

Michael said, "We should get you to the doctor."

"I need to shower. It cannot wait."

"I don't think that's wise. If you . . . saw what you looked like right now, you'd understand."

"Now, Michael," I said. I grabbed at my chest. I was on the verge of hysteria. "I don't care what I look like. Right now, I need this one thing. I cannot handle anything else."

My father drove quickly over the broken Port-au-Prince streets using his horn liberally. I stared at his hands, or the outlines of his hands, all I could see in the darkness.

When I was a little girl, I thought my father had the biggest, strongest hands in the world. When I was a little girl, I followed my father everywhere, always wearing little dresses with matching hair bows because he liked little girls who looked like little girls. As the youngest, I was the child my father knew best because by that point in his career, there was less travel, more time at home. I asked questions, so many questions, even started walking like him, mimicking his mannerisms. My father called me *ma petite ombre*, his little shadow. I always smiled when I was with my father. He was good to me when I was very young, kind and gentle. He had always worked hard. He woke every morning at five, ran four miles, then dressed and went to work. He spent his entire life having to prove over and over again that he was the best, the brightest, the kind of man who could build a tower into the heavens. Though he would never admit it, my father's life had been exhausting. In America, he worked six days a week, arrived early, left late. Only once did he get sick, a flu so terrible he only made it to his car in the garage before he realized he could hardly stand. He called for my mother in the kitchen making breakfast for me. Mona and Michel were already at school. My father had to lean on my mother as she helped him back into the house, back into bed. For four days, he was sick and feverish, vomiting until his body had emptied itself completely. I stayed by his side the entire time. I was only four. I sat with him and brought cool compresses and drew pictures and sang him songs. I napped with my father, my head on his chest, my small hand in his. Years later, my father told me that during those days when he was so sick, he caught me staring at him with a frown, my eyes filled with worry, like a tiny adult. When my mother tried to shoo me from my father's side, I refused. I did not rest until my father was able to get out of bed, bathe himself, stand outside for a few minutes to take in some fresh air. "It is an amazing thing," my father once told me after Christophe was born, "how much a child loves a parent. That kind of love terrifies me." That may be the only true thing my father has ever told me.

On that fourteenth day, in the dark empty of my salvation, I saw the hands of a weak, stubborn man. I saw the hands of a man who could not love his daughter enough to save her when there was still something of her left to save.

I still held the picture of the boy who was known to be my son. It was hard to focus but it still felt important to be awake, ready for what might happen next. I crossed my legs and leaned forward, resting my forehead against my knee. I was still in my cage. I was still beneath the sweaty bodies of men who were not my husband. I was still torn apart and cut open. Michael started rubbing my back. He was tearing what remained of my skin from my body. I didn't recognize his touch. I said, "Don't," more sharply than I meant to. His hand stilled but he didn't pull away, refused to pull away. The warm pressure made my bones ache. I tried to hold myself together until I could wash myself clean. I would never get clean. There was not enough water.

‖‖‖ ‖‖‖ ‖‖‖
‖‖‖ ‖‖‖

Instead of returning to my parents' home, we drove to a modern-looking office building in Pétionville. I vaguely recognized it from a picture on the website of my father's company. The man was everywhere. The office was dimly lit and empty as we walked in, me flanked by these men, still at the mercy of men. The doctor was a friend of my uncle who was also a doctor. He smiled gently. I stared at the floor of the waiting room and muttered, "How could you do this to me, Michael?"

"You're not . . . rational right now. This is what you need."

I shook my head and began muttering. I didn't know what to do with my hands. The doctor tried to take me by my elbow but I hissed, practically spitting on him. He smelled like cigarettes and hand sanitizer. This was new, understanding men by their smells. I knew so many.

He stepped away and said, "Please follow me to the exam room."

I looked around, needed some means of escape, but Michael steered me to the exam room and we stood, waiting.

I tried once more. "I need to shower, Michael. Get me out of here, please. Please." I was ready to fall on my knees.

Michael reddened, wouldn't meet my eyes, tried to caress my face but I slapped him away. The doctor appeared in the doorway and handed me a gown. I couldn't bear the thought of taking off my clothes for yet another man my body did not care to know. My hand shook as I took the gown. The doctor excused himself and I set the gown on the exam table. Without turning around, I said, "You cannot be here for this." Michael stepped toward me, started rubbing my shoulders. I said, "Don't. Please don't."

His hands stilled. "I can handle it."

"I can't," I said.

His silence was a measure of the distance between us.

Alone, I shrugged out of my clothes, what remained of them, and stepped into the gown and stepped into something much more like I had recently known. I was not free at all. There was a light knock and the doctor peered in. When he closed the door behind him, I swallowed a scream. A sharp pang rose from between my thighs into my stomach. I gripped the exam table.

There were so many things he could do to me and the room was so small and Michael was too far away. I feared he would not hear my cries. I looked around for something, anything I could use to make my stand. All I could see was a glass jar of tongue depressors on a small counter next to a jar of large cotton swabs. I could break the jar, I told myself, and use the shards of glass. I needed a plan.

"I'll make this as quick and painless as possible," the doctor said, as if the sincerity of his lie could comfort me.

I lay on the table, my legs in the stirrups. My chest grew tighter and tighter. I looked at the glass jars on the counter, wondered how long it would take me to reach them. I stretched my arm out but could not quite reach the counter. I clenched my jaw until it locked. He gently tried to force my knees apart. I held them shut.

"I can't do this," I whispered.

"This is for your own good," the doctor said. "You have no choice."

He was right. I had no choices and the truth of that was too much. The doctor wore latex gloves, the strange smell of them filling the room. I was choking on everything. He began gently tracing the fresh burns. "What caused these?"

My vision blurred. I saw the Commander standing between my legs, a thin stream of gray smoke drifting between us. I snapped my legs shut.

When the doctor tried to force my knees open again, I jumped off the table and grabbed the jar of cotton swabs, the glass slipping in my hands.

I threw the jar at him, not nearly as hard as I wanted, and he quickly stepped to the side. "Stay away from me," I gasped, trying to breathe without a sharp pain in my chest. The jar shattered when it fell to the floor. I reached for another jar, tongue depressors, and held it high in the air. "I cannot do this." I wanted to break everything in that room, tear it completely apart. The shape and dimensions of my anger frightened me. I closed my eyes. When I opened them, the doctor was close, too close.

The doctor held his hands out. He said, "Please." He said, "You must. There are things I can tell just by looking at you and things I cannot."

I ached so terribly, in so many places, but I could not show the doctor those wounds. My wounds were mine. I needed to keep them to myself. Pain could not break me. My body knew that now. My body knew there were no limits to what it could endure. I wanted to tell everyone I met, *you have no idea what I can take*. I wanted to tell the doctor, *you have no earthly idea what I can take*.

I was not going to let him touch me, examine me, try to fix me. He had no right to any part of me. The doctor implored me to let him draw blood. I refused. He asked if he could at least take X-rays. I agreed, reluctantly, and in another room, lay flat beneath the machine, shaking as it burned the image of the ways I was broken beneath the skin.

Finally, the doctor left me alone again to get dressed. I stepped into my jeans, quickly, but as I was removing the gown, trying to keep myself inside my skin, the door opened behind me. I spun around, and hissed, "Get out. Get out now." I tried to cover myself or make myself invisible but it was too late. Michael could see. He could see everything. "Oh my God," he said. He didn't leave. I couldn't move. I suddenly felt like I was very small in a very large, dark room. I couldn't hear anything. He sprang into action, finished dressing me like a child, very gently.

In another office, the doctor sat behind a desk, detailing all the injuries he could see, the ones he couldn't see, what might be lurking. He gave me burn ointment. "For your thighs," he said.

"Jesus. What burns?" Michael asked.

"It's nothing," I said, digging my fingernails into my palms again.

"It's not nothing," the doctor said. "The burns are quite serious. All your injuries are serious." I had fractures on three ribs, heavy bruising, and internal injuries he couldn't assess without a proper examination. Michael frowned, cracked his knuckles. He asked why I hadn't been properly examined.

I stopped listening. Their words did not concern me. Michael shook me, said something about needing to be examined immediately. I drifted away again. The doctor gave me painkillers and antibiotics and a pill that would make an unwanted pregnancy disappear, told me I should go to the hospital in the States immediately, that I might need surgery. He gave me Valium. My mother often jokes that everyone in Port-au-Prince takes Valium. "How could they not?" she says.

Twenty minutes later, we pulled past the gates of my parents' home, my father's castle in the sky, and drove up the long steep drive. I sat up. The decadence disgusted me. The way I had once enjoyed such decadence disgusted me. Armed guards stood near the gates, holding machine guns across their bodies. Another set of guards stood watch near the front door. When we stopped, Michael got out and held his hand out to me. I leaned into the seat and sighed.

Michael ducked his head into the car. "Do you need a minute?"

"I just want to sit here." Michael stood near the open door. "I just want to sit here," I said to myself. "I just want to sit here."

My father and the negotiator went into the house. I listened to the sounds of the city—cars passing on the street below, crickets, music, a woman yelling angrily. I could sit in the backseat of that car as long as I wanted. I could sit in the back of that car until my skin fused to the leather.

Michael ducked back into the car. "It's getting cold, Miri. You're shivering."

"I am?"

He removed his shirt, a white button-down, and handed it to me. He was wearing a wifebeater underneath. "Put this on," he said.

I clenched my teeth as I pulled Michael's shirt on. My arms were so sore, the muscles stretched, shredded. The shirt was warm and smelled familiar. I lay on my side, holding the cuffs of Michael's shirt between my fingers, trying to begin to find my way back to the woman I had once been.

"I don't want to rush you but we should go inside. I think we'll all feel better with you in the house." He paused. "I will feel better with you in the house, near me. I am never letting you out of my sight again."

I sat up again and was instantly dizzy. Michael held his hand out to me. I took a deep breath and slid my hand into his. He squeezed, hard, and I squeezed back. I wanted to run my fingers through his hair, but I was afraid to touch him like that.

As we walked up the stairs leading into my parents' house, I said, "Wait." I stood on the step above his. "Put your hands in your pockets."

"What?"

"Please, Michael."

He slid his hands into his pockets, looked at me expectantly. I held his face, trying to memorize his features, trying to believe he was real, that I was his wife, that I was safe. Michael's heart was beating fast. I could hear the steady bass of it, the *thump thump thump*. He started crying and I tried to wipe his tears away but there were too many. I said, "I love you." I said, "I know you were taken too." I said, "Please don't move your arms, please don't touch me," and he didn't. He cried harder, said he was so sorry, so so sorry. I said, "Hush, baby." I leaned into my husband's body and wrapped my arms around him, fitting into him the way I always do. He was my one true thing. I held on to him as tight as my arms would allow. He stopped crying and we stood, alone. He did not rush me. We did not speak. We did not need to. For a moment, I thought it might be possible to be whole again. I did not know how long it would take to get there. I did not know how to find my way.

||||| ||||| |||||
||||| ||||| |

My parents' house was quiet and empty. An older woman with my face held a beautiful, sleeping child. She stood, approached me, still holding the child. She tried to hold her hand to my face but I did not let her. I could not look her in the eyes. I was uncomfortable beneath the lights. I wanted to run away from these people who would know too much about what happened to me if they looked at me too carefully, these people who could not recognize a stranger in their midst, these people who allowed me to become a stranger. She tried to hand me the child but I crossed my arms across my chest, tucking my hands beneath my armpits, staring at my feet. Michael leaned down and whispered something in her ear. She frowned. "Mireille, I am your mother, this is your child, your son, Christophe. Here, hold him, such a beautiful boy."

"I know who you are," I whispered, though I wasn't entirely sure that was true anymore.

I would not dare touch that child until I was clean even if he was not the child of the stranger before him. I would not touch him with any part of what I had become. He was perfect. He would stay that way. I would see to that.

We stood within that uneasy impasse, a mother, a mother, a father, a father, a husband, a husband, a sleeping child, a broken child. They wanted to ask questions. There was nothing I could say. I could not bear the taste of my mouth. I needed to vomit. That's all I would do for months, trying to purge myself. I held my stomach, swayed unsteadily. I said, "Excuse me," and ran up the metal staircase to my room. I don't know how I knew my way through that enormous house. I was reminded, again, of the wisdom of the body. In the bathroom, I fell to my knees and heaved into the toilet. I stayed there, like that, like a prayer.

When I stepped into the weak stream of lukewarm water, still dressed, I beat my fist against the tiled wall. I said, "Are you fucking kidding me?" I had hoped for hot water from the cistern but knew it was not likely so late in the day. I beat the tile again. My clothes clung to my body uncomfortably so I peeled myself out of them and scrubbed myself with a white washcloth and a bar of pink French soap. I washed myself until there was no soap left, until the water was ice cold and then I sat on the shower floor, letting the water wash over me weakly. A stream of reds and pinks, my blood, circled the drain for a long while. Every now and then I would hear a knock at the door and I said, "Leave me alone."

I needed to be alone. It is easier to be alone when you are no one. The longer I sat there, the more I remembered of the woman I had been and would never be again, the woman I would have to pretend to be even though I was no one. After several rounds of this call and response, the bathroom door opened. I pulled my legs against my chest. Through the glass, I saw the outline of Michael's body. He leaned against the bathroom sink.

"You've been in here for a long time."

"It's not nearly enough."

"I will sit with you, keep you company."

I didn't have the energy to protest. I sat until the water ran out. I had known there would not be enough water. I asked Michael to hand me a towel. I asked him to leave. He sighed softly, and stepped out. As I dried myself, I stared at my reflection in the mirror. A thick shock of silver, inches wide, ran through my hair on the right side of my head. The streak would never go away. Friends would later call it distinctive. Michael would say it made me even more beautiful. My face was nearly unrecognizable, misshapen—two black eyes, contusions, bruising. A constellation of small bruises lined my collarbones. There were darker bruises wreathing my neck, my shoulders, my thighs, my back, my stomach. A series of small cuts marked my left calf. There were cuts across my back, a very fresh cut between my breasts, wide, open and weeping. There were so many burns. I studied the attentions of unkind men. My fingernails were ragged and broken. I fought so hard. I was proud. I would have that, always.

When I was ready, I pulled the bathroom door open a crack and asked Michael to hand me some clothes. It was a relief to wear something clean, something of mine—a long-sleeved T-shirt and flannel pajama pants. It was a relief to feel the air-conditioning against my damp skin. Michael sat on the edge of the bed in a T-shirt and boxers. I stared at the hair on his pale legs. I love the hair on his legs, tufts all the way down to his ankles. My hair was wet and heavy against the back of my neck. I tried to twist it into a loose bun. My arms ached.

"Can you believe my hair?" I pointed to the silver streak.

Michael smiled softly. "It's beautiful. You are beautiful."

"You'll say anything to charm me. We both know I look hideous right now." I pointed to the bruises on my face.

"What do you need?"

I shook my head. "Michael, I have no idea." His name felt good on my tongue.

He nodded slowly. "Do you want to see Christophe?"

I did, very much, but shook my head. I went to the window and looked out onto the mess of the city below, blocks of concrete stretching from the mountains all the way to the ocean. I wrapped my arms around myself. My mouth still tasted terrible. My jaw ached, was loose.

"Come to bed," Michael said.

There was the weight of TiPierre's arm, so heavy draped across me as he slept. Panic wormed through my body so sharply I doubled over. I wanted to hide. I wanted to sleep alone so I could be safe. Michael rushed to his feet, held me by my shoulders. "Are you okay?" he asked. I felt another sharp pang. I tried to free myself from his grasp. My body was coming apart. "Please," I begged. "Please don't touch me, Michael. I'm sorry. I can't handle it." He immediately pulled away, looked at his hands as if they had betrayed him.

"I'm sorry," he said. "I don't know what to do."

The walls were closing in; this new cage was getting smaller and smaller. There was a leash around my neck. The leash was heavy, choking me, reminding me I was still in that room, alone, with angry men. "I want you to pack our things so we can get out of here in the morning."

Michael backed away slowly, sat on the edge of the bed, tucking his hands beneath him. He nodded to the side. "Sit with me." I was thankful for the blessing of a king-sized bed. I sat as close to him as my leash would allow. It was not close at all. I looked at the floor, tried to make sense of the marble patterns.

"You look so skinny."

"I haven't eaten much lately."

"Do you want me to make you something?"

"What took so long?" I asked, quietly.

My husband bit his lower lip and shook his head. "We should talk about this later."

I threw my hairbrush against the wall. "What took so long? You abandoned me. How could you?"

"I did not abandon you, Mireille. I tried everything. Everything."

"But?"

He shifted uncomfortably. "Maybe we should talk about this after you've had some rest."

"What happened? Why didn't you come for me?"

"I tried," Michael said. He started crying again. I wanted to comfort him but didn't know how. I wished tears would come so easily to me. "There were complications."

I nodded slowly as the air in the room shifted. "I don't understand. Money was not the problem. What aren't you telling me?"

Michael sucked in his chest. His voice took on a tone I had never heard, tight with fury. He stood and began pacing. "Your father insisted on handling the negotiations. He wanted to prove a point. He said if he capitulated too easily, his words, those *animals* would try to take everything from him, everything he built. I threatened to kill him. I tried to work around him but I don't know anyone here, I don't speak the language that well, no one would help me. No one would fucking help me. It was like I wasn't even there but I looked for you with your cousin. We nearly tore the city apart."

"What are you talking about, Michael? Which cousin?"

My husband shook his head. "Nothing for you to worry about. I just mean to say, I did not sit idly by."

I was missing something but I couldn't quite figure out what. "I told them on the very first day my father wouldn't pay." My voice broke. "I was right. I knew he wouldn't want to pay. His principles matter more." I paused, trying to swallow the uncomfortable shape of this new truth. "Why did he finally pay?"

"Who knows? Your mother, maybe. Or his conscience finally got the best of him."

I exhaled loudly, My chest tightened. I didn't realize I had been holding my breath. I was not going to cry. I would not cry. "Thirteen days is a very long time."

"A lifetime," Michael said. "I know."

"No, Michael. You do not know. You have no idea."

I crawled to the edge of the bed and stretched out as best I could. It still hurt to breathe. It hurt to think. It hurt to be in this new cage. The leash wrapped itself ever more tightly around my throat. Carefully, I rolled onto my side and faced my husband. He stared and stared at me as if he were trying to read my mind. I knew he needed something from me, something to hold on to. I barely had the energy to give him anything. I said one true thing. "I missed you so fucking much." He smiled widely, tried to reach for me but I grabbed his wrist, tried to make the gesture seem affectionate by rubbing my thumb over his knobby wrist bones. I was not convincing.

Michael fell asleep quickly but I did not, did not trust I could sleep, did not trust what I might say in my sleep, did not trust what could happen while I slept. Michael started to snore. His sounds, the shape of his body near mine, made me feel closer to whole, however fleeting the moment. Tears welled. I would not cry. I slid out of bed and walked to where Christophe slept in a crib my mother bought the moment she heard I was pregnant. My son sleeps exactly like his father, on his side, his fingers curled into loose fists, one arm stretched behind him. He looks like his father more than he looks like me if you're paying attention. They have the same nose and cheeks and toes. My son has my eyes. I leaned into his crib to touch the perfect dimples on his fingers but stopped myself. I still did not trust myself to touch my child but I held my hand against the rapid rise and fall of his chest. I would not touch him again for weeks and weeks. I said, "I love you so much."

I listened to the boy's soft snoring until morning, watched how his lips trembled every so often. I thought about how simple things were in a country like Haiti. There were no authorities to notify about my release, not really. In the morning, the police would visit, yes, but I doubted much would come of it. I wasn't going to stay in Haiti one moment longer than I had to. There would be no evidence collected, no trial, no justice and without justice, there was no crime. It was almost a relief. I was no one so nothing happened to me.

When Christophe stirred, I quickly left his room. I did not trust myself to keep it together around him. Michael was still asleep. I looked for my phone, which I hadn't seen in two weeks. I found it next to Michael's on the end table. I sat on the floor and watched him sleep too. He looked older. I imagine I did too.

There were dozens of missed calls and my voice mail was full. I saw several messages from Mona and listened to them. She called me each day I was gone, explaining why she wasn't in Port-au-Prince waiting for me, explaining that our mother and her husband demanded she stay in the States. I listened to her voice and tried to remember the shape of her face. I refused to cry. My hands shook as I dialed her number in Miami. She answered on the first ring.

"Miri, Jesus Christ. I miss you so much."

"Mona," I said, stuttering. "Please come to the airport tomorrow. Please be there."

"Of course, Miri."

"I don't remember anything, Mona. I mean, I do but I don't. I listened to your messages. You didn't forget me."

"Forget you? Honey, you're all we've thought about."

"They abandoned me."

"No one abandoned you. I know you don't believe that, but it's true."

"I'm tired, Mona. I have to go."

"Don't hang up," Mona shouted, but I ended the call.

After a final look at Michael's sleeping form, I took my soiled clothes, the ones I wore for thirteen days, the ones covered in piss and tears and semen and blood I could not wash out even though I tried. They were still damp from the shower. I threw those filthy clothes holding those memories of my body into the fire pit behind my parents' house and watched the clothes smolder.

Eventually, I looked up and saw Michael's silhouette in the light of the fire. He watched over me but left me alone. When all that remained was gray ash, I threw more wood into the pit, watched the flames reach high into the night. I held my hand close to the heat. I knew what it meant to burn, how it felt, how the right amount of heat can make your skin rise and how the pain rises with your skin until it spreads through you and when the pain starts to spread, it becomes easier to endure. I closed my eyes and fell forward but Michael grabbed me by the waist. He pulled me away from the fire. He wrapped his arms around me. I tried to fight his embrace but he was stronger. He whispered into my ear. He said, "No, Mireille. No." He held me as I fought. He gave me someone to fight who wouldn't fight back. He let me fight until I ran out of energy. I did not cry.

We sat on a teak bench next to the pit. I lit a cigarette, offered him one. He accepted even though he doesn't smoke. We stared into the fire. I looked at my left hand, so naked. "They took my wedding ring and my engagement ring."

Michael tried to reach for me but I pulled my hand away before I had to suffer his skin against mine.

"They're just things. I will get you new ones," he said.

"They mattered to me."

"And they mattered to me, but you matter more."

"I fought, especially when he took my rings. I fought."

"Who is he?" Michael came close, close enough for me to feel the warmth of his body. Sorrow pulsed from his skin. "What did they do to you? Tell me. Give me something so I can do something. God, Miri. I want to kill somebody."

The most honest words locked themselves in my throat. I tried to push something out that might make sense but the harder I tried, the more the words twisted themselves into tiny, stubborn knots. I shook my head, covered my mouth.

"I understand," Michael said. "When you're ready, I am here to listen. There's nothing you can't tell me, baby."

"I am never going to be ready, Michael. Not ever." My spine stiffened.

"It must have been terrible."

I turned to look at my husband. "What is it you want to know, Michael? Do you think I don't know what you're asking? If there's something on your mind, just say it."

His features rearranged themselves in new ways. "I want to help you."

My mother has often told me there are some things you cannot tell a man who loves you, things he cannot handle knowing. She adheres to the philosophy that it is secrets rather than openness that strengthen a relationship between a woman and a man. She believes this even though she is an honest person. Honesty, she says, is not always about the truth.

I rubbed my forehead and looked away so I could tell him an honest lie. "It was terrible, Michael but not as terrible as you might think. They certainly did not hesitate to knock me around but other than that, they left me alone in a small, hot room with greasy walls and a narrow bed. They didn't feed me much so I was hungry all the time and I missed you and the baby. My milk dried up. That was the worst of it."

Michael nodded slowly. I waited for him to say something, hoped he would want to believe me enough that we would never have to discuss what happened. The mere thought of telling him the truth made my throat lock up again. There were no words that would make him understand what had happened or what I had become. The necessary vernacular did not exist.

"You have to tell the police something in the morning."

"No, I don't. I have nothing to say to anyone. We are getting our kid out of here."

He threw his hands up. "I won't argue with you. It's probably a waste of time anyway. You know, you haven't cried at all. You can cry if you need to."

"I wasn't waiting for your permission, Michael. I don't need to cry."

I felt him shrinking away. I reached for him and his fingers found mine. I ignored how my skin crawled. I held his hand so tight. When I pulled away he said he was going back to bed, that he was exhausted, and I said I was going to stay outside. I did not want to be surrounded by walls. I couldn't breathe in my father's house. As he walked by, Michael put a heavy hand on my shoulder. I winced. "You didn't have to lie," he said. "You could have just said you're not ready to talk."

I didn't look at him as I sank into the bench. "That's not what you wanted to hear, is it?"

He left but I did not notice. Sometime later, there was rustling in the corner near the kitchen's entrance onto the courtyard. I wrapped my arms around myself and stared into the dark shadows. Slowly, Nadine stepped into the light of the fire. I slid over on the bench and made room for her.

When she sat, I turned to look at her. She had once been beautiful or she still was, only beauty now resided in her features differently. She was nearly as old as my mother, late fifties, her hair streaked with gray, her eyes bright and her eyelids sagging. She should not have still been doing the work of cleaning up after a family like mine.

"I've been a maid for nearly forty years, have worked for five families."

"What you must think of us."

"Some families are better than others. Your mother treats her staff generously," Nadine said.

"That's my mother, generous."

"I have never seen anything like this." Nadine reached for me, grabbed my arm. When I tried to pull away, she held firm. "Your father is not so generous. He should have paid much sooner." She sucked on her teeth. "Much sooner."

Again, the leash around my neck tightened. Beads of sweat broke out across my forehead. It was unnerving to hear someone say what had gone unspoken since my return.

Nadine took my hand between hers. The palms of our hands were soft together. "Kenbe fèm," she said. Hold steady. Stay strong.

She said these words as if strength were still a possibility for me. I was grateful for her words. I knew how far beyond my reach strength was.

꧁꧂ ‖‖‖‖ ‖‖‖‖ ‖‖‖‖
‖‖‖‖ ‖‖‖‖ ‖‖

There was something calming about packing, putting things in order. Order. That's what Michael needed, that and to put some distance between his family and this place. He had always known that something like this would happen. He watched the news. He had eyes. But first, home. They had to get home, their flight left in five hours. Packing was the first step in making that happen. He looked down at his hands, the knuckles raw, nearly bloody. No one had noticed and he was grateful for that.

As Mireille sat on the corner of the bed, staring at the wall, Michael folded their clothes carefully, making neat piles. Fabienne stood in the doorway. Her hair, normally pulled tight in a French twist, hung in loose strands. She twisted her wedding ring back and forth.

"It would be good to stay longer, Mireille. Please talk to your father. We were so worried."

Mireille didn't respond, just kept staring at the wall. Michael paused his folding. It was unnerving, how still his wife sat. He wanted to shake her.

"We are getting out of here," he said brusquely.

Fabienne was undeterred. "I am speaking to my daughter. Stay out of this." More softly, she said, "It would be best to put this incident behind you, Mireille."

Mireille turned to look at her mother, eyes dull. "Incident?"

Michael normally stayed out of Mireille's relationship with her parents. He didn't understand how they worked, how often there was more said in what was not said between his wife and her parents. "Normal families," he once told Mireille after he met her parents, "actually say what they mean and feel." "We're Catholic," she replied, and they laughed. It seemed funny at the time, almost charming.

He looked up from the pile of Christophe's clothes he was folding with strangely timed precision, forcing his hands to work steady. "That is total bullshit. And there is no *out of this* for me. She is my wife. You can't will me away because that would be more convenient for you."

In the before, Mireille would have said Michael's name sharply and he would have understood that American husbands are to be seen and not heard. Mireille said nothing, resumed staring at the wall and began rocking back and forth.

Fabienne frowned, began twisting her ring harder. "Your ordeal is over, Mireille. We can move on from this."

Her clinical vocabulary fascinated Michael—it was like his mother-in-law was talking about a mild inconvenience. This was all madness. He looked at his wife, whose hands were shaking.

"I'm sure you can move on from this," Mireille said, "but I will never move on. I am still where they kept me; I am in that cage."

Mireille ran into the bathroom. There was retching, silence, and more retching. Michael winced, and after the retching stopped, followed his wife. She stood in front of the mirror, holding a pill bottle. She placed one pill on the tip of her tongue and swallowed.

"Are you okay?" Michael asked.

Mireille placed another pill on her tongue, swallowed. "I don't know what the hell I am," she said.

"Babe, what does that mean? I'm really worried."

Mireille finally looked up. "It's like I can't remember my name or my life but . . . I can. I mean, it's all there but I can't quite reach myself. I am so tired."

"We're going home, baby, and we'll get you to the hospital and we'll figure out how to get you better."

She laughed hoarsely. "B-E-T-T-E-R." She studied herself in the mirror for a moment, shook her head, and slid past Michael. "I need some air."

Before she could leave the bedroom, Fabienne took firm hold of Mireille's elbow and pulled her close.

"Let go of me," Mireille snapped.

Fabienne relaxed her grip and traced her daughter's hairline with her fingertips. "You are my youngest daughter. You are loved. I am sorry this happened."

Mireille stared blankly again. "I'm no one's daughter, not anymore."

"Look at me."

Mireille faced her mother.

"You are my child. You hear me? You are mine and you will always be mine and nothing can change that. I made you."

The air was so thick and still. Michael blinked, and he was back on the street, surrounded by armed men. Mireille was being torn from him, Christophe was crying, the horn, the stunned silence as he ran toward the house with his son in his arms, one would help. His headache returned, a sharp and steady pain behind his eyes. He wanted out of Haiti, forever. He wanted away from Mireille's parents, all these people who said one thing and meant another.

"You may have made me but he left me to rot and you let him and now, I am rotten. Your child is all gone," Mireille said.

Michael blinked again and resumed packing though he was done with neat folding. It didn't matter. "We are getting the fuck out of here," he muttered, stuffing the rest of their things into the suitcases.

Fabienne looked past him at Mireille. "Your father loves you very much."

"Don't speak to me about that man and love. What they did to me."

"These kidnappers are businessmen. From what I understand, most of the people who are taken are treated reasonably well."

Enough was enough. Michael threw a shoe against the wall and it left a thick black mark. He pointed at Mireille. "Does she look like she was treated reasonably well? Open your eyes for once in your precious life."

"You should leave this country before they come for you," Mireille said.

"My place is here, with your father." Fabienne faltered. "Mireille, there are things you cannot understand right now but he loves you very much. He loves all of us. He has suffered here as much as anyone."

"That's not how I remember it," Michael said. Mireille turned to look at her husband, and for a moment, he saw a flicker of life, but then her eyes dulled again.

Mireille stood. She looked at Fabienne and Michael. "He didn't come for me. None of you came for me. You all let me rot," she said, and limped out of the room, Michael calling after her, even though he knew his words could not reach her.

Fabienne tried to regain her composure and turned her attention to her son-in-law. "You have no understanding of the world. Don't you dare try to come between my daughter and her family."

Michael snapped the suitcase shut and look a quick look around the room. "With all due respect, Fabienne, you and your husband did that all on your own and if understanding the world means being okay with what my wife has been through, I'm fine not understanding a goddamned thing about it. We're done with this place, forever."

"How American of you, this being done with the birthplace of your wife's parents, as if such a thing were possible."

"You know, Fabienne, being American is feeling pretty good right now. This would have never happened to us in Miami, or anywhere in the States and don't you forget that."

Fabienne closed the distance between them and dug her fingernails into Michael's arm. "I lived more than half my life in the United States. You are being quite selective about the merits of your country and how nice that must be for you, Mr. America."

Michael looked down at his mother-in-law's hand and shook his head. "Thirteen days, and you can stand there and lecture me?"

"You cannot come between us," Fabienne said again, as Michael grabbed the suitcases and stormed out of the room. There was little conviction in her words.

$\cancel{||||}\cancel{||||}\cancel{||||}$
$\cancel{||||}\cancel{||||}|||$

ur goodbyes were formal and impossible. There was a fracture that could never close. I stood near the front door trying
to stay quietly in my rage, trying to control my fear about every
hideous thing that could happen to me, my husband, my child,
between my parents' home and the airport. My mother held
Christophe for a very long time, pressing the palm of her hand
against his face as if she were trying to memorize his features
with her skin. My father stood next to her with his hand firmly
against the small of her back. He would not look me in the eye
but he stood tall. My father always stands tall.

I tried to remember how much I once loved that man. I
couldn't. All I could see in his face were thirteen days spent
in the company of seven men who undid me. His pride burned
everything good between us and he stood, defiant still, letting
me choke on his ashes.

My mother looked so small standing next to my father. I wanted to reach across the raw fracture but the way she stood next to him, the way she fit her body against his was more than I could forgive. We kissed lightly, once on each cheek, and she handed Christophe to Michael. I leaned into her and I whispered, "I love you," because I did not want that to go unsaid, not after everything. There was a fracture between us but for my mother and me it was not impassable. She grabbed my hand as I turned away, squeezing tightly. She took a long time to let go. She said, "You will survive this." I had never known her to be an optimist.

I said nothing to my father. My father said nothing to me. His will is absolute and mine had become absolute too. Michael said nothing to anyone but I knew what he was thinking and I loved him for it. Our bags were brought to the car. As we walked out, my father cleared his throat. He called my name but I didn't look back. He called my name again, louder. I tell myself I heard desperation in his voice. I may have heard what I wanted to hear. I kept walking even though each step hurt more than the one before it. Michael and I sat in the backseat behind two armed men, with our child between us. I wanted my father to run after us, to try to explain himself, to tell me he loved me, to tell me anything at all, but he didn't. He simply called out my name as if that were the *grande geste* I needed from him.

As we approached the airport, all I could see was the swarm of dark, sweaty bodies shouting, reaching, shouting, reaching. I worried one of my kidnappers, maybe more, were there, waiting to take me again, waiting to extract more ransom, more penance where there was none to give, waiting to end me as they already should have. There's no one you can trust in a country run through with anger.

We pulled up to the terminal and I grabbed Michael's arm as he moved to open the door. "Wait."

"Why? I want to get us the hell out of here."

"It's not safe." I looked around nervously. Strange faces kept peering into the car, trying to see through the dark tint covering the back windows. I donned a large pair of dark sunglasses. I tried to ignore the shock of pain running through me, my God, the constancy of it. "It's not safe," I said again. I fumbled through my purse for the painkillers and swallowed three, dry, and waited to feel something like numb.

The men in the front seat turned around but Michael waved them off. He nodded affably, moved to stroke my arm but stopped himself. "We can sit here all day if we need. We have air-conditioning." He looked down at Christophe, who was sleeping. "And the baby is sleeping so he won't even know the difference." Michael smiled and this time I recognized him, my husband from the before.

I leaned back and closed my eyes, sank into the leather seat, waited and waited and waited to stop feeling the pain between my thighs and in my heart and in my back and in my head. Slowly, the bruises loosened and the world muffled. It was more difficult to focus. I spoke slowly but my words were slurred. "I think we can go now."

Michael nodded and tapped one of the armed men on the shoulder. The driver opened my door and helped me out of the car. I steadied myself against his arm. His jacket opened. There was a holstered gun, nestled against his rib cage. I wanted a gun for myself, one that would never be pointed at me or thrust in me, one I could hold. Michael carried Christophe and we walked behind the security guard, who cleared a path. I tried to keep my head down. I tried not to hear or see or feel. I ignored the stares, and what those people were thinking, what they could see written on my body. We were quickly ushered through the diplomatic check-in area. I was still my father's daughter even though I was no longer my father's daughter.

When it came time to pass through security I stopped just before the metal detectors as I watched one of the security agents giving a passenger a vigorous pat-down. "I can't do this."

Michael, a few steps ahead of me, paused, turned around. "What do you mean?"

"If they have to pat me down, I will die, again, Michael."

He looked at his watch. "We have to go, babe. You'll be fine."

"I will die," I said, quietly.

"If I did not think you could handle this, I would try and figure something else out, but you will be fine. This is the last terrible thing, I promise."

"You have no fucking idea what I will be," I snapped. "And you have no business making promises." Every time I spoke to him I said something I regretted, but I had so little kindness left in me and no patience at all.

Christophe stirred then settled again against his father's chest. I wanted to hold my child so badly I could feel it in my arms, how the weight of his small body always fit against me but then I thought of the me I had become touching that child and I took a step away from Michael.

"I want to understand why this will be hard for you," Michael said, "but I also know this is the only way home."

"Home." I shook my head. "I hate you," I said, instantly regretting the words but I walked right past him holding my passport and my plane ticket. As I walked through the metal detector I shook so hard my elbow accidentally brushed against the side and the sensor beeped. I glared at Michael through the detector and he looked down, his face red.

"Madame," one of the security agents said, lifting his arms, motioning what I should do. I held up a hand, said, "Please, let me just walk through again."

He shook his head, said something about security protocols. I wanted to laugh. No one in that country knew anything about security. The agent stepped toward me and I shrank. Michael tried to walk through the detector but the man with the wand held his hand up.

"She's my wife," Michael said. "She needs my help."

The security agent pretended not to understand English. He turned to me and raised his arms again. I tried to find the words to explain to him that I could not be touched, that if he touched me I would shatter and I would die more and I would never find my way home. I faced Michael and stared at him as I raised my arms, slowly. The muscles were sore, stiff. I looked at my wrist, still raw and abraded. There was so little left of my skin.

Michael nodded and half-smiled. "Mireille, look at me. You're going to be fine."

I wanted him to stop saying that; the way he lingered on the *f* with such confidence, it was just too much. The security agent stood in front of me, tried to block my view. I looked past him. I looked into Michael's blue eyes. I wanted to tell my husband I was still so in love with him, that despite everything I knew that to be true. The security agent smirked and set his wand down. I could smell his spite. Men like him do well in such positions of impotent authority. I was close enough to claw his eyes out, to dig my fingers into his eye sockets, to pull those soft, pulpy masses away from his skull, to tear at the fibrous bundles connecting his eyes to the rest of him since he was so clearly incapable of seeing the state I was in. My arms trembled but I stood my ground. I surprised myself. I had a little fight left. He started at my wrists, pressing my body between his hands. His hands were sweaty, calloused.

The floor tilted as he patted down my chest, pressing his hands too long, too hard against my breasts, so very sore. I whimpered as quietly as I could. I bit my lower lip until I tasted blood. The security agent's hands slid lower. It was getting difficult to keep count of the men who had no right to my body taking liberties. The agent crouched to the ground and leered up at me. I ignored him. He pressed my ankles between his hands, my calves between his hands, my thighs between his hands. The agent's hands were a blade, peeling me apart, slowly separating what remained of me. I felt everything. I looked into Michael's eyes. The leash around my neck was so tight, the ringing in my ears so loud that my world reduced itself to nothing.

"Look at me," my husband said again. He was eerily calm. It would be months before I understood he had no choice, that he had a singular purpose that day, to get me home, to make me safe. Christophe blinked slowly and yawned, waking up; my son smiled at me. I tried to return his smile but could not. Fresh bile bubbled in my throat.

When he was finished, the security agent returned my ticket and passport. Michael walked through the metal detector without incident and glared at the agent as he retrieved the stroller, our carry-ons. We sat at the gate and Michael tried to talk to me, to reach me but I was no longer there, I was no one again, surrounded by strangers, sitting next to the husband and child of another woman. On the plane, I recognized almost everyone in the first-class cabin. They stared and whispered. I hid behind my sunglasses. The plane took off and I stared out the window at the sparkling ocean. Nowhere is Haiti more beautiful than from high in the sky.

After a time, the captain turned off the seat belt sign. I stood and stepped into the aisle.

Michael moved to follow me. "Where are you going?"

"The bathroom. What are you, the hall monitor?"

He sat back down. "I am just trying to help."

"Leave me alone if you really want to help."

He ignored me, said, "I'll be here, waiting."

I sighed, so tired, so sick of everything. "We're on an airplane. Honestly, where else would you be, Michael?" I walked away.

In the cramped bathroom I stared at the stranger in the mirror. I was taken aback by the weight I had lost. My clothes hung from my body like they belonged to a woman twice my size. The wide streak of silver seemed even brighter. I filled the small metal sink with water and washed my face and my hands. I wanted to wash my entire body again. I was never going to get clean. I tried to count the number of hours between that moment and when I could take a shower in my own bathroom. There were too many. I dabbed water against my dry lips and sat down on the toilet. I leaned forward and tried to forget about the leash around my neck or the walls of the bathroom closing in on me. There was knock at the door.

"Baby?"

"What?

"Are you okay?"

"No, Michael, I am not."

"Open the door."

I ignored my husband. I counted to one hundred. After the first week, I started to believe my release was imminent so I played counting games. I thought, "I will count to one thousand and then I will be free." I counted over and over again and hours would pass and I counted more. I paced the length of my cage and counted. I counted the number of cars that sped by while the sun was out. I counted how many of them were playing the radio loudly. I counted the cracks in the walls and ceiling. The Commander or TiPierre came and used me and I counted through that, the number of thrusts, the number of times they ran their hands or tongues over my body, the number of times TiPierre told me something unbearable and romantic, the number of times he slid his tongue between my lips, the number of times the Commander ran his knife across my back or held his burning cigarette between my thighs, elsewhere. When they were done, I started counting again, how long until they returned. I counted to one thousand in the hopes that in so many moments, I would be free. I lost track of the number of times and the number of banalities and indignities I counted.

Michael knocked again, louder this time. "Open the door, baby."

I counted to ten and slowly opened the door. He stepped inside. It was the two of us in a viciously small space. A small cry escaped my lips. I looked around frantically. Michael looked at me, confused. The shaking started again. I tried to fold myself into myself so no parts of our bodies were touching but it was impossible. I knew he was my husband but I did not know. He was a man.

"Don't hurt me," was all I could say.

He looked stricken. He held his hands behind his back. "I could never hurt you. I just wanted to check on you."

I stepped back toward the toilet. There really was no room. I wondered how I might tear through the walls. I held my hands in front of my body. I no longer recognized Michael.

"Don't hurt me," I said again. "Whatever you do to me, don't hurt me." Surrender was all I had left.

Suddenly it all became too much, being trapped in too finite a space, a cage, with a man, any man, the security agent, my father, the rise of my skin beneath heat, the rise of my body beneath seven men for thirteen days, everything broken inside of me, the wail of the horn, the ringing in my ears, the leash around my neck, the cries of my child as I was torn away from everything I love. My knees buckled. I fell into a quiet place where I felt nothing.

Everything was silent and suddenly there was a rush of noise, muffled, and stale air. I opened my eyes, and slowly realized I was in Michael's arms as he pressed a cool cloth to my forehead. I looked around and could see the aisle to my right and the closed cockpit door to my left. My face flushed brightly. I sat up quickly, too quickly and grabbed Michael to steady myself.

"This is embarrassing."

"Shhh," Michael said. "This is nothing of the sort."

"Where is the baby?"

Michael smiled tightly. "He's fine; one of the flight attendants is looking after him. He's charming her to death."

"I would like to not be on the floor anymore."

He pushed me forward, carefully, then stood and helped me to my feet. I wobbled but he held me firmly. He would not let me fall. As we walked the few steps to our seats he said, "You need to eat something and we're going to the hospital as soon as we land."

I shook my head so hard it made me dizzy. "I'm not putting myself through that. It is not going to happen."

"Okay, okay. One thing at a time."

"One thing, my ass, Michael."

"Mireille, you are in no condition to make decisions for yourself right now. We are going to the hospital and that's that."

I shook my head. I would run when we entered the terminal. I would run away. He could not make me go to any hospital. I said nothing.

Michael helped me into my seat, fastened my seat belt, and soon a flight attendant brought me a meal. I ignored her pity as she handed me the small tray. I sank into the seat. It was so overwhelming to understand what was required of me. I looked out the window at the thick whorls of cloud surrounding us. Michael excused himself and returned quickly with our boy.

"Eat something," he said, nudging the steaming tray toward me.

I kept looking out the window. "I don't know how."

I heard the sound of plastic being removed, smelled something that seemed like food. I did not want to eat. I did not want anything inside me.

"I'll help," Michael said.

I sat quietly and let him feed me because I was too tired to protest. I didn't care about the other passengers murmuring and staring. I simply opened my mouth when he told me and chewed when he told me and swallowed when he told me and sipped when he told me. I tasted nothing, felt nothing, was nothing.

||||| ||||| |||||
||||| ||||| ||||

Even though there were camera flashes going off and so much shouting, so many bodies wanting something from me, I knew Mona was near. There is a secret language between sisters who are close. After we made it through customs, a gaggle of reporters waited, shouting questions, wanting to know what happened, if I would ever return to Haiti and on and on. I had no answers. All I saw was the red of their lips and open mouths, the whites of their teeth, how they swarmed around us, trying to trap me in a new cage.

Michael covered Christophe's head with a blanket and I clutched his arm, hiding behind my sunglasses as we made our way to baggage claim. I did not answer their questions. I said nothing. I simply stared at the ground, tried to count how many steps it would take to get out of the airport, to get home, to get away. When a reporter got too close, Michael growled, literally growled. I felt the tension in his arm, how he was coiled, ready to lash out at anything. We were both feral now.

Mona was standing by the luggage carousel with her husband. I saw her, my sister, the keeper of my secrets, and I let go of Michael's arm and walked toward her. I thought, "If I can get to my sister, I will feel better, I will feel alive." I counted the steps. Mona smiled, tried to hug me but I flinched, shook my head. She nodded, said, "Let's walk." We began moving toward the deserted end of the terminal. Michael tried to follow but Mona waved him away. As we walked, I stared at the small groups of people on the curb waiting for loved ones to pick them up. We sat near an empty carousel that was still revolving slowly. I held the arms of the chair as I lowered myself, wincing softly.

"I'm glad you're home, Miri. I cannot begin to know what you've been through but you are alive. We will fix this."

A sharp pain shot through my heart. I grabbed my chest. I tried to find the words to explain to my sister that I was not alive, that the sister she remembered was dead. A man wearing a blue jumpsuit walked past us pushing a loud floor buffer. We watched him and sat silently for a long while.

"It should have been me. I'm the one who's in the motherland all the time. I wish it had been me," Mona finally said.

I turned to face her. "Don't. Do not say that. This shouldn't happen to anyone."

Mona gently traced a bruise on my right cheek. Her touch was so gentle it made me think she could wipe all my bruises away. "You look fucking terrible, kid."

"He took thirteen days to pay for me, Mona. Thirteen days. He abandoned me." I tried to breathe but the memory of a pair

of strong hands wrapped around my throat made it nearly impossible. I gripped the arm of my chair.

My sister sucked the air sharply. She nodded. "I know. There's
nothing I can say to make this right. I don't understand how this
happened."

I grabbed her arm, gripping her tightly. "Don't ever go back
there. Promise me. They'll take you too and they will hurt you
in ways you cannot imagine."

Mona covered my hand with hers. "Oh honey. We are going to
get you through this."

I looked toward the other end of the terminal, where Michael
stood with Christophe and Carlito, surrounded by our baggage.
"I want you to promise me something."

"Anything, Miri. Anything."

"If something happens to me, don't let the child forget who
his mother was. You're his godmother, and if I can't . . . If I cannot take care of him, be the mother he deserves."

Mona took my hand between both of hers and brought it to
her lips. Her touch was soft. It was nice, in that moment, to
smell her and feel the warmth of her skin and to hear her voice.
"Don't talk like that. You are safe now."

"There's no such thing as safe," I snapped. "Just promise me
you could love that boy like he was your own if I needed you to."

She slid closer to me, pulled me into her arms even though
I resisted at first, even though her touch made my skin crawl
and my body shudder. Mona kissed the top of my head. "I already do love your son like that, you know I do." I had no fight
left. I stopped trying to pull away and let my sister hold me. I
wrapped my arms around her, my body curving into hers the

way it always had, like we were two halves of one whole. I did
not cry but I held on, so very tightly.

In the car, Michael said, "We're going to the hospital," but he
was less confident than before.

I grabbed the car door as we sped along. "I will throw myself
out of this car if you do not take me directly home."

Michael gripped the steering wheel tighter and I opened the
door, wind buffeting us. He reached across my body and pulled
the door shut, cursing. "Jesus Christ, Miri."

"I am not going to the hospital. If you drive me there, I will
run and you will never see me again, so you decide."

"Fine," Michael grumbled. "We'll go home for now."

When we pulled into the driveway, Michael shut off the car
and said, "We're here."

I choked on something sharp. There was no place where I
belonged. "I don't have a home anymore," I said, dully.

He reached for me and I shrank away, jumped out of the car,
and walked to the edge of the driveway, listening to the sprin-
klers quietly watering our lawn.

The house was quiet, the air stale, when we finally made
it inside. Christophe was asleep in his father's arms and Michael took the baby to his room, got him settled. I went to the
kitchen, reached in the third ceramic jar next to the stove where
I stashed cigarettes. I poured myself a tall glass of gin, dropped
in a few ice cubes, watched as they sank and slowly rose back to
the surface.

Out on the lanai, gray wisps of smoke slowly rose up around
me. I held my drink against my forehead and wished for the leash
around my neck to loosen. I drank my gin slow and steady until

there was only a thin sliver of ice rolling around the bottom of the glass. I lay back on the chaise longue, enjoying the numbness in my face. For the first time in a long time, nothing hurt. I rolled onto my side and curled into a tight ball. It was a warm night, only a light breeze. Every once in a while, the leaves from the palm trees above rustled softly. There was a time when the sound made me smile. It was nice to be outside, to be free from walls, to be out of a cage. I felt like the smallest little thing beneath the great Florida sky. The leash loosened. I could breathe again.

The pale light of morning sun woke me. I shivered. A blanket covered me so I pulled it tightly. Michael lay in the chaise next to mine, clutching a baby monitor in his hand. "Today is Tuesday," I thought. I ached even though I was dead.

I reached over and shook Michael awake. He stirred slowly. "What are you doing out here?" I asked, softly, as if I didn't want to wake him up too much.

He rubbed his face, the morning stubble making a scratchy sound. "You were here."

I held my hand against his shoulder. I didn't trust myself to do anything more. "I'm going to get ready."

"For what?"

"It's Tuesday. I have to go to work."

Michael looked at me like I had lost my mind. I did not appreciate it. "That's completely insane, Mireille."

"Don't you call me crazy, Michael Scott Jameson. Work is the only thing I know how to do right now."

He gaped as I walked away. I heard him muttering, "Don't act crazy, then."

I took a long, hot shower, grateful for American plumbing, and dressed carefully, trying to choose clothes that would mask the evidence of my *ordeal*—a long-sleeved white blouse and gray slacks. My clothes were very loose. I tried to cover the bruises on my face as best I could. I never was good at applying makeup, usually relied on Mona or a girlfriend to make me prettier when an occasion called for it. Michael paced the bedroom as I dressed, making idle threats. I ignored him. I had a job, one I was good at. At work, things would make sense.

When I finished dressing, I turned to Michael, who stood in the bedroom doorway, his large body filling the frame. I tried not to panic. I forced myself to smile. "How do I look?"

Michael shook his head. "You look like shit and completely exhausted. Babe, be reasonable. I can't allow you to go to work."

I stood across from my husband, and tried to raise myself to my full height, which is not much. Fortunately, I was wearing heels. "Allow me?"

He shut the bedroom door and it suddenly became harder to breathe. A thin sheen of sweat spread across my chest, my blouse clinging to my body.

"What are you doing?" I asked, my throat dry.

"I am doing what's best for you," Michael said.

My hands started shaking and I looked around the room for something, anything, tried to assess how I could protect myself and make my way out of this new cage.

Michael held his hands out to me. "You're in no condition to go to work. We are going to the hospital, and together, we will start to figure out what we need to do to get you better."

I held on to the wall behind me. "I've fucking told you about the hospital. Shut up about it, already." I looked down at my feet. "Please get out of my way."

He crossed his arms across his chest, stood his ground. He was a bully.

"I basically spent the past two weeks," I said, my breath coming faster and faster, "locked in a cage, and you're seriously going to try and keep me trapped in my own house?"

Michael snapped. "You wouldn't have been in that situation if we weren't in that hellhole in the first place but you had to drag us down there when we could have gone anywhere else for vacation."

I was stunned. "How soon the truth comes out. You blame me for being kidnapped." I bit my lower lip and nodded. "That's rich. Wow."

We were silent for several moments.

"I'm sorry," Michael said. "I didn't mean it like that, not at all. I just want to get you looked at. Miri, you look terrible."

"So you've said but that is beside the point. You cannot trap me in this room."

"I'm not trapping you, Mireille. I am trying to help you."

I looked to our bedroom window, two stories up. Below, there were hedges, Bermuda grass, too long. I raised my head and looked Michael in the eye. "You know me well enough to know I will throw myself right out that window if you don't get out of my way." I pounded the wall. "You can't keep me locked up."

"I am not locking you up," Michael said. "I am keeping you safe." The calm confidence in his voice enraged me.

"You know nothing about keeping me safe. You showed me that the day I was taken, too, so don't sit there and lecture me on something you know nothing about."

Michael gasped, his face darkening. "That is incredibly unfair. You don't know what I went through. Even you said I was taken too. Come on."

"What you went through?" I said. "What you went through. Please spare me how hard this is for you right now. Please." I ran to the window and opened it, looked down at the ground, did not care how far I might fall. I needed to be out of that room with the closed door and the walls that threatened to fall in on me and the man I barely recognized, the man who could hurt me. Michael rushed to me, gathering me as gently as he could in his arms, my back to his chest.

"Don't do that," he whispered into my hair.

I kicked wildly. "Put me down," I shouted, even though my voice was ragged, hoarse, and not very loud at all. "Get your hands off me." I gasped, trying to swallow air. A loud ringing filled my head. If Michael didn't let me out of the room, I was going to lose it completely. I tried to figure out what he wanted from me, what I needed to say for him to let me go, for me to open the door, for me to get away. I started babbling. I don't even know what I said.

When I had worn myself all the way out, Michael said, "I am going to let you go if you promise not to do anything crazy."

I nodded, went limp in his arms.

Michael loosened his grip a little but didn't let me go. "Promise?"

"I promise," I said. "I can't leave the house. I understand."

"Do you?" Michael asked. I nodded again. He let go of me and turned me around. "We need to get you examined, and then we can figure out how and when for you to get back to work. You need time and doctors and . . . time."

I wanted to tell Michael he had no idea what I needed because I had no idea what I needed. I looked at the door to my right. It was only a few steps away, no more than ten feet. I was fast, or I had once been fast. I was faster than Michael with his big, corn-fed body that lumbered when he ran. He was still too close. He had long arms. I had to be smart. I was no one. I could do anything.

I reached up and pressed my hand against his cheek, stood on the tips of my toes, kissed his chin. "I don't know what I was thinking," I said. "I guess I just want to feel normal."

Michael's shoulders dropped. He covered my hand with his, rubbing his thumb across my knuckles. "Of course you do, and you will."

I took a step back and then another. "I should change before we go," I said. "Work clothes aren't hospital clothes." I tried to smile. "What are hospital clothes anyway?"

Michael nodded, forced himself to laugh, and went to sit on the edge of the bed. As soon as his knees bent, I ran for the door. I ran even though it hurt so much I nearly burst into tears. Michael lunged after me. My hands were still shaking as I fumbled with the doorknob and flung the door open, letting a rush of cool air into the room. Finally, I could breathe a little. I ran into the hallway and down the stairs, Michael thundering after me, shouting my name. I ran into the kitchen to find my keys and Marisol, our nanny, was standing near the microwave, holding Christophe. Michael plowed into the room after me, and stopped.

I smoothed my hair, tried to appear normal or what I remembered as normal. "Good morning, Marisol."

"Mireille," she said, nervously. "It's good to see you. I am glad you're home safe. I was so worried."

I forced myself to smile wide. "I am fine."

"Shouldn't you have breakfast?" Michael asked, his voice strained, clearly trying to salvage the situation without making a scene.

Christophe stared at us from Marisol's arms, looking from Michael to me and back to Michael, his mouth open in a little O. The keys were sitting on the edge of the counter. Michael and I looked at them as if we were each willing the keys toward us.

"You should sit and eat," Michael said. "Your clothes are hanging off you."

I was the kind of hungry I did not know was possible but in its way, the hunger felt good. It was a comfort to be so empty. I had to hold on to that emptiness.

I straightened my clothes. "I don't want to sit because right now sitting hurts and I don't want to swallow food because right now swallowing hurts. Do I need to explain why or will you take me at my word?"

Michael reddened. "Mireille, don't do this. We will go to the hospital and come home, and you can get some rest."

Marisol began patting Christophe on his back. She looked as uncomfortable as I felt. "I should take him for a walk," she said.

I limped to the end of the counter, grabbed my keys, and was so flushed with relief when I wrapped my fingers around them, I could hardly stay standing. "I am going to work," I said. "Today is Tuesday."

As I ran out of the house, Christophe started crying and Michael kept shouting my name over and over.

I drove out of the neighborhood and followed the familiar route to my office, the steering wheel slick against my sweaty hands. Nothing seemed familiar. It was quiet in the parking garage as I pulled into my space. I took a deep breath and studied the distance between my car and the elevator entrance. I calculated everything that might happen to me over that short distance. I opened my car door and planted one foot, then the other on the ground. I stood and closed the door softly behind me. A car slowly drove by and headed for the exit. I straightened my spine and tried to keep moving toward the elevator. I began sweating everywhere, my blouse clinging to my body. When I reached the elevator, it slowly hissed open but I couldn't bring myself to step inside, to put myself in a cage from which there was no escape. I slowly backed away, then turned on my heel and ran back to my car.

I didn't stop shaking until I was safely locked inside. I refused to look at myself in the rearview mirror. I couldn't go to work. I couldn't go home. I could drive, though. I drove to I-75 and I drove out of Miami. I kept on driving until I stopped seeing palm trees.

‖‖‖ ‖‖‖ ‖‖‖
‖‖‖ ‖‖‖ ‖‖‖

Georgia was tacky billboards—porn stores and fruit stands and Asian massage parlors and cheap hotels. It was dark as I neared Atlanta, sprawling strip malls and chain stores stretching into skyscrapers. I knew Michael would be terrified, livid. I did not want him to worry for me, for someone who was nothing. I wanted to call him to explain but I had no explanation so I sent him a text message that I was fine, that I loved him and I kept driving.

In Chattanooga, I got a room at a Holiday Inn Express. I put the DO NOT DISTURB sign on the doorknob and pushed a chair in front of the door and set one of the water glasses on the narrow arm so I would hear it fall if someone tried to enter the room. I saw that in a movie once.

There were ten voice mail messages on my phone and twice as many text messages. I texted Michael I had stopped for the

night and was safe and said I couldn't come home and I loved
him and was sorry so very sorry. He texted back, "UNAC-
CEPTABLE. I AM FREAKING OUT." I typed, "I am too," and
turned my phone off. I pulled the curtains shut and sat on the
bed, emptying my purse to take inventory of what I had with
me—painkillers and Valium, a tampon, a pen with the name
of my law firm engraved on the side, an iPod and headphones,
three different shades of lipstick, a half-wrapped stick of gum,
a Leatherman tool, an envelope with family photos we had taken
at the mall as a joke, in the before, a hairbrush, my wallet. I had
enough to start over. I took out one of the pictures of Michael,
the baby, and I sitting in front of cheesy sunset backdrop, my
husband and I grinning like idiots and curling our fingers into
gang signs. I remembered taking the picture. As the flash went
off, Michael shouted, "WESTSIDE!" I removed my shoes and
set them neatly next to the bed and slid beneath the cover. I fell
asleep holding the picture of my family to my chest, trying to
pull the best parts of us inside me.

The hotel room phone rang in the middle of the night. The
sound startled me, covered me in a cold sweat. When the ringing
wouldn't stop, I answered but didn't say anything.

"You are in Chattanooga."

A wave of nausea made me lean forward. I heaved. The Commander had found me. I couldn't think. I didn't know what to
say. "Who is this?" I whispered. "How did you find me?"

"Mireille? It's Michael, your husband, who is losing his mind
wondering what the hell is going on."

"Michael?"

"Yes. Of course it's Michael. Please tell me you understand
why I am freaking out."

"I understand."

"I am coming to get you."

"No . . . no," I stuttered. "I am not fit to be around other people. I am an animal. Just forget me, Michael." I needed him to understand I was dead. I needed him to bury me, move on.

"Of course you are fit to be around me. You are my wife, Mireille."

"I can't do this. Forget about me."

"We are not having this conversation."

"You're right," I said. I hung up. I quickly returned my earlier inventory to my purse and checked out. I texted Michael I was leaving Chattanooga. I went to an ATM and took out five hundred dollars. I got back on the interstate and drove.

Tennessee had mountains, the interstate curving through them with jagged walls of rock on either side. I hit a wall in Kentucky where the land flattened and there was little to see.

I was driving and suddenly I found myself swerving across the road. A truck's horn blared. I remembered the blaring of the car horn on the day I was kidnapped, Michael's bleeding and broken head on the steering wheel, Christophe in his car seat, his eyes wide, his lower lip trembling, and me trying to reach them, trying to hold on to them, having no choice but to be taken away while countless people stood, silently, watched, did nothing to stop any of it. I couldn't breathe. I started sweating again, muttering the word *no* over and over. I pulled off at the next rest area a few miles ahead, made sure the doors were locked, and climbed into the backseat, where I curled into myself. I swallowed a handful of pills and tried to sleep, trying to sink into nothing, tried not to feel or remember my life before, or what happened when I was taken, when no one came for me. The windows quickly fogged. My breathing slowed. I was cold, couldn't stop shivering. I clutched my phone in my hand, wanted so badly to call someone but I was not sure who would want to hear from me.

I called home. When Michael answered, I said, "I am so tired," and he said, "I know baby, just tell me where you are baby. I'll come get you." Baby, baby, baby. He said that word so many times. "I want to listen to you breathe," I said. "Let me listen to you breathe." I held the phone, hot and sticky against my ear, listening to my husband breathe. That's how I fell asleep, pretending we were in the before, pretending I could still sleep next to him without being choked by terror.

A loud rapping on the window woke me. I sat up quickly, disoriented, cold. My phone fell off the seat. I picked it up, held it to my ear. There was no sound. I pressed a few buttons. The battery was dead. Again, the loud rapping. I wiped condensation from the window and saw a highway patrol officer staring down at me. He motioned for me to get out of the car. I was paralyzed. The rest area was deserted. I was alone. The sky was dark gray, nearly morning.

"Move it," the officer said, his voice muffled.

I straightened my clothing and got out of the car carefully. I stared at my feet, shoved my hands in my pockets, my hair falling into my face.

The officer pointed to a nearby sign. "No overnights allowed."

I nodded, stepped away from him, slid along the car toward the hood.

He grabbed my shoulder and I whimpered as his fingers gripped my broken skin. "Where do you think you're going?"

I looked up and his eyes widened. "I just stopped to rest before heading on. I'll be on my way," I said, carefully.

"I'm going to need to see some ID."

I had ID, a plastic card with the picture of the woman I used to be bearing her name and age, hair color, eye color, height and weight. She is an organ donor. She is supposed to wear glasses when she drives. I reached into the car for my wallet, my hands shaking as I pulled my license out. I handed it to the officer and stared at my feet, wanting to create some kind of distance between his body and mine, between how he could hurt me and how hurt I already was. I hoped he wouldn't notice that the license belonged to another woman. He read the relevant information into a radio attached to his shoulder.

As he waited for the dispatcher to get back to him, he said, "You don't look so good; you look like you've been knocked around a heck of a lot. Do you need to go to a shelter?" There was a slight twang in his voice. He had kind eyes.

I was still afraid of what he might do to me. He could throw me over the hood of my car and tear my clothes off. He could drag me behind the rest area or into one of the bathrooms. He could force me to my knees. He could make me put my mouth on him. He could take me in the backseat of his car. He could use his gun or nightstick and try to reshape my body in new and crueler ways. He could gut me or shove me in the trunk of his patrol car and take me into the deep Kentucky woods. There was nothing left for him to take from me but there were a great many things he could do. For the rest of my life, I would always calculate the worst possibilities of being alone with any man but my husband. I would always be prepared.

I held my arms across my chest. I said, "I'm fine." I said, "Please don't hurt me." Those four words were my mantra; they would be for years as I came to terms with my fragility, how weak we really are.

Warbled speech filtered from the radio. The officer said something back, handed me my license. He stepped closer. I bit my lower lip, closed my eyes tightly, shrank away from him as best I could. I prepared to fight. There was a pattern of oil stains beneath my feet. I stared at the oil, how it spread away from me and toward the curb. My blood, I thought, would spread in a similar pattern, would spread thin and wide. Eventually it would fade or it would burn beneath the slow rising sun.

"Is there someone I can call?"

It was so hard to hold on to names, to remember who I was and whom I belonged to and what I tried to erase and who I had become. I wanted to tell the patrol officer there was a man, a tall country boy with pretty shoulders who moved to the big city just to follow me, that this man was good and true and sang to our child while he changed diapers and danced with me even though he had no moves and was waiting for me, worried, needing to find me. I finally looked up at the officer. I said, "No, there's no one you can call."

The officer tugged on the brim of his hat and returned to his car. My knees went weak. I gripped my car, then quickly got back behind the wheel, locked the door. He sat in his car staring at me for a long time. I waited for him to leave first. I did not want him to follow me. He was a man. He was dangerous. I was not safe. When I got back on the interstate I continued heading west, until I was surrounded by endless acres of corn, the stalks standing tall and green.

stood at the base of the stairs leading up to the farmhouse. The white paint was chipped in places, flaking or hanging loose. I made a note to tell Michael so we could make a trip out to repaint. It was a hot July afternoon, the air heavy with moisture. In the distance, cows lowed softly. I could not outrun the heat no matter where I was. I sweated and waited without knowing what I was waiting for. My body was stiff and sore. I drove for so long, barely stopped save for gas and going to the bathroom, didn't want to have to leave my car or be where people could hurt me. I just wanted to get somewhere safe.

Michael's mother, Lorraine, appeared in the screen door, holding a dish towel in her hand. She tucked the towel into the waist of her pants and stepped outside. She did not look surprised.

"Miri, I am glad you are here. You were done wrong. You were done real wrong," Lorraine said. "The older I get the less the world makes sense."

"I couldn't stay at home and I didn't know where else to go," I whispered. "I'm sorry I didn't call." My legs felt heavy but they were the only things holding me to the world. I sank slowly to the steps.

"Don't be silly." Lorraine pulled a pack of cigarettes from her pocket. She always kept them in a vinyl cigarette pouch with a gold clasp. She lit a cigarette and offered the open pouch to me.

I took a cigarette. "You shouldn't be smoking," I said, lamely.

Lorraine sat close but not too close. There were yellow bags under her eyes. She was thinner, her skin hanging looser on her bones. We had that in common. "I'm not going to deny myself with whatever time I have left," she said.

I rolled my cigarette between my fingers. A few scraps of tobacco fell out of the end, slowly drifting to my leg. I lit my cigarette and held the burning end close to the palm of my hand. There was a comfort to the focus of the heat, a familiarity. I held the burning end of the cigarette closer. The pain calmed me as the burn traveled along the lines etched into my palm.

"Don't do that," Lorraine said, softly.

I shrugged, stopped, and took a long drag on the cigarette.

"I expect you'll be staying awhile."

I shrugged again.

"You've got my boy going crazy with worry. I am going to tell him you're here. They need you, my boy and your boy. We all do. I can tell by the look of you Michael has no idea how wrong you were done but you're going to have to find your way out of wherever you are for you and for them."

I pressed my lips together tightly but stared ahead. Lorraine stood, dropped her cigarette to the ground, stubbing it out with her shoe. The extinguishing sound made my skin crawl. "We'll be having dinner in a couple hours." She turned, then paused. "You are welcome here." Just like that, she was gone, the screen door slamming behind her.

Later, Michael's father rumbled near the front door, asking, "How long is she going to stay out there? We should get her to a doctor. She doesn't look good at all."

"She'll be out there as long as she needs," Lorraine said, calmly.

Night fell slowly, the dark sky holding itself closer and closer to the earth, almost within reach. The air chilled. In the house, the television was on, a sitcom with a laugh track. I couldn't move. My body still felt so heavy and yet so hollow. The night grew darker, colder. The screen door opened.

Someone neared and I shrank into myself as much as possible; I willed myself to disappear.

"It is just me, child," Lorraine said.

I lowered my head and nodded. She draped a wool blanket around my shoulders and this time sat right next to me.

"Look at me."

I refused, just stared down at my feet.

"I spoke to Michael."

The mere mention of his name made my heart contract. I missed his face and his voice and how, in the before, he held me like an extension of him.

"He is ready to jump on the next plane."

I shook my head violently, struggled to breathe, my throat closing.

"Calm down. It took some doing but I got him to sit still. You have some time to find yourself out of wherever you are right now."

Her kindness, the unexpectedness of it, was more than I could bear. Before I realized what I was doing, I leaned into her now-narrow frame. She held me and kissed the top of my head. I didn't cry, and I didn't speak and Lorraine didn't speak. We just sat there. I remembered, for a small moment, what being safe felt like. I longed for my own mother but she was not safe and could not nor would not keep me safe.

I woke up screaming. My throat was still raw, torn, but I had become accustomed to that discomfort. I had become accustomed to many discomforts. Lorraine ran to my room, Michael's room, Glen right behind her with his twenty-gauge cocked and ready. I sat up in Michael's childhood bed, unable to remember where I was, unable to find the light switch, unable to understand anything around me. I couldn't remember my name. That was all my life seemed to be in the after, trying to orient and reorient myself in new geographies.

Once Glen and Lorraine realized there was no intruder, no danger they could see or understand, Lorraine shooed her husband away. There was a rocking chair in one corner. It creaked then quieted as she settled and covered herself with a quilt.

"I'm going to turn out the lights in this room but leave the door open and the hall light on. I'm guessing sleep isn't coming easy but you should at least close your eyes."

I fumbled for my purse, palmed a few Valium, and swallowed them dry. I waited for the hazy cloud to fill me up and turned onto my side, facing away from my mother-in-law.

I didn't sleep but everything muted. It was a relief. I imagined Michael in the cold, empty space behind me, how his arms might feel around me. It made me nauseous and still, I longed for him. Lorraine fell asleep quickly. Her light breathing, the occasional softness of a sigh, comforted me.

Sleep did not come easy. Sleep did not come.

In the morning, I smelled coffee, heard the day rising from downstairs. Pale shafts of light flooded the room. When I opened my eyes dust hovered in midair. I sat on the edge of the bed, staring at my bare feet. The sharp, familiar ache between my thighs and up through my navel returned. I had a dull headache. I bit my lower lip, angry that everything still hurt, hurt worse, that the bruises were deeper, uglier. I wondered when the pain would disappear. "I will not cry," I whispered. I rapped my knuckles against my skull. I heard a cough, looked up, and realized Lorraine was still in the rocking chair. I felt naked in my tank top, a pair of Michael's boxers. The bruises and scars and cuts were lingering brightly, freshly. My body was unwilling to allow my skin to forget. Thirteen days is a long time. I heard a sharp intake of air. Lorraine took in the mess those men made of me. I didn't bother to cover myself, not this time. I wanted a witness. I wanted someone to see even though she could not really see.

"What did they do to you?"

I swallowed hard and looked up. "Everything."

My mother-in-law stood, slowly, and stepped toward me, her hands held open like she might pull all the hurt out of me. I backed away, trembling. She stopped. "It's okay. You can talk to me."

I held my hand just above my navel and shook my head.

Lorraine nodded. "You stay here as long as you need." Her voice cracked. "As long as you need."

I dressed in Michael's old clothes—a high school gym T-shirt and sweatpants I cinched around my waist as tightly as possible. They were still too big. I tried to find his smell in between the worn threads. The clothes hung on my frame awkwardly, made me feel gaunter than I looked. I was a woman without a country or a family or a name. I was no one. I took the stairs slowly gripping the banister. My body was still stiff and each step pulled at something violently tender inside me. I paused as a strong wave of nausea caused my knees to buckle. I started sweating. I covered my mouth with my hand and quickly finished making my way down, two stairs at a time. The front door was closer than the bathroom so I made my way to the porch, leaned over the railing, and heaved as a thin stream of something clear and vile spewed from my lips. I pressed my forehead against the railing, damp and cool with morning dew. My lips were dry, cracked.

"You need to see a doctor," Lorraine said from behind the screen door. "Michael says you haven't received proper medical attention. Also, you look like shit."

My forehead still pressed against the railing, I angled back to look at her. "Thank you, Lorraine. I'm not going to any doctor. I'm fine."

"I am not sure you know what those words mean. You are clearly everything but fine." She opened the door, extending an arm toward me. There was a cordless phone in her hand. "Michael's on the phone. If you can't talk, you can't talk, but you can listen."

I wiped my mouth with the back of my hand. I reached for the phone and crouched down, my lips pressed to my knees. I held the phone against my ear.

"Are you there?"

I didn't answer.

"I don't know what to say," Michael said. "I don't want to say the wrong thing again. I want to help you. I want to be with you. Christophe wants to be with you. Your parents think I'm hiding you from them. Should I tell them where you are?"

Even though he couldn't see me, I shook my head.

"I miss you so much and I am going out of my mind. Your sister has been in and out all day. We are all freaking out. At least let me see you."

I groaned as I stood, and went into the house. I found Lorraine in the kitchen and handed her the phone. As I walked away, I heard her say, "This girl is a fucking mess, Michael. She's a real fucking mess. It's going to take something mighty to get her right."

I hovered awkwardly in the hallway just beyond the kitchen. I didn't know what to do with myself.

"I know you're out there," Lorraine shouted.

I shuffled back into the kitchen.

"If you're going to be here for a spell, you can make yourself useful."

I wanted to smile but when I tried my cheek muscles refused to respond. I nodded instead.

"You ought to take a shower. We can go into town later, get you some real clothes. You're too small for anything of mine. I washed what you were wearing. Your clothes are on Michael's bed."

I nodded again and did as I was told. I stood in the shower for a long time, until Lorraine knocked on the door. "We run on well water, my dear."

I sighed, turned the water off, longed for a way to remove my skin and cover my body with something better, unbroken.

Back in the kitchen Lorraine handed me an apron. "I'm canning this week. I don't suppose you know anything about canning." She didn't wait for me to answer. "Just do as I tell you and hopefully it will all turn out okay. Just know that if you go wrong when you're canning, you can get people real damn sick. Let's try not to do that."

I nodded again.

The kitchen table was covered in bushel baskets of tomatoes, green beans, cucumbers. The vegetables smelled fresh, were still covered with dirt. I ran my fingers over the small knobs on one of the cucumbers, felt dirt gathering in the whorls of my fingerprints. My stomach growled and was emptier than ever but I didn't want to eat, didn't want to have to swallow anything. I was afraid to let my body do what it needed. I hungered.

We worked quietly for several hours. When Lorraine directed me to a task, I performed it as best I could. I wanted to be useful. Every strange sound made me tense and every sound was strange. It wasn't long before I was exhausted. The screen door slammed as Glen came in for a late lunch and I dropped the Ball jar I was holding. I stood in the center of a kaleidoscope of broken glass, shaking. I leaned down and began picking up shards of glass frantically.

"I'll get that," Lorraine said, calmly. "Glass breaks."

I ignored her, continued picking up glass. I looked at my arms, still covered in tiny cuts from being shoved face-first into a mirror by a man who wanted me to thank him for the privilege of relieving myself. I didn't even notice when blood began oozing from the palm of my hand, between my thumb and forefinger, and along the back of my hand.

Lorraine took hold of my wrist gently. "Drop that glass, Mireille; you've gone and cut yourself."

I looked at my hand; the flesh gaped a bit near the center of my palm, the edges of the parted skin puckering. I felt nothing. My body was once again forced open by something sharp. The Commander had a fondness for the blade of a sharp knife; he talked to me calmly as he drew his blade in neat rows, not too deep but deep enough, over and over across the small of my back. I refused to scream for him. I refused to let him know I felt anything at all. I felt everything, absolutely everything.

The shards of glass fell to the floor. "I'm sorry," I said. "I'm so sorry." I stood and ran up to Michael's room. After shutting the door, I hid under the bed, all the way against the wall, so I might feel safe, if even for a little while.

The floor was cold.

Lorraine cleared her throat. I opened my eyes and saw her sitting on the floor, peering at me. "You've been out for more than a day. On the floor. Under the bed. That is strange."

My mouth was dry, sour.

I crawled out. She handed me a plastic tumbler of water. I took a long sip and then another and another. I reached for my purse and felt an uncomfortable relief when I wrapped my hand around the plastic bottle of Valium. I took three, maybe four, and another sip of water.

"You sure are taking a lot of those little pills."

I put the bottle back in my bag and fell into the bed. I wanted to say something, something important, but I couldn't. Lorraine pulled the covers up around my shoulders. I drifted asleep.

When I opened my eyes again, I saw a Post-it note stuck to the tumbler of water—"My back hurts. I'm in my room if you need me. Michael sent you some things via that Federal Express. They're in the closet."

I couldn't move. I was paralyzed. My heart was paralyzed. Stiffly, I reached for my pills, for the silence they promised. I couldn't find the bottle. I felt a white stab of anger toward Lorraine, sat up, emptied the contents of my purse onto the bed and finally the orange bottle rolled out.

I tried to calm down. My hands trembled as I opened the bottle, held it to my lips and swallowed some pills, I don't know how many, I didn't care, enough to let me sleep a little more, forget a little more, wrap myself in a perfect haze a little more.

On the fourth morning, Lorraine stood at the end of the bed, her hands on her hips. "Don't you run? At the very least, don't you bathe?"

I sat up, rubbing my eyes.

"I don't think you're up for running, but you should at least get yourself clean and get out there and sit in the fresh air, get some color. You look even worse than when you showed up."

It was hard to think clearly. I had nothing to wear.

"A box of your stuff is in the closet," she reminded me.

I squinted, slowly remembered the note, my husband, my child, my life, but what was really the husband, child, life of another woman. I had no idea what to do with myself, how to move forward from one moment to the next, how to be alive.

Just after breakfast, Lorraine called me to the kitchen.

"We are going to bake today. I want you to make the dough with me."

"My father waited so long to pay for me my milk dried up," I blurted out. "I can't feed my son."

My mother-in-law nodded. "That must be a hard thing, Mireille. I am so damn sorry to hear it."

"I couldn't think of anything to keep my milk. I didn't know what to do. I didn't think it would go so fast. The pain," I paused, my voice cracking, "was really too much. There was this constant ache." I tugged at my shirt.

She took my hand. "There was nothing you could do but what you did. Do you hear me?"

"This would not have happened if he paid the ransom sooner."

Lorraine held her hand against my cheek. I flinched, but she said, "You're safe here, relax. And yes, there's a lot that wouldn't have happened if the ransom had been paid sooner."

"Do you think my son misses me? Like, is he old enough to miss me?"

Lorraine looked at me strangely. "Of course Christophe misses you."

"I wish I could be with him. I wish I had anything to give him." I looked down at the table and tried to remember the last time the woman I had been nursed her son. We were sitting in my parents' courtyard, early morning, already hot. Christophe nursed drowsily, holding my breast in his hand, smiling every once in a while. Michael joined us with his coffee, held the mug while he gave me a sip. He wrapped his arm around me and said, "Sometimes, this really does feel like home," and I leaned into him, brushed my lips across his and we sat together, quietly. I prayed I wouldn't forget that morning.

Lorraine stood in front of the counter with a large sack of flour. She took a small handful and began sprinkling it on the linoleum floor. I looked down and noticed she was barefoot, wiggling her toes.

"You wouldn't believe how good this feels. Take off your shoes, try."

I looked at my feet. "I can't. My feet are cut up. I don't want to get your floor dirty."

"Are they now?" Lorraine pointed to the empty chair behind me. "Sit."

Slowly, I lowered myself into the chair, gritting my teeth. Lorraine pulled a first aid kit out of the pantry that sat across from me. She patted her lap. "Let me take a look."

I shook my head, fidgeting in my chair. I tried not to panic. Lorraine touched my hand softly. "I am not going to hurt you."

My mother-in-law is stubborn and right then she had far more fight. I raised my legs, resting them in her lap. She held my ankles gently, carefully removing my shoes. She shook her head, hissing softly as she inspected the bottoms of my feet. "It is no wonder you're limping around here like an old lady. You should have said something."

I looked away, gritting my teeth harder. Tears started streaming down my face and once the dam broke, I couldn't stop sobbing. Lorraine didn't bring any attention to my tears. She dabbed alcohol on a handful of cotton swabs and carefully cleaned the cuts on my feet, wrapped them in fresh gauze. She hummed as she worked, Willie Nelson. When she was done, she patted my calves. "You should let me look at the rest of you, let me take you to the doctor. I can see you're bleeding elsewhere."

I shook my head.

"Fair enough. At least now you can feel the flour with your toes."

Lorraine resumed her place at the counter and I stood slowly, my feet still tender. I stood behind Lorraine and wrapped my arms around her, pressed my chest to her back and we stood there for a long while. She was something safe and good I could hold on to. I held tight. I allowed myself that.

We got back to work, and Lorraine handed me a bowl and the necessary ingredients, watching as she directed me in the correct proportions of flour, salt, yeast, and water. She sprinkled flour on the counter and told me I was going to knead the dough. I had no idea what I was doing. I began rolling the dough around, watching as the sticky mass collected flour. My feet were sore but the silky flour felt nice on my heels and toes, soft and clean.

Lorraine put her hands on her hips. "Not like that. You've gotta get rough with the dough. Get angry at it."

I didn't want to get angry, was afraid of what might happen if I gave in to my rage.

"Your anger is plain to see and right now it's all you got. No use pretending it ain't there. Hell, I'm angry too."

Lorraine slammed her bony fist into the dough and it sighed as it gave way and spilled around the sharp angle of her closed fingers. She squeezed the dough back into a ball, then slammed her fist into the dough again.

"Your turn."

I closed my eyes and rolled the dough back into a ball like Lorraine had. I punched the dough lightly.

"You've got more spit in you than that."

I flexed my fingers, then balled them into a tight fist. I started beating the dough with both hands. I didn't think or talk. I just pounded the dough over and over until I started sweating and breathing harder.

Finally, Lorraine held a hand up. "Well, you sure taught that dough a lesson. It is good and ready now. Let's make a couple more loaves."

We baked all afternoon, made enough bread to feed a small army. My arms ached from all the kneading but it was nice to stand at the counter in Lorraine's big, airy kitchen with the window open and fresh air and the smell of bread baking while I buried my fists into something that always gave way to me.

had been alone with Lorraine and Glen for what seemed like an eternity even though it had been only nine days, fewer days than I was held captive. In the after, days were not the same. They were long and indistinguishable and uncomfortable. I wanted to see other faces. I was tired of the stale smell of Lorraine's cigarettes and Glen's heavy breathing and the rooster reminding me, each morning, how little I slept. Talking was too difficult, too exhausting. I took to writing notes when asked questions or when I had a question. Lorraine said she was glad I had worked something out because she wasn't a mind reader. They kept me busy with chores around the farm—repairing fences, baking pies, building a new chicken coop, even planting seeds in Lorraine's garden. They pretended I was being useful even though I could barely lift my own head. Most nights, there was dirt beneath my fingernails. My body still hurt, constantly, but it was a relief to have something to do, to be given clear, manageable tasks, and otherwise be left alone.

Michael and I settled into a routine where I called him several times a day and he talked to me, just talked and talked and talked, no matter what he was doing. When I heard his voice, the leash around my neck, the leash woven by the Commander's hands, it loosened. He would say, "I miss your voice," and I would want to say, "I do too," but I could only listen.

This time when Michael answered, Christophe was crying in the background. Michael sounded tired, irritable. He started talking about his day and then he stopped. He said, "You know what, I just don't have it in me today, Miri. Your sister just left. Our son is teething. He needs me. We need you. There's not much else that matters, is there?" I heard Christophe wail even louder. I pictured his little face, bright red, his eyes angry with tears. My breasts ached anew. I wanted to beg Michael to talk to me. I wanted to tell him his voice was holding me together but the words could not come out. He sighed heavily. "I'm sorry but I don't know what to do and I'm sick of this." He hung up.

I listened to the dial tone, the persistent whine of it. It sounded so much like the wail of the car horn. I listened until the busy signal began to repeat and then I too hung up. I held the phone, wondered how I could fold the world in such a way as to erase everything terrible between us, the time, the distance, the damage. Then I got angry, so angry I stalked out of the house with only a few dollars in my pocket and my keys. I sped off the farm and onto the country highway. I didn't slow down for the winding curves in the road. I didn't slow down until I pulled into the parking lot of the one bar in the one-stoplight town.

When I walked into the bar, a Brooks and Dunn song was blaring from two speakers in the corner of a small dance floor. Several men and women, mostly my age or younger, some a little older, were hunched over the bar drinking light, foamy beer in glasses covered with beer sweat. I shoved my hands into my pockets and ignored the stares and took a seat at the bar. The bartender set down the lemon he was cutting and looked at me hard. "I know who you are," he said. "You're married to the Jameson boy; you're the one who got taken in that one country. I heard about it on CNN." I set my hands on the bar, looked down. He gave me a slight nod. "I was in the army," he said. I didn't understand the connection but he meant well. I took a thin square of a bar napkin and wrote "gin and tonic" in big block letters with a black dry-erase marker resting near the drink specials board. I pushed the napkin toward the bartender. He smiled and poured me a tall, stiff drink. "You drink for free tonight," he said. I forced something that was supposed to be a smile but probably ended up looking like palsy. Every once in a while, he would talk to me, mostly about his time in the military, his girlfriend Tracy, their three kids, how he wasn't sure he was ready to settle down even though he was plenty settled.

I drank the first drink fast, so fast my teeth ached down to the pulp and I felt a tight pressure between my eyes, making it hard to focus on anything. The bartender continued to talk and I learned about how he loved to play the clarinet and not many people knew that about him. I drank the next cocktail a bit slower but not by much. I never let the ice cubes melt. I was hungry, but I ignored the persistent gnawing in my stomach. It was still too difficult to eat regularly. I put food in my mouth when Lorraine insisted but never very much or often enough and I always threw it all up.

The bar was filling fast and a deejay played popular Top 40 hits intermixed with country music. The combination was disconcerting but the patrons seemed enthusiastic, spending most of their time on the dance floor, alternating between line dancing and movement that tried to approximate the dancing you might see in a rap video.

A tall blond man slid on to the bar stool next to me. He was not handsome. He was not quite ugly. He had a choppy haircut and his hair hung shaggily over his ears, with a blunt shape along his forehead. His jeans were dirty and he wore a T-shirt with a hole in the left armpit. He offered to buy me a drink and I let him.

"You don't talk much," he said.

I shook my head.

"Fine by me. There's nothing more annoying than a woman who talks a lot but ain't got nothing to say."

His comment was so common it wasn't worth rolling my eyes. He said his name was Shannon; he hated having a woman's name, insisted he was all man, offered to show me just how. I wondered what it was about me that compelled men to be so confessional. I took a tiny red sword from his drink and stabbed the palm of his hand. "I like them feisty," he said.

I stabbed him once more with my tiny red sword. He smelled raw. He inched closer and closer to me and talked and talked and didn't seem to care that I only nodded. He said he worked for a meatpacking plant in the slaughterhouse. It made sense. He said I was Prime Grade. I offered nothing in return. He didn't care. I was meat, lean meat, but meat nonetheless. He pulled me on the dance floor. I could barely stand. The bar was terribly hot, the air thick, the walls pressing in on me. We started moving, our bodies always touching. He hooked his fingers into my belt loops, pulling me more tightly against him. My skin felt like it was rolling in waves trying to separate itself from the fat, bone, muscle beneath. I slid my hands around his waist, swiveling my hips. He said, "Damn, you're sexy." He was a liar. I felt heavy and loose and the leash seemed almost invisible. I threw my head back, shaking my hair out. I wanted nothing to do with this man. I wanted everything to do with this man. I thought about Michael hanging up on me, about how I was losing him so soon into our after and we both knew it. I grinded myself against Shannon even harder.

After several songs we returned to the bar. He bought me another drink. He leaned into me, resting his hand on my thigh, digging his fingers into my thigh. His breath was hot and wet and horrible against my neck. He laughed coldly, said, "We should take this outside."

I would let this man with a woman's name break me again so I might be properly healed. I stood carefully and began walking toward the back door, focusing on placing one foot in front of the other. I paused, turned, looked at Shannon, nodded toward the door. He threw a couple of bills on the bar and came after me. By the time we made it outside, I was leaning against him. He didn't care. My father didn't come after me. My husband didn't come after me, but a redneck meatpacker named Shannon, a man with a raw dead stink, he did.

The night air was cold. When I placed my hand against the brick wall, it hummed with the bass of the song playing in the bar, music from another room. Shannon stood in front of me. He was much, much taller but fleshy. His girth repulsed me. I was meat. I did not want this but I did not leave. I waited, hoping he would break my bones, needing him to break my bones even though they were already broken. He leaned down until his lips were practically touching mine. I turned my head slightly. He could not have my mouth. I was defiant. He tapped my chin with a calloused finger. "I bet you like it real rough."

I lowered my head, grateful. I tried to relax my entire body to make it easier for him to break me. I wondered how his fist might fit against my chin or in my gut or how his hands might span the circumference of my neck or how much pressure he would apply to my throat before none of this mattered anymore. I wanted to say, "Put me in the ground. I am already dead."

The back door opened and three girls in silk camisole tops, high heels, and tight jeans stumbled out, laughing loudly. They paused, saw us, and giggled some more before heading to their car. Their perfume was still sharp and it lingered long after they were gone. I hoped they might come back for me. I was like them once.

I waited. I waited for Shannon to do what needed to be done. He did not take long.

He grabbed me by my shoulders, digging his fingers into me hard. I closed my eyes. I knew, by then, how to surrender, how to surrender to being broken, how that could be fighting. He pushed me against the brick wall, tried to push me into the wall. The bruises on my back brightened. He kicked my legs apart and grabbed me by my hair, yanking my head back. He shoved a hand into my pants. He stared at me. I did not look away. I felt nothing as he jammed two fingers inside me. I was dry, very tender. He said, "Yeah, baby." He licked my cheek. I swallowed the sharp acid that rose. He slid a third finger inside me. I closed my eyes even tighter. I felt nothing but the pain was not bearable. He started moving his fingers in and out of me. I could feel him hard against my thigh. "You are so hot," he said. He was still a liar. He was a man. I was meat.

He released his grip on my hair and started to tug my jeans lower. I hoped the cover of night would hide the marks I did not care to explain. He thrust his fingers especially hard. The pain was perfect and necessary. I wrapped myself around it. I was still dry. "You know," he grunted. "You could help me out." I shrugged and he stopped. His features changed, rearranged themselves into something more dangerous. He wrapped a hand around my throat, answered one of my questions, closing his hand tightly. I did not gasp. He said, "You're going to give me what I'm due," as if I were putting up a fight he couldn't quite make sense of.

My bare thighs were cold. Goose bumps spread across my skin.

Shannon slammed me against the wall again. "What the hell is wrong with you?"

I shrugged once more. This time, though, I smiled.

He shook his head and started unbuckling his pants. "Fucking women."

A large rodeo buckle held his belt together but he did not give me the impression of a man who had ever ridden rodeo, who had ever put himself in a circumstance where he might be broken. He reached into his pocket for a condom, tore it open with his teeth. I watched us, me against the wall, the mark of his fingers around my throat, standing there, spread open, waiting for him to take me. It was such a relief for something to finally make sense. He pulled my hand to his cock. "You feel that?" I swallowed as I felt the heat and length of him in my hand. He wrapped my fingers around him, covered my fingers with his. I squeezed lightly. There were tears at the corners of my eyes. I refused to cry.

I prayed for mercy from him, for myself. I opened my hand, stretching my fingers. I did not want to touch him.

That first night the seven men came for me, after the first phone call where I told my father and husband lies about my safety and they told me lies about my safety, when I lost count of how many men used me for hours and hours, I prayed because I had faith, because I needed faith as much as I needed to fight. I prayed because I was always taught that through prayer I would find salvation. I prayed for mercy and I prayed for more, for a breath of cool, dry air, for someone to come through the doors, to pull the men off me, to undo what had already been done. I prayed to forget. No one came for me. I prayed and no one came. I remembered everything. There was no salvation. But here, I could save myself.

I planted a hand against Shannon's chest, tried to pull my jeans up with my other hand. "No," I said. My voice was hoarse. I hardly recognized the sound of my voice.

Shannon laughed. "Playing hard to get?" He pulled at my neck with his teeth.

I swallowed huge gulps of air. He pushed my jeans back down, held me against the wall with his arm to my throat. I started clawing at his chest. I wanted to scream but my voice was still too new. "No," I said.

His body was wholly pressed against me. I was meat. He was going to take me because I asked him to.

"What kind of game are you playing? You know you want it."

"No."

Suddenly the back door swung open again. I whispered, "No." There was a rush of cold air. When I opened my eyes, the bartender was holding Shannon by the collar of his shirt.

"The lady said no, so you best leave her be."

"She's a fucking cock tease," Shannon said, pulling his jeans up. He left the condom on. He spit on the pavement to his right, wiped his mouth with the back of his hand, and pointed a finger in my direction, looked like he might run up on me again.

"No, sir," the bartender said. "She is not. Go on home. This was a misunderstanding and you'll live."

I tried to pull myself together, my fingers stiff as I fumbled with the buttons of my jeans. I fell to my knees and then I fell farther still, resting my forehead against my hands.

Someone finally came for me. I still had no faith.

In the morning, I wrote Lorraine a note telling Michael to come get me. My husband found his way to me faster than I thought possible. I was sitting on the porch swing wrapped in a blanket, hungover and sore. I felt crazy. I was crazy. A maroon Dodge Charger sped along the gravel road leading up to the farm and then Michael was out of the car and up the steps. He stopped, breathing heavy.

He looked at me like he was afraid of me. "Can I hold you?"

I stood, the blanket slowly falling from my shoulders. "Where's Christophe?"

"With your sister."

"I see." I wanted to lean into him until I remembered our last conversation. I stepped back. "No, Michael, you can't touch me. You are sick of this. That's what you said. There has barely been any *this* and you are already sick of it."

His arms fell limply at his sides. We stood, staring at each other. He did not apologize.

At dinner, we sat silently around the table—me, my husband, his parents. I watched as Lorraine and Glen and Michael ate—roasted chicken and cauliflower from the garden and a salad. My mouth watered. I hungered. I refused to eat. I traced the edges of my knife with my fingers, over and over.

Michael pointed at me with his fork. "You need to eat."

I shook my head. "I don't want anything inside me."

He set his fork down. "What is that supposed to mean?"

"Michael," Lorraine said, sharply.

I stared down at my plate, the skin of the chicken glistening warmly. My mouth watered more. "I do not want anything inside me. What do you think it means?" This time, my voice was barely more than a whisper.

"Babe," Michael said. "You've lost too much weight. You look terrible."

I bristled. A semblance of my vanity was still intact. "Stop saying that. Guess what? You look terrible too. Your shirt is ugly. How many times do I need to tell you to throw that horrible shirt away?"

"My shirt?" Michael slammed his fist against the table, making my silverware jump.

His anger was too much. He was too close. He could hurt me. I got up and ran out of the room.

"Miri, I am sorry," Michael called after me.

"What the hell is wrong with you, boy," Glen said. "Get your head on right."

"I don't know what to do," my husband said. "She is completely unreachable."

"How else is she supposed to be?" Lorraine snapped. "What she's been through."

"She won't tell me what she's been through. How can I help if I don't know?" My husband started crying and I paused, looked back and saw him bent over, his face in his hands. His entire body shook. His sobs were deep and ugly and filled the room. Glen went to his son, gently placed his hand on Michael's shoulder. I wanted to turn and go to Michael, to kiss his face and his pretty shoulders, to brush his hair from his face, to offer him some kind of solace, some kind of promise that we could find our way back to our fairy tale.

"I am so sorry," I said. "I have to go."

The volley of our apologies was wearing.

I stopped in the mudroom and found a flashlight. The walls of the house threatened to collapse on me, vibrated as they readied to close in. Even though it was a cool night, I walked out of the house to get away from the grief I was causing and the cage trying to trap me. I walked until I no longer felt the throbbing in my feet because the pain had radiated everywhere. It hurt to breathe. I heard the Commander's men laughing in the near distance and then I heard him, his lazy drawl explaining what he was going to do to me. "No," I whispered.

There were footsteps behind me. I started to walk faster. Someone called my name, a deep voice. I ran, even though I was so tired, so weak, my mouth so dry. I hungered. The cold night air made my bones ache. I looked up at the sky. There was no cross to guide my way, only moonlight. I could not tell if I was in Port-au-Prince or in Nebraska. On both sides of the gravel road, high stalks of corn. My name again, the footsteps, louder, closer. I turned, shining my light from side to side. A man, tall, moving toward me. I couldn't think clearly. Panic began winding through me. I screamed. The Commander had found me. I knew it. I ran faster. My feet were hurting again. Dampness in my shoes, cuts newly opened. He told me to stop. I looked around for someplace to hide. There was nothing but open fields. I veered right and ran right into the stalks of corn.

"Dear God, don't go in there," the voice said. "It's not safe at night."

I shouted, "Stay away from me. I'm not going back in that cage. You can't trick me."

"You're not safe in the fields," the voice said. He sounded as scared as me. I did not understand.

I ran, stalks of corn hitting me in my face. I turned off the flashlight so he couldn't find me. I had no idea where the field would end. I stumbled and tripped, falling hard to my knees, new bruises. I got back up, kept running.

There were outbuildings dotted along the edge of the property. As a teenager, Michael and his friends would hang out in the sheds, drinking beer and smoking weed they grew in small plots between the rows of corn. "It was the purest stuff," he once told me, "made from the best soil on earth, Nebraska soil."

The Commander's voice, it had to be him, was farther away now, echoing into the night. So much corn. My thigh muscles threatened to tear. Finally, I reached another service road. I was soaked with sweat, my clothes clinging to my bones. I smelled the stink of my fear. I did not know how the Commander had found me so far away. I hoped Michael was safe in the house, was almost relieved the Commander was chasing me so my husband and child might remain free. There was no place I could ever hide from the Commander; I knew that. I looked up at the sky again.

During one of our first trips to the farm, Michael and I had walked around, late at night, the air still and warm. The sky was clear and full of stars. It was the first time I saw a constellation and didn't have to pretend I could see the handle of the Big Dipper. He told me how to find my place in the world using the stars. I no longer heard the Commander calling my name. I needed to think clearly. I needed to hide. I wanted to lie down; I was so tired. I tried to remember what Michael said about which star to follow, how my hand felt in his, the small way he laid claim to me by pressing his fingers against mine. I picked the brightest star and walked toward it. It still wasn't safe to use my flashlight so I moved carefully through the dark.

Finally, I came upon one of the outbuildings. I quietly opened the door, praying it wouldn't squeak. Inside, I turned my flashlight back on and looked around. There was a bag of seed, a large wheelbarrow, a roll of barbed wire, equipment I didn't recognize. In a toolbox, I found a pair of wire cutters. I climbed into the wheelbarrow, pulling a tarp over me, leaving only my eyes exposed. I clutched the wire cutters, holding them out in front of me. I stared at the door. I tried to breathe shallow. I waited. I did not blink.

It got harder to stay awake. Every time I heard a noise, I waved the wire cutters in front of me. My eyelids grew heavier. It was so cold. I curled into a small ball, wrapped the tarp around myself more tightly. I waited. My eyes were so dry. When I started falling asleep, I jerked myself awake. I had never been so tired. It was not long before I couldn't fight sleep anymore. Something dark and heavy covered me.

There was a noise, voices. My eyes flew open. A truck idling, a door slamming shut. I covered my mouth with my hand, tried to make sense of where I was. In my other hand, something, I blinked, wire cutters. I was cold. My body was stiff. Thin plastic covered me. I lifted it up slightly. Thin shafts of light poured in. Suddenly, I remembered where I was. The Commander was out there with his men. He hunted me down like a dog and I was alone, at his mercy, at the edge of a vast farm. No one who could help me knew where I was. The door to the shed opened, a man standing in the doorway, behind him, blinding light. I unfolded myself, every joint aching. I waved my arms wildly in front of me, stabbing into the air with the wire cutters. This time I would make him bleed. The wheelbarrow tumbled backward and I fell to the floor. I ran to the corner and huddled into myself, covering my head with my arms. I wanted to die but I was already dead. I couldn't bear the thought of the Commander taking me to a new cage. A woman was screaming and she sounded peculiar—hoarse and hollow and hopeless. My skin crawled as I realized I was the woman screaming.

It took an hour to get me out of the shed. Michael and Glen and family friends had spent all night searching for me. It was Michael who followed me but in my terror, all I heard was the Commander. I stayed huddled in the corner, screaming, as the men tried to approach me. It was too much, to be in so small a cage once again, so many men hulking over me. Finally, someone went and got Lorraine. She shooed the men away and closed the door so we were alone. She knelt next to me, and pulled my arms down from over my face. She said, "There now," as she carefully pried my fingers loose from the wire cutters. She held my hands gently. She told me my name and that I had a husband and son waiting for me. She told me I was safe and I was loved. She said these things over and over until I was able to believe them.

Finally, I looked up. I said, "I am Mireille Jameson," with what remained of my voice.

Lorraine wrapped her arms around me, kissed my cheek, her lips warm and moist. "Yes," she said. "Yes, you are."

I could barely stand. Lorraine helped me to my feet and I leaned against her. We moved slowly.

"One step at a time," Lorraine said.

Outside, the sun was bright and high. I held my hand over my eyes. Michael and Glen stood next to Glen's truck. Michael was haggard, his eyes red, dark stubble covering his face. He had been crying again. He held a blanket in his open arms and I walked into him, let him wrap the blanket around me. We sat in the truck bed and Glen and Lorraine sat up front. I was so tired, so hungry. I leaned against his chest and he kissed the top of my head. At the farmhouse, Michael carried me inside and Lorraine told him to take me to the kitchen. There was a large pot of something on the stove and she ladled it into a bowl and sat across from me. Michael hovered, his body humming with nervous energy.

"You've got to eat," Lorraine said.

I shook my head frantically. "I want to be empty," I said. "Please."

"This is just soup," she said. "It won't make you feel too full." I looked at the bowl, a thick broth of some kind. Lorraine filled a spoonful, looked at me sternly. I pursed my lips together. "I really do not want to force-feed you," she said.

"Please don't."

"That was a bad choice of words. This will be good for you. I know you're hungry. You've gotta eat."

I was desperately hungry. I wanted to bury my face in the soup but I finally felt hollow enough to not feel those men and what they did to me. I didn't want to lose that.

"This soup is made from fresh beef, hearty stuff, and vegetables you helped pick," Lorraine said.

I wrapped the blanket around myself more tightly and remembered the first time Glen told me we were eating their livestock. "Circle of life," I said, quietly.

Michael started laughing, a deep, chesty laugh that made me want to smile. He pulled up a chair next to me. "I knew you were in there," he said. "I knew it. Please baby, eat just a little." He sounded so mournful. I nodded. He clapped his hands together. "Hot damn."

Lorraine fed me slowly, treated me with such kindness, kindness I needed greedily. The soup was delicious, silky and warm and full of flavor. It had been so long since I had eaten anything, days. Each time Lorraine told me to open my mouth, I did. Each time she told me to swallow, I did. When the bowl was empty, she asked if I wanted more and I nodded. She tried to make me eat some bread, too, but I refused. That would have been too much. After Michael washed my bowl, Lorraine told him to help me up to the bathroom. I leaned against my husband as we walked up the stairs. He leaned down and whispered into my ear, his breath tickling my neck. He said, "I love you." I didn't want to talk but I squeezed his arm so he would know some part of me heard him.

Again, Lorraine shooed him away so we could be alone. I sat on the toilet as she ran a warm bath. I was mute. When I refused to remove my clothes she said, "No problem." I stepped out of my shoes and climbed into the bathtub in my jeans and T-shirt. The water held my tender skin and quickly bloomed pinkly as the fresh blood from my feet fell away from my body.

"You are safe," Lorraine reminded me.

The second time she tried to undress me, I raised my arms over my head and she removed my soaking-wet shirt. She helped me out of my jeans, my underwear. It was terrible to be so naked. I pulled my knees to my chest, hugged myself, lowered my head.

"Don't look at me," I said. "Please don't look at me. You shouldn't have to see this."

Lorraine began gently scrubbing my back with a soft washcloth. The scent of apples filled the bathroom. She pulled my arms open and washed all of me. She said, "You have nothing to be ashamed of." She said, "Your body will heal."

"I'm no good anymore. I am dead."

Lorraine squeezed my shoulder. "There's so much good in you, it can't possibly be gone. And I believe you feel dead right now but you won't always."

We sat there for a long time, Lorraine saying kind, necessary things.

The following night, my husband and I lay in bed. I reached for Michael, rested my hand against his bare arm. "Are you going to leave me?"

"What?" he asked, his words sticky in his mouth.

"Are you going to leave me? Because if you are, I'd rather you do it now."

"That's ridiculous." He growled. "Don't ever ask me that again."

I slid toward him. A thousand tiny hooks pulled at my skin. I clasped the back of his neck and pulled his mouth to mine. I kissed him softly, so softly. I took in his breath, traced his lips with my finger, tried to memorize their softness, their shape. I kissed him again, harder. I thought, "This man is my husband," and repeated those words silently so I would not forget, so I could love the man I was with despite the men who were with me. He responded shyly, kept his hands to himself. I pulled his arm around me, my tongue inside his mouth, tried to remember the taste of him and forget the taste of too many others.

Michael gently pulled away, held my face in his hands. "What are you doing?"

I pressed myself against him, his thighs to my thighs, our hipbones pressed together. I loved his body, how much bigger he was, but in that moment, I hated his body and how he could drown me. I kissed his neck, pulled at the skin softly with my teeth. He moaned softly, found my lips again. I tried to relax, tried to ignore the panic, the way my skin ached. I ran my fingers through his hair and rolled onto my back, pulling him on top of me. He was so heavy; he was pressing me through the mattress. Michael slid his hands beneath my tank top, pressing his fingertips against my ribs. He dragged his lips along the curved bone of my chin to the hollow of my throat, down between my breasts. I gritted my teeth. I needed to give him this. I needed him to stay with me more than it would hurt to do what needed to be done to make him stay. This was my new ransom. I braced myself for the pain. I thought, "I will show you what I can take."

"Is this okay?"

I lied. I spread my legs wide, tried to push his boxers down. He put his mouth on my nipple. He kissed the constellation of fading bruises along the underside of my breasts, my navel, just above my pubis, tried to kiss me between my thighs.

"Don't do that," I said. "Just fuck me."

He laughed, kissed the flat of my stomach. "That doesn't sound like you." I fought my body's urge to start shaking. I was so tired of fighting.

I pressed my hand to his shoulder. "Please," I said. "Let's just do this."

Michael crawled back up my body, stretching himself alongside me. He kissed my shoulder and inched my thighs apart with his knee. An ugly sound trapped in my throat and Michael pressed his lips against mine so hard, my lips swelled. I opened my mouth to his, to him, to holding on to him.

He slid his hand between my thighs, stroking me softly. I squeezed my eyes shut, tried to keep my legs open. I covered my eyes with my forearm so he wouldn't see the truth of the moment. Hot tears fell down my face and into my ears. I tried to make myself go through the motions, raising my hips to meet his fingers, trying to feel to forget to fight to feel.

His fingers stilled. "I don't want this."

I sat up on my elbows and glared at him, my hair falling in my face. "Really? Are you kidding me?"

"I know when my wife wants to make love."

I pulled the sheet up around me. "Right. And now I am damaged goods."

His brow wrinkled. "Nothing could be further from the truth."

"Then fuck me, Michael. Jesus. I am throwing myself at you."

Michael held my wrists and pinned them over my head with one hand. He knelt between my thighs and I stopped breathing, preparing myself for him to force himself inside me, for all the ways it would tear me apart. "Is this what you want?" There was an edge to his voice. I finally felt a pang of desire so sharp and pure it disgusted me.

"This is exactly what I want," I said, angrily. I tried to wrest my hands free, tried to make him fight me, take me. I tried to make him into a different man. "I need this. I don't want you to leave me."

I pushed him onto his back and started sliding down his body, wanted to offer him something, anything, my mouth, my hands, but he grabbed me by my shoulders. "Mireille, no. Not like this. That's enough."

The relief I felt was sudden and complete. I quickly pulled my clothes back on and turned away from Michael. I listened as his breathing slowed. The distance between us expanded steadily. "I hate you for saying no."

"You won't always hate me," Michael said.

After he fell asleep, I hid in the bathroom and I lay in the bathtub. I smelled TiPierre and the Commander and the others, the sharp stench of them. Their bitter sweat ran down my neck and into my eyes and my mouth, the taste of it fresh with their own barely controlled rage. I felt TiPierre's greedy hands grabbing at my breasts while he fucked me, how there was no elegance to how he used me. I thought about the Commander and his cruelty, the calmness of it, how assuredly he assumed he had a right to my suffering. As I slept, I was consumed by the dreams of the woman I had become.

I was kept in a cage inside a cage inside a cage. I became an animal, baring my teeth, throwing myself against the bars, ignoring the pain. I would have broken my own body but the cage became smaller and all I could do was rock back and forth, hissing. Men who were also animals, poked at me with sharp things. They bled me for sport. They fed me bloody meat I tore with my teeth and fingers. The meat was slick and bland in my throat.

I was kept in a glass box inside a glass box inside a glass box. I could see everyone I loved and they could see me. They were happy. They smiled at me as they walked by my glass box inside a glass box inside a glass box. I tried to shatter the glass with my fists and only shattered my bones. I stripped myself naked, pressed my body to the glass. I forced those beyond the glass to bear witness.

I was suspended from an iron bar chained to a vaulted ceiling inside a room inside a room inside a room. The muscles in my arms unraveled. My bones stretched. I grew longer. I grew longer. No matter how hard I swung my body, I never reached a wall.

I had no choice and in that there was freedom. There were seven angry men with tightly muscled, long, lean bodies. Their skin was dark and shiny slick with sweat. They used me in the worst ways they could imagine. I had no choice so I surrendered my body to it. The more they hurt me, the harder I came. The more they hurt me, the more I changed, the more I became what they wanted me to become. They left me gaping, open, wet, wanting.

I woke up thrashing wildly, Michael staring at me, finally seeing me for the stranger I had become. I hated him for the look on his face, too.

Lorraine and I sat on the porch drinking coffee, smoking cigarettes. It was our morning ritual. Glen and Michael were in the barn doing some maintenance on milking machines.

Lorraine looked at me hard, the way she often looked at me, with a slight trace of confusion, some bemusement.

"You're not ready to go home," she said.

I watched a perfect stream of gray smoke leave my lips. I shook my head. "Oh, I'm never going to be ready."

"But you're going to leave with him."

I picked at a torn cuticle and thought about how I no longer smelled the manure on the farm. "I love him. I don't want him to leave me. He's completely fed up already." I swallowed the urge to cry. I could not cry—not over this.

"That boy isn't going anywhere. He's not acting right but he loves you and he is true."

"He needs me to go home with him. He needs his wife and things to go back to normal. My son needs a mother."

"I'd say you've still got time to be thinking about what you need. This is just the beginning."

I nodded and we continued rocking, sitting in silence, smoking her Parliaments. At some point she reached for my hand with her arthritic, reddened fingers. Her skin was dry but warm. I did not pull away.

I don't know what Lorraine said to him but that afternoon, Michael flew back to Miami. He did not say goodbye, nor did I. He left a note—his first honest words since I was returned—"I love you. This is so much bigger than me. I don't know if I can do this."

ⵘⵘⵘⵘⵘⵘ ⵘⵘⵘⵘⵘⵘ ⵘⵘⵍⵍ

wanted to remember what it felt like to move without being chased. There were things inside me still not set right. My feet were still tender like the rest of me, but the pain was bearable, unlike too many other things. I put on my running clothes and found the iPod Michael brought me and I started a slow loop on the gravel road circling the farm. It was hard going at first. I had been smoking too much so my chest tightened uncomfortably as I tried to manage breathing and moving at the same time. I turned the volume high, so high I wouldn't have to think. My body settled into a comfortable rhythm. After an hour, I finally stopped and finished my last lap walking, my hands on my waist.

I called Michael from the kitchen, leaning against the counter as I drank water from a canning jar. When he answered, I was quiet but he knew it was me. I focused on one word at a time. I said, "I ran today." I hung up before I heard his voice. We had nothing, really, to say to each other but I wanted him to know.

After I showered, Lorraine asked me to drive with her to Lincoln. She had a doctor's appointment and shopping to do. I agreed. As we walked into the medical complex, Lorraine said, "You know, you could stand to see a doctor, too. I took the liberty of making you an appointment right after mine."

I stiffened, felt out of breath. I stopped, gripping the railing next to me. "I don't need to see a doctor," I stuttered.

"Why don't we let the doctor decide that?"

"Sometimes I really don't like you."

Lorraine pulled her purse tightly against her chest and smiled. "I don't care."

I followed her inside like a sullen child. When she handed me a wooden clipboard with various forms I needed to fill out, the words seemed to rearrange themselves. I was suddenly one of those people who have suffered brain injuries, who have to relearn everything in order to start living again.

"You're a lawyer. You should be able to handle pointless paperwork."

"Very funny."

She pointed at the top of the form. "Put your name there."

I tried to remember my name. Sometimes it was with me and sometimes it was just beyond my reach. My hands sweated. I heard the voices from inside my cage, loud and laughing and drunk.

"I don't know what to do," I said.

Lorraine pointed to the top of the form again. "Write Mireille."

I did as I was told, gripping the pen tightly.

Line by line she helped me complete the form, then took it to the reception desk. When she returned, she said, "That wasn't so hard."

"Where's your form?"

Lorraine looked at me. "I don't have an appointment, dummy."

I leaned forward, resting my forehead against my knees. Lorraine began rubbing my back exactly the way her son did as we sat in the backseat of my father's car, speeding away from an empty church. This time I didn't pull away.

When the nurse called my name I tried to remember how to stand. Lorraine held my elbow and we stood together. She steered me toward the waiting nurse. When she turned to walk away, I grabbed her arm.

"My Lord, child," she said. "You're shaking like a leaf."

"You're welcome to come back," the nurse said to Lorraine and I nodded eagerly.

In the small examination room, I sat on a round, rolling stool, shifting from side to side. Lorraine sat in a chair and began flipping through a magazine. As the doctor walked in, she smiled widely and extended her arm, shook Lorraine's hand, said her name was Dr. Darcy, but to please call her Evelyn. She offered me her handshake too but I took a half step back. She smiled softly. "I hear you've been through an ordeal. Can we talk about that a little?"

I said nothing but there was something about her I liked. There was kindness in the doctor, in the cadence of her voice. I hoped I could entrust my body to her. I needed to entrust my body to her. I was hurting so much and didn't know how much longer I could hold out. She said she was going to take really good care of me. She asked Lorraine to leave the room. I changed into a gown and then the doctor and I were alone. I prayed I wouldn't vomit all over the doctor's pretty face. Before I could stop myself I said, "I might throw up on your pretty face."

She laughed again. She struck me as the kind of person who was easy with laughter but always genuine. "I'm a doctor. I can handle it. Can you talk about what happened?"

I shook my head.

Dr. Darcy nodded and patted the examination table. "No problem," she said.

I wanted no part of any exam but I also knew Lorraine wouldn't back down. I knew I needed help. I concentrated on making it to the table and climbing up. As I lay back, I squeezed my legs together. My knees shook, all that tension working its way through my body. The doctor lightly tapped my knee. She said, "I know this is hard but I need you to relax, just a little."

I tried to relax, tried to pretend this was a normal annual visit but I couldn't spread my legs apart. Something hot and wet trickled into my ears, down my neck. I sat up on my elbows. "If I freak out, please just do what you need to do because I can't handle doing this a second time." I still didn't open my legs.

"I'm sorry I have to do this," Evelyn said softly, "but I will be as careful as I can."

I was so sick of sorry. Slowly, I began to inch my legs apart, my body opening. Evelyn gently placed each of my heels into the stirrups. She began to explain what she was doing but I couldn't hear. I couldn't care. It hurt more than I expected but I didn't know how to say anything. I did not know how to say *stop, please, stop.*

There is nothing I cannot take.

The doctor swallowed a sharp intake of breath, muttering, "Oh my God," and then there was the sound of metal against metal. I stopped hearing or feeling anything. I went limp. My arms fell to the side. My eyes rolled back. I suddenly felt like I was a very small person in a very big room far away from anyone or anything that could hurt me. I was almost happy. Finally, I figured out how to leave my body.

There were hands on my shoulders and they shook me. Someone called my name. I could hardly make it out. I was still very small in the very big room and I didn't want to leave because I felt nothing.

There were hands on my shoulders and they were shaking me. Someone called my name again. The voice was clearer now. I opened my eyes and several unfamiliar faces peered down at me. I tried to remember where I was, tried to make sense of yet another geography. I looked down at my body. I wore a hospital gown. My face and neck were slick salty wet. I was very tired.

An unfamiliar face loomed closest. Slowly her features became less and less fuzzy. "Glad to have you back," she said.

"I didn't go anywhere." I was groggy.

"Can you sit up for me?"

I frowned. "Of course I can sit up." As I pulled myself upright, I was overcome by a wave of dizziness. I reached back to steady myself. "Where am I?"

She held a small penlight in her right hand and looked into my eyes. She said, "I'm Dr. Darcy, Evelyn. You're at the clinic."

Instinctively, I wrapped my arms around myself. "Why is everyone staring at me?"

The doctor nodded, then shooed the others out of the room.
After she closed the door behind them, she turned back to me.
"You gave us quite a scare."

I stepped off the exam table and reached for my jeans, trying
to stand and dress at the same time. I steadied myself by grabbing the table. "I'm fine."

"Why don't you sit down?"

I finished pulling on my jeans and sat in the closest chair,
crossing my legs.

She sat on the rolling stool and pulled herself closer. "I'm
glad you came in," she said. "You've definitely been through a
lot. There's a reason why you're in so much pain."

"I never said I was in pain."

"Mireille, I am a doctor." In a matter-of-fact manner, the doctor carefully explained what she had found. I was back in the
very big room. I felt everything.

"You also really need to talk to someone," she said. "You are
exhibiting all the signs of post-traumatic stress disorder."

"Really," I said, drily. "That's a crack diagnosis."

Evelyn smiled. "I have a list of great people who can help."

I nodded tightly. "I can't. I don't. It's too much. I will be fine.
I don't want anyone inside me in any way."

The doctor patted my knee. "We'll revisit this. Meanwhile,
I'm going to run some tests, have you come back tomorrow."

I nodded and finished getting dressed and tried to forget
everything the doctor told me.

The next day, the doctor seemed smaller behind her desk, younger, still kind. I fidgeted in my seat. Lorraine reached for my arm, steadied me. "Calm down," she said. I tried but I couldn't stop shaking my leg. The doctor opened a manila folder bearing my name.

She smiled. "I got the sense you didn't hear much of what I said to you yesterday so I thought it might be easier to talk in a less clinical setting. Your blood work came back clean. You'll want to be tested again in six weeks, three months, and six months just to be sure."

I clasped my forehead. It was a small miracle. I held that small miracle in my hand as I listened to the rest. I needed a reconstructive procedure, she said, to repair my vaginal canal. The damage was extensive. I thought about the ugliness of her words. They would keep me in the hospital for a night or two, could fit me in this week.

"You're saying I have to be in a hospital, on an operating table?"

The doctor nodded.

"I cannot do that. I just cannot."

"This is not optional. If you want to have a normal life, or something like a normal life, it is not optional."

"Goddamnit. I cannot deal with this. When will this be over?"

Dr. Darcy leaned forward. "I understand how you're feeling. I do, but this surgery is one step toward getting better, hurting less, being whole."

I imagined being in a hospital, being paralyzed, being cut open again and shook my head so violently, I gave myself a headache.

"You look here," Lorraine said. "When I was sick as a dog and refusing that chemotherapy, you were the one who said my family needed me to get better, who was so stubborn and sat with me day after day in that hospital, with all those tubes running in and out of me. Now it's your turn to do what has to be done because your family needs you. We need you."

The doctor continued talking, telling me about the procedure, how the best doctors would be helping me. I sat still and pretended to listen. I hoped for something to go terribly wrong. If they put me under, and I was lucky, I might never wake up.

On the way back to the farm, Lorraine said, "Should you call Michael or should I?"

"I'll do it," I said, dully.

When we pulled up to the farmhouse, I jumped out of the truck and walked toward the barn, walked until I couldn't see the house rising above the cornfields anymore.

He answered the phone after only one ring. "It's never going to be over, Michael."

"What's wrong?" He was tired, impatient.

My terror overwhelmed me. All I could think of was everything that could happen to my body in a hospital. "I don't know if you want to know but I need to have surgery."

His voice changed. Suddenly, he sounded terribly serious, his words clipped and precise. "What kind of surgery? Why? When?" He fumbled for a piece of paper.

I tried to remember the doctor's words, tried to explain them to Michael carefully. He took notes, his pen moving furiously. I knew later he would call every doctor he had ever known.

"I don't want to do this," I said. "Please don't make me."

"I'll be there tomorrow. I should have never left."

"You don't have to fly back out here," I said. "You just left and I'm not an infant. Stop saying what you think you're supposed to say. I can't take it anymore."

"I'm not going to fight with you. I have fucked this all up but I am going to get better at taking care of you, I swear."

I was silent. I looked up into the sky, clear and blue, the sun high and bright. A flock of birds passed overhead. I raised my arm high above my head. I wanted to grab hold of their dark feathers so they might lift me from the ground, take me away.

"Miri," Michael said. "Are you there?"

"You have been somewhat of an asshole. I need you to know that and I need you to be nicer to me." I hung up on him again and it felt good. I waited a few moments and called Michael back. Neither of us said anything for a long while. We breathed.

Finally, I said, "I've always been the fighter and that has worked for us but I don't . . . I can't do it right now. You need to be the fighter. You need to fight for me and for us, or you need to walk away."

"You make it sound like this could be an easy decision."

"It is mostly easy, Michael. Either you can fight for me until I . . . until I can find my way back or you can't. And if you can't that's fine. Or it's not fine but it is out of my hands. I'll let you go. You'll let me go. Eventually, we'll work out what's best for Christophe."

Michael flared his nostrils. "Here you go again, making decisions for us without letting me into the process, not even a little bit."

"That's not what this is. I can't fix me and us at the same time."

He grunted. "I guess you've given me a lot to think about."

I swallowed my irritation. At least I had that. "I guess I have. Goodbye, Michael."

This time, when I hung up, I didn't call him back. There was a quiet finality to our conversation, one I could live with. He didn't call me back, either. The birds disappeared past the horizon. They left me. Nothing would take me away.

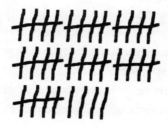

Everything was out of control. Michael knew that.

The morning after they found Mireille in the outbuilding, his mother had a long talk with Michael while Mireille slept.

"Everything comes easy to you, Michael," Lorraine said. "It always has. That's not your fault but now, something isn't coming easy to you and you are acting like a damn fool. There's nothing easy about what you're dealing with but you need to face that and step up."

Michael didn't know what to say to his mother so he shrugged, his eyes burning at the edges. He couldn't bring himself to look Lorraine in the eye. "I don't think anyone could step up to something like this. My wife was kidnapped but I went through something too."

Lorraine gave him a look he had never seen from her. Michael wasn't sure if it was disgust or disappointment or a little of both. "You are breaking her heart. It's written all over her face."

"I'm the last thing on Miri's mind right now, Mom. She barely even talks to me."

"She talks to me. She doesn't say much but most of what she has to say is about you and the baby and how much she wishes she could be with you both."

"Right. The baby she ran away from," Michael said. "She left us, without a word, right when I got her back." He yanked at his hair. "I keep losing her."

Lorraine's eyes narrowed. "I don't even know you right now."

"I don't know myself, either," he said, storming out of the house, his face burning. For hours, he walked along the dusty paths between the house and the barn and a cluster of out-buildings. He called Mona to check on Christophe and avoided answering her questions about Mireille. Later, his father inter-rogated Michael while they were in the barn, fixing one of the milking machines.

"This is not how you were raised," Glen said, "and I think that's all I really need to say about the way you're acting."

Michael kicked at a rotting board. "You and Mom think you know so much. You have no idea what I've been through. Every second she was gone I was dying. Every single second. Honestly, I still feel that way."

Glen removed his hat and began squeezing the bill. He grunted. "You take a look at those bruises around your wife's neck and every damn where else?"

"I'm not blind, Dad. I'm supposed to just suck it up because I don't have any bruises?"

"You are not behaving like the man I know you are, Michael Scott."

Michael paled. "I'm not making myself clear. I just . . . I need help, too. I don't even know where to begin. I don't understand half of what she's saying. I look at her and just want to cry because she's hurting so bad and I can't fix it."

Glen pulled his hat back down on his head, sank to his haunches, and resumed his tinkering. "You're still thinking this is about you, Michael. Don't get me wrong. You've been through hell. I'd lose my mind if your mother were hurt like that. But you should have seen your wife when your ma was sick, the things she did to help us even though your ma was ornery as hell. It makes me sick to say this but thank God we didn't have to depend on you. Everything would have fallen apart."

Michael chewed on the inside of his cheek. "Don't say that. I'm trying my best. I don't know how to get us past this."

Glen stood again, wiping his hands on his overalls. "What makes you think you need all the answers right now?"

Michael smiled wearily. "I'm an engineer, Dad."

His father chuckled, but quickly grew serious. "I remember when you were in eleventh grade, doing real good in wrestling. That year, we drove down to Lincoln for the state championship. Your ma and I were so proud because you were unbeatable, pinning guys fast and doing all sorts of crazy things on the mat. We had no idea where you got all that from. You got a look at your first opponent and all of a sudden, you didn't feel well, started holding your stomach and mumbling some horseshit about the flu. It was the first time you had come up against a guy bigger than you. Your coach told you to walk it off and you did fine but I still remember how you wanted to walk away, as

great as you were. I had hoped you finally learned how to stand
up to something bigger than you."

Michael lowered his head before clapping Glen's shoulder.
"I'm doing the best I can."

Glen looked Michael up and down and shook his head. "I
don't think you are. I don't think you're even close."

There was nothing Michael could say or do to explain himself. When he closed his eyes, he heard his wife screaming. When
he opened them, she was gone, always gone. He was on his own.
On his way back to the house, Michael kicked the barn door
over and over until he couldn't lift his leg anymore. Back at the
farmhouse, he wrote Mireille a note. He left.

Now, he was alone in Miami, with Christophe. Michael's eyes
were dry and his neck and knees ached. He slept badly on the
two flights back to Miami, a middle seat for both legs, nowhere
to fall but forward. Walking through the airport to the parking
garage made him sick to his stomach. The Miami airport was a
horrible place, he decided, always sending people to or returning them from sorrow.

There was the right thing to do. Michael knew that. He was
supposed to stand by his wife, this woman he barely recognized,
the one who was normally poised and confident, maybe even
a little arrogant but always captivating. She was his compass
point.

But this woman was a stranger. He hated himself for thinking it but it was the truth. His wife was a stranger. Or he was
the stranger. He had failed her from the moment she was taken
until the night she was returned. He couldn't stop replaying
that afternoon, wondering how he could have stopped those
men, wondering how he didn't.

★   ★   ★

That night she was returned, after finding Miri outside by the fire, he got a phone call from Victor, who told Michael to meet him on the street outside Sebastien's gates. Victor was alone in his car, the radio humming.

"What's up?" Michael asked as Victor put the car into gear and pulled away.

"We're going to handle some business."

Michael's stomach flopped and he cracked his knuckles, leaned forward in his seat. "You know who did it, don't you?"

They pulled up to the same squat house they had visited days earlier. It was late, soon morning would rise, and the street was empty, no lights on in the house.

"There's a crew that suddenly has all kinds of money. This motherfucker we talked to lied and now we're going to fix him good."

Michael looked around. A stray dog ambled past, growling softly. "I don't know if this is such a good idea," Michael said. "We should report this to the police or something."

Victor got out of the car and slapped his hand against the roof of the car. "You don't think that the men who did this wouldn't own the police too? Now shut up and get out."

Reluctantly, Michael stretched himself out of the car and stood, swinging his arms in front of his chest the way he used to before wrestling matches.

"Follow me," Victor said as he strode right up to the door and began pounding. There was silence, then a light and the door unlocking. TiPierre opened the door and peered out, his eyes half-lidded.

"Victor, what the fuck?"

Victor pulled his gun out from his waistband and shoved his way into the house. Michael followed, adrenaline burning through his skin. Victor cocked TiPierre's forehead with his gun and the young man grabbed his face as it began bleeding. "You shouldn't have lied to me."

"I didn't lie, and Laurent is going to fuck you up for this," he whined. "Why do people keep messing with my face?"

In the dim light, Michael and Victor noticed the bandage on TiPierre's cheek. Victor tapped the bandage with the barrel of his gun. "What happened there?"

"Cat got me. Fucking pussy."

Victor ripped the bandage from TiPierre's face, studying the wound, still fresh and open and angry and red. "That doesn't look a cat scratch, not at all. It looks like someone took a bite out of you."

TiPierre shrugged. "I don't know what to tell you."

Victor cocked him with the gun again and kneed TiPierre in the stomach. He hunched over, wincing. "You better stop or we're going to have a real problem."

"What the fuck is going on?" Michael asked. "Who is this guy?" Everything was moving too fast.

TiPierre finally looked at Michael. He sucked his teeth. "Who is this *blan*?"

Things were slowly starting to make sense. Michael's knees nearly buckled. All the nervous energy he had been bottling inside threatened to explode out of him. "You know who took my wife," he said. "You know."

"I have no idea what you're talking about, but you better get out of here before you find real trouble. Victor, get this *blan* out of here."

Victor handed Michael his gun. "He works for the man who took your wife. He was in on it. Handle this."

Michael looked down at the gun, marveled, not for the first time, at how easily it fit in the palm of his hand, how easy such a destructive thing was to hold. His finger curled around the trigger and Michael exhaled. He lifted his arm up, tried to hold steady as he pointed the gun at another man. That too was easier than he imagined. He closed his eyes for a moment, remembering the first deer he killed with his father, that youthful sorrow over the loss of a once-living thing. And here was this man, nearly at his mercy. And suddenly, he understood, that this man had hurt his wife. He could see it in the eyes. He could smell it on the man. Michael was incandescent with anger. His arm began to tremble and he felt the veins in his neck bulging.

"Okay, okay," TiPierre said, backing away. "Laurent took the bitch, but it was just business, Victor. Don't act like you don't do business. Walk away, man, and no one will know you were here."

His body moved before he could stop himself. All the air rushed from Michael's chest as he threw himself at TiPierre, fists flying, shouting with such force, spittle punctuating every word. The men fell to the concrete floor. TiPierre put up a good fight, at first, but Michael's muscle memory was stronger. Soon he had the younger man pinned on his back. Michael brought his fists to TiPierre's face over and over until his knuckles were raw and TiPierre's face was a pulpy mess. The man on the ground gurgled, and Michael stopped, heaving as he held the man's shirt in his fists.

"Here," Victor said, handing Michael the gun once more.

Michael took the Glock. He was strangely calm as he released the safety and pressed the barrel beneath TiPierre's chin and still, he wanted to cry. He wanted to be home with his wife. He wanted this to have never happened. He wanted there to be some kind of justice in the world. Michael looked into the other man's eyes, nearly swollen shut. He dared to imagine what this man had done to his wife, the mother of his child, who couldn't hide what she had been through. He dared to imagine how this man's face had been wounded. Michael's finger trembled against the trigger. He could do this one thing for Mireille. He could offer her this small justice. A child started crying and when Michael looked up, he saw a woman, holding a crying boy on her hip, maybe a year old. Her eyes were wide with fear as she looked from Michael to TiPierre on the ground.

"If you're going to do it, do it," Victor said, tightly. "We've got to get out of here before there's real trouble."

"Fuck," Michael shouted. He shook his head, shoulders slumping as he shoved the gun into his waistband. He brought his fist to TiPierre's face one more time and stood, slowly. "I can't. We'll tell the police or we won't. I don't know."

"By the time we tell the police, this guy will be long gone."

Michael grabbed Victor's wrist. "We're not doing this," he said. He nodded to the woman and said, "You are with a very bad man. He hurts women."

She nodded, pulled her child closer as his crying subsided into sorrowful hiccups.

They sat in the car for a long while when they pulled up the long driveway of Sebastien's house.

Victor turned to Michael. "You could have killed that guy. I thought all you Americans were gun-loving cowboys."

Finally, Michael said, "I couldn't kill a man in front of his son. I would have but for the child."

Victor nodded. "I get it, man. I don't know if I could have done it, either. We're not killers."

The sun was rising and from their vantage point, the city they looked out onto was a beautiful place, fragile and draped in pale blue light. "We're not killers," Michael whispered, already hating himself for not pulling the trigger, for not setting down the proper path of vengeance.

And now, Michael couldn't stop thinking about that night, his weakness. His knuckles had scabbed over and healed but all he thought about was the power he let slip through his fingers. How could he be with Mireille, this woman he didn't know and couldn't face or fix, when he was too weak to avenge her? His impotence consumed him. One day passed and then another and another. And then it was a week and then it was two.

He worked, staying at the office later and later, taking advantage of the nanny's generosity. He knew it and she knew it but neither of them said anything about it.

It was late but Michael didn't want to go home to his big empty bed and his empty house and terse messages from his mother and silence from his wife. Brett, one of the architects in his firm, appeared in the doorway, grinning.

"A bunch of us are going to a gentleman's club. You gonna join us?"

Michael shook his head, looked down at his wedding ring, but then he changed his mind. He was a man. He could have a little fun.

The club was loud and dark and the air was thick with the smell of stale cigars, body spray, and boozy breath. On the main stage, a woman gyrated slowly to a hip-hop song Michael once loved but now barely recognized. He couldn't remember the last time he heard music. He sat with his coworkers in a low-slung leather banquette, and once the waitress started bringing them bottles, he let go all the way. He had whiskey. He had ice. This was all he needed.

On the table stood a beautiful woman, or what could pass as a beautiful woman. She was tall, long blond hair, probably a wig. There was a wide hollow between her breasts, slicked with glitter. Some electronic song was playing now, one he recognized as a song Mireille ran to. No. He was not going to think about his wife, or, rather the woman he remembered as his wife. She was gone. He took another sip of whiskey and grinned up at the stripper, whose knees were now touching his, her hair draped over his face. He couldn't stop staring at the sharp valley between her breasts, so sparkly.

He had no recollection of how he got home, but when he opened the front door, he found Mona waiting on the stairs.

"What the hell are you doing here?" Michael asked, his words slurring. He tripped as he closed the door and fell flat on his ass. "This is not what it looks like."

Mona rolled her eyes. "This is very common, Michael."

Michael giggled. "You are just like your sister."

Mona sighed, stood, and helped Michael to his feet. "She wasn't kidding when she told me you giggle when you're drunk."

Michael nodded solemnly. "What are you doing here?"

"Your nanny called. She is not a slave, you know." Mona walked Michael into the kitchen and sat him down on a stool at the breakfast bar before handing him a bottle of water. "Look,

I'm not going to bullshit with you. Decide if you're going to step up or not and if you're not, leave Miri now, while she's still a mess, so she only has to put herself back together once."

"This is none of your business," Michael said.

"You made it my business when you started being an asshole."

Michael stood, running his fingers through his hair, over and over. "Is the way I'm dealing with my fucked-up, kidnapped wife not good enough for you?"

Mona sighed, then smiled, sadly. "No, Michael, it isn't. And I'm pretty sure it's not good enough for you, either."

He loosened his tie and sat back down. "I failed her, Mona. I let her get kidnapped. And then I almost killed a man. I had his blood on my hands and I held a gun to his head in front of his child but I couldn't do it. I couldn't make things right."

"Get off the cross, Michael. You didn't let anything happen," Mona said as Michael finished his story.

"You don't understand. We found one of the guys."

Mona sat down next to her brother-in-law. "What the hell are you talking about?"

Haltingly, Michael told Mona about his excursion with Victor on their last night in Port-au-Prince, about TiPierre and nearly breaking the man's body with his two hands, about how little he knew about the world and how little he was able to do when his wife needed him most.

"Damn," Mona said as Michael finished. She laughed lightly. "Trust Victor. That guy sure gets around." Mona clucked her tongue. "I wish I could have been there to see you giving it to that animal. I'd have joined in. I'm willing to get my hands dirty for the cause."

Michael choked up. "Victor is the only one who treated me like I mattered the whole entire time. He's the only one who listened to one goddamned thing I had to say."

Mona took Michael's hand. "My sister didn't marry a man who would kill another man, not for any reason. She married you because you wouldn't, besides which, the world is full of dangerous men. You can't kill them all to keep my sister safe."

Michael clenched his jaw. "I could try."

"You could," Mona said, softly. "But you could also try just being there for your wife here, and now. She needs you around more than she needs to be avenged. Besides which, we both know my sister. She'd eventually be pissed you didn't let her have at the guy herself."

Michael couldn't help but smile. "She is fucking impossible."

"You married her."

He looked around the kitchen in the home he and his wife had built—the counters, the stainless steel appliances, the dried flowers on the table because a home should always have fresh flowers, she said, and the last grocery list Miri had written, still tacked to the refrigerator with OREO COOKIES in capital letters at the top and bottom. "That I did," he finally said.

HHH HHH HHH
HHH HHH HHH
HHH HHH

When I closed my eyes, I was no one. I was the woman who forced herself to forget her husband, her child, all the joy she had ever known, who carefully stripped herself of her memories so she could survive. I was no one in a house filled with angry men. I dreamt of the Commander cuffing me to his bed, stretching me apart, digging his elbow into my breastbone, how the pressure of it made me think he would shatter my rib cage. I turned onto my side, held my hand over my heart, tried to strip myself of these darker memories but they could not be stripped. They were not yet old enough to be memories.

A kind voice said my name softly. I turned toward my name, felt a warm weight beside me. I opened my eyes, and saw Michael smiling back at me from the end of the bed, his hand wrapped around my ankle. I gasped and rolled off the other side of the bed, crawled into a corner, pulled my knees to my chest.

Michael remained calm. He knelt in front of me, lifted my chin with one finger.

"It's Michael," he said.

"You're here." I swallowed. "What are you doing here?"

He sat next to me and pulled a big blue velvet box from his pocket. When he opened the box it made a soft popping sound. "I am an asshole but I choose you, every single day. I will do the fighting we need done."

I looked at the gleaming rings in the soft velvet box, traced them with my fingers. I closed the box, pushed his hand away. "Michael, don't. No one expects you to stay with me. No one would choose me right now. Don't insult me by saying what you think you're supposed to."

He held my left hand gently. "I choose you today, yesterday, tomorrow. I swear." He opened the box again and slowly slid a beautiful diamond ring along my finger and then a thin wedding band that matched his. He closed his hand over mine. "I'm here because I have to tell you something. I went to a strip club."

I lightly punched his arm. I can be pettily jealous and he knows it. My irritation brought me back to myself, at least for a moment. "What the hell, Michael. Seriously?"

Michael threw his hands up. "Hear me out."

I punched him again.

"I was in a not good place and I don't know, I wanted to do something stupid. Anyway, I was there with some guys from work and it was fine, whatever, but the girl who kept dancing at our table, she had glitter between her boobs. It was crazy. And all I could think was, 'Miri would love to see this sparkle.'"

"If you think about your wife at a strip club, you are doing it wrong."

"That's my point. I was surrounded by all these incredibly beautiful women and I wanted to tell you about the glitter boobs. I wanted you there with me. I wanted you."

"You aren't really thrilling me with this story. Please tell me more about these beautiful women while I sit here, looking like shit."

He grinned. "It's a little funny. Admit it."

I rubbed my face. "God. I am so angry, Michael. I am completely fucked-up."

Michael ran his fingers through his hair. "We need help, real help and we'll get it, starting with your surgery."

"Stop being mean to me." I clutched at my chest. "I can't handle mean right now."

"I get mean when I'm scared."

I picked at a fingernail. "I've never seen you mean before, talking to me the way you did, treating me the way you did."

"I've never truly been scared before, not like this. I've never been so terrified in my whole life."

I uncurled a bit, stretching my legs out, pulling my hair into a loose knot. "We have that in common."

"We have a lot in common." He rubbed his hands together. "Wait here."

Michael jumped to his feet. He disappeared for a moment, then returned with Christophe, the baby taking awkward, tentative steps, his arms stretched forward.

I stood and pointed. "He's walking?"

Michael grinned, proudly. "Goddamned right. A little more than ten months old. Fucking genius."

"Mama," Christophe said, grinning before rushing into his baby babble.

I crossed my arms across my chest and smiled down at my son as he made his way awkwardly across the room. "Why are his arms stretched out like that?"

"Oh that. I am teaching him to walk like a zombie."

I arched an eyebrow. "You are teaching my child to walk like the undead?"

"We've had a lot of time on our hands while I've been . . . getting my head right."

Christophe stopped when he reached me, clapped his little hands and threw his arms up the way he does when he wants to be held.

"Go on, hold him," Michael said.

I shook my head. "I don't want to hurt him. I don't want to make him dirty."

"Open your arms, baby. You will not hurt him."

I looked at my hands, realized they had been closed into fists. I unclenched my fingers and slowly stretched my arms out and leaned down to pick up my child. I held my breath. I tried not to shake, muttering, "I don't think I can do this."

But then, I did. I held my child and my arms remembered every inch of him, the weight of his body, the tiny folds of his skin. My body could never forget the memory of my child. I held my boy, his forehead warm and soft against my neck. He smelled so sweet and good and clean as he yammered happily. I offered silent gratitude for the resilience and obliviousness of tiny children.

Christophe grabbed hold of the neck of my T-shirt, something he often did when I held him. I traced his tiny lips with my finger. I tried to give myself that moment. I tried not to think of anything but my husband and child, these best parts of us.

That night, I couldn't sleep. I slipped out of bed, where Michael lay, dead to the world, Christophe next to the bed in his Pack 'n Play. I went to the kitchen, sat down, and stared out the window at the clear night sky, all those stars. The house creaked in the way of old farmhouses. I tried not to flinch at every little noise.

It wasn't long before Lorraine padded into the kitchen. She sat across from me and smiled. "I thought I heard you. You and sleep are strangers, that's for sure."

"When I close my eyes . . ." I shook my head.

Lorraine reached across the table and took my hands in hers and I didn't pull away.

"I see you are wearing a wedding ring again. It looks good on you."

I shrugged. "Michael is trying to do the right thing even though I don't think he wants to. I can't live with that, knowing he's staying with me out of some sense of obligation."

"That simply isn't true," Lorraine said.

I hunched forward, pressing my forehead against the kitchen table, my shoulders shaking as the tears came. "I'm no one, Lorraine. I'm nothing. I don't know how to be in a marriage like this."

Lorraine stood and came around the table, sat down on the chair next to me. "Maybe you don't know who just yet but you are someone. Stop saying you aren't. And you don't need to know how to be in a marriage. Hell, I've been with Glen for forty-five years and I don't know how to be married to him from one day to the next."

I couldn't help myself. I laughed and sat up, rubbing my face. "Glen never talks. That would drive me crazy. Michael never shuts up. At first I wasn't sure about all that talking but it grew on me."

"Listen here. The night after he met you, that fool son of mine called Glen and me at midnight. It nearly gave me a heart attack, the phone ringing so late like that. He talked a mile a minute, said he met the most amazing woman. I knew right then he was far gone. He's not doing the right thing because it's the right thing. He's doing the right thing because it's what he wants to do. The real question is, will you let him?"

I looked at Lorraine, hiccupping a bit. "He really called you the day we met? I wasn't very nice to him."

Lorraine laughed. "He told us that too."

I looked out the window again. The moon was high and bright. I traced a constellation against the glass pane. "I will never forget how you've opened up your home to me."

"Oh hush," Lorraine groused. "Just hush."

We talked quietly until we both began to yawn and then we walked up the creaky stairs to the men we didn't know how to be married to.

Michael was sitting up in bed, staring at his phone. He looked up. "I thought you had run away again until I heard you and my mom talking."

I shook my head and climbed onto the bed, straddling his lap. He looked at me, arching an eyebrow. I ran my hands along his shoulders, down his arms, tucked his arms behind his back.

"Don't touch me," I whispered.

Michael nodded.

I kissed his chin and drew my lips along the line of his jaw. "Please don't touch me," I whispered again.

"You're safe with me," he said. "I will not touch you."

"I need to tell you what happened before you decide if you will stay. Do you want to know?"

"I do," Michael whispered.

I ran my fingers through his hair, trying to memorize each strand. I kissed him, reminded my mouth of his taste. At first our lips were soft together and then they weren't and I wanted to fall into him as much as I wanted to pull away. I needed Michael to know I still belonged to him and only him, no one else, not ever.

I pressed my chest against his, my cheek against his neck, my lips barely brushing his ear. There were many truths to share. Softly, softly, I told Michael the best truth I could, the one we could both live with so he could someday be freed of whatever he imagined about those thirteen days, so I might someday be freed of the truest truth.

||||| ||||| |||||
||||| ||||| |||||
||||| ||||| |

I spent nearly six months with Lorraine and Glen, who watched over me the way my own parents should have watched over me. Michael visited when he could. Mona sometimes came with him and chattered endlessly about how quaint it was in the country, about Carlito and what he was up to, about all the things we would do when I returned to Miami. She and Lorraine got along famously. Mona never tried to make me talk about what happened. She did not push. She was just there. Sometimes, Michael left Christophe with me; sometimes, he didn't—it depended on if I was closer to dead or alive. I spent a lot of time alone, locked inside myself, while the people who loved me most tried to reach me.

I did only one interview, for an evening news program, with a journalist I hoped would not ask me stupid questions. She mostly didn't. There were no other interviews, no books, though someone made an unauthorized movie that airs regularly on a cable network. People love a real tragedy when they think it cannot happen to them. At the end of the movie, in white block letters, the epilogue reads, "Mireille Jameson practices law and lives in Miami, Florida, with her husband and son." I have seen the movie more times than anyone knows. It comforts me to imagine my kidnapping had been that neatly endured and resolved.

Five years later, I had seen several therapists. Some sent me to psychiatrists who tried to fix me with complex cocktails of drugs with very long names I cannot pronounce, drugs that made me listless and tired, always so tired, unable to think or work or be a wife or mother. Others told me I simply needed to talk, as if all it would take was the recitation of my horrors for my anger and my grief and my terror to disappear. Only one therapist told me the truth. She sat in one of those expensive, uncomfortable chairs you see in modern design magazines. She set her leather-bound notebook on her desk and leaned forward, her elbows on her knees. She said, "I am going to come clean with you, Mireille. You will get better but you will never be okay, not in the way you once were. There is no being okay after what you've been through."

That truth freed me. I said, "Thank you," and I meant it. I was lighter and cleaner and calm. I still see her once a week, sometimes twice. Sometimes Michael and I go together. I never say much but I show up.

We tried, unsuccessfully, to have another child. We spent a shocking amount of money and saw specialists across two continents but carrying a child was something my body was no longer capable of. No amount of reconstructive surgery or time or money or hope would fix what was damaged. The sorrows piled themselves silently around us, nearly choking us, choking me. But. We eventually found a surrogate to carry our baby, a little girl. She is a beautiful creature with wide eyes and scrawny, bowed legs. Lorraine says, with so much pride, that our daughter is *advanced* even though she's not yet two. We named the baby Emma Lorraine and like Christophe, I rarely let her out of my sight but not in a way that would make her helpless or weak. Girl children are not safe in a world where there are men. They need to learn to be strong.

There was an earthquake. Haiti split open and all that remained were gray piles of rubble and hundreds of thousands of people with nothing to hold them to the world, living in tents hungry, hungering and somehow, still faithful, holding their hands to the sky, praising God for their salvation. It was a new sorrow, a fresh break in an already broken place. The tents are still there, providing no shelter. Women are in even more danger. There is no water. There is no hope. My parents survived and for that I was grateful, in spite of myself. My father's buildings stood strong while the rest of the country fell. I imagine he is proud of his work, these standing monuments of his resolve.

In the weeks after, Michael gently suggested we go to Port-au-Prince even though that was the last place either of us wanted to be. There were so many funerals. So much mourning was demanded of us all. I could not return to the motherland, land of my mother and my mother's mother. I tried. We bought tickets and he packed our suitcases and we went to the airport but as we stood in the frantic, mournful throng at the ticket counter, the familiar shaking returned. I could smell my kidnappers and feel how they used me over and over. The memories in my body were too fresh. I wanted to go, to mourn, to help in some small way, to see if enough time had passed that I might enjoy that native sun on my skin, but I could not. My body would not let me. We sent money instead and it was then I felt like a true American.

My sister finally convinced me to return to Port-au-Prince. "At least once," she said. "You need to see our father. He has changed. He always asks for you. He wants to make amends."

I did not believe Mona. A man who would sacrifice a daughter was not a man capable of change. I agreed to return to the place where I died because my sister had done so much for me, for my family, when we needed her most. She was a mother to my son when I could not be and a friend to my husband when I could not be and my best friend, always. At first, Michael objected, reminded me of the last time we tried but he relented after my therapist assured him *I could handle it*. The night before we left I reminded him too. I said, "There's nothing I cannot survive," and he said, "That's what terrifies me."

We bought our tickets, packed a small bag, and left the children with Mona and Carlito after a great deal of kissing their little faces and promising we would be back in two or three days. I hate to travel without them but I hated the thought of them with us, in a lawless place, even more.

As we descended into the capital I took two Valium so I could hold myself together, so I could breathe, so I could feel a little less. Michael shifted uncomfortably, his leg shaking wildly. I offered him a Valium and grabbed his thigh to calm him down. I said, "I'm not going to fall apart." He covered my hand with his. While the plane taxied, I stared out the window at the tarmac, the ever-present waves of heat rolling across the concrete. I felt nothing and I felt everything. I remembered the Haiti of my childhood, the complex but unadulterated joy of feeling like I had a second place to call home. I remembered the country Haiti became for me, the sorrow.

"If I am cursed enough to be kidnapped again, don't bother trying to save me." I feigned a laugh. We both knew I wasn't joking.

"Oh baby," is all Michael said.

The airport looked the same. The city looked the same. The city looked completely different. I saw no part of myself in the country I once called home. Everywhere, even two years after the earthquake, there was rubble, and broken buildings, bent at their knees, yearning for mercy. The presidential palace had collapsed in on itself—a fallen man, unable to rise. We drove past a tent city, teeming with people walking down the long corridors between tents, sitting in front of their canvas homes, staring at the cars driving by. Heat rose through my neck as I looked away. Still, I was shamed by how little I truly understood or could ever understand about this country.

I closed my eyes and said, "I really do not want to be here." I said, "Michael, please, please don't let anything happen to me," and he said, "I swear to you, I won't." I needed to believe him to keep breathing.

I was nauseous as we drove up to my parents' house, the familiar rolling sensation in my stomach making me dizzy. Even with the air-conditioning blasting, our bodies were practically sticking to the leather seats. Michael's face was red as it always is when he gets too hot. The walls surrounding their home were higher, the tops of those walls covered in barbed wire and thick shards of broken glass that glinted in the sun. I donned my sunglasses. We waited while the gates opened. The nausea grew stronger. My chest tightened. Two cars sped past us. We waited.

Michael tried to hold my hand but I shook my head. He nodded and looked straight ahead. "This goddamned place."

Finally the gates opened and we lurched forward and slowly up the steep hill. My chest loosened.

"I'm going to be sick," I said calmly as the car stopped at the top of the driveway. My parents stood on the front steps. They leaned into each other. They were smaller, older, but still, together they painted a distinguished portrait. I opened my door and steadied myself as I stepped onto the pavement. A blanket of heat wrapped around me. The air was heavy with salt. Sweat trickled along my spine. I walked to the edge of the driveway and leaned against a tall palm tree with a thick trunk, breathed deeply, and then I hunched over and vomited.

Michael stood behind and held my hair. I was grateful. In the after, we were different people but we still worked; we were good together, lock and key.

When I finally felt empty enough, I stood and smoothed my shirt, my hair, and turned to face him, rolled my eyes. "They probably think I'm a freak."

He handed me a bottle of water, and I eagerly wet my mouth. He stepped closer, lifted my sunglasses, and perched them on the top of my head. He smiled.

"You're okay," he said. "Who cares what they think? You are not a freak, at least, not *that* kind of freak."

I couldn't help but laugh. I slapped his chest. "You are such a pig."

Michael held my chin and kissed me. "I am."

"I'm never coming back here."

"I know," Michael said.

He wrapped his arm around my shoulder and I let him and we walked slowly toward my parents. My mother beamed and even my father allowed himself a small smile. He opened his arms and I stopped, stiffened.

Michael shook his head, moved in front of me. "She doesn't want that," he said.

A shadow flickered across my father's face but he stepped aside. I leaned into my mother and kissed her once on each cheek. Her perfume filled the air around us. Michael and I walked between my parents and into the house. The four of us stood in the foyer with the gleaming marble floors, the walls bearing beautiful art, a stand with a mahogany sculpture. We stood for a long time. We no longer knew who we were to each other.

"You look very thin," my mother said.

"This is my body. I'm a runner," I snapped. I hated people commenting on my body, stating the obvious. In the after, it was strangely difficult for me to gain weight but I wasn't abnormally thin anymore.

My mother squeezed my arm and sucked her teeth, making her disapproval clear. "Are you eating?"

"I am eating," I muttered, shoving my hands in my pockets, pulling away.

She drew her fingers along the wide streak of silver that refused to go away. "Why don't you color this?"

Michael pushed my mother's hand away. "My wife is happy with the way she looks."

"Let us sit in the living room," my mother said, finally done with her assessment of my appearance.

Michael and I sat on the couch while my parents sat across from us on another.

"Can I offer you a drink?" my father asked.

We both nodded.

"Something strong," I said.

Nadine brought us rums and Coke. As she handed me my glass, she touched my shoulder, gently, and I took her hand, squeezed. I said, "Thank you very much."

I drank my rum quickly, letting the warmth of the sweet liquor spread across my chest. Between the Valium and the drink, I was almost numb. I reached for Michael's glass and drank his too. I dared my parents to say something.

My father cleared his throat. "It's good to see you, Mireille. You have been missed."

"I'm here because Mona asked."

My mother reached for my father's hand. There are no limits to her compassion for that man.

"I want you to understand I thought I was making the best decision for this family, because I love my family so much."

I closed my eyes. Three SUVs surrounded my family and me on a hot afternoon. We wanted to go to the beach and lie in the sand and play with our son in the ocean for the first time. That is all we wanted. It didn't seem like too much.

I twisted my glass against the palm of my hand. "I'm glad we're not wasting time with small talk."

My father shifted. "It would seem we have passed that point."

"You left me to die and that's exactly what happened." I looked up. "I died."

My father leaned forward. "If I paid, I had no way of know-ing if they would return you. I had to think about your mother, your sister, my sisters, the rest of our family. Paying for you would sacrifice them too. It killed me to imagine what you were going through but I am responsible for many lives."

He slowly told us the story of his best friend Antoine Deus and how they came for his daughter-in-law and sister and cousin and son and even his wife, how Antoine Deus paid each ransom asked of him until there was nothing left and he was left des-titute, his family nothing more than ghosts of the people they once had been. My father sat across from me and explained that he could not see everything he worked for given over to animals, how he believed that if he took the right stand, he might do more good than harm. "I truly believed that when the kidnap-pers realized there was no money to be had, they would set you free," he said. "I believed you would come back to us whole."

Michael tensed. His arm muscles practically bulged through his shirt and he said, "You are unbelievable."

"You sacrificed me," I said. I slammed my glass on the cof-fee table and the sharp sound echoed through the room. "You were willing to rob my son of his mother." I pointed at him, my pulse racing. "Your grandson. My husband. Do you have any idea what it has taken for me to pull myself back together? How could you?"

My mother turned to look at my father. Her expression was inscrutable.

He didn't even look away. My father looked into my eyes, and held his hands open, the strength of his conviction hovering between them. "In impossible circumstances one is faced with impossible choices."

I understand impossible choices; there were so many I had to make when I tried to forget everything I loved because the memories made surviving that much harder. There are moments even now when I am laughing with my husband and children. A phrase or a smell or a sound makes me forget where I am and who I am and how I belong to the people around me. I sit, frozen and lost, until someone helps me find my way back.

"Thank you," I said. "Thank you for telling the truth."

I returned to Port-au-Prince for one reason—to tell my father everything that happened to me, the whole, filthy truth of my kidnapping, even the parts I hadn't told Michael. I wanted my father to know how for months after my release, I starved myself so I could feel empty, so I could forget the brutal ways the men who held me filled my body. I wanted my father to know about the nights I still wake screaming because it is so hard to escape that cage and the men who trapped me there. I wanted my father to know I died and had only just started to feel alive again. I needed him to know what his sacrifice cost me most of all, but also my husband, our children.

When my father's eyes started to water, I shook my head. "You do not get to cry, not in front of me."

His skin took on a gray pallor. I wanted to tell him I would never forgive him, that his *impossible* choice had killed all my love for him, but when I looked into his face, all I saw was an old man who made a terrible, weak choice and had to live with it for what remained of his life. He did not deserve the truth of how I died.

I looked at my father, the man who had been the uncompromising measure for all things in my life for so long. There was still good in me. He did not need to know the truth for me to feel more alive.

"I came here to tell you I forgive you," I said, as firmly and clearly as I could.

Michael and I exchanged looks; I squeezed his hand.

I thought, "I am free," and for the first time, believed it.

My father's eyes widened and his hands trembled. He quickly folded them in his lap. He shook his head. "I don't dare ask for your forgiveness."

"I do not need your permission. I forgive you nonetheless."

Sebastien Duval crossed the room and I stood, my arms hanging limply as he pulled me into a loose, awkward hug. I gritted my teeth, counted to five, all I could handle, pulled away. I would never let him touch me again. When I shrugged out of his embrace, my mother held my father and kissed his cheek. She studied me, her eyebrow slightly arched, until I looked away.

After dinner, my mother motioned for me to follow her into the courtyard. We sat, alone. It was warm, quiet. Her blooming roses filled the air fragrantly. I lit a cigarette and released a thin stream of smoke, my chin tilted upward.

"You told your father a kind lie," she said. "I thank you for that, I truly do. You have always been a good daughter."

That night in bed, I couldn't sleep. Every sound made me jump. Every shadow was an angry, righteous man coming for me, taking from me, hurting me, punishing me for all our fathers' sins. I remembered how the Commander would stare at me, into me. I sat up and leaned against the headboard, turned on the light. I reminded myself of everything I knew to be true, something Lorraine taught me to do, years earlier, in those moments when I couldn't be sure about when and where I was.

My name was Mireille Jameson née Duval.

I was married to Michael Jameson.

I was a lawyer.

We had a son, Christophe, and a daughter, Emma, the still points in my turning world.

I was loved.

I was safe.

I was safe.

Michael slept soundly. I shook him but he kept on sleeping. I shook him harder and he slowly opened his eyes.

"Are you awake?"

He rolled onto his side and faced me. "Of course. Come here."

I breathed a sigh of relief and slid closer to him, rested my cheek against his chest. He sleepily rubbed my back in slow circles the way he usually does when I wake up from a nightmare. I kissed the bone of his jaw and his neck and the base of his throat. We were so frantic and fevered together the first time we visited my parents. We were so young then. We had somehow stumbled back to that same place.

Over these years, Michael waited for me. He showed me how to be touched again when I could hardly handle being touched. He showed me how to be loved again. We showed each other how to be loved again.

I slid my hands beneath his T-shirt and traced the thick muscles of his shoulders with my tongue, quickly shimmied out of my pajamas. I grabbed at his earlobe with my teeth and pulled him over me as I rolled onto my back. I said, "Make me forget, baby." Michael traced the edges of my face, touched me so softly everywhere, made me shiver and arch into him and want him fiercely, feverishly. And then we were not quiet or gentle. We were true.

After we were sated, I lay with my head on his chest, our bodies fitting damply. Michael asked me why I forgave my father.

I didn't forgive my father. I lied because that lie cost me less than the truth would have cost him.

There once was a king who met a miller, a vain man prone to deceit. The miller told the king his daughter could spin straw into gold and so the king locked the daughter in a room full of hay even though the only thing the daughter could do with hay was hold it in the palms of her hands. She had to make a deal with a devil in order to satisfy the king, make promises she could not keep. No one ever says what happened to the father who was willing to trade a daughter for the favor of a king. I know what happened to the daughter. I know.

I said, "I didn't want to lose whatever was left of the good in me."

"You're better than he deserves," Michael said.

Early the next morning I kissed Michael's forehead as he slept, then dressed and walked down the steep driveway to the street. There was a light fog slowly lifting. The steel gates were open. It was quiet, so many high walls holding the wolves and their bloody, bared teeth, at bay.

A dark SUV drove by, the windows tinted. I didn't shrink away. I thought, *you have no idea what I can take*. There was so much wildness just beneath the surface of my skin. I was not afraid to show it. The car kept driving and disappeared around the bend.

When I heard footsteps I knew it was Michael. His arms were open and waiting for me when I turned around.

He cupped my face with his hands. "Are you okay? What are you doing?"

I pressed my hand over his heart. "I still love this place but my roots don't reach here, not anymore. It can never be home again. I hate that he took that from me."

"The Commander?" Michael asked.

I shook my head. "He would be much easier to forgive."

"I'm sorry," Michael said.

It was all that needed to be said.

A few weeks after we returned from Port-au-Prince, Michael and I went to brunch with Mona and Carlito. We sat on a sunny patio of a popular restaurant at one in the afternoon, slightly hungover from drinking and dancing the night before. We all drink a little more in the after, just enough to dull the constant reminders of how our fairy tales have been rewritten. The restaurant was crowded, loud. The day was sunny and warm, a perfect Miami moment. I wore sunglasses. I always wear sunglasses when I am not at home. I am always hiding in plain sight. I do it out of respect for the living. I wore a long summer dress, bared my arms, finally felt comfortable enough to do something other than shroud my body in layers of dark, heavy clothing. The bruises have long faded but scars remain. In certain outfits, people stare but I pretend they cannot see me or these truths, so written on my body.

Mona looked at me over her menu, offered a reassuring smile. She does that a lot, checking in with me in small, intimate ways, letting me know I belong to people who love me, letting me know I am safe, trying to hold and keep me in the world.

At first, I did not recognize the busboy. He wore black khaki pants and a short-sleeved, white button-down shirt over a T-shirt. There were sweat stains under his armpits. He was quick with his work, clearing tables, carefully setting plates covered in runny eggs and syrup and fluffs of leftover butter and fresh salmon in a gray plastic tub. He came to our table to refill our water glasses and when I looked up, I saw the scar beneath his left eye, still pulsing like it was trying to move across his face. I thought, "This is not possible," and then I thought about my work and how many people build all their hopes on the promise of living in this country. I thought, "Of course." I grabbed Michael's hand, squeezed so tightly he winced, said, "Babe, what's wrong?" He studied me carefully, worry in his eyes.

My throat locked. I wanted to shield his body with mine or shield mine with his. I moved my chair closer to his. I could not speak. The leash around my neck tightened. It had been some time since I last felt that leash. Michael patted my hand, returned to his conversation. He and Carlito were engaged in a heated debate about a mayoral candidate. The busboy paused, looked at me. I stared at him. He could not see me behind my sunglasses but he knew me. He quickly finished pouring our waters. His hands shook and he spilled some water on Michael's slacks. I could not release my grip on Michael's hand.

The world is the smallest of all places. You are never safe. When he leaned over my shoulder, I smelled him. His smell is always with me. There is no escape from it. None. Mona stared at me too. She could not see my eyes, so she could not see my fear. She could not see how we were in danger but she knows me. She tried to make sense of what was wrong.

The busboy left and I looked around, tried to find him again. I needed, very much, to understand his exact location in relation to mine. I looked at my sister and her husband and my husband. They were not safe. I needed them to be safe because they were my whole world. I stood, slowly, my legs rubbery.

Mona stood with me. "What's up, kid?"

I didn't say anything. I walked away from her. She tried to follow me but I waved her off. I walked through the noisy restaurant and into the kitchen. At first no one noticed me. It was hot and loud, cramped and crowded. The air was even more humid, steamier than outside. A waiter finally noticed me, said I couldn't be back there. I focused on what I needed to say. "I'm looking for the man with the scar." The waiter nodded, pointed me toward the back of the kitchen. I walked past the line cooks shouting rapid Spanish to each other back and forth across the line. I saw the back door to an alley, cracked open. I walked through it and found the Commander standing, leaning against a concrete wall, smoking a cigarette. He was waiting for me. He was no longer a boss, no longer the king of his world, sitting on his red satin sheets watching American sitcoms. He was no longer a blade digging into me, his fresh wound.

I did not know what to say. I did not know what I was doing, alone, in an alley with him. I raised my sunglasses, resting them on the top of my head. I did not need to hide from him. He was the architect of my fear. I wanted him to see the woman he made, the steel of my body he helped forge. I wondered how long it would take Michael and Mona to realize something was wrong. I hoped. I dared to hope they wouldn't take long. I lifted my chin, exposed my throat. He had the chance to put me in the ground.

I called him by his given name. I said, "You should have killed me after you killed me."

He said nothing. His face betrayed no emotion but his eyes were calmer than they once were, older. I thought about tearing that thick scar from his face. I thought about what I might find beneath the dead braid of tissue. I stared at the scar and it hissed. I was calm and then I was not. I was crazy. I was all the crazy held in my bones for five years. I pounded his chest with my fists and he didn't resist. He didn't try to defend himself. He stood still, his arms hanging loosely at his side while his cigarette burned. He let me bruise his body and break the blood beneath his skin. The din of the kitchen grew quieter. My arms were tired so tired but I was wild with rage and nothing would stop me. I would break his skin and break his bones beneath the hot Miami sun. I would leave his carcass on the pavement. I would.

I made an ugly, wheezing sound, a desperate sound. A strong pair of arms pulled me off him, lifted me into the air. I still tried to hit the Commander with my arms, my feet, with anything. I clawed at him, tearing his skin apart. I looked up and saw Michael, Michael who finally came for me. Mona appeared, her eyes narrow, flashing. "What's going on?" she said, practically shouting. I pointed at the Commander, and made a new, sharper sound but I could not find words. I could only make that horrible sound. I was a wounded animal. Michael tightened his grip as he tried to make sense of the situation. It did not take long. "You should have killed me," I shouted. "You should have killed me." My voice grew hoarse. "Let go of me," I shouted. "Let me go."

Michael refused, said, "Miri, Miri, sweetheart, calm down."

"You calm down," I said, squirming. I was strong. I worked very hard five years into the after to be strong, to fight even harder.

Michael loosened his grip and spoke softly into my hair. "I am going to let you go but I want you to stand still."

I nodded and he let go of me. I lunged for the Commander again, dug my fingernails into his face, tried to pull off his hideous scar, left a deep red fissure of broken skin bleeding beneath it. I stilled. The wail of the car horn filled the alley and the air around us.

The Commander looked at me and his lips curled into a little smile and I remembered everything he did to me. The memories filled my body at once, threatened to spread through me like a malignancy, destroying everything I had done to become closer to alive again.

Shaking, I reached for Michael's hand. My husband stood in front of me. His muscles tensed and he stared at the Commander real hard. "What did you do to her?" he asked.

Some of the kitchen staff began hovering in the doorway. I was a spectacle. I was garish. The Commander looked at my husband, my husband who is strong and big and who keeps me safe. Michael let go of me, turned me around, studied my face, and looked at the Commander. Michael reached for the man who so wholly changed the course of our lives, his hands trembling, his body finally understanding. The Commander ran. He ran like a coward. He ran because he was no longer the man with a gun keeping a woman in his cage. He did not have his knife or his kingdom or the men who served him. He only had his scar and the stained apron around his waist. He ran because his life was in danger. Animals know when their lives are in danger.

Michael started after him but I held on to my husband with both hands, with both hands now. I said, "Don't leave me. You don't know what he's capable of."

We stared at the Commander running away until he disappeared from our sight.

Michael pulled me against him. "Yes, I do," he said.

The last time the Commander forced himself on me, after my ransom had been paid and I was not released as had been agreed upon, he told me his real name—Laurent Charles. He told me his was a good name, a strong name, one he wanted to give his son. I lay on his bed, handcuffed, my arms stretched above my head. My body settled easily into this human bondage. The body adapts more willingly than the mind. I knew it would be the last time I had to endure his body on top of me and inside me, his sweat, his tongue, his spit, his skin. I had that to hold on to, the knowledge that there would be a last time between us. I would not belong to him. I would be free of him even if I could not be free of him. It was the last time but I wanted mercy. I needed mercy. The body adapts but the mind has limits. I was shattered.

The Commander lay next to me, his body stretched along mine, his skin sticky against mine, as he drew his knife between my breasts over and over. You do not feel the pain as your skin comes apart. There is an uncomfortable sensation strangely absent of discomfort when the blade first pierces the skin. The pain comes when the knife cuts deeper, through the fat, what little there may be, when your body is open and bloody. That pain is breathtaking. Blood trickled along the undersides of my breasts and down my sides. I spoke his name, firmly, clearly. I said, "Laurent, please grant me mercy." I said, "Forgive me for my father's sins."

He stopped, set the knife on the bed next to my ear. The blade was so sharp it hummed eagerly. "You want mercy?" His voice was drowsy with desire. I never hated him more.

"Yes, Laurent, I do. Please grant me mercy."

He thought for a moment, rubbing his hand across my stomach. "I will grant you mercy if you do not fight."

I bit my tongue. This was the real sacrifice, my life for my life. I gave him one kind of pain to avoid another. I killed myself to save myself. I would not have survived otherwise.

I told him to uncuff me; he did. I wrapped my arms around his shoulders. I kissed his forehead. I died. I kissed his cheekbones, sharp. I died. I told him he was the son of L'Ouverture as I gently grazed his neck with my teeth. I died. I pushed him onto his back and lay on top of him. I bled onto his body, dead but still dying. I pulled his arms around my waist. This was mercy. I pressed my lips to his chest, slid down his body, tracing along his center with my tongue, tasted my blood on his skin. I died. I traced the deeply carved muscles of his trembling thighs with my lips, my fingers, my tongue. I said, "You shall know kindness even though you have shown me none." I died. When he said, "I want you now," I lay on my back. I did not fight. I died. When he said, "Look into my eyes," I did. I died. I did not fight. This was mercy. This was my sacrifice. He said, "Say you love me," but that I could not do. Anger coursed through him. It was a bitter thing for him, understanding I would never belong to him. He fucked me harder and harder. I did not resist. I relaxed my whole body around him. I made him believe I wanted him, that there could be an us because I understood what he wanted. There was nothing breakable left inside me. I let him take me. I let him kill me. He said, "Say you love me." Again, I refused. He punched my face. The ringing in my ears grew so loud, rattled my skull. I took his hand, his raw knuckles, raw from the abuse he had inflicted on me and I kissed each one. I died. He said, "Come for me, let me pleasure you." I refused this delusion too. I could not have even if I tried. Only one of us misunderstood what was happening. He punched me again. I smiled up at him, held him gently, touched him gently. He grabbed me by my shoulders and shook me violently, made me think what little held my body together would finally be ripped apart. I said, "Hush." I said, "You shall know kindness even though you have shown me none." I showed him kindness. When he was done, I went to the bathroom and prepared a wet cloth. I returned to his side and washed him clean as he lay in the middle of his bed, his limbs heavy. I wiped his face and his chest and between his thighs. I knelt at the foot of the bed and cleaned his feet, massaged them gently. I rubbed his entire body with lotion and lay next to him. I died. I threaded my fingers between his and lay my head against his chest. It was not long before he wanted me again. There was so much fight swelling just beneath the surface of my skin. I ignored it but it was there. He tried to kiss my lips and I turned my head. I let him have me again. It did not matter. I was already dead. He said I would see my family again soon. I showed him kindness. He remained an animal. That is how I died even though Laurent Charles, who called himself the Commander, did not possess the kindness to kill me.

In Greek mythology, Hades fell in love with Persephone. In one version of the story, Hades wanted Persephone and had to have her so he abducted her and forced himself on her and kept her with him until Zeus ordered him to release her because her mother, Demeter, forbade the earth to bear fruit until she found her daughter and the people were hungry. Hades was so desperately in love with Persephone that he deceived her, plied her into eating pomegranate seeds while she was in the underworld because he knew that if one eats while in the underworld, they are doomed to spend eternity there. Hades released Persephone to her mother as he had been ordered but she was forced to return to the underworld for a time each year. She was free but she was not free. Persephone paid a steep ransom for eating six pomegranate seeds.

When he was finally done with me, I could not allow myself to believe I was being released. I had no idea where my shoes were. That's what I focused on as they walked me out of my cage. My feet were bare. The Commander and three other men put me in an SUV. I sat in the backseat between the Commander and another man. The Commander held my thigh possessively, like we shared a certain bond. When I tried to shove his hand away, he squeezed harder. I leaned back and closed my eyes, tried to sit so still he might forget me altogether. I did not want to incite his desire.

We drove from one neighborhood I did not recognize to another neighborhood I did not recognize. Eventually, we stopped on a deserted street, far less dense than the alleys of Bel Air. He ordered the other men out of the car. They stood, huddled a few feet away, smoking cigarettes, laughing loudly as they joked.

I wanted the Commander to hold his gun to my head and pull the trigger. I wanted him to put me in the ground.

He sighed. "It did not have to be this way. Normally, I am a man of my word. I am a businessman. I do not harm women during the course of these negotiations." He brushed a strand of loose hair from my face, tucked it behind my ear. "The only person to blame here is your arrogant father."

I did not move. I did not believe I could be free.

The Commander opened his door but paused. "Perhaps next time you are driving through the city in your expensive car, you will look at the city around you instead of looking through the city around you."

I stared at my bare feet. "I could say the same thing to you and the way you ride around in your expensive cars."

The Commander chuckled. "You do amuse me. You know how to fight. You have a mouth on you. You should stay, be the boss's woman. You're no good to anyone else now." He shrugged, rubbed his chin. "I ruined you for any man but me."

I shook my head like I was having a seizure and slowly slid toward the door because if I made it past the door, I might find my way to the woman I had once been. He was probably playing a game and I did not want to give him the satisfaction of fooling me. And still. I wanted to be free. The Commander tried to help me out of the car but I slapped his hand away. I stood next to him and he tried to hold my arm.

I stepped away. "I would have never belonged to you."

He nodded, sneered at me in the moonlight. The Commander grabbed me, digging his fingers into my arms. He pressed his lips to mine, his tongue thick and wet in my mouth. I tried to bite him but he did not pull away until he was satisfied. The man was, in all things, merciless.

"Run," he said. "Run until you cannot run any farther. If we see each other again, I hope you will say hello. We are friends now. We have shared so much."

The Commander kept talking but I did not listen. I did not want to hear his voice. I took a step away from the Commander and his men. I took another step. Every nerve in my body was raw, exposed. I took another step. I started walking quickly.

"I will not forget you," the Commander shouted. "And you will not forget me."

I wanted to tell him, "Yes, I will," but I did not need to have the last word.

Instead, I ignored the pain, how it made my body feel open and completely worn-out. I ran and I ignored the Commander still shouting, his voice rising in pitch. I ignored how he sounded almost sad and lonely. I ignored how maybe we were both broken in similar ways. I did not look back. I listened for his footsteps behind me but there was only the sound of my terrified breathing and my bare feet on the ground. I ran faster. I finally dared to hope.

Acknowledgments

My parents, Michael and Nicole Gay, have made so much possible for me in so many ways. My brothers, Joel and Michael Jr., are okay, I guess; they have adorable children. My sister-in-law Jacquelynn is awesome and reads everything I write and seems to like it; her support never goes unnoticed or unappreciated.

My agent, Maria Massie, has so much faith in my writing and is a tireless champion. She has fabulous hair and impeccable taste.

Amy Hundley is a cherished editor and friend. She understood exactly what this book needed to find its shape and brought *An Untamed State* along with fierce intelligence and gentle hands. She too had faith, she took a chance, and I am grateful. She also has great boots that I want to steal but our feet are not the same size.

I also thank:

- My Twitter friends for making procrastination worthwhile
- Channing Tatum for his neck
- My *PANK* co-editor and friend, M. Bartley Seigel, for too many reasons to list

- Brad Green and Ethel Rohan, early readers of this novel who pushed me to make it better
- The members of my local writing group, Daiva Markelis, Mary Maddox, Letitia Moffit, Angela Vietto, and Ruth Hoberman, who read and gave invaluable feedback on early versions of this novel
- My boss, Dr. Dana Ringuette, who makes it possible to be both a teacher and a writer, and the extraordinary creative writing faculty at Eastern Illinois University: Daiva Markelis, Olga Abella, Ruben Quesada, Lania Knight, and Charlotte Pence
- Steve Himmer, editor of *Necessary Fiction*, for setting all this into motion by taking the story "Things I Know About Fairy Tales," which eventually became this book
- Megan Lynch, for insight and friendship
- Tayari Jones, a friend and mentor like no other
- Edwidge Danticat, for her grace, generosity and being a leading light for Haitian writers
- Karolina Waclawiak, who kindly listened to all my neuroses as this novel was birthed
- Alissa Nutting, who kindly listened to all my neuroses as this novel was birthed
- Jami Attenberg, who kindly listened to all my neuroses as this novel was birthed
- Michelle Dean, who kindly listened to all my neuroses as this novel was birthed and is one hell of a friend
- Tracy Gonzalez, my best friend who is more than a best friend, in this life, and if I am lucky, the next